ABBY ROAD

ABBY ROAD

a novel

ophelia london

Entangled Publishing, LLC
2614 South Timberline Road
Suite 109
Fort Collins, CO 80525

Visit our website at www.entangledpublishing.com.

Edited by Stacy Abrams
Design and typesetting by Neuwirth & Associates, Inc.
Cover design by Alexandra Shostak

Print ISBN: 978-1-62061-244-6
EPub ISBN: 978-1-62061-245-3

Manufactured in the United States of America
First Edition March 2013

To Taylor Swift and No Doubt.
Thank you for keeping pop music relevant.

PROLOGUE

How could there be no valet parking? This was Los Angeles. After circling the building a second time, I finally found a space. Even though parallel parking was not my forte, I managed to snake in and then did that reverse-forward-reverse-forward trick about ten times, trying to straighten out. I glanced through the passenger-side window, inspecting the population of the sidewalk. Hmm—busy, lots of business people and shoppers dodging one another. Hopefully no tourists, though. My stomach felt queasy at the thought.

I sat back in my seat, closed my eyes, and breathed slowly. *In through the nose . . . out through the mouth . . . Repeat until pulse steadies. . . .*

If I were late to my appointment, I'd tell Dr. Robert it was because I was practicing a relaxation technique. He knew agoraphobia wasn't my current paranoia, however, so he probably wouldn't buy it. So, after one more inhale, I adjusted my huge round sunglasses, took a last look through the window, and opened the car door.

I was careful not to slam it shut—no need to draw unnecessary attention. I walked around the car. And I was fine. I stepped onto the sidewalk. Still totally fine. Dr. Robert's

office building was only about fifty paces away. Dead ahead.
If I looked down and walked fast, no one would—

"Abigail? Abigail Kelly?"

I froze in place. Bad idea—I should've kept moving. I
turned toward the voice. It was a girl, maybe about sixteen
years old. She was pointing at me with one hand while her
other was clapped over her mouth. Probably stifling one of
those ear-splitting teenage squeals *I* would have been good
at eight years ago

"It is. It's *you!*"

"Hi there," I said, forcing my mouth to turn up into my
"charming smile." Before she even reached me, I was automatically poised to take whatever scrap of paper she handed
over. It was a movie ticket stub this time. I glanced at the title,
but I'd never heard of it. Occupational hazard of being on
the road and out of the country for the past eleven months.

"What's your name?" I asked, then scribbled my best
wishes followed by my signature, including the trademark
loopty-loop on the *y* at the end.

By that time, three other girls—friends of girl number
one, presumably—had joined us.

"Seriously. I just *love* you!" one of them said, beaming.
"Your songs are, like, all my favorites."

"You're so much prettier in person," declared another.

I was nodding and smiling and loopty-looping as fast as I
could, keeping one eye on the building entrance a few yards away.

"Your hair," girl number one said, "is so totally beautiful. How do you get it that blond and shiny?" She actually
reached out and touched my head.

I allowed it. Not that I was used to having total strangers
pet me on street corners, but it was like I'd been nine months
pregnant for the last five years, and everyone thought they
were allowed to rub my belly.

"Yours is gorgeous." I smiled. It was true; it was the kind
of red you can't get out of a bottle. "Never change it," I said,
signing the last piece of paper. "Grow it long. You'll rule the
world. Trust me."

The girls gathered in a buzzing huddle as I started to walk away. Not too petrifying that time. Four autographs, probably a couple of cell phone pictures. Nothing that was going to make tonight's news. I clutched my purse strap over my shoulder and exhaled. Home free.

"Hey, Abigail." It was a man's voice this time. "C'mon, give us a big smile now."

When I looked over my shoulder toward the voice, I didn't find just one man, but three, all dressed in their typical L.A. daytime street garb: shorts, wrinkled T-shirts, ball caps on backward, and cameras strapped around their necks.

Suddenly they were one arm's length away from me.

The paparazzi really had no sense of personal space. Looked like I picked the wrong day to run a simple errand alone, without Shugger, my bodyguard, or even Molly, my personal assistant. I wondered for a frightening second if I should call Max and have him send in the troops to pull me out; managers were very good at things like that. But I dismissed the idea—causing a scene might have been worse.

"Hi, guys." I waved in what I hoped was a friendly manner, even though I was dying to turn and run. "I'm sorry, I have to go." I pointed toward the building. "I have an appointment."

"With the 'Psychiatrist of the Stars' again?" one of them said, his snapping camera literally three inches from my face.

Really, I shouldn't have been at all surprised that they knew, even though I'd gone in to see Dr. Robert only one other time—the rest of our sessions had been done over the phone because I was out of the country. Not that they were doing much good, if you asked me. When I'd tried to convince him I was simply having a quarter-life crisis, he didn't believe me.

Maybe he was smarter than I'd thought.

"What do you talk about with him, Abigail?" another paparazzi asked.

I shook my head, playing mysterious, and backed away.

"Yeah, c'mon, you can tell us. It'll be *our* little secret, right?" He snickered while moving his camera to a different angle.

Knowing this had already gone on too long, I turned on my heel and started to walk off, ignoring the warning bells chiming in my head. The three men followed me, saying things I tried to ignore. All the paparazzi were really after was a reaction—they wanted to snap a picture of you crying or yelling or adjusting your bra strap.

"Yo, Abby," one of them called out, stepping in front of me right before the entrance. "How's Christian these days, huh?"

My stomach dropped to the floor and my throat felt like a long, slippery snake was choking off all my oxygen. His question was a low blow, even for them, but I did not react. Christian was my one button the paparazzi knew they could push—even though what happened to Christian was a year ago. That didn't matter to them. In fact, they would sink as low as they had to, dig up the most painful part of my past and twist it into something even uglier, just to get the response they wanted. But I refused to give it to them.

Instead, I swallowed hard and said nothing. When I tried to step around them, the photog in front blocked my way again.

"How does it feel, Abby? To know you killed your brother?"

I wasn't sure when I realized that my forward motion had stopped. Half of my brain was screaming to remain calm, *Do not react, Abby*, while the other half was painfully aware that the clicking sound of the cameras had suddenly tripled. There was no part of my brain that could give the command to retreat.

The next sound I heard was my own gasping. I felt tears on my cheeks when I pressed a hand over my mouth. Blood rushed to my head as I bent forward, my other hand braced on the front of my thigh. My eyelids were clenched so tightly that all I saw was black . . .

The next thing I was fully aware of was sitting on the small sofa in Dr. Robert's office. He was staring from a wingback chair a few feet away while some hidden machine was playing sounds of the ocean, and there was a steaming cup of something minty smelling on the table next to me. I looked down at my lap toward an area of acute pain. Both fists were white-knuckled—nails digging into my palms. When I swallowed, my throat felt uncharacteristically raw. I tried to think back, wondering if I'd really just broken down like that. In the middle of rush hour. For the whole world to see.

"Are you ready to talk about it?" Dr. Robert asked, clicking his pen. "About your brother?"

I took a breath and opened my mouth.

But then I closed it, sealing my lips together. No, I was still not ready to talk about it.

Dr. Robert crossed his legs. "All right, then."

I reached over for my drink and took a sip, then another, staring down into the mug. The liquid inside looked like tiny tsunamis as my hands shook.

"Okay," Dr. Robert said, lowering his notebook. "Let's talk about something lighter for a while." He stroked his short beard. "When was the last time you felt happy?"

I chuckled darkly and rolled my eyes, about to explain to him that I hadn't had one moment of joy since Christian died. But then I thought of something else and realized that wasn't the truth.

"Three . . . three days ago," I began, my voice sounding scratchy. "We were in Paris. The band was exhausted—it was our ninth show in nine nights. We were running on adrenaline." I returned the cup to the table and looked toward the window past Dr. Robert's head. "During the acoustic set, it was just Hal and me onstage. The song was slow—a love ballad from our first album. We were sitting on stools. Hal was on guitar, and I was behind a standing mike. Toward the end of the song, I remember closing my eyes." I closed my eyes then, reliving the memory. "I could actually feel the music pulse through my body, down to my toes, under my hair. I've never felt so . . . *alive*." I sat forward, leaning toward Dr. Robert. "My voice, the band, all the instruments were blending perfectly that night; everything was clicking. As I sat under the spotlight, I felt the energy of fifty thousand friends singing along with me, singing their hearts out. That massive venue was suddenly intimate, like we were *all* in sync. I wondered if they knew we were experiencing something extraordinary."

I pressed both hands over my heart. "Hal and I snuck a look at each other at the end. We were grinning like idiots. Right then, I knew I was doing exactly what I was meant to do, what I *love* to do, every day, every minute. I felt it in my bones. And I was *so* . . ." I broke off when my voice cracked. "I was so perfectly happy."

I opened my eyes and looked at Dr. Robert, pleased that I'd done what he asked.

"And now?" he said. "How do you feel today?"

I felt my chest go instantly tight and my hands ball up as before.

chapter 1

"A DAY IN THE LIFE"

"Yellow Submarine" was playing from my jeans. I knew who was calling by the ringtone, but I didn't answer right away. It couldn't be too important; we'd already spoken five times.

By the second chorus, I moved to a corner of the bookstore and fished out my cell. "Hi, Molly," I half whispered. "What's happening on the home front?"

"Hold on, Abby. Just a tick." Behind her voice I heard traffic, the radio, and a single horn honking: Molly's. "Bloody *move it*, Tiny Tim!"

I bit my lip in amused pity, imagining some poor waif on crutches trying to cross the street without being mowed down by the beautiful, impatient brunette in the convertible Mini Coop with the Union Jack paintjob. Despite the British accent, Molly's creative potty mouth was legendarily dirty.

"Move your bloomin' *arse!*" she called out, probably while stopped at a red light on Hollywood Boulevard, reminding me of Eliza Doolittle's similar outburst.

The urge to crack up tickled my throat. I stifled it, stood on my toes, and reached for a biography about Janis Joplin on a top shelf. Sure, Molly could be abrasive, but I happened to find it hilarious. She knew her colorful Cockney swearing was known to make me laugh at highly inappropriate moments. She claimed that part of her job as my personal assistant/best mate was to treat me to ten belly laughs in each twenty-four-hour period, even on a day like today when we were on two different sides of the country.

But that was "before." These days, it took a lot to get me to laugh.

My life had changed since the shooting. It had been a year, and there I was, chopped into bits, organized and separated like items on the dinner plate of a finicky eater. Nothing touching, no overlapping. Compartmentalized survival mode at its most dysfunctional. Doctor Robert would've been *so* proud.

"Anyhoo," Molly finally said to me, "Where was I?"

"We hadn't gotten past hello." I replaced the Joplin book and grabbed one about Julie Andrews. Snowcapped mountains were on the cover. I liked that.

"Hello, Abby, *darling*." Molly chimed, bright and sparkly, exactly the way I'd needed her the past five years. "Where are you now? Still at your sister's place, yeah?"

"No. Pensacola, at a bookstore." Hearing whispers on the other side of the bookshelf, I quickly moved to the end of the biography aisle, getting that hot-and-prickly feeling up the back of my neck. I couldn't see anyone, but I knew I was being watched. I guess my cover was blown.

After a beat, Molly asked, "You're out in public? And are you out-out," she continued, using our *very* ingenious code language, "or just out?"

"Just out," I reported, adjusting the dark aviator sunglasses that covered practically half my face. My long hair was pulled back, too, tucked inside a baseball cap. I tried, but I'd never been very creative at the whole *disguise* thing.

"You're out in public," Molly repeated. "On your own?"

"Doctor's orders," I sing-songed. "He said if I took this trip to Florida alone, I couldn't just hide in Lindsey's house all summer. He made me promise to get out among the people."

"He's a quack," Molly muttered.

I nodded in private concurrence and then dropped the Julie Andrews book in my shopping bag. "It was the right decision, though, to stay away from L.A.," I conceded aloud, knowing that Molly's protective/venomous dislike of Dr. Robert was for my benefit.

"It *was* impulsive," Molly admitted slowly. "Less than a week ago, you were onstage in Paris."

"True." I lowered my voice. "But for the past year, you know how everyone's been saying I need support—the familial, *unconditional* kind." I paused to roll my eyes, wondering if Molly would disagree with this diagnosis as well. When she didn't, I jumped back in. "I suppose they're right. Or maybe I got tired of arguing. I don't want to even think about ... *it* ... anyway." I paused again, stuffing down the sick feeling that came every time I thought about Christian.

"I've been here only one day," I continued, after quickly crossing from behind one bookshelf to another, "but Lindsey kept watching me with those big eyes, so I called her a bad word, grabbed her car keys, and started driving."

"What word?" Molly asked, a wicked smile in her voice.

"You don't want to know. But let's just say I won't be given any sister-of-the-year awards."

When I heard another sound behind me, I glanced over my shoulder. But again, no one was there, only whispers from around the corner. I heard my name more than once. I sighed.

"What's wrong?" Molly asked.

"Cockroaches," I answered. "The lights came on, and everyone scattered." Of course I should've been happy about it—that no one was pawing at me for a change. But for some reason, knowing that I was being watched was worse than being approached. Since my public meltdown on the street two days ago, I suppose people were afraid to venture near.

"Start flapping your arms around, then," Molly suggested. "And scream like a banshee. See what happens."

"Nothing will happen. They'll be too stunned to speak, or they'll say, 'Isn't that *her*? Didn't she used to be that famous singer? Such a shame.'"

I paused, staring blankly at the shelf in front of me, listening to the sounds of the bookstore: shoppers, clerks, background music. "An hour ago, the place was pretty much empty. Now it's packed. I'm afraid to come out of the fortress of books I constructed in the back corner."

"That bloody *stinks*, babe," Molly said sympathetically.

I smiled, but it hurt my face. Frowning felt more natural. Evidently my mood-altering happy pills weren't doing their intended job.

"But how clever of you. A whole book fortress? Aww, and the tabloids claim you're a one-trick pony. Ha! One trick, indeed," she muttered. "You should give an impromptu concert, right now, in the middle of the store. Rock their socks off."

"Now there's a thought," I joked, positioning myself in front of a row of thick books with glossy black covers.

"Seriously, though," Molly said after a moment, "do you want me to have Max send in some muscle men to pull you out of there? He has connections everywhere. Like the mob."

"No!" I exclaimed, then dropped my voice. "We promised each other I would be manager-free this summer." I slid the hot-vampire-meets-socially-awkward-teenager book back into its place on the shelf and glanced down the aisle. "It's not like I'm being assaulted by psychos jumping out of corners, so why cause a scene?"

"I'm your biggest fan, Abigail Kelly," Molly quoted in her best Kathy Bates stalker voice.

"I'll leave soon," I promised, mostly to myself. "I'm just not ready to go back to Lindsey's yet. She'll have questions I don't want to answer."

There was a silent beat before Molly exhaled a noncommittal, "Yeah."

I immediately felt the vibe of our conversation darken. I bit my lip, hating how disconnected and gray my life had become.

After another stretch of silence, Molly said, "So, Abby? I called you for a reason this time, actually … b-because …" After some uncharacteristic stammering, her comments changed direction. "Well, anyway." She exhaled. "I have to ask, you still taking your meds?"

My stomach dropped. I knew she was just doing her job, but I hated being treated like a mental patient. "Yes, Molly," I reported, busying myself with the growing stack of books in my bag. "Every morning," I practically cheered. "Every morning for three hundred and sixty-three days—" The last word caught in my throat.

I had no idea why I tried to make a joke out of it. Reciting the exact number of days since Christian died was *not* totally hilarious. And suddenly, I couldn't breathe. That year-old noose, that long, slippery snake was slithering up my throat, coiling around my insides, choking me until I couldn't—

"Well!" Molly cut in brightly. "You'll be happy to hear that the stalkerazzi are still 'round your house here. And you haven't even been up in Malibu for, like, what? A year?" She scoffed. "So completely *stupid*."

I caught my breath, listening to her complain unintelligibly for a while, her slurry Eliza Doolittle lost on me again. Since Molly and I were practically joined at the hip, the paparazzi pissed *her* off as much as me.

"Any guys around?" she asked, veering us toward a more pleasant distraction subject. "Describe them, please. It's high time you got a little action."

I shook my head but played along. "There's a tall gangster wannabe behind the computer games," I reported in a low voice while leaning against the end of the bookshelf. "He's holding his hand over half his face trying to make it look like he's not totally ogling." I whipped off my sunglasses and made a point of holding direct eye contact with the guy. His face went beet red before he backed up and disappeared.

"How ugly is he?" This was always Molly's first question about anybody.

My reply to her was always the same. *"Butt,"* I answered. "Gold chains, wife beater, fedora. He looks like 2003's Justin Timberlake puked on him."

"Hot."

When I moved my phone to the other ear and turned around, I noticed *him*, standing alone, right across the aisle at the end of Sports & Outdoors. I did a double take, which didn't happen often, because except for the ones with wicked-tall blue hair or an exceptionally nice posterior, I hardly noticed the existence of guys anymore. Occupational hazard of living in L.A., where everyone was perfect, plastic, and beautiful.

But I did notice this guy. He was laughing out loud at whatever he was reading.

That's what hooked my attention, the laugh. I wished it were contagious. Before I fully realized that we were staring at each other and that maybe I should have, I don't know, smiled or something similarly human, he tucked the book into the crook of his arm and walked away.

"Listen." Molly broke into my thoughts. "I'll pay ya ten bucks to walk over and kiss him. Right now. Chop-chop."

"What?" I gasped, feeling a little fluttery. "No way, Molly." As I spoke, I couldn't help standing on my tiptoes to see where Laughing Guy had gone.

"Go on, then," Molly continued. "March up, tear off his stupid fedora and gold chains, close your eyes, and think of England."

That's when I realized who she was talking about. "Oh. Har har. Here I go. Alert the media." It was a joke, but even back in the day when I was milking my celebrity for all it was worth, I never would have sauntered up to a stranger and attacked. After another quick glance around, I realized Laughing Guy had left my section of the store. I sighed, a bit disappointed.

"You've been out of the VIP scene for too long," Molly said.

"He's gone, anyway. So much for all men fainting into a heap at my feet."

When I heard Molly's chuckles turn to snorts, I started laughing, too. I absolutely adored her—she was as close to me as my sister, Lindsey. While running my fingers along the skinny spines of Dr. Seuss, I calculated how long it had been since Molly and I hit those VIP clubs on our rare nights off.

Not long enough.

"The very idea of the club scene is exhausting, it'n it?" Molly said, continuing my thought.

I answered with one confirming chuckle.

"At twenty-four," she went on, "your partying days are over."

I chuckled again, only bleaker. Another confirmation.

"So, what books have you collected so far?" she asked, probably realizing that my thoughts had strayed toward the dark again.

"Well . . ." I sat down on the long bench in front of the magazines, pulling from the tote bag my potential purchases one at a time. "A coffee table book about Maui," I reported.

"For Hal?" Molly exhaled one humorless laugh. "At least it will give him something to read besides *Rolling Stone* or *Lead Guitarists' Worst Hair Weekly*." I could almost hear the roll of her eyes. Then she beeped her horn at something— probably a mother pushing a baby in a stroller. "He's been tweeting every few minutes," she continued. "The boy needs a hobby. It doesn't sound like the band is up to anything useful this summer."

With one finger, I traced the line of breaking waves on the cover of the Maui book. "The guys are never productive when I'm not around," I mumbled. Then I bit my lip, considering something else. "Molly?" I looked up. "What if fans lose interest because we're taking the summer off? What if we never sell another record? That kind of thing's happened before. I've seen those shows on VH1." I clutched my phone, allowing myself two seconds to imagine the consequences. Then I sprang to my feet. "I need to come home. Today. Right now. Can you get me on the next flight?"

"Abby? *Abby!*"

In a panic, I swung to grab my purse, nearly knocking over my shopping bag of books.

"Abby? Listen to me. Abby—*stop!*"

Molly's voice had the stern tone she saved for emergencies. Hearing it grounded me in place, and I didn't dare move. "We talked about this. You deserve this vacation, okay?" she said, speaking much calmer. "We all do."

I exhaled, but my heart was still pounding in my chest.

"And don't worry about the lads; it's not your fault they bought that gigantic mansion up in the hills. Your fans aren't going anywhere, either. They can't wait to buy the next record, okay?"

I nodded, blinking back sudden tears.

"Are you all right, then?" she asked. "Abby?"

"Can't you hear me nodding?"

Molly laughed approvingly. I wouldn't have survived this without her. She held me together, above and beyond her job description.

"Doctor Robert said this summer needs to be about me," I said in a small voice. "Like a test to see how I survive without a crew of people telling me what to do and where to go and what to wear." When I took in a deep inhale, my lungs shook. "So far . . . I'm failing."

"Give it time, sweetie," Molly soothed. "Collect your things, yeah? It's time to leave the store."

I nodded once more and then obeyed her gentle command.

"Leave the magazine area. Do it straightaway, okay?"

"Why?" I asked, knowing Molly was excellent at steering me from tab rags with bad press or pictures that made me look fat. "Is there something new?"

"No," she said immediately. "Well, yes and no. It's not *new*, per se."

I was already on my feet in front of the rack, scanning the covers for what she was warning me about.

Then I saw it. It wasn't *my* face on the cover, but it might as well have been.

"Are you talking about *Recognise*?" I tore the magazine

from its stack and then stared at the picture on the cover. "Huh. I haven't seen his face in almost a year."

Molly huffed. "Your ex is a moron," she uttered flatly. "Why is it that the more symmetrical the face and perfect the abs, the more idiotic the personality? Look at the title of the cover story."

I read it aloud: "'Miles Carlisle's Tortured Heart.'" Now *that* was a laugh. "Still tortured after almost a year? Maybe he needs to write a song about cheating on his girlfriend and then swear it isn't autobiographical. That used to make him happy."

"He needs to be castrated," Molly stated. "Don't call him."

"Like I would." I sat down, crossed my legs, and opened the magazine. "I'm on dating ice, anyway. Until I find a combination of Clark Kent and a young Paul McCartney, I'm out of the game."

"You'll be single for a while, *chica*."

I chuckled, mindlessly flipping through the magazine. That's when I noticed the large, ice-blue eyes of the girl on page five stared back like I was gazing into a mirror. I remembered this photo shoot. It was five years ago, right at the beginning of my new life. Against my better judgment, I flipped to the center.

There she was again.

I leaned forward. "I'm in it, too."

"I know," Molly said. "The article is total crap, though. Taking that idiot Miles's side. Horrid cow of a writer."

I rubbed a fist into my forehead, massaging away a new headache. "Ya know, a year ago, Christian would have bought up every copy in the store and hidden them in the trunk of his car."

"I know." I heard a sad smile in Molly's voice.

I was smiling, too.

"I never knew what he did with all those," she said, "but I'm sure he recycled."

I started to laugh but choked instead as reality resurfaced:

Christian isn't here now. He'll never be here again. I felt the magazine shaking between my trembling hands.

"Grab the stack," Molly ordered, almost as if she'd heard my thoughts. "Grab them, Abby."

I walked toward the magazine rack, quickly looked around me—no one was close by, of course—and snagged the few mags that were left.

"Drop them on the floor."

I did.

"Now kick the lot of them under the rack."

I paused for a moment, then obeyed. As I stepped back, I wiped my hands on my jeans like I'd just been touching something dirty.

I'd driven almost ten miles toward Seagrove Beach when Molly announced that she had arrived at her apartment. This was the same moment that my cell beeped, warning me of the low battery. Molly had surely been talking to me the whole time, but my mind hadn't been on our conversation.

"I'm FedExing a new charger straightaway."

I told her I had one with me.

"Do you know *exactly* where it is, Abby?"

I frowned, picturing my still unpacked heap of suitcases in Lindsey's guest bedroom.

"It'll be at your sister's house by tomorrow. Plug it in—I need to be able to contact you via mobile."

"Thanks," I said.

When I didn't say anything more for a few minutes, Molly suddenly asked, "Do you want me out there?" I heard forced enthusiasm in her voice. "I'll fly out tonight if you want. We'll veg on the beach all summer. Just you and me. You know, since your brother—"

"No." I cut her off.

But then I didn't know how to continue.

After I fell silent again, Molly said, "Okay, Abby, okay."

Her upbeat tone turned defeated. "But please, call if you need me. Please."

The touch of pleading in her voice made my throat feel tight and snaky again.

"Day or night. Promise me?"

I promised, then quickly ended the call.

ASSOCIATED PRESS, NEW YORK CITY: Music in Me held its eleventh annual concert in New York's Madison Square Garden last week. The charity event raised more than five million dollars for the music and art departments of inner-city schools throughout the country. Those most notable in attendance were . . . Abigail Kelly (of Mustang Sally). This year marked Kelly's fourth to perform at the event and her second as co-host. Mustang Sally has been voted Best Pop Group at the three major music award competitions four years running. No other group has held such high honors.

chapter 2

"HELP!"

Lindsey's house was bright yellow, with a wrap-around porch big enough to accommodate everything from four large wooden rockers, a gas grill, every Tonka truck known to man, and a secluded corner reserved for sunbathing.

Her garage door magically opened as Lemon Drop— Lindsey's vintage yellow Beetle that I'd borrowed earlier— proceeded cantankerously up the driveway. I parked beside her silverish-greenish Volvo. Probably hearing Lemon Drop's final sputter, Lindsey threw open the door to the house. Her bright, smiling face looked fresh and lovely, making me wish for two hours in a makeup chair to catch up.

"You were just on the news!" She beamed. Seems she'd forgiven me for stealing her car and taking off like that. "My little starlet." Over her white skinny jeans, tailored pale-blue button-up top, and hot pink leather flip-flops, she was wearing a white apron with her name embroidered in large red script surrounded by daisies. She could've been the front cover for *Better Homes & Gardens* as well as the Victoria's Secret catalog.

"For what?" I asked, hauling myself out of the car.

"That charity gig last week." She leaned in and started confiscating my shopping bags from the back seat. "I didn't know you wanted to save the rainforest. How noble of you."

"Is that what that concert was for? They never tell us."

I heard my sister's "har har" from inside the car.

Lindsey whistled a tune as she continued pulling out my bags. I stared at the back of her glossy blond hair. How was it that she always seemed so organically happy? This made me recall the earlier conversation with Molly when she'd offered to call Dr. Robert to change my prescription. Maybe she should have.

His name wasn't really Dr. Robert; it was Craig, I think. It was sort of an inside joke. "Doctor Robert" is the name of a Beatles song, the one about the lads being all nice and fixed up on drugs. Well, *one* of those songs. I've been stealing from all things Beatles since I was sixteen.

Anyway, I digress.

Meanwhile, back on Penny Lane . . .

"Why is it so quiet?" I asked, hooking my arm through three shopping bag handles. "Where is everyone?"

"Steve will be home late," my sister replied, "and the boys are out back." She gestured toward the yard. "Running through the sprinklers till dinner." She showed absolutely no leftover frustration from the battle she and her husband had fought against their four-year-old twins that morning.

As we entered the house, I told Lindsey about a photographer I'd spotted in the parking lot across from the bookstore.

"Those people are such *parasites*," she said, the corner of her lip curling in disgust.

"At least he wasn't hanging out in your hedges," I offered cheerily, with only a touch of cynicism. "I do give him props for initiative; his telephoto lens was bigger than the Hubble Telescope."

"Shoulda rammed him with Lemon Drop," Lindsey suggested. "That car's one tough broad. And that dude, he was probably from one of *those* magazines." She crinkled her nose like she smelled something foul. "And they call themselves *journalists*."

We nodded at each other in unspoken accord.

Those reporters didn't even attempt to get the truth

anymore. They caught a whiff and then ran with it. I'd learned to ignore it, to grow a thick skin, but it became intolerable when those stories started to include my brother and how I wasn't at his funeral.

"My cell died," I blurted, needing to distract myself before I got that snaky feeling in my throat again. "Did anyone call for me? Max has your number, so any of my guys can get it."

"Are you expecting to hear from Max?" Lindsey crinkled her nose again. Another foul stench.

"Eventually." I kicked off my sandals by the door.

"I *hate* that guy," she muttered under her breath. "Hal called my cell looking for you." She turned and fluttered her lashes at me.

"What'd he want?"

"We talked for only a few. Sounds like he's missing you."

"He's bored," I said, which was much more logical than her explanation.

"He's *madly* in love with you," Lindsey trilled over her shoulder while I followed her down the hall. "I've been telling you for years."

"Hal and I are buds, Lindsey. Ease up on the match making."

"Don't break his heart—he's sweet."

Now my nose crinkled. "Hal?"

"He cracks me up. He's so witty."

"Are we talking about the same person who recently tweeted 'I just ate some noodles' and 'My toenails are amazing'?"

"Funny, see?" Lindsey laughed and flipped her hair. "And so cute." She stopped to restart the clothes dryer. "Don't you think he's cute?"

"Kind of." I shrugged. "But not the type of cute that makes me want to rip his shirt open."

"Like Miles Carlisle, you mean?"

I dipped my chin, staring at my sister through my eyelashes. "Lindsey. I broke up with that idiot almost a year ago. Again, stop with the match making."

My sister pulled an innocent expression, complete with

big, round eyes. "Okay, okay. But if *you* don't tell me what's going on in your life, then I'll have to get my information elsewhere, and my sources say he's hooked on you." She gestured to the tall stack of magazines behind me next to the picture window. Despite everything they printed about our family and all those other crap-filled stories, Lindsey relied on the tabloids way too much.

"Max is my manager," I said, skipping back to our earlier subject, "and he'll be calling me at some point."

"I thought you were on an official vacation." She dumped the contents of my bags onto the kitchen table to examine the day's purchases.

"I *am* on vacation." I rubbed my nose. "I just don't want Max to think I'm hiding from him."

"You should be hiding. One whole summer off after five years nonstop?" She chuckled sarcastically. "How *generous* of him." She lifted her perfectly sculpted eyebrows at me as she held up a jumbo-sized conch shell coated with cheap mother-of-pearl. "I get you for *three whole months*," she reminded. "That's the deal."

I nodded, unwilling to argue at the moment. She returned the tacky shell to its blue tissue paper. "When you showed up here last night, you looked like death."

"Gee, thanks," I said, running my hands through my hair.

Upon further consideration, however, I probably *had* looked freakishly ghastly when I'd appeared on Lindsey's doorstep, because I'd yet to wash off the gaudy stage makeup from my performance fifteen hours earlier or remove the several feet of pink extensions woven through my hair. I probably looked like something that was dug up then left out to rot.

Lindsey claimed I looked like death. Okay, so at least my outsides were catching up to my insides.

I held my breath and glanced at my sister, willing myself not to break into sobs. There was so much she still didn't know. That sob hung in my chest, torn between the agony of holding in and wishing that I could've told her everything.

"Ah! *Muchas gracias* for this!" Lindsey suddenly exclaimed, flipping through my one purchase for her from the bookstore. "I've been dying to read this."

"You're welcome." I smiled.

After returning my other souvenirs to their bags, Lindsey turned her scrutinizing eyes back to me. In response, I pushed my fingers through my hair, vainly attempting to appear non-dead.

She tipped her head to the side, eyebrows raised. "Don't they let you sleep on that tour bus? Or eat?"

My spine stiffened, causing my proverbial panic-and-retreat alert to kick into high gear.

"Your hair's thinner, Abby." She planted her hands on her hips, continuing to study me.

I felt my face getting hot.

"You've lost more weight, too." She bit her thumbnail, looking guilty. "Seriously, what's happened to you? I saw you six months ago; you looked fine then."

Fine? I wanted to ask. Six months ago, I'd been merely a tragic caricature of my once happy, normal self. Now I didn't even have the energy to keep up the façade.

"I *told* them," Lindsey continued when I remained silent. "I *told* them you weren't strong enough. I told them we shouldn't have let you go back out on the road alone."

"I wasn't alone," I corrected automatically, not bothering to disguise the misery in my voice. "Not for two seconds am I *ever* alone."

She continued to chew her thumbnail, not listening. "But we didn't know what else to do, ya know? And you wouldn't let Mom or Dad help or . . ."

Just breathe, Abby. Just breathe. Let her talk. She'll finish in a minute.

I stared into the middle distance between us, trying to make it look like I was listening, when I was really counting backward from one hundred in my head.

My focus was pulled when I felt something cold on my palm.

"I'm being a bad mom," Lindsey said, after placing a bottle of water into my hand when I apparently didn't take it. "I'm fixing mac and cheese for the boys." She displayed and shook a blue box of dry noodles and powdered cheese. "Seriously contrary to Doctor Oz."

"I'm telling your Mommy Group," I warned, folding myself into a kitchen chair.

"And I'm being even lazier and making a dumbed-down version of Rachel Ray's Cobb salad for Steve and me. I'll fix you whatever you want. Sky's the limit."

"Food." I gulped, feeling woozy just speaking the word. "Food is the last thing—"

"Then don't worry about it," she said, filling a saucepan with water at the sink. "You'll have to eat sometime. I'll try not to worry about you. At least not *openly* worry about you. I know how much you hate that."

I leaned over, reaching for one of the glossy magazines. At a glance, I realized I'd met every single person on the cover. I grabbed a pen off the counter and idly start filling in black teeth on Angelina.

Lindsey dried her hands on a red kitchen towel then tucked it into her apron. As she examined the magazine over my shoulder, she played with a chunk of her shiny blond hair, looking exactly like pictures of our mother at that age: both natural, effortless beauties. Unlike me. I had to work like a maniac to keep my booty in check. The men in the family were just as genetically fortunate, father and son, movie star good looks, spitting images twenty-five years apart.

Falling last in line, I'd been born a hodge-podge of all four. My hair is naturally dark, and so is my skin. My peepers turned out an odd grayish-blue and larger than sometimes look normal for the size of my face. My neck is long, my face round, and my feet big. I'm also the shortest in the family by several inches, shooting up to five foot six when I was fifteen, all sharp knees and elbows.

I used to beg Mom to give me highlights so I would look more like Lindsey, but it never happened. Of course, the color of my hair was the first thing I was required to alter after I signed Max's contract five years ago. That makeover experience was my own personal *Miss Congeniality* transformation. Out of that salon I'd stepped: new hair, new eyes, and new clothes. Malibu Abby, made by Mattel.

After that, every photograph of me was as a blond in colored contacts—an ice-blue so dramatic it reminded me of the sky in the Van Goghs I'd obsessed over in my painting classes during my last semester of college. At first I thought my eyes looked too phony, but like most things, I got used to them. Then they became my trademark.

"You did get one other phone call," Lindsey began again, pulling me back to the present. "Mom." She stood very still in the middle of the kitchen, waiting to see my reaction.

"Oh?"

When she didn't get the response she was expecting, Lindsey turned her back to resume her task. "Just checking on you," she continued from over her shoulder. "Making sure you arrived safely. You should give them a call when—"

"I will," I cut in. "When I get the chance."

And with that, Lindsey let the subject drop.

Lazily, I glanced past her at the refrigerator, covered in photos and drawings, some with crayons, some with markers or finger paint. I felt a little lump in my throat, slightly jealous of the normal life she was living, and feeling pained at the same time, knowing that I'd basically forfeited any kind of traditional normalcy to live *my* life.

Something caught my eye. "Lindsey?" I rose to my feet. "Why do you have *that* up there?"

Lindsey followed my stare to the magazine page taped to the side of the fridge. "I think it's hilarious." She grinned as she regarded it. "It was taken the night before I left you in Amsterdam, back in January. Remember?"

I stood before the picture. "I remember," I said, smiling at the memory.

The picture was of Mustang Sally—all four of us in the band. At the far end of that ornately decorated Dutch hotel hallway, Hal and the guys had thrown a sort of cul-de-sac after party our last night in Europe. That photo captured the scene: ice buckets, pizza boxes, some random girls behind us out of focus, and visual evidence of the aftermath of a multicolored Silly String war. The guys had unleashed a surprise attack on Lindsey and me.

"Hey, they airbrushed you out." I pointed at the photo. "You were right there next to me. You had Jordan in a headlock."

"I know." Lindsey shrugged, wiping down the counter.

I turned back to stare at the picture. Cameras don't lie, but computers sure can be deceptive. Not only deleting my sister, but also adding what looked like strategically placed items of beer bottles and ladies' lingerie. I'd been there that night, and I knew the guys were drinking nothing more than Mountain Dew. In their own ridiculous ways, the guys did try to play their parts—dating models, racing motorcycles, and other equally mature endeavors. But we weren't your typical rock stars.

I examined the picture more closely. "It's kind of endearing, if they weren't so infantile."

"I love it. Because *look*." She pointed at the photo. "You're laughing."

And I was. Huh.

Frozen in time, the four of us were covered in a rainbow of sticky, wormy webs, and my mouth was wide open. Laughing. Unabashed.

No, cameras don't lie. But I also remembered the guilt I felt right afterward, knowing that before that night, I hadn't laughed in months. I didn't deserve to laugh after what I did.

"What do you want to do tomorrow?" Lindsey asked, probably catching the change in my expression. I tore myself away from the picture to look at her. She was chopping bell peppers with an orange-handled chef's knife on a turquoise plastic cutting board.

"Absolutely nothing," I answered, returning to my chair. "I intend to be an über beach bum for the first month." I let my head drop onto the table and then rested it on one cheek. "Just flip me over twice a week so my tan is even." I closed my eyes.

Lindsey dropped something loud into the sink.

"Why?" I asked, popping one eye open. "What do you have going on?"

"Cleaning house," she said. "Early in the morning before the boys are up."

"Need help?"

She looked at me with a grin. "Abby. Please . . ."

We har-har'ed in unison, knowing the domestic gene had totally skipped me.

I propped my head on my elbow and flipped through the magazine in front of me, not really looking at the pages. I let myself be distracted for a while, my attention shifting from the magazine to watching Lindsey bustle around her kitchen, always on the go, always on top of everything, chatting away.

"Around eight o'clock," she said, "I'm taking the boys into Panama City for haircuts, and then we have their four-year checkup in the afternoon. Steve's meeting us for dinner at a new place that just opened on the water. Why don't you come along? We'll make a day of it."

"Sounds like fun." I yawned, shoving the magazine aside so my head could drift down to the table. "But I should probably lay low around here, if that's okay."

I felt Lindsey at my side. She swept the hair off the back of my neck and laid her cool fingers on my skin, exactly like our mother used to do. "Why don't you go up to bed?" she suggested. "After all those frantic pop-sprints you do on-stage, I'm sure your body is exhausted."

I pulled myself to my feet, heading in the general direction of the guest bedroom. "Just so you know," I said over my shoulder, "that maniac performer is the *old* me." My legs felt so heavy, it was exhausting to climb the stairs. "I'm much more boring now. No tricks, no surprises, no—"

Before the words had completely escaped my mouth, I

stubbed my toe halfway up to the landing and fell face first onto the plush carpeted stairs.

As I began my slow and helpless slide back down, Lindsey went from gasp to laugh to cackle. By the time I reached the bottom, she was bent in half, tears streaming down her cheeks. "Abigail Kelly, ladies and gentlemen. No pictures, please!"

It was exactly 9:02 in the morning when I caught myself watching the clock. Lindsey and her boys had been gone barely an hour, and I was already bored out of my skull.

After drifting from room to room, I slid open the glass door at the back of the living room and stepped out onto the deck.

The Gulf of Mexico was bright blue, like sun hitting stained glass in a church window. Florida always seemed so clean to me, probably because I spent my quality time—if and when there was any—in small, secluded places like Seagrove Beach and her sister city Seaside, instead of Miami's South Beach or Tampa's club strip.

Tipping my chin up and to the east, I closed my eyes, allowing the morning sun to hit my face straight on. Yellow and black sunspots danced inside my eyelids. I clutched the railing of the deck, swaying back and forth.

Something fluttered in my stomach, and I realized my palms were sweaty.

I know what this feeling is . . .

The desire to be out in the world—free at last!—if even for a little while, was suddenly overwhelming. The same desire had hit me yesterday and inspired my impromptu fieldtrip to Pensacola, which had turned into a big, fat fail. Before then, I hadn't really been out in public since the day I went to see Dr. Robert in L.A. Another fail.

I pressed my hands against my stomach and opened my eyes, staring into the different levels of blue. When my tummy flipped again, I realized I'd concocted a plan.

Before I could change my mind, I spun on my heel and headed back inside the house in search of my sandals. While strapping them on, I spotted my cell being charged on the counter. I unplugged it and slipped it in my pocket. With shoes properly on feet, I hustled out back to the shed behind the house, hauling out my sister's monstrous red beach cruiser—balloon tires, wire basket, the whole works—and the accepted and preferred mode of transportation in South Walton County. A Dodgers baseball cap hung on a nail next to the door. I plopped it on my head and yanked down the bill.

At a leisurely pace, I pedaled along the bike path that followed Scenic Highway 30A. Houses to my right, Gulf to my left. It was one of those perfect Florida days, the kind you read about in *The Best Places to Go* travel books and hear in those old Beach Boys songs about turquoise waves, white sand, and surfer babes.

A few other bikers, joggers, and dog walkers were out on the path, all of whom nodded to me as we passed each other. Across the street, two women were speed walking. One was in a purple T-shirt, and one in a red windbreaker, both in matching yellow visors and round sunglasses. I was enchanted by how typically Florida they seemed.

Lindsey and I used to be chummy like that, I thought as they speed-walked ahead of me. Sometimes when she came to visit me in L.A., we used to creep around shopping malls, me in deep disguise until an ultra-observant fan inevitably busted us. Then we'd run like mad, giggling until we cried.

I bit my lip and squinted up at the sun. Lindsey and I didn't laugh like that now. Like so many other things in the past year, I'd also learned to live without my sister.

Behind the walking pair strolled a man and a woman, hand in hand. When they stopped for a little cuddle, he patted her belly, rubbing the swelling baby bump. I didn't bother to hide that I was drinking in their private moment.

As I got closer, I found that I was wondering if the daddy-to-be was cute. Then, for whatever reason, I thought about that idiot Miles. Even though the relationship was ancient history, there was something reassuring about knowing that once upon a time I'd been able to feel a romantic connection. I wondered if that would ever happen again.

What really interested me now was the lofty idea of meeting someone with whom I could have an interesting, non-celebrity-centered conversation.

Dream big, Abby!

I glanced at the happy couple again.

And now they're kissing. Great. The one thing I actually miss about dating.

I knew I shouldn't have been daydreaming about romance, because I was trying to get my head straight. Kissing should've been the last thing on my mind. So with a flex of my abdominal muscles, I mentally forced that yearny feeling down my legs and to the bottoms of my shoes. When I paused at a crosswalk, I stomped my feet, just to make sure I got it all out.

Back on the bike, I coasted in and out of little beachfront neighborhoods with names like Gulf Glades and Seashore Shades. Lush greenery lined the streets, along with flower patches and quaint cookie-cutter homes, reminding me of the candy house from *Hansel & Gretel*. I was grateful Lindsey lived in a place like Seagrove Beach. I could disappear here.

Skidding to a halt at a three-way stop, I had the monumental decision of which direction to take next. Left was sugary white sandy beaches, right was a string of T-shirt shops, and straight ahead was Seaside Town Square.

I smiled and adjusted my hat, setting my course dead ahead.

chapter 3

"DAY TRIPPER"

The big red cruiser rattled and jarred as I rode over bumpy cobblestones. While still in forward motion, I swung my leg over one side of the bike, landed on both feet at a little jog, then walked us both up the sidewalk. I leaned the bike against the front window of Modica Market; no chain, no lock—something you could still do in Seaside.

It was pretty early, and there weren't many people out yet. Feeling at ease, I strolled up the sidewalk, peering in the different store windows as I passed, just like any other shopper might do. For a while, I lost myself in shark teeth on strings, paintings of tropical settings, homemade fudge, and hand-crocheted baby blankets.

When I heard the characteristic muffled and thumping bass line of pop music, my attention was drawn to a blue minivan pulling into a parking space a few yards away. The side door slid open, and out poured approximately twenty teenage girls. It was like one of those clown cars at the circus—they kept coming and coming and coming.

And I froze, except for the wind whooshing from my lungs like a deflating balloon.

I knew if I were spotted, my clandestine outing, and quite possibly my entire vacation, would be dashed beyond all human repair. I also suddenly remembered what I was wearing. Max would have a brain seizure if anyone published pictures of me in my sister's off-the-rack jean cutoffs and a yellow tank top that read "I'm a Woo-hoo Girl" across the front. Also, I didn't have my blue contacts in, and I was sure my hair was a windblown disaster.

Not taking the time to weigh my options, I lowered my chin and ducked toward the first shop I came to. I pushed, but the stupid glass door wouldn't give, as if it were swollen from humidity. Desperate and frantic, I gave it a few more mighty shoves with my shoulder and then stumbled in.

A Chinese gong clanged overhead as the door closed behind me.

"I'll be right with you," a voice called out.

I raised the bill of my ball cap, stealing a quick glance around. The store appeared to be devoid of any customers. My first stroke of good luck.

"That's okay," I answered into the air. "Just looking." Seemingly out of harm's way, I took off my hat, ran my fingers through my tangled hair, and observed my surroundings.

The store was one big square. Merchandise was sparse but organized and aesthetic. *Save the Manatee, We Take You Fishing!* and *Calcutta Bait* posters plastered all walls and windows, along with numerous colorful, attention-catching flyers advertising everything from dog walkers to worm diggers. Lavishly painted surfboards, black wetsuits, instruction manuals, and maps filled in the rest of the perimeter. Clothes — shorts, T-shirts, and bathing suits — hung from neat, round silver racks in the middle of the floor.

From a shelf displaying other similar sea-life statues, I picked up a three-inch blue crystal figurine of a dolphin. A fancy white tag was attached to it with a gold string. The description on the tag was in one of those Scandinavian languages, Danish, maybe. Still not 100 percent used to a seven-figure salary, I turned it upside-down to check the price.

"*Six hundred dollars?*" I said aloud, incredulous. "For this piece of — "

"That's an original."

I gasped and whipped around.

He was tall—I noticed this first because I felt myself looking up.

"It's a Hans Schoster. Just arrived from . . ."

He was talking, but I was concentrating on something else because, after his height, what automatically registered next in my brain was the angular bone structure of his face and the early June surfer-boy suntan that covered his athletic body.

"I take it you've heard of him?"

"Well . . ." I did try to answer, but I was preoccupied by his hair now, dark and wavy, cut conservatively but rumpled enough to give the impression of a vacation on the Riviera or having just rolled out of bed.

He was saying something else while gesturing to the display over my shoulder.

Tall and built, he reminded me of a much younger version of the hunky Australian actor who played Wolverine, minus, of course, the shredded wife-beater, sadistic glares, and clear need of a manicure.

"Obviously," Wolverine continued, "six hundred is a steal. And if you'll notice . . ." He was off again, pointing at the dolphin in my hand. Something in his diction made him seem older than he looked.

When he stopped talking, I blinked. He blinked, too, drawing me into the color of his eyes. They were bright green, the prettiest this side of Ireland.

"Are you a collector?" he asked.

Yes, I knew he'd been speaking the whole time, and when I realized I hadn't uttered anything coherent, my face felt much too hot and my pulse banged in my chest like a kettle-drum. I wondered if I was about to have a heart attack, right there beside the bikini rack.

The guy dipped his chin and chuckled.

That's when it hit me. It was the guy from the bookstore yesterday.

Oh my. He's completely gorgeous up close.

To join my other pulmonary embolism symptoms, I broke out in a sweat. As I was about to clutch my chest and beg him to call 9-1-1, I realized I wasn't about to stroke out. The simple fact was: I was standing in very close proximity to an incredibly hot man and having a *normal human female response.*

I relaxed and exhaled.

"If you like dolphins," he said, "I can show you something in a different price range."

I stared at his hand, which was outstretched and held open, presumably waiting for me to hand over the statue. "I like this one," I finally said, "but thanks." Although my mouth had moved, the rest of my body seemed to be stuck in place. Wolverine's green eyes widened. I tried to offer a breezy little laugh, but it came out as a hiccup.

For whatever reason, my attempt at composure was failing. In fact, I felt myself going redder in the face and sweatier down the back. In a last-ditch effort, I sealed my lips, spun around, and walked away, almost running head-first into a clothing rack. The prickle under my hair informed me that the guy was watching my retreat. All casual-like, I started twirling a strand of hair around one finger while pretending to examine a purple beach towel draped through a wooden hanger.

"Would you like me to hold the Schoster at the register while you look around?"

When I turned back, the expression on Wolverine's face was readable. He was skeptical, probably wondering how a twenty-something woman wearing cutoff jeans, a campy graphic tank, and a Dodgers cap could afford a six-hundred-dollar "original."

"I'm not going to *steal* it, if that's what you're worried about." *Nice. Well done, Abby.*

The guy with the green eyes said nothing.

Stalling for time, hoping the coast would soon be clear outside, I meandered to an adjacent wall with a variety of hats hanging from hooks. Being a closeted hat aficionada,

I put down my baseball cap and dolphin statue and pulled a floppy forest green fishing number off a hook. *Hmm, not quite right.* Next I tried on a leathery Indiana Jones–type fedora, but it swam on me. After experimenting with something that resembled an English cricket cap, I maneuvered closer to the exit and took a peek through the glass door. The blue van was still parked outside.

I twisted my lips and sighed.

"Try this one," Wolverine said, coming up behind me. He was holding out a pretty straw hat with pale blue and yellow flowers dotting the wide, floppy brim. "I think it might go with your eyes."

I cocked my head. "Is that some kind of line?" I said, automatically going on the defense.

"Um, no." He seemed puzzled at first but then he lifted a slow smile.

He looked like he belonged in a men's magazine selling razors or aftershave—the kind of face you're just dying to slap with both hands to see if the skin's as tight as it looks. After the slap you're supposed to grab the face and kiss it, right?

He waved the straw hat in front of me.

I took it and moved to a mirror. "I don't think it looks right," I said after putting it on.

"Because you've got it sideways." He stepped directly in front of me, reached out, and made the necessary adjustments.

I had nowhere to stare except at his chest. He smelled great, freshly soaped and shaven. After living months at a time on a tour bus with a bunch of musicians of questionable hygiene, I forgot that guys could actually smell nice. And this guy smelled more than nice.

"Now what do you think?" he asked, stepping back and putting his hands in his pockets.

"Yeah, better," I replied without bothering to consult the mirror.

He was wearing gray flip-flops, khaki cargo shorts, and a blue T-shirt—all items looking suspiciously like the new Resort line from Emporio Armani gracing the pages of *Vogue*.

I silently compared his Italian beachcomber garb with my string of binding haute couture that I was usually forced to parade around in. And I envied him.

Suddenly, he took another step back and folded his arms.

I swallowed hard, knowing what was probably coming next.

"Do you live around here?" he asked.

Here we go ...

"Just visiting," I offered nonchalantly. Like that ever worked.

"But you've been here before," he stated, rather than asked. He'd seen my face somewhere. *Of course* he'd seen my face somewhere. "I recognize you."

"Yesterday." I dropped my chin, preoccupied by my fingernails. "I saw you ... at the Pensacola Barnes and Noble."

"Oh, is that it?" When I looked up, he was tapping his chin. "No, no. Somewhere else."

I shrugged, briefly intoxicated by his accent now. It was foreign, very subtle, not exactly British or French, but he certainly didn't have that Floridian twang.

"I've got one of those faces!" I exclaimed. This was followed by an overexcited chuckle. Knowing that I was probably going mildly hysterical, I figured I should start backing toward the exit.

"Aren't you forgetting something?" He held up the blue dolphin between his thumb and index finger. But then he lowered it and scratched his chin, looking frustrated. "You're sure we haven't met formally? I could swear—"

"Yes—quite," I cut in smoothly, copying his proper dialect. "I'm positive." After another manic chuckle, I reached out and unbuttoned a red-and-white Hawaiian shirt on a mannequin with no arms or head.

It sucked. No, it *really* sucked, but I knew the drill, and it was only a matter of time before my cover was blown and I was forced to hole up in Lindsey's house, dodging cameras and reporters until I was driven out of hiding and shipped to L.A. I wasn't ready to go back yet.

"Can't I just buy the thing," I mumbled, "without the twenty questions?"

He opened his mouth but then closed it, his green eyes holding on me with even more frustration. After a few seconds, he let out the breath he'd been holding, and something on his face changed. Apparently he'd given up on uncovering my identity.

"You got it," he said, strolling to the counter. "That's six plus tax." He punched buttons on the register. "Paying with paper or plastic?"

I couldn't help noticing a little smile tugging at the corner of his lips as he talked. This was rather distracting. He lifted his eyes to me like he was expecting something, but I had no idea what he'd been saying. I'd been wondering what his neck smelled like. Was that where the aftershave was? Was he shirtless when he'd splashed it on that morning?

The sound of his tapping a finger on top of the register shook me awake. "Oh! My wallet." I touched my hands to the front of my hips. "I left home in such a hurry." I dug a hand into the front pocket of my shorts, pulling out a thin, flat five-dollar bill that Lindsey probably forgot was in there before she washed them. "Do you have a layaway plan?"

His mouth was still fighting that smile.

"No, really. I have the money for it. I just need to come back later." I gestured to the wall with hooks. "I'll take the hat, too."

"I thought you didn't like it."

With a skip, I returned to where I'd left the pretty straw hat. "It's what everyone in Paris is wearing this summer." Properly positioning the hat on my head, I turned up the side brim and struck a pose. "*Regardez-moi*."

It's funny how everything can change.

Just like that.

Behind me, reflected in the mirror, his big green eyes—and his mouth—were wide open.

chapter 4

"ACT NATURALLY"

"Wait a minute." The green-eyed guy was pointing a finger at me. "Aren't you—"

"No, I'm not," I interrupted, backing away, bumping into a rack. Plastic hangers clattered. "Seriously, I'm not her. Okay?"

After a few seconds lapsed, he tilted his head to the side. "You sure?"

I nodded in confirmation and peeled off the straw hat. Turning to the clothes rack, I started straightening the hanging T-shirts. "I'm really not, though." I waved a hand dismissively. "I swear."

"You look just like her."

"Oh, I know." I pulled a turquoise T-shirt off a hanger and pretended to examine it thoughtfully. "I get that *all* the time. Such a drag."

When I sneaked a glance at him, he was grinning. "Right . . ." He drew out the word.

It was a game. I knew it and he knew it, but he didn't seem to mind joining in.

"I'm not surprised in the least," he continued. His arms were crossed in front of him, one finger tapping his chin.

"The resemblance is extraordinary. Maybe you should get a job as an impersonator."

This made me cackle out loud. The irony. I knew the gig was up, but instead of my normal desire to flee the area, shrieking in hysterical panic, I felt okay, more *relieved* than terrified. After all, the guy seemed friendly enough—not the type to call the local tabloid and claim the two hundred big ones for ratting me out.

"How about this," I said and stepped toward him. Standing on my toes, I plunked the straw hat on top of his head. The wide brim hung over his eyebrows. When I was through, I rubbed my palms together, examining my work. "Hmm." I squinted at him. "Perfect. Now *you* look more like her than *I* do!"

He chuckled and extended his hand. "I'm Todd."

"Abby," I said with a laugh—a genuine one this time—as we shook hands.

"I know." From under the shadow of the hat brim, he winked.

I dropped his hand and looked down, feeling hot blood rush up to my cheeks. *You're blushing in front of a cute guy, Abby. It's totally normal behavior. Relax, enjoy it!*

"I'm sorry I was rude before." I pointed my chin outside. "I was waiting for some kids to walk by."

Todd's gaze held on me for a second before it moved to the front window.

"People, you know? The public? It can get crazy." I exhaled a tense laugh, my nervous panic returning, and commenced tugging the ends of my hair.

He took off the hat and gave me a concerned look. "Are you okay?" He ran a hand through the top of his hair, mussing it up, which made him look tremendously cute.

"Umm . . ." Why couldn't I manage to construct more than two real sentences in front of this guy? "It's just crowds. Crowds make me jumpy, and I kind of freak out."

Well, that's obvious.

I was painfully aware that I was on the brink of babbling

on about my potential panic attacks to a total stranger. After a nod, Todd started folding a pile of tank tops on the table beside him.

After giving myself a few moments to breathe, I went on. "So, I don't remember this store from when I was here last. Do you work ... I mean ... is it yours?" The question seemed weird. I knew he couldn't be more than twenty-eight, but for some reason he seemed older.

Leaving an impeccably folded stack of tanks, Todd moved to another part of the store. As he walked, he straightened oars of different lengths and colors hanging off wires from the ceiling. Below them was a small square table stacked with brochures and flyers about fishing, camping, and boating expeditions.

I followed behind, taking the opportunity to check him out from behind. *Abby like.*

"I've slowly been adding my own merchandise," he offered after what I took for a nod of concurrence at my question.

"You grew up here?"

Todd shook his head, leaning against the front counter. That's when I noticed the long, wooden sign above his head. *Todd's Tackle.* "But I've lived just about everywhere else."

"Army brat?"

He laughed, mostly to himself. "You could say that. My father was in the military, but I've been around the block as well."

I stood next to him, resting an elbow on the counter. "And these worldly travels of yours have somehow made you an expert on women's casual beach headwear?"

He grinned, but then his expression turned mock serious. "As I was watching you pacing around and around"—he pointed his chin toward the center of the store—"my mind was searching for a failsafe opener, something that wouldn't sound horribly corny, yet would express something less common than 'Nice weather we're having.'" He shrugged, running one hand through the side of his hair. "The best I could come up with was, 'Hey, you, put on this hat. Now.'"

"Very smooth," I congratulated.

"Oh, sure." He chuckled. "I was confident I'd eventually win your attention with my irresistible combination of wit and hats." He moved to the other side of the counter, pulling out a bookkeeping notebook held together with rubber bands. "The previous owner was severely behind the times," he said as he dropped the notebook on the counter, "so it's not exactly the way I want it yet." He glanced around his store, reminiscently, as if flipping through old family photos. "But it will be someday. I have a list of things I want to do in my life. Some are here." He glanced around again. "Some are far away. I add to my list every day." He looked at me now. "I've got all the time in the world. And I'm very patient."

With that, he walked to another part of the store, leaving me with my elbows on the counter and my head full of questions.

All the time in the world, my brain repeated. *What must that be like?* Even there in small-town Florida, I was unmistakably reminded of how different I was from everybody else.

While fingering a keychain in the shape of a shark fin, I tried not to eavesdrop as Todd excused himself to take a few phone calls, booking two fishing tours for later in the week. His cell on the back counter was also buzzing with incoming messages and calls, during which I saw the minivan full of its tweener passengers load up and drive away.

"I guess I should be going," I said, as it appeared I had no further excuse to be lingering. Todd was busy, and I should probably get out of his way. "But," I added quickly, "I'll be back for the dolphin." I raised my right hand. "I promise." And I meant it.

With that, we walked toward the exit.

"Come any time," Todd said when he reached the door. "I'm here most days. But you might want to wait until I'm open next time."

I looked at him quizzically. "Your store's not open yet?"

"Not until ten. It's early in the season, but I sometimes *do* have paying customers, you know."

"Why wasn't the front door locked?"

"It was. You barged in. I heard the floor lock snap." He lifted an eyebrow. "Sure, it's a little rusty, but you must be stronger than you look."

"Oh, gosh." I laughed in spite of myself. "Sorry. I was pretty desperate to take cover." I turned toward the window, mortified.

Todd opened and held the door ajar in front of me, displaying one of his beautifully sculpted biceps. "Be careful out there," he offered as hot, sticky air rushed inside the cool room. "Because you know what Sinatra always said."

"Yeah? What did he say?" I asked as I took a quick glance out the door to investigate the population of the sidewalk. It appeared to be as empty as before. I exhaled, relieved, but when I moved my eyes back to Todd, I found him staring at me. His brows were knitted, like he was confused about what he was seeing. It was completely unsettling, yet somehow, my heart picked up speed in the way it does when it knows you're about to get kissed.

Wait. I suddenly panicked. *Do I have something stuck between my teeth? Is that why he's staring?* I sealed my lips. *Or maybe he actually expects me to know what Frank Sinatra said. Who the hell knows* that?

"Everything okay?" Todd asked in a smooth voice. When he took a step toward me, my heart beat even faster. "Here. Don't forget your disguise." He held out my Dodgers cap.

"Oh." My muscles unclenched. "Um, thanks." After that, I didn't know what else to say, and his staring was making me sweat again. "So, I . . ." I cleared my throat in a way I hoped was subtle. And then I managed to ramble off two or three sentences in a language I wasn't even aware that I knew. My accent was probably worse than sub-par.

When I finished, Todd blinked and kind of flinched. "What was *that*?"

I lifted my shoulders. "It's what's written on the tag attached to the dolphin."

Todd looked over his shoulder toward the counter, then back at me. "You speak Danish?"

I shrugged again. No, of course I didn't speak Danish, but I could say "Good night, thank you for coming" in seven languages. The necessity of memorizing song lyrics on the fly had become second nature. Yes, my memory was pretty good.

"You looked at that tag for five seconds and could repeat it verbatim fifteen minutes later?" he asked.

I didn't say anything, just tucked some hair behind one ear.

He smiled, kind of dubiously, and folded his arms. "Do you know what it means?"

"Of course," I said, annoyed by the way he was grinning, like he thought I was lying—even though I was. Fact was, I had no clue what the stupid tag said; I'd only recited it phonetically.

"So?" His grin widened, annoyingly, charmingly. "What does it mean, Abby?"

I cleared my throat, stalling. Then I cleared it again.

Come on. You're Abigail Kelly. Act like it!

Just as I was about to admit the truth, inspiration struck: *What would Molly do?*

Quickly I did an instant recall of all the times I'd seen her flirting with pilots and shoe salesmen and record executives. If I could copy Danish, surely I could copy Molly. I lifted a gradual smile, showing my teeth. After that, I performed this little chin jerk thing that resulted in my blond hair curtaining half of my face. As I snatched my ball cap out of his hand, I made sure to lightly brush him with one finger.

"Later, if you're lucky, Todd's Tackle, I'll tell you *exactly* what it means." I paused to pucker and then twist my lips to the side. "But you're going to have to track me down . . ." I skimmed a finger across the front of my hair, flipping it over one shoulder. "And *beg*."

With that, I walked out the door.

chapter 5

"DO YOU WANT TO KNOW A SECRET?"

"How ugly is he?"

"Butt." I laughed. "Totally, totally butt."

Molly moaned approvingly into the phone. "And you met him at a surf shop?"

"*His* surf shop," I corrected. "He owns the place."

"Blimey. When was this?"

"Two minutes ago, right before you called. I swear, Molly, he's . . . he's so—"

"You didn't spaz out, did you?"

"No," I said, but of course I'd just told a big one.

"Good, good. So now what?"

I lifted my chin and twirled a little *pirouette en dehors* as I headed toward my bike. "I'll go back tomorrow and buy the statue thingy." I bit my lip. "Should maybe learn a little Danish, too. But what if he's not at work in the morning? What then?"

Molly made theatrical gagging noises.

"What?" I asked, recognizing her disapproving tone. "You think I should've pounced on him when I had the chance, don't you?"

"Abby, listen to me." Even her accent sounded frustrated. "I want you to turn round, march back, and give that boy your phone number."

I slowed my pace, considering her suggestion. "But I don't know my phone number."

After some more incoherent muttering, Molly shrieked. "I give up. You're such a bloody conventional *Yankee*. Next thing I know, you'll have run off with one of those creepy ponytail lads with a Darwin fish on his bumper, then move to a farm in Idaho to raise alpacas."

I lowered my cell and stared at it. "What?"

"I think you know what I mean, missy."

I laughed again and hung up.

The heat of the morning had kept most of the day-trippers off the cobblestone streets of the Seaside Town Square. Instead, they sought shelter in backyard swimming pools, air-conditioned restaurants, or bigger cities with malls. I passed by two long rows of brightly colored bicycles—cruisers, like mine, with big tires and a basket hanging between the handlebars. The man running the rental stand sat off to the side under the shade of a tree, his nose in a book, fanning himself with a magazine.

I looked over my shoulder, thinking of Todd. So cute, so *un*Hollywood. Tomorrow I'd go back for the dolphin, for sure. Then the next day, maybe I'd just sort of pop in for no reason, all breezy-like. Guys love that. My smile stretched, and I was suddenly in the mood to make out in the balcony of a theater.

When I arrived back at Modica Market, my bike was un-moved, leaning against the outside of the store. I reached for the handlebars, about to pedal down the sandy sidewalk, re-tracing my path from an hour ago. Instead I stepped over it toward the front window. Cupping my hands around my eyes like a quintessential Peeping Tom, I peered through the glass. Behind the solitary, non-computerized, punch-in-the-keys cash register at the front, the little store was packed with fresh produce, local specialties, and 1950s-style wooden shelves stocked to the ceiling with cans, bottles, and jars of every color, shape, and size.

I knew what my next adventurous mission was going to

be: I would spend that machine-washed five-dollar bill on one jar of Modica homemade jam. Lindsey knew I died for the stuff, especially red currant. She used to send it to me wherever I was, in squatty jars with scalloped labels. I hadn't had any in more than a year, not even a lick off the back of a spoon. Sugar equals fat, you know.

Oh, screw it, I thought, *I'm on vacation.*

After a long, preparatory exhale, I pulled the door open halfway and then froze when a little bell tinkled above my head. An older man with a bushy gray beard and a stiff red apron glanced my way, nodded, and returned to his work. He looked like Santa. I liked that. I leveled my chin and crossed the threshold, allowing that little bell to tinkle its heart out as the door closed behind me.

The display of preserves was right by the entrance. Score! I knelt in front of it, scanning the shelves, but alas, no red currant. As I was about to turn and ask a clerk if there might be any in the back, I spied a jar behind a row of elderberry. Just as I was reaching, a small brown hand jetted out for it.

"Hey," I complained indignantly. "That's mine." Before I knew what I'd done, I snatched the jar back, right out of the hand.

"Mummie, Mummie. She took my jelly." I turned my eyes to find a little boy, his pouty lips quivering, empty hand still outstretched. "Ees *mine*!" he squealed through a colorful island accent. He backed away and wrapped his arm around someone's leg. I looked up.

Her black dreadlocks were swaddled in a purple and orange hair wrap that matched her bright floral dress. She was obviously his mother, all tall and exotic and striking, and she was glaring absolute daggers at me.

The bell on the front door tinkled as someone new entered the store. Great. I kneaded my forehead, worrying for a quick second about the scene I was causing. Max would be irate.

"Aw, of course it's yours," I said quickly, smoothly, smiling up at the glaring mom and then at her pouting kid. I balanced the jar on my open palm. The kid's little hand grabbed it and snapped back faster than a striking cobra. The mother took a step forward, still staring me down.

"I'm sorry . . . about that." I dabbed my forehead with the back of my wrist. No one spoke or moved. "I'm sure there's another jar in back, so I'll just . . ." The kid kind of smirked at me, so I reached out to give him a high five, a seemingly friendly gesture.

"No! No!" he yelped, brown eyes wide, backing away like I was some freako child snatcher. "She try to take my jelly. Mummie!"

"Tom-Tom," the woman said gently, patting his head. But wee Tom-Tom would not be shushed.

The bearded man in the red apron appeared, probably wondering what all the yelping was about.

"Don't let her take it! Don't let her, pleeeeease!" Excellent. The precious little nipper was now pointing a chubby finger at me — no more than three inches from my nose — as he wailed.

The man in the apron scanned me up and down with a scowl. I was now thinking of him as "Evil Santa," and this thought was cracking me up, which made his scowl deepen.

"No-no-no," I implored, biting back another laugh. "I'm not trying to *take* it. I just wanted some . . . uhh . . ." I chuckled nervously. "Some red currant . . . jam stuff."

The mother and Evil Santa stared at me like I was speaking Martian.

"Okay, then, how about I get dibs on the *next* jar? Or, you know, we can thumb wrestle for it." I looked at the kid and laughed. "Ha ha, I'm sure you'll win!"

Evil Santa shifted his weight defensively when I turned to him.

"So, I . . . The jam, if you see any more sitting around, right? Na-ha-ha." Okay, I had no idea what I was saying, and I suspected that my sounding like a mustache-twirling villain wasn't helping the situation. I sat back on my heels, completely out of ideas, with an overwhelming desire to go lie down in the middle of a busy freeway.

"Trouble, Bob?" someone asked from behind me.

I flinched in surprise, immediately recognizing the distinctive vocal timbre of the new speaker. It was burned on my brain, as was the scent of its owner's similarly distinctive aftershave. And for about the tenth time in an hour, I felt myself flushing from head to toe and becoming positively speechless—this time because I was trying to come up with a logical explanation as to why Abigail Kelly was (heh-heh) squatting in the middle of the floor trying to scam a five-year-old out of a ten-ounce jar of high fructose corn syrup.

"No trouble," stated Evil Santa. "This young lady was *just leaving*."

Yeah, I got the hint.

Slowly, I turned my head toward the new voice, displaying my best doe-eyed look of innocence.

Todd didn't so much as blink as he stepped between Evil Santa and me. For a second I thought maybe he hadn't recognized me, or if he had, maybe he was positioning himself to cause a crafty diversion for me to escape. At the very least, he was sure to challenge Evil Santa to a duel to save my honor.

Todd did none of the above. He stood and stared, just like the others. After what felt like an eternity, he sighed and said to Evil Santa, "May I remove her for you?"

"Please," Evil Santa answered and then escorted his malicious minions away from the scene of the crime.

Todd frowned at me like a disappointed father before extending his hand to help me up.

"Thank you," I mumbled, winding a strand of my hair around one finger. "I don't know what just happened. I swear, I was—"

"Stealing candy from a baby?" he whispered. "Abby, how cliché."

"I wasn't stealing," I hissed, wishing for that busy freeway again. I dipped my chin self-consciously and glanced around. "Just please get me out of here."

Todd nodded to the door sporting the tinkling bell.

With long, stiff steps, we filed down the sidewalk shoulder to shoulder, practically at a run. I didn't care where we were going, as long as it was away from *there*. After about a minute, Todd shot me a glance. I lifted one shoulder in reply. He suddenly stopped walking, doubled over, and commenced to howl a laugh so loud it was like he'd been suppressing it for hours.

I stood beside him, arms folded. "Some nerve," I observed. This made him laugh harder.

My own lips started twitching, fighting back a building smile, as I watched him losing it in the middle of the footpath. "I'm *so glad* my public humiliation made your day." My attempt at a sarcastic sulk was pitiful; I was about to lose it myself.

"That might've been the funniest thing . . . I have ever seen." He panted. "Looked like Bob was about to blow a gasket. That bawling kid, his mom glaring curses at you, and you crouched there . . . that panicked expression on . . ." He cackled again.

"Well, I . . ." But it was only a matter of seconds before I grabbed my stomach and squatted in the middle of the sidewalk, letting loose my own hysteria. We remained there, laughing and trying to speak for what felt like hours, until, through my tearing eyes, I saw Todd finally straighten.

"As your liberator," he said, slightly calmer, "I insist you tell me exactly what just happened."

I pushed my hair back and opened my mouth.

"And . . ." he added before I got the chance to dodge the question, "don't even *think* of leaving out a single gruesome detail, or . . ." When he laid one hand on my shoulder, I forgot about pretending to be aloof. "Or I'll throw you back to the sharks without a thought." He grinned, showing straight, white teeth.

That's when I noticed the dimple on his left cheek. It was all I could think about while I begrudgingly conveyed the last ten minutes of my life as we started down the sidewalk. "So," I said when I'd finished, attempting to talk about something besides his dimple, "were you at Modica to save the day or to pick up some red currant jam? Let me save you a trip back—they're out."

"I caught that much." He extended his arm in front of me, forcing us to stop at a crosswalk. "Actually, Chandler's on duty the rest of the day. I stopped in because I promised him lunch." He shot a quick glance in my direction. "But I think that can wait for now." He lifted one hand to shade his eyes from the sun as he scanned both ways for traffic.

"Who's Chandler?"

"One of the local kids who helps out at the store." He touched my elbow, leading us into the crosswalk. "Fearless kayaker. Since he turned eighteen last month, I let him lead all the tours."

"You kayak, too?"

"Yes, ma'am," he answered in a phony southern drawl, "but he's not hitting the water today. I'm forcing him to stay indoors, while also making sure he works extra shifts to earn college tuition." There was that dimple again. "He's a great kid. I really should grab him lunch." He gave me a look. "Think you could sneak back and snag a pastrami on rye?"

"I only steal jam from children. I thought that was clear."

Todd turned his head to laugh.

Not until the bottoms of my sandals were filled with sand did I notice how far we'd walked. "Where are we?" I stopped in my tracks. "My sister's bike. I left it in front of the market." I made an automatic about-face to retrace our steps, but Todd didn't follow.

When I turned back, he was still standing in place, his hands on his hips. His blue T-shirt sleeves were taut around his well-defined arms, and I could tell, even through his shirt, that his chest and abs were just as toned. I wondered if he was one of those guys who obsessively pumped iron, or if he was naturally built lean and mean like a professional soccer player.

"If you're heading back to the Square," he finally said conversationally, "I'll go with you and grab Chandler a sandwich for later." He took a step toward me. "You've eaten at Modica?"

"Not for ages, and never under threat of being scowled to death."

He chuckled. "You're funny." But he said it like he was surprised by the fact. "You should try their tuna," he continued. "I don't eat it, but some call it ambrosia."

"Why don't you eat it, then?"

"No fish unless I catch it myself. A rule I have."

"Tough guy," I said, picturing him all macho on the bow of a boat, rough waves, pole clutched in his hands.

"So?" he said, wrenching me to the present. "Want some lunch?"

"Food?"

He laughed. "That's usually how it works."

I pushed out my bottom lip, taking a quick consensus of my inner condition. No signs of barfiness. No bile. All systems go. My hand patted my empty and suddenly ravenous stomach. "I haven't had tuna in a long time. Ambrosia, you say?"

He nodded. "It's my treat. I insist," he tacked on, not actually giving me an opportunity to object. "It's the least I can do for our town's inexcusably shoddy treatment of a . . . visitor."

I smiled. It felt good to be treated like a lady for a change.

"Lunch sounds great, actually. Thanks." As we smiled at each other, I felt a weird kind of sizzle up the back of my neck. Well, not *that* weird. I knew exactly what it meant. "So, where to?" I asked, forcing myself to speak and not just pin him against the wall.

"Modica's, of course."

"What? Are you crazy?" I screeched. "I am *not* going back in there. Evil Santa will call the cops."

"Who?"

"Evil Santa."

Todd looked perplexed as he translated my description. "Oh. Well, Bob likes to bark, but I'm sure he's forgotten the whole red currant scandal by now. I'm a very loyal customer." His green eyes widened, kind of pleadingly. "So . . . ?"

"Well." But it was no use. I was melting under his eager gaze. "Okay," I finally relented. And with the plan settled, I bounced to his side.

"What should we talk about on the way?" he asked. "Weather? Politics? Your choice."

"How much time do we have?"

He looked down at our slowly pacing feet and then up at the sun, pretending to gauge Galileo-style. He rubbed his chin. "Approximately seven point five minutes, at this rate."

I tried not to crack up at what automatically popped into my head. "Anything?"

"No subject off limits."

"Tell me, then," I began, not missing a beat, "why did your last relationship end?"

This comment was me bypassing small talk and going right for the jugular. I was about as subtle as a southern hurricane. I believe Molly would've been proud.

Todd didn't seem fazed, however. He merely slowed his pace. "Aha." He faced me, looking both surprised and impressed. "You don't mess around, do you?"

"So says Mister I-Catch-My-Own-Tuna."

He chuckled and hooked his thumbs through his belt loops. A few people passed by on the footpath. I barely noticed them. "Okay." He cleared his throat. "Well, there were a number of reasons why it ended. How elaborate would you like me to be?"

"Spare me anything I can use against you in court."

"She was a safe bet. I was into safe bets at the time." He shrugged. "But recently, I promised myself . . . well, let's just say I don't take safe bets anymore on anything. Ever."

"Why?" I asked, surprised at his sternness.

One of his hands clutched the back of his neck and then went running up his head, scratching the top. When I'd spotted him yesterday at the bookstore, I'd zeroed in on his classic good looks. But now the lines of concentration etched into his face made him a different kind of handsome. More real. I could tell that Todd was someone with life experience and stories to tell. I couldn't wait to hear them. He slowed his pace again and turned to look me in the eyes.

"What I want now in a relationship, Abby— No." He shook his head, correcting himself. "Forget what I *want*. What I *know* I *must have* is a woman who takes my breath away."

Okay . . .

"And not just the figure of speech, but truly takes my breath away. Then we're free-falling together. Spinning circles. Out of our minds."

I stared at his face, feeling the need to swallow, but my throat seemed a bit paralyzed.

"I'm not naïve enough to expect that kind of intensity to last forever," Todd continued. "But if nothing else, we all deserve at least *that*—to occasionally be knocked breathless by the one we love most, don't you think?"

Honestly, I didn't know what to think. I was too busy wondering how it would feel to be spinning freely through space, out of my mind, breathless. I made myself look down at the sidewalk, overly aware that I'd trip over my own feet if I let my mind continue its free fall.

Before I could steady myself, he went on. "Think of a first kiss, that moment immediately before lips touch, that hitch in your breath. Know what I mean?"

I nodded, and then I felt a similar inhale catch in my chest when Todd touched my arm to stop us on a corner.

"Comfortable nervousness," he added, almost in a whisper. "Butterflies in your stomach. Christmas Eve as a kid. That's how I want to feel when I'm with her. The purest kind of bliss." After a beat, he looked away, squinting toward the street. "Basically, Abby, we broke up because we didn't love each other anymore." He glanced at me and cracked a smile. "I would elaborate further, but I think you've had enough."

I looked down and saw that I'd been twisting and tugging at the neck of my tank top. It was wrinkled and stretched. How did I get so classy?

"You seem a little distracted," Todd observed.

"No. I'm . . . just . . ."

He grinned.

"Oh, shut up." I laughed, and we crossed the street.

Up ahead, my red cruiser was leaning against the glass window of Modica. Three other bikes were beside it now—one, a yellow tandem with pink fringe dangling from the handlebars.

"Well?" Todd asked when we stopped outside the door.

"Well, what?" I was stalling, of course.

He nodded toward the door in reply.

But I couldn't do it. I couldn't move. "I can't go in there," I admitted quietly.

Todd gave me a look with those same melting-my-knees eyes. "Come on."

Over his shoulder, I looked through the glass. Hardly any customers. No reason not to, I guess. Crap. My heart started to pound with adrenaline. I took in some deep breaths and shook out my hands like I was psyching myself up for the high jump.

Todd watched with a bit of a smirk, apparently amused by my fretting.

After another minute, he bent down to my ear, so close I could breathe in his lovely aftershave. Or was that his natural smell? "It's okay," he whispered, causing my heart to pound even more. "You're with me this time, and I swear to you, I am safer than an armored car." The nearness of his face made my mouth water. "But, please, first just promise me something."

He pulled back and looked me in the eyes.

"What?" I whispered, thinking of about a hundred things I would have promised him at that moment.

"Don't trip on your way in. You'll embarrass me."

He pulled the door wide open, spun me around, and pushed me in.

chapter 6

"HERE COMES THE SUN"

"Back already?" Bob asked. "Your little helper's called twice looking for you."

Ignoring my squeaks of protest, Todd muscled me toward the deli in the middle of the store. "Has he?" he said, pulling a BlackBerry out of his pocket and checking the face. "I'm getting his lunch now." With his free hand, Todd positioned me in front of the deli glass.

Bob popped up behind the counter to assist us. "Pastrami on rye?" he asked Todd.

While those two discussed the economy or the tides or whatever, I found myself transfixed, ogling at the rows of fresh meats, cheeses, and salads on the other side of the glass. It was a regular Garden of Eden *al fresca*. Although my food allowances had changed during the last five years, my food *preferences* certainly had not. Anything greasy, sugary, salty, or fatty was a constant craving.

When I looked up, Todd was grinning at me, probably noticing my gluttonous expression. "Hungry much?"

"Yeahhh," I gushed, throwing manners to the wind.

"Good." He turned to Bob. "Give me roast beef with mustard on wheat, no cheese. And how is the tuna today?"

The proprietor didn't have to think twice. "Best on the

Gulf," he bragged through fluffy whiskers, wiping his hands across the front of his red apron, "but we're already out."

Todd huffed and slid his gaze back to me. "Hmmm." He squinted, studying my face, index finger tapping his chin.

Maybe he thinks he can detect my craving by staring at me hard enough. Yeesh, I certainly hope not. Talk about embarrassing . . .

"She'll have smoked turkey with cheddar— No, scratch that," Todd corrected, eyes still on me. "Swiss cheese, on a hard roll. Tomatoes, pickles, avocado . . . sprouts."

Bob went to work, chopping, smothering, and smearing.

Todd turned around and rested his back against the glass, looking mentally exhausted, like he'd solved a long-division problem in his head.

"And they say chivalry's dead."

"Did you mind my ordering for you?"

I shook my head. Sure, Max had bossed me around for the past five years, but Todd's bullying me through the door and deciding what he thought I'd like for lunch—that felt different. "How did you know, though?" I asked, leaning against the counter beside him.

"Know what?"

"I prefer Swiss cheese and sprouts."

He smiled first and then chuckled, replaying something funny in his mind. "I would say you're an open book, Abby, but I wouldn't want to insult you."

I smiled back as the heavenly scent of fresh food mingled with the memory of his aftershave. A part of me wanted time to stand still, to live in the simplicity and normality of the moment, while the frantic part of me was torn between shoveling food in my face and/or tackling this guy to the floor and smothering his bread with something other than mustard. Sometimes my physical cravings were difficult to differentiate.

This was forgotten when I got a familiar prickly feeling up the back of my neck. It was a girl around twelve with curly red hair and a short yellow skirt a few aisles over, staring at me. She whispered to a boy a year or two older. I forced the corners of my mouth to smile and waved my fingers.

At my simple acknowledgment, the girl let loose a loud shriek. "Told you it was her!"

More giggling ensued until an adult shushed them.

I knew Todd caught the whole thing. I wished he hadn't. I wished *I* hadn't.

Bob handed Todd two bags over the counter. "Any sides?"

Seeing the huge size of the sandwiches through the bags, I shook my head. Todd ignored my protest and leaned over to me. "We're ordering more food, okay? You seem pretty ..." His eyes looked me up and down discreetly. "Hungry."

When his gaze dropped to my mouth for just a split second, my throat went completely dry.

"Do you want salad or pasta?" he asked. Before I could open my mouth, he said, "I think we'll take both."

"Dessert?" Bob asked him as if I weren't standing there.

"One slice of key lime pie. Two forks." I felt Todd's hand on my arm. "You'll thank me later."

No doubt I would.

We left the market, taking the three hundred steps across Town Square back to Todd's Tackle. Todd led the way as we paraded through the gonging front door.

A very tan young man with shiny white teeth and a blond, bleached-out mop of hair glanced up. He waved from behind a pile of colorful board shorts he was attempting to fold.

"What's with the dang holdup, boss man?" he called out with goofy enthusiasm. A pair of neon green shorts hung off the tip of the finger he pointed at Todd. "I'm starvin' like Marvin!"

"Minor detour first," the boss man replied.

"It was my fault," I inserted as I emerged from behind Todd.

Startling me, Todd whipped around so that his body was blocking Chandler's view of me. "Are you sure?" he whispered, his face bent down to mine. "I can just drop this off, if you'd prefer." Between our two bodies he was holding the bag with Chandler's pastrami sandwich inside. "Just give me two seconds, and we'll be off. He doesn't have to, um, bother you."

"You *claim* you're safer than an armored car," I whispered back. Then I snatched the bag from him. "Prove it."

Todd lifted one eyebrow. "Oh, you're good."

Without taking his eyes off me, he said, "Chandler, I'd like you to meet—"

"Hold up."

In unison, Todd and I turned toward the goofy kid.

His finger with the hanging shorts was now pointing at me. "You look exactly like—"

"Chandler!"

The kid jumped about a foot, almost as high as I did, but his eyes obediently fixed on Todd.

Todd took a beat—after knowing he had his employee's complete attention—and cleared his throat, staring the poor kid down like a lion tamer.

It was easy to see that Todd was very good at holding someone's attention when he wanted to. I'd already fallen under that spell a few times that day, and it was pretty obvious poor Chandler was no match, either.

"Chandler." Todd's voice was deliberate and controlled now. "This. Is. Abby." He was holding his hands out in front of him, the tamer approaching the beast. "Okay?"

Oh, brother. Such drama. I stepped between them and extended my hand. "Hi, Chandler." I beamed. "It's very nice to meet you."

He didn't lift his hand to shake mine. In fact, the kid didn't move at all. I lowered my hand to pick up his, which was hanging like a dead thing at his side, and gave it a hardy shake.

"Uhh, nice to meet me," Chandler garbled. "Oh, I mean I love you, I mean . . . umm, er, uh?" He swore under his breath and pulled his hand from mine, his tan face turning the same shade as the bright pink T-shirt he was wearing.

Todd glanced at me, showing his bottom teeth. "We don't let him out much."

"Don't worry about it." I waved dismissively. "Here, we brought you lunch." I handed Chandler the bag.

He looked like he was on the verge of another out-of-body freak-out. "Abigail Effing Kelly," he spoke slowly, "is bringing me lunch?" He lifted his chin and let out one loud cackle. "*Totally* off the *chain*! Wait'll the guys hear this!"

I shot Todd a look.

"Hey, be a mate," he said to Chandler, "and don't mention this to anyone. *Capiche*?" Todd sounded plenty stern as he continued to reel in his overly enthusiastic employee, but then I noticed something a bit more threatening in his expression when he laid one hand on Chandler's shoulder.

Chandler, who had turned slightly green, seemed to understand the gesture. He looked from Todd to me and then back to Todd. Again, his excitement mellowed under the steady gaze of the tamer.

A moment later, Todd shook Chandler's shoulder in a friendly way and stepped back. "You finally sold the ruby longboard," he observed.

His employee nodded timidly.

"That's great work, man. Really great. Congratulations."

Chandler's youthful animation returned as he described to Todd his big sale of the morning. They were friends with mutual respect; I could see that. When Chandler looked up to greet a customer, Todd glanced at me, pointing a thumb at his own chest. "Armored car," he mouthed.

I lifted a hand to cover my grin.

"Well," Todd said a few minutes later "we'd better shove off."

I bid *adieu* to Chandler and walked to the front door. When I turned back, Todd had his hand clamped down on Chandler's shoulder again, speaking low, looking him directly in the eyes in that . . . way.

Funny, Chandler was eighteen and Todd was probably ten years older, yet the authority he commanded made me feel like I was in the presence of a crown prince. Or a mafia don.

"What was all that?" I asked Todd when he joined me outside.

"That?" He kicked some rocks off the sidewalk and squinted up at the sun. "Oh, I merely explained to Chandler in graphic detail what will happen to his job and the rest of his existence if he tells any living soul about your being here." He grinned sardonically and then ran an index finger across his throat.

"Poor Chandler."

Todd rolled his eyes. "He'll live."

We crossed the street toward the beach. "Please say we're eating soon," I said, my eyes following a seagull overheard as it glided on the breeze.

"I'm trying to think of a good spot," Todd explained, then stopped walking. "Somewhere public, but you know, off the beaten path." He plunged his free hand into the back pocket of his long khaki shorts and stared toward the horizon. "Hmm." His profile was pensive. And sexy. Pink mouth, straight nose, those emerald eyes. What a unique and glorious combination bestowed upon one lucky face.

I was hearing music now, swirling around us like in a movie when the tension builds. It was the love theme from *Romeo & Juliet*, or maybe that crap song from *Titanic* that everyone hates. Oh man, I loved that crap song.

"Hey, there," Todd said, yanking me from my reverie. I stared at him and smiled. He chuckled lightly and glanced toward my midsection. "Are you going to answer that, or do you expect me to go in after it?"

I was wide awake now, hearing the actual song that was playing. Suddenly all romantic notions evaporated. It wasn't *Romeo & Juliet* I was hearing, but The Beatles' "Helter Skelter," the ring tone I knew very well; it was attached to only one person's incoming calls.

I tried not to appear as shattered as I felt as I fumbled for the cell in my pocket.

"Hello? I'm here. Hi, Max." I spoke in a rush. "How are you?"

"Yeah, okay . . . in a minute. You, grab me that . . . no, *that* one there. Hey, babe." He sounded distracted, like he was multitasking and I was an afterthought. "You were supposed to call yesterday."

I pinched my eyes shut, then pictured him—his famous "annoyed with Abby" smirk; his tall, thick, built like an ex-NFL linebacker body; his piercing brown eyes; and his mouth gnawing one of those nasty cigars.

"Sorry," I said, attempting to blink out that "enticing" image. I turned my body slightly away from Todd, trying to simultaneously shelter him and hide him. "I forgot to call. Lindsey and I . . . we . . ."

Todd tapped me on my shoulder and pointed away. "Should I wait over there?"

"No," I whispered, lowering the cell from my ear. "It's my manager." I held up one finger. "I'll just be a sec."

"Hey!" Max called through the phone.

I slapped it to my ear. "I'm here," I said. "Sorry. Sorry."

"Who is that you're talking to?" His simple question was riddled with preconceived insinuations and assumptions. I knew the tone. Max was a master at sending passive-aggressive shame. He could rival any Catholic grandmother.

I wished I didn't have to answer. I wished I could've returned to watching Todd walk and talk and smile at me.

"It's no one you know," I offered, turning my chin to glance at Todd. "He's a . . . friend."

Todd smiled at me warmly, his hair blowing in the breeze. I had the overwhelming desire to hurl my phone into the Gulf like a shot put.

Max sighed. "Babe, don't make me remind you how—"

"I know, Max," I said, cutting him off.

We both fell silent. I shut my eyes, pounding a fist against my forehead. My mistake was interrupting Max Salinger. That was never done, you see.

"Everything's fine!" I exclaimed before things got tense. "Nothing to worry about. It's all good."

Todd tapped my shoulder again and gestured toward Town Square. "I'll be right back." He took off running.

"Wait!" I called after him, feeling a little panicky at the thought of his absence. He stopped mid stride and turned around. "Where . . ." I lowered my voice. "Where are you going?"

"I'll be right back," he repeated. Without another word or a chance for me to protest, he shot up the sidewalk like a silver bullet, leaving me on the street corner.

I stared after him, wondering if he used to be a runner. Maybe he still was. Maybe he ran marathons in his spare time. *Maybe—*

"Hey! Are you even listening to me?"

"Sorry, Max, sorry. I was in the middle of something, uhh, important." I leaned back against a skinny tree and stared south toward the water. It was limpid blue and sparkling with bits of golden sunlight, calling to me like the sirens to Odysseus or like those Austrian hills did to Maria, while my cell phone felt like an iron-hot brick against my face.

"I'm sorry," I repeated, kneading my forehead, "that I didn't call like I promised. It won't happen again. I swear."

Max sighed loudly into the phone. "Dammit, babe, I was hoping this break would be good for you, but you sound even more distracted, if that's possible. You know what happens when you're distracted."

I missed the old Max, the one who might have asked about my day or my flight or if I'd seen that annoying movie star, the one we both thought was majorly fuggly, on the cover of *People* magazine. For years, Max was practically a member of the family, albeit a very bossy member, which was probably why he could guilt trip me into anything if he pushed the right buttons.

I sighed softly, away from the phone. "I know; don't worry. Everything's fine." I was beginning to sound like a broken record.

"Listen to me," he said. "I'm allowing this break for you to get yourself together. We need you back here at the end of the summer, healthy and ready to work hard. You're getting it together for me, right, babe? Or do I need to go shopping on *American Idol* for your replacement?"

That little jab made me smile. "Low blow, Max."

He chuckled. "All right, babe. Go crash on the beach or paint your nails or whatever it is you do to kick back. But I'm calling you tomorrow to discuss something else, so keep your damn phone with you."

"Okay, I promise."

We hung up a few minutes later after he, again, reviewed what had happened, what could happen, and what *would* happen if I didn't return in better mental shape. His final statement was, "Do you hear what I'm saying?" This was kind of a joke to me because what Max actually meant was this: "Do you hear what I'm *not* saying? Read my mind." Over the past year or so, he had become an impossible riddle that I stopped trying to solve. Sometimes it was better to just shut up and obey.

I stared down at my cell, flipping it over and over in my hands, wishing I hadn't brought it along this morning. Wishing a lot of things. That phone call had been exhausting. Even though I wasn't at work, talking to Max made me feel tense, like I *was* at work.

When I looked up, I noticed a car slowing down. My muscles locked even tighter. If the paparazzi found me here, I had nowhere to hide.

The car stopped just past me and then thankfully continued after only a few camera flashes sparked from an open window. I watched it drive away, realizing that the occupants were simply taking pictures of the Gulf behind me.

Even still, my tense muscles wouldn't relax. I wanted the world to go away. I wanted to run and hide somewhere private and safe, somewhere magical, like inside the peaceful hues of a landscape painting, or maybe inside the serene melody of a song I loved. Paul McCartney's lulling "Golden Slumbers" was my personal favorite for times like that, times to hide. Christian had known how to calm me down. Sometimes it took only a look from him or a few words.

But I was on my own now.

I sank to the sidewalk, leaned back against a tree, pulled in my knees, and tucked my chin, ball cap over my eyes. I probably looked like a *señorita* catching a morning siesta.

Because of that phone conversation, my mind turned to David, my last "distracting" dating experience with someone outside the business. The time had never seemed right for me to be in a real relationship with a real person. Other than that idiot Miles, who Max probably had a man-crush on, my manager had never appreciated my having a boyfriend at all. He said it didn't fit my image. It escaped me how my personal life had anything to do with my professional image.

Max definitely would have vetoed my spending a day alone with Todd. Maybe he was right.

My knees cracked when I stood up. As I brushed bits of sand off the back of my shorts, I wondered if perhaps it might be better if I sneaked back to my bike and pedaled out of this guy's life forever. *Better for him,* I thought, trying to ignore the squeeze of disappointment in my chest, *and better for me.*

Before those thoughts had time to leave my mind, Todd came up from behind me, slightly winded and holding something behind his back. "You forgot this." In his hand was the pretty straw hat I'd admired at his store.

The noonday sun shone down on him like a spotlight, but not the kind I was used to living under. Todd looked warm and glowing and completely buoyant. That unpleasant squeeze inside of me released like an unclenching fist.

After I put on the hat and adjusted it properly, he tilted his head. "Pretty cute," he observed. "I'm beginning to see what all the fuss is about."

chapter 7

"IT'S GETTING BETTER"

"Why does this house have a name?" I asked.

Todd and I were stopped in front of a tin-roofed cottage the exact color of a Creamsicle, peachy pink with white trim. Nailed to the picket fence was a white sign with loopy blue script.

"Most of the homes in Seaside have names," Todd answered. He hefted our bag of lunch over his shoulder as we looked at a house called Wandering Thoughts. "I believe it began as a throwback to antebellum plantations. There's a book about it; I've got a copy at home. You're welcome to borrow it if you'd like."

Something about his offer made me feel very normal. And very good.

The neighborhood we were strolling through had no traditional front lawns, just different types of gardens. The front garden of Wandering Thoughts consisted of yaupons with red berries, purple beautyberry bushes, and woody goldenrods, like a tangled jungle of summer colors.

At first glance, the charming houses appeared identical, like each was a scoop of rainbow sherbet in a never-ending glass dish of ice cream. Todd explained the same developer had built them all.

"Where do you live?" I asked as I leaned against the fence, running one finger across the name plate.

"Here, in Seaside."

"In this neighborhood?"

He shook his head. "Way too touristic." He reached up, picking at the fan-like leaf of a coco palm hanging above his head. "They're picturesque little cottages, but . . ." Something a bit darker crossed his face, an expression I couldn't read and hadn't expected. His gaze moved past the tops of the tin roofs toward another neighborhood. "When it came time for me to buy, I wanted something completely my own, away from all of that. Something real."

"I know exactly what you mean," I said. My tone automatically morphed into serious to match his. "I have a house, too, in Malibu. I bought it four years ago. Actually I was twenty when I bought it, so it's under my brother's name." The thought made me laugh, though I didn't know why. "It's pretty lacking in furniture right now. Everyone keeps telling me to hire a decorator because I never have time. It's just sitting there, basically empty." I moved my hand up to my hair, knotting a strand around one finger, a nervous habit. "It didn't used to be empty. My brother and I, we lived there together, before he . . . he — "

I stopped short, surprised that I'd just disclosed so much to a stranger, almost without meaning to. I was lost for a moment, unable to block out images of Christian the last time I saw him. And before I knew it, mental anguish crashed over me like a tidal wave. I had to grab hold of the fence for a moment. When I looked at Todd, his brows had pulled together. For a second I wondered if he also had been thinking about what happened last year. Or if he even knew.

Of course he knows. My thoughts fired back. *Everyone knows the story.*

"Why don't you hire a decorator, then?" he asked, his expression still puzzled.

I echoed his words back to him. "Something real. Something completely my own." I forced out a long exhale. "And I want to do it myself. I think I'd be good at it. Someday."

Just then, we both turned to see a black convertible backing out of the driveway of Wandering Thoughts. The man behind the wheel leaned out his open window, probably to query as to why we were loitering around his front yard. The woman in the passenger seat lifted her sunglasses, took one look at me, and said something to the driver. The car sat idling in the middle of the street.

And let the staring begin.

"Does your house have a name like these do?" I asked Todd, trying to jerk his attention away from our audience.

"Yes," he answered, his focus stuck on the black convertible's taillights when it finally drove away. He cracked a smile, turning his attention back to me. "But it's hideously kitschy. It came with the house, and I haven't gotten around to officially changing it yet."

He pulled my Dodgers cap from our bag of food. "Mind if I wear this?" he asked, sliding it on his head. The bright blue made the color of his green eyes pop. "Once I'm inspired, I'll change the name of my house to something more rock 'n roll. Something like Fly Me to the Moon or Summer Wind."

"*Very* rock and roll," I teased, arching one eyebrow. "You're a big Sinatra fan, I take it?"

Todd grinned and ran his fingers under his chin.

I couldn't think of another jab, so I dropped the subject.

A few minutes later, we crossed the street, heading south toward the water. Leaving the main road, we ventured onto a dirt footpath that ran through a shady, wooded neighborhood. I could make out a few houses here and there tucked back in the little wilderness. Sounds of children splashing in swimming pools and dogs barking floated through the thick, protective oaks and tall golden fronds of pampas grass. I picked a few flowers and threaded the stems through my hat. A little farther on, the trees cleared and we were in a new neighborhood right across from the beach.

Because I'd lagged behind, Todd stopped and turned. I quickly removed my attention from his exceptional butt.

"Am I too fast for you?" he asked.

I cleared my throat and caught up.

"We're trespassing now," he added, "so shhhh."

"What?"

He held one finger over his lips.

"Oh," I mouthed, then followed behind him as we quietly crept along the side of a white house called Cherry Pie Place. All the shades were drawn, with no cars in the driveway. I hoped the owners were gone and wouldn't catch us sneaking through their property. As we passed by the back yard, a black lab padded toward the fence. Despite myself, I shrieked before having the sense to cover my mouth with both hands.

"Stay close," Todd whispered over his shoulder. "Here." He reached back.

I exhaled, more than grateful to take his hand.

After weaving our way through a maze of tall shrubbery and brittle scrub oak in a side yard, we finally made it to the base of the boardwalk. We passed the public shower off to the left of the path and then climbed the wooden-plank stairs up and over the tall dune that separated the houses from the beach.

At the top of the platform, Todd suddenly crouched into a squat. "*Down.*" He whispered the order like a drill sergeant. I dropped to my knees beside him, knowing we were attempting stealth.

When we started down the stairs—still in a crouch—I caught my first glimpse of the view. This particular beach had big, sun-bleached boulders speckled along the shoreline, jetting out into the blue water. I could see for miles and miles down the beach, out to the water, up the shoreline. Really cool. To our left, east of the beach, stood a cluster of high-rise condos and other manmade developments. No one was swimming in the water, but I could make out a few white sails on the blue horizon. If I'd been back in one of my college painting classes, I would have replicated that view, favoring a delicate rainbow of watercolors—no messy, overstated oils here—with a subtle, upsweeping of brushstrokes to emphasize the pearly beach and green-blue Gulf.

At the foot of the stairs, I pulled to a stop, wanting to take in the moment fully. I peeled off my hat and let the refreshing wind dance through my hair. With my eyes closed, I inhaled a few slow breaths, body and soul feeling in harmony with the world for the first time in quite a while.

"This reminds me of a Monet," I whispered, my voice blending with the wind and waves. "The one with the water lilies. I've always wanted to dive into that painting and just kind of . . ." I sighed tranquilly. "Float away."

When I opened my eyes, Todd was looking at me, seeming a little lost in his thoughts, too, but then he cleared his throat and dropped my hand. I had *not* forgotten he was holding it.

"On a clear day," he said, crossing his arms in front of him as he looked toward the edge of the horizon, "you can see all the way to the South Pole." He made his way down to the boardwalk that led out to the beach and then to the sea. "You can leave your shoes here," he said, sitting down and kicking off his Locals.

But I felt pained, and my hand kind of stung from the way he dropped it. I bit my lip, wishing for a moment that I was plain old Abby Kelly from Arizona and not some untouchable celebrity.

When I looked down at Todd sitting cross-legged, wearing my baseball cap low over his eyes, my heart warmed. He was just about the most adorable creature I'd ever beheld. I knew then that it was up to me. If I wanted to have any kind of normal day with him, I was going to have to chill out and resist my natural urges to mistrust or act like a babbling idiot.

I plastered a smile on my face and joined him on the end of the boardwalk, unfastening my sandals that laced up and around my ankles. "The sand looks like sugar," I said, deciding that it was my turn to point out interesting observations.

Todd hopped to his feet. "It does," he agreed, taking a step onto the beach, "but it gets wicked hot. And watch out for sharp rocks."

I hot-footed it behind him as he led us to a mini Stonehenge circle of rocks a few feet from the shore. He sat down, his back against one of the rocks. I did the same.

"Where were you born?" I asked, deciding to veer away from my earlier plan of innocuous chitchat. This was my attempt to nonchalantly pry for personal information. Much more fun.

"Highland Falls, New York," he answered.

"Was it a nice place to live?"

He shook his head while unloading our lunch. "Not for a kid. West Point Military Academy. I was three when we left." He passed me a napkin. "Until college, I'd never lived in the same city for more than a year or two."

"Which college?" I asked.

He looked up but didn't answer right away. "A school in Maryland," he finally offered, digging in our bag of food. "I finished my MBA two years ago, but I took some time off before business school." He sent me a lightning-fast glance. "Marine Corps."

I sat back on my heels. "Wow. That's . . ." I was about to blurt, "That's just about the sexiest thing I've ever heard," but instead I said, "That's hardly *time off*."

We sat in silence for a bit, me extracting information from a part of my brain I never thought I'd use in casual conversation. "So," I said, folding a napkin, "is this school in Maryland you mentioned *Annapolis*, by any chance?"

He nodded.

"*Ex Scientia Tridens*," I added, putting on my serious face. "That's the Academy motto, you know. It's Latin for 'From Knowledge, Seapower.'" I paused, waiting for his reaction.

His stunned-into-muteness expression was very satisfying.

"Navy will have a pretty decent team this season, don't you think?" That little sports nugget was thanks to Hal. "Oh, and *Semper Fidelis.*" I straightened my spine and offered a very smart salute.

Todd blinked, brows still furrowing, looking more shocked than if I'd yanked out an Uzi and started field-stripping it blindfolded. "How do you know that?" he asked.

"Oh, I know a bit about you Marines." I leaned back, arms balancing my weight behind me.

"And?" Todd didn't break his stare; apparently my off-handed explanation was not enough.

"To tell the truth, a copy of Oliver North's autobiography was left under my hotel bed a few years ago. It was the only book I had with me, and for a while, I became a little obsessed with him and his service years." I shrugged, gazing out at the sea.

Todd passed me a bottle of water. "It wasn't *Under Fire*, was it?" His tone was drenched with disbelief.

"That's the book," I confirmed, "and don't sound so *shocked*. I'm not illiterate."

"No, no, it's not that," he insisted, handing me a bag of chips. "I read that book for the first time last summer. He became a sort of hero of mine. Made me want to re-enlist."

"Once a Marine," I sing-songed, "always a Marine."

"Exactly." Todd fell pensive again, staring down at his sandwich. "You do realize that book is more than twenty years old? Interesting that we both read it recently."

"I find the whole thing rather . . ." *Careful, Abby . . .* "Heroic."

"Agreed." Todd smiled. "I was hardly like Ollie, unfortunately." He formed his fingers into a gun, firing imaginary shots at a flock of low-flying seagulls. "After boot camp and officer's training, I spent a lot of time in the grunts, doing my job. Nothing glamorous."

But very noble, I mentally added. And then my overly imaginative mind found it difficult *not* to picture him in desert-blasted digicams. Gun on his shoulder, sand goggles, American flag on his sleeve, defender of the free world. Macho hot stuff.

"Do you ever miss it?" I asked, holding the water bottle up to my cheek, trying to cool down surreptitiously.

Before answering, Todd looked puzzled; maybe he was thrown by such a nosy question. "I've never considered that," he replied after a moment. "I suppose I do, though, in a way." A corner of his mouth pulled back. "But I get my fix every now and then. I secretly love killing my father and sisters at paintball." He took a long drink of his water and looked out at the Gulf, smiling reminiscently.

"I was three semesters away from getting my degree," I said.

Todd handed me my turkey sandwich.

I sat it unopened on my lap, suddenly worried about what he'd think. He had his master's degree and probably military medals, and I was basically a dropout.

"You went to college?" he asked. The left side his mouth was full of roast beef.

"You sound surprised again."

Todd took another bite of his sandwich, mustard squirting out the other end. He chewed for a moment and then stopped. "Before either of us says anything more, will you do me a favor?" he asked. "Eat." His eyes pointed to the untouched sandwich on my leg.

I unwrapped it and took one bite just to satisfy him. Oh, buddy, it was delicious. The bread was the perfect combination of chewy and hard, the veggies were garden fresh, and the avocado was like edible velvet. Where had this food been all my life?

"Enjoying yourself?" Todd asked.

I laughed, careful not to blow bits of half-chewed bread out of my mouth.

After I wolfed down half the sandwich, Todd went back to his own. "So, your college days?" he prompted at the exact moment when my mouth was completely full.

I'd been asked that question before in interviews, and it always made me uncomfortable. But Todd's curious expression was neither mocking nor probing, which made me willing to share. "Yeah," I said, still chewing. "I enjoyed it at the time, my classes and labs. I was going for a degree in fine arts, but I wasn't sure what I wanted to do with it, painting or drawing. Maybe teaching." I sighed. "Math was my strong subject, though. Those long algebraic equations came really easily."

"I'm not surprised," Todd said after wiping his mouth with a napkin.

"Why?"

He lifted a smile. "I saw your photographic memory in action firsthand earlier, how you rattled off Danish like that." He shook his head. "That's crazy impressive." The way he was looking at me was almost like admiration. *He* was the one with the MBA.

"It was never my intention," I said, my voice low, "dropping out like I did. I guess I really didn't have a choice; the music stuff happened so fast." I looked out toward the water. "I wonder sometimes if that was a mistake."

Todd rested an elbow on his knee. "You make it sound like your life is over. How old are you? Twenty-four?"

I nodded.

"Well, I've got you by four years, and I'm still making decisions I regret. That's life." He balled his napkin in his fist then tapped his chin thoughtfully. "If this helps at all, at the end of my deployment in Iraq, I didn't know whether to continue in the military or go back to school. I was stuck at a crossroads with absolutely no plan."

"Really?"

"Totally vacillating. I considered the FBI for a time, went as far as applying."

"Did you get in?"

He only smiled, still chewing, at my question.

"Ah. Of *course* you got in."

He took a long swig of water. He was so cute; it took everything in me not to dive over and pin those big shoulders to the sand.

"So the CIA didn't interest you?" I joked.

"Not for long."

I froze mid-chew. "You approached the CIA?"

"Actually they approached me." He slowly leaned forward, looked over his shoulder, and then back at me. "But the rest of that story is classified. If I told you, I'd have to kill you." He reached out and grabbed me by the arms. "Then *eat* you."

We stared at each other. The touch of his fingers made my skin tingle.

"You're so . . . full of it," I whispered, breaking the silence. "They probably wouldn't take you because of all your dirty little secrets, right?"

Todd let go of my arms and sat back. "Not a chance." He looked down at the spread of food between us. "I'm rather squeaky clean, I'm afraid."

I couldn't stop smiling, tickled that this big, tough, sexy guy was apologizing to me for being abnormally normal.

He leaned back on one hand. "Seriously, though, I think the Feds were mostly interested in my sniper background." A different kind of smile sat on his lips now; something in it made the little hairs on my arms stand up.

Sniper shooting? In Iraq? Gosh.

"I seemed to have inherited a kind of . . ." He shrugged. "Unique hand-to-eye coordination. But in the end, I decided to go the civilian route, which made my mother very happy." He handed me a fork so we could share the key lime pie. "Most of my heavy-duty assault rifles are locked up." He sliced into our dessert. "For the time being, anyway."

I rolled onto my side. Todd was on his back. For the moment, neither of us was speaking. The sun felt so warm, mirroring the feeling in my soul. I sighed lightly as I watched him stretched out on the sand next to me, and I wondered what would happen if I accidentally tucked myself into the crook of his arm . . .

Saved by the bell, "Octopus's Garden" started singing from my pocket.

Todd rolled his head to look at me. "It's Hal," I explained.

"Richardson?" he asked, sitting up. Todd knew the last name of our guitarist. Yep, we were *that* famous.

I nodded. "Should I answer?" I wondered aloud, asking both of us. "I get a lot of calls when we're split up like this. Such a pain."

"Take the call," Todd said. "I don't mind. Would you like some privacy?"

"For Hal?" I scoffed, pushing the button to accept the call. "Stay right where you are." I slapped the phone to my ear. *"What?"*

"Molly called." Hal's voice was low, monotone, all business. "Said you met some dude."

I sighed impatiently, draping my free arm over my eyes. "And?"

"Are you too busy vegging on the beach to talk to me, or what? Is the dude right there with you?" Hal cackled.

I could practically feel Todd at my side. I tried hard not to grin. "Maybe he is."

Silence. "Lemme talk to him, duchess."

I moved my arm off my eyes to see Todd looking down at me. He'd heard the request—Hal's voice was always very loud through the phone.

"Ha-ha." I scoffed. "Not happening, Hal."

"Duchess . . ."

I rolled my eyes and sat up. Todd shrugged and nodded simultaneously, then extended his open hand.

"Hal, do *not* be a moron," I warned.

But Hal only chuckled like he was up to something.

"Sorry," I whispered to Todd as I passed him my cell. "He'll keep bugging me."

"Hello?" Todd spoke, his gaze moving to the sky. "Yes. Well . . . yes." He looked confused first, and then he chuckled. "Yes, I know." He looked at me, listening hard. "She is, and I will." He laughed again before saying good-bye.

"Sorry." I shook my head. "Hal's the product of what happens when cousins marry."

"I didn't realize he was a *gangsta*."

"He's not." I snickered. "I think he was trying out his tough-guy persona on you."

"Scary." Todd smiled as he handed back my cell. "He's awfully protective of you, isn't he?"

My brows wrinkled as I slipped the phone into my pocket. "What did that ingrate say to you?"

"Something about breaking my face if anything happens today."

"Happens?" I repeated. "What does that mean?"

Todd shrugged. "He's *your* crazy friend, not mine."

I laughed, trying to picture scrawny, skater-boy Hal breaking anything on Todd. "He *is* crazy," I confirmed.

I looked past Todd's shoulder, out to the water, remembering that just over a year ago, I sat across the room from Hal and the other two guys of Mustang Sally on the day Max announced that "Satellite" was going to be the first single off the new album. Hal had winked at me inconspicuously and wrinkled his nose. He'd been hiding it, but I knew him, and he was disappointed.

"When you kids become more established," Max had said, "you can record your own songs."

I'd wondered what could be "more established" than four multi-platinum albums and four sold-out world tours in a little under four years.

"So," I said to Todd, eager to get back to the last bit of our earlier conversation. "You were telling me about when you lived in New York." From the details he'd allotted so far, I was beginning to piece together his story.

Todd was in the middle of two sisters who both lived in New York City. His mother was from Sicily, a full-blooded Italian; his father was third-generation Marine Corps. Todd's evident yet nondescript accent was a direct result of his family's travels through his schooling years.

"Right," Todd said. He reclined onto the sand.

I did, too.

"After grad school, I landed as a financial analyst on Wall Street."

(Cue scenes of Todd in a dark suit, power tie, hair combed back, briefcase, black town car. Very "Mr. Big.")

"For how long?"

"Less than a year. I didn't really need the job at the time, but that wasn't why I left. I realized pretty quickly that it wasn't what I wanted to do for the rest of my life."

Todd's family was obviously loaded. Though he didn't flaunt it like some of the other Richie Riches I knew, it was plain to see the evidence of old money. He simply had that way about him. Classy.

A few years ago, before I witnessed on more than one occasion actors hooking up with their makeup artists and debutantes running away with their chauffeurs, I would have considered Todd unequivocally out of my league. Celebrity or no celebrity, he *totally* outranked me.

"Then what?" I asked. "Like, what were you doing a year ago?"

Todd leaned forward. "What were *you* doing a year ago, Abby?"

"One year ago I was on my way to England," I began without having to think, "five shows in five days in five cities. Then Europe. Then Asia." I folded my arms. "Top that."

"I was climbing Everest."

"Oh," I sputtered and then swallowed, recalling a blurb I'd read on the back of a pamphlet once: Mount Everest is 29,035 feet. One hundred and twenty corpses are still stuck up there, frozen in the ice, until I don't know, global warming sets them free? And it cost upward of $65,000 even to *attempt* the climb.

I carefully regarded the man at my side—he was like a sexy Jack Bauer. "Did you make it all the way?" I asked.

"To the summit?"

I nodded eagerly.

He chuckled. "Of course not."

"How high?"

"Camp One, twenty thousand, fifteen feet. Then my buddies and I literally crawled back down the mountain to base camp." He paused and scratched his chin. "I spent the next week puking my guts out, crying for the stuffed dog I had when I was four." He ran one hand through his hair and grinned at me. "Admit it, Abby. You're totally turned on right now, aren't you?"

chapter 8

"IF I FELL"

To catch more of the cooling wind, Todd and I moved up to a twin pair of the bleached-out rocks a few feet from the breaking waves. Little tidal pools dappled the sand here and there, and I dug my feet into the cool, wet grains. Todd looked straight ahead at the water, his fingers laced behind his head, hair and clothes moving in the breeze. I wished I knew how to use my camera phone so that in months to come I could remember how he looked. I snapped a mental picture before turning back toward the water.

The waves were calm and smooth, making the grand Gulf look more like a sleeping lake. A tiny sand crab inched its way near my feet as I kept perfectly still. With its white, almost translucent shell, it looked like a phantom against the pale sand. It crawled over my buried toes then continued on its merry way along the water's edge until it disappeared into the sand.

The heat was welcoming, like a big hug, and the sun was a warm kiss on my face. Or maybe it was just a hug and kiss I was craving as I sat with my toes in the sand.

"Do you like it here?" Todd asked.

"So awesome," I replied, tipping my chin. "How do you know about this place? Isn't it private property?"

"I know a guy who lives over there," he said.

Like me, Todd had buried his toes in the sand—such a playful, childlike thing. I resisted the urge to lean up against him, even though I knew the feeling of our sides together—and maybe his arm around me, too, if I let my fantasy wander—might have been just what Dr. Robert ordered.

I unburied my right foot and tapped the top of his left with my toes. His eyes moved to mine, and he smiled. I recognized that kind of smile; it made my pulse throb in my lips. His expression turned serious as his eyes dropped to my mouth. The carnal impulse sweeping over me was hard to hold back because it felt like my lungs had caught fire.

I was relieved, yet disappointed, when Todd stood and waded a few inches into the water.

"This is perfect to swim in," he said without looking back. "Especially if you don't like high surf." He folded his arms tightly against his chest.

I stared after him, still feeling rather hot and bothered.

Needing to extinguish my inner fire before I imploded, I didn't fight my next impulse. I had the presence of mind to first toss my cell phone and new hat over my shoulder, before dashing past Todd, straight into the water. As I ran hard, splashing in the shallow surf, I heard him call out something from behind me. I took a few more strong running steps and pitched headfirst into the oncoming wave, pulling myself forward under the water.

The pressure hit my ears like descending in an airplane, arresting my exhale until my body grew used to it. In full-on mermaid mode, I broke the surface for a quick breath before jackknifing for another deep dive. Years of intense vocal training had strengthened my lungs, and I could hold my breath for a fairly long time. Underwater, I opened my eyes, blinking through the initial salty sting. Schools of tiny iridescent fish fearlessly swam around me. From the ocean floor, I picked up a broken piece of starfish. After breaking surface for one more inhale, I body surfed the next foamy wave into Todd's feet. He'd waded out a few yards to meet me.

"What's the matter?" I panted, blinking up at him, my eyes blurry and stinging. "Afraid of the water?"

"Yes," he replied through his teeth. "There's a level red today. See the red flags up all the poles? That means sharks. That's why no one's out there."

"Sharks?" I yelped, bumping into Todd's legs, scrambling to my feet as we both backed out of the water. "Why didn't you tell me?"

"I tried, but you kept running." He laughed tensely, peeled off my Dodgers cap, and let it fall from his hand onto the wet sand. "You didn't surface right away, and then you dove again and didn't come up." He shut his eyes, pressing his index finger over the bridge of his nose. "I was just about to go in after you."

"You would've done that?"

He lowered his hand and opened his eyes, turning to me. "Abby, in a heartbeat."

Okay. I'm only human.

One step was all it took. I leaned in the rest of the way, wrapping my arms around him, not caring for one second if he thought I was a lunatic. "Thank you," I whispered, hoping my words reached his ears. He didn't respond vocally, but first one of his arms went around me and then the other. This spoke volumes.

I smiled into his warm shirt, my limbs softening, melting like hot honey. His hands moved across my shoulders. Seawater dripped from my hair down my face. It was probably damaging my retinas to the point of mutilation and blindness, but I didn't care.

His hands slowly slid from my shoulders to the small of my back, pulling me ever so slightly into him. I felt a hitch in my breath, the kind Todd had described earlier, the kind that precedes a perfect first kiss. I knew I wouldn't contest what was coming next . . . salt water or no salt water.

But all at once, I was released.

"Sorry," he whispered, his arms going slack as he took a step back from me. He chuckled tightly, shaking his head.

"Sorry." He looked down at the tiny waves bubbling at his tan feet, hands safely back in his pockets.

"It's okay," I mumbled, taking my own step away, feeling ridiculous and a bit trampy for having hurled myself at him. Embarrassed and frustrated, I turned around, stumbling back to where I had been sitting just a few minutes ago, a naughty child banished to her bedroom.

You idiot! I inner-scolded, as I pulled my knees in front of me, fingering my toe ring. *The man shows an inkling of not wanting you to be eaten alive by Jaws and you attack him like it's prom night!*

I couldn't see the front of him, but the back of Todd's shirt was plenty drenched thanks to me. I shook my head, ashamed by my idiotic bravado. So not my style. I would never be Molly.

"I'm not normally . . ." I started to explain, but stopped, not knowing how to finish without making it worse. I attempted to run my fingers through my wet hair, but had to settle for twisting it into a loose, dripping tangle down my back. Todd was still looking out at the water.

"Have you ever seen a shark?" I asked, choosing to totally ignore the proverbial elephant in the room.

"All the time," he answered, "when I'm diving." He sat on the rock next to me, but not as close as before. He'd learned his lesson. "They won't hurt you unless you give them a reason."

"You're brave."

He shook his head. "Hardly."

It was all too awkward and stupid, and the hot summer air felt heavy and thick and choking all around me. I didn't have time for tense silence, so I pulled forward Abby's most comfortable panic defense mechanism: The irrepressible blab. "My favorite color's brown," I blurted from out of nowhere, and Todd's brows pulled together like he was missing something. I blinked, a little startled myself. "You know, 'cause it reminds me of dirt, and I like dirt—*love* dirt, always have, as long as I can remember." I hoped I was making sense but couldn't slow down to make sure. "I like to plant things, too," I went on, "and water them, and watch them grow. Hands digging in the dirt, dirt between my fingers, caught in my nails. That's something I really miss about home. Arizona's dry and dusty and dirty and . . . and—"

"Brown?"

"Exactly!" I laughed, finally taking a breath. "I love wearing brown, too, even though *apparently* it's not the right tone for me anymore. I used to be an autumn, but now I'm a spring." Todd was staring at me with a funny look. I realized I'd derailed myself again. "I don't know." I sighed. "Wearing brown makes me feel . . ." I wrapped my wet arms around my wet legs and continued. "Protected and warm, so . . . yeah."

Winded from talk and fresh out of ideas, I set my gaze on the bright blue water, waiting for my next brilliant streak of conversational inspiration to strike. It didn't, and it became quiet again, only the sounds of the wind, the lapping waves, and an occasional bird.

"Well, *I* heard," Todd began a moment later, "that your favorite color is pink. I read about it in a magazine once." When our eyes met, his expression was both guilty and inquisitive. He leaned his face closer to me. "Or," he whispered, wearing no smile now, "should we continue with this little charade of my not properly acknowledging who you are, Abigail Kelly?"

My stomach fluttered, feeling both grateful and terrified. "No." I finally said. "Whatever we do, let's not pretend."

Todd nodded in unspoken concurrence. As we smiled across at each other, all of that stupid awkwardness evaporated like so much sticky sea water on my skin.

"So, pink?" He lifted his eyebrows and leaned back.

"Are you sure you want to hear this?" I asked. "You might lose all respect for me."

"Eh-hem." His eyes flashed to the front of my wet clothes. "I believe we're way past that, Abby."

I looked down, then quickly pulled and shook out my damp yellow tank top, which had been rather see-through and molded to my purple bra.

"Pink," Todd prompted, looking only at my eyes now, like a gentleman.

Appreciating the distraction, I theatrically cleared my throat. "My favorite color in all the world is *pink*," I recited, turning toward my audience (the water), gesturing with jazz hands. "Any season, any reason, it's such a pretty, cheerful, *dreamy* color, and pink's a girl's best friend." I winked flirtatiously at the invisible camera over my right shoulder. "I'm always in *love* when I'm in *pink*." I blew a kiss into the air.

Breaking character, I chortled, feeling the full stupidity of it.

"I had to say that," I explained, "for this perfume I endorsed a couple years back. *Moulin Rouge.*" I drew my wrist to my nose, inhaling the nonexistent bouquet, further demonstrating my pitiable acting skills.

"Impressive." Todd chuckled, applauding in short, brisk claps.

"'Twas nothing," I assured him, giving a little bow. "I've actually come to despise that color. But I tell the magazines pink over brown every time. It's in my contract."

"That's interesting," Todd said distractedly as he leaned forward to look past me. I turned and followed his gaze.

Right down the beach from us, a mother and two little girls were setting up camp. All three wore red bathing suit cover-ups and matching hats. The mother was attempting to pitch an aqua sun umbrella. Todd was suddenly on his feet and jogging over to them. The wind was blowing their way, so I couldn't hear what he was saying, but I did see him take the umbrella, hold the pole straight up over his head, and then jam it into the sand with a shockingly mighty force.

Oh my.

Down on his knees, he shook the pole, making sure it was secure. After an adjustment, he stood up and opened the shade wide. It didn't escape my notice that, after a glance in my direction, he angled the shade so it blocked where I was sitting. This made me smile.

The woman produced another umbrella, and Todd began

setting that one up. It was rather mesmerizing to watch. Of course I couldn't see from where I sat, but I imagined how his biceps stood out like rocks while he worked and his abs flexed with effort. I almost thought about going over to help, just so I could get a front-row look at those muscles in action. But I stayed put. And fanned myself.

When Todd was through, the woman motioned to her cooler. He held up both hands, palms out, refusing whatever she'd offered him. Arms crossed, he chatted with her for a few moments and then motioned to me. Even from my distance away, I could see the woman's posture slump a bit. After Todd crouched down to say something to one of the little girls, he waved to the mother and trotted back to me.

He was wearing a carefree smile, the kind worn only by legitimate do-gooders, when he sat next to me.

"Do you know her?" I asked. "*Them*, I mean," I quickly corrected.

"No." He shrugged. "Why?"

"No reason." I couldn't help smiling. How was it that his natural happy-go-lucky-ness made him even more appealing? I wondered if there were any more umbrellas he'd be willing to pitch . . .

"So do you really make up things for interviews?" he asked, jumping right back to where our conversation had left of

"Um, sometimes," I replied, grabbing the front of the rock with my hands, leaning back in a suspended sit-up. "It's the only way I feel like part of my life is private." I dropped my feet, shuffling them in the sand. A gust of wind filled the sail of a white boat straight ahead. I smiled when I heard the passengers whooping and cheering as the boat picked up speed.

"They turn on you." My throat suddenly felt scratchy and my voice dropped a notch. "They act like your best friends, then two seconds later, they've said the ugliest things. They write whatever they want, even if they know it's a flat-out lie." I paused, remembering something from the past, and shuddered. After what felt like another too-long pause, I looked at Todd—for approval maybe, or for understanding. He was watching me, expressionless. I turned toward the water and stared into the distance, getting another disconnected-from-the-present feeling.

"It's like being sucked into a hurricane," I went on. "Instead of meeting a million new people, I feel isolated. My family and close friends are all I have, and after Christian, my family won't even ... They don't—" I stopped short, pulling myself away from where my dark thoughts had been headed.

Todd's head tilted as he watched me, a flattish smile on his face. He was trying to understand, but I knew I wasn't making sense.

I tried to smile back at him, but my lower lip was wobbling. "I'm in full-blown survival mode these days," I whispered through the wobble.

"What do you miss the most?" he asked. "About *before*, I mean." He leaned back on one hand. A lock of dark hair had fallen across his forehead. He looked innocent, wholly un-jaded by life. I wasn't used to seeing that quality in people anymore.

I exhaled, taking a cue from his calm. "I miss the excitement of traveling," I answered. "Moving around like I do, I never get to *experience* where I am. I've been to Ireland three times, and I've seen only the inside of rooms and cars." I shrugged. "I'd really like to go back someday; I've heard the grassy hills are an indescribable color of green. That landscape might be fun to paint." I sighed wistfully. "I should probably start one of those bucket lists. Oh, and you know that real sugary orange soda? I might miss that most of all."

Todd laughed approvingly. The way he was watching me brought back a memory of my little nephews listening to a bedtime story. I felt the urge to tuck him in but immediately flushed hot at the thought. Hadn't I already pushed things to the edge of appropriate manners with someone I just met?

"What else?" Todd inquired. The manner of his voice was unobtrusive.

I stared down at the sugary sand, watching a circus of sand fleas bounce up and down on a small piece of driftwood then fly away. "Right now," I said, my fingers twirling the ends of my wind-drying hair, "I miss real life."

I could feel the air shifting around me as he leaned forward. "Meaning?"

The sharp ticking of my heart begged me to take a chance, that it might be a good idea to share my feelings with him. With anyone. That was what my therapist had said, anyway.

"I sometimes wish," I spoke in a whisper, causing our faces to automatically draw together, "that I was back in my dorm room studying bio. I wish I was trying to decide what to wear on a date, or singing Beatles at a karaoke party, or hoping the guy next to me in English would ask me out. I wish I had those kinds of things to worry about instead of . . ." I sighed in spite of myself. "A lot of people rely on me now. That's all."

"You're a pretty tough cookie, Abby." Todd smiled. He scooted an inch closer. "Heavy lies the head that wears the crown."

"How true," I agreed. "But, it's *uneasy* lies the head."

His lips peeled apart, but he didn't speak.

"You know Shakespeare?" I asked.

"A bit," he said after a moment. "*You* know Shakespeare?"

"A bit," I echoed. "That's from *Henry the Fourth*." I looked down, poking the tips of my feet into the sand. "He was made king at a young age. I can relate."

Todd's foot reached out and touched my toes.

The tiny hairs on my arms stood up. "My sister says I carry the world on my shoulders." When I looked at Todd, his lips were trembling, like he was trying not to laugh. Then he *did* laugh—one chuckle into the back of his hand, like a cough.

"Sorry about that," he said. "What you said struck me as funny."

"Funny?" I repeated the word, trying not to sound indignant.

"*Ironic* is a more accurate word," he amended when he noted my crushed expression. He leaned back, bracing his hands on the rock behind him. "I've been accused of having the exact opposite tendencies." A pause. "Relationships," he said, slowly shaking his head. "Sometimes no matter how hard you try, they don't work."

I leaned forward an inch, trying to read his expression. It was solemn for a split second and then lightened up. "Enough of that. I wouldn't want to bore you."

I was about to list off the dozens of reasons why nothing he could say would bore me, but just behind Todd, a pair of barefoot joggers approached from the right. I was feeling fairly incognito at the moment, but to be on the safe side, I dove over and buried my face in Todd's chest.

Okay, I knew this was unconventional, probably unnecessary, and I was most certainly asking for trouble, but I simply could not stop myself. "Those runners?" I asked. "Are they past us?" My voice was muffled while my nose took the opportunity to build a memory of the smell of his shirt. It felt warm against my cheek and was fresh and a bit spicy—that unique cologne again.

"Not quite," Todd reported. I felt his chin on the top of my head and the hard muscles of his chest. "Not . . . quite." One of his arms went around my back and then the other. Relaxing into our position, I breathed out, imagining that I could have comfortably remained in that very spot for hours. But it wasn't hours, maybe just a minute—a happy minute.

"Hey," he began a moment later, "how long will you be in town?"

"That's a good question." I pulled my head off his chest. I noticed new splotches of wet down the front of his shirt, transferred to him from my wet clothes. "Sorry," I said. "That was way out of line again."

"It's okay. I get it," he said quickly, then lifted a smile. "I'll do better at concealing you next time."

I returned to my rock, and my eyes found the joggers. They were way down the beach, so he *could* have released

me much sooner, right? Which meant he must have been enjoying our close encounter as much as I was. I couldn't stop
myself from grinning.

"So? How long?"

It took me a few seconds to remember his question. "The
whole band's on break till September. It's our first summer
off in five years."

"Where are you staying?"

"With my sister, Lindsey, in Seagrove Beach, a couple
miles from the Seaside Square. She really wants me to stay
the whole summer." I chewed on the inside of my cheeks;
they were still sore from when I'd chewed them raw yesterday on my drive home from the bookstore. All that stress
and misery seemed like a million years ago. "I kind of promised her."

"But you don't *want* to stay." It wasn't a question. Todd
was perceptive. He just had no idea why I wished I could
avoid every member of my family.

"I have a hard time hanging around one place," I offered,
since this response seemed entirely reasonable. "We just
wrapped a sixty-two-city tour. On and off, I've been away
from home for almost two years straight. You would think
it would turn me into a complete homebody when I'm not
touring, but it's the exact opposite." I gave him a sheepish
smile, feeling alien again.

"But you *could* stay if you wanted to?"

I considered and then nodded.

Todd dropped his chin, looking down at our feet, side by
side atop the white sand. They resembled baked pretzels
sprinkled with sea salt.

"Well, if you ask me," he offered matter-of-factly, "I think
you should stay."

"And why is that?"

He bumped his shoulder against mine. "I think it might be
fun rescuing you from sharks all summer."

chapter 9

"ACROSS THE UNIVERSE"

I gazed out at the late afternoon sky above the water; it was beautiful and swirly. The occupancy of the beach had nearly tripled. Couples were strolling along the shore, children splashed in the shallow waves, and even a few brave swimmers had taken to deeper waters, despite the red flags whipping in the wind. Todd and I were semi-protected on the ground, nestled inside our circle of Stonehenge rocks.

It was easy to share with him under these conditions. He was easy to talk to and open to hearing about my crazy life. My filter had all but disappeared.

"So I've been sitting here, trying to plan my summer."

Todd smiled, flicking sand in my direction. "Your summer *here*?"

"Maybe." I smiled back. "I haven't thought much about what being away for so long will really mean." Pensively, I sifted some sugary grains through my fingers.

"Think aloud," Todd suggested, sitting up. "Maybe I can help."

"With no ulterior motive, of course."

He chuckled. "I'm pretty good at talking to either side of an issue, but for this, I'll listen for now."

"Okay." I sighed. "Well, there'll be conference calls with Max and the team, weekly at the very least."

Todd nodded.

"And they'll send out music for me to work on. Hopefully no press," I added, openly cringing. "My diet's already blown."

"You're welcome." Todd smiled proudly.

I leaned back against the rock and exhaled. *Okay, maybe staying for the summer really is doable.* "Oh, and I might get a movie script. Max would love that. He wants me to break into legitimate acting."

"Really? Is that what you want?"

"What do you mean?"

After a moment, he repeated the question. "Is that what you want?"

"I guess," I answered, looking away from him. "It's part of Max's career plan for me." I started digging my hands into the sand on either side of my thighs. "I'll never get the part," I added. "It's for the new Bond girl. Max would probably love for me to have surgery first, probably this summer."

"What kind of surgery?"

My hands froze and I turned away, scrunching my face. *Too much information, Abby.*

Todd cleared his throat—a subtle request for an answer.

I looked over and gave him a sharp look. "What *kind* of surgery do you *think* someone like me would need to be a Bond girl?"

His eyes narrowed in thought, but he didn't answer.

"Obviously I don't currently have the . . ." I didn't know how to finish, so I just looked down at the front of me. "I'm not particularly, I mean, I don't want—"

"That's ludicrous," Todd cut me off. His disapproving voice was almost a growl. "You don't need anything like that." One side of his mouth pulled back. "From what I've seen of you, you're very nearly too perfect."

My stomach dropped at his words. *From what he's seen of me? Great. He thinks that glamour girl in those magazines is the real me.*

Nothing could have been further from the truth. Suddenly every muscle in my body pulled tense like a piano wire.

"Thank you," I replied politely as I burrowed my hands deeper in the sand. The cold, sharp grains dug under my fingernails, a stinging pain. I burrowed deeper.

"You don't like being told that?" From the tone of Todd's voice, he was obviously confused. "Sorry," he added when I didn't respond, "but I'm not about to take it back. I stand by my opinion." He chuckled, but then must have caught sight of my pained expression, because he immediately stopped.

I pulled my feet in, sitting cross-legged, my shoulders hunched forward, my body attempting to curl itself into an invisible ball. I kept my eyes down, preoccupied by my pedicure. It was a vile pink. I loathed pink.

"Abby, what's wrong?"

I could only shake my head, feeling Todd's eyes boring into my face, studying me again. I couldn't bear the thought of his looking at me like that, discovering that the Abigail Kelly he saw on TV and in magazines was nothing more than a freak behind a mask of ice-blue contacts, bleached hair, and painted-on smiles.

I was about to plaster on one of those phony grins and tell him, ever so brightly, that nothing was wrong. But I didn't have the heart to pretend. Instead I kept staring down, digging, wondering if I could escape the scene by digging my way to China. Then I felt something on my foot. I looked up to see Todd's finger, tapping.

"You're uncomfortable," he said. "I see that, but I'd deem myself unmanly if I didn't tell you that, personally, I consider you—"

I opened my mouth to speak, but I was cut off. "Nope. Still my turn." He tugged gently at my foot. I uncrossed my legs, stretching them out toward him. "Okay?" he asked.

I nodded.

"Okay then," he confirmed. "And I was about to say that this morning, I was surprised. Your face and your . . . your eyes, especially."

I still couldn't look at him, knowing I'd once more become a disappointment to somebody.

"You don't look a thing like your pictures."

"I know," I blurted out, choking on sudden tears in my throat. "Those *pictures*—it's like I'm another person. It's me, but a flawless me, a *perfect* me. Abigail Kelly without blemish. She's a *freak*!" My voice broke. "A freak who doesn't really exist."

It was absolutely mortifying to know that Todd thought the same thing. I faced the wind, holding back more tears. Surely he would cut his losses now and head for the nearest tiki bar. Could I blame him? I was a basket case.

"You don't realize it, do you?"

Hearing his voice, for a moment I was surprised he was still sitting there, methodically brushing sand off the bottom of my foot. I closed my eyes, trying to focus on the feeling of his touch and not the knot of self-disgust in my stomach. I nodded obediently at whatever his question was.

"Obviously you don't," he argued, his hands gripping around my foot. "Those photos are misleading. Abby, in person you're absolutely stunning."

Slowly I opened my eyes, staring first at my foot between his hands.

"Stunning?" I whispered, wondering if that word had a negative implication in this context. I kept my eyes down and shifted uncomfortably, hyper-aware of how I'd jumped into the ocean with all my clothes on and then proceeded to bake under the sun like a pickled herring. I tried to slide my foot away from him, but nothing doing. His grip was ironclad.

"You can go back to your pouting when I'm finished. But right now, I need you to believe me, and . . . I would really like you to look at me."

When I did, I was surprised at what I saw. Instead of some goofy smirk to cheer me up, Todd's expression looked a little anguished.

His glance was the one that fell away first this time. "If you want," he said, his voice dropping lower, "I'd be more than happy to share what was running through my mind when I first saw you at my store, *before* I realized who you were." His index finger ran over the arch of my foot. When my leg trembled, a satisfied little smile returned to his mouth. "I took a full minute before approaching. You intimidated me."

I rolled my eyes. Clearly nothing intimidated Todd.

He looked down, concentrating on drawing figure-eights over my skin. "With little effort, Abby, you're driving me completely mad."

"Ditto," I whispered back without even thinking.

Todd's finger stopped circling. When he lifted his eyes to me, something hot shot through my chest, landed, and burned. I could clearly picture how I was about to act upon this sudden chemical reaction: lean in, crawl over, scale him like a Mount Everest Sherpa.

Then I noticed Todd's expression change. He was frowning at something in the air over my head. His arm shot straight up. When he brought it down, he was holding a red Frisbee. He stood, muttered something under his breath, and whizzed the red disk to someone way behind me who hollered a faraway, "Thanks, man!"

Todd looked down at me, hands on his hips. "Abby, I was thinking—" But that was all he got out, because the next second, the red Frisbee clocked him square on the bridge of his nose. Stunned, he stumbled back, falling into a sit on the rock behind him.

I shot to my feet. "Are you all right?"

He was nodding, one hand over his eyes. When he lowered it, his gaze flashed to something over my shoulder. After muttering a single swear word, he grabbed my wrist, yanking me forward, down onto his lap.

I was too shocked to do anything but gasp.

The next second he threw one arm around my waist while the other hand was at the back of my head, shoving my face into the side of his neck.

I squirmed to get away. Silly reflex. This only made his grip tighten.

"Shh-shh," he whispered. "Hang on."

That's when I heard the running footsteps from behind, heading straight toward us.

"Yo, sorry, dude." Male. Probably early twenties. My spine stiffened. "Oh. Hey, Todd." I could feel the dude's eyes on me now—or on the *back* of me, at least. Thanks to Todd, he couldn't see my face.

Realizing what Todd was up to, I decided to relax and play along. I slipped my arms around his back and snuggled in, to make our sexy cuddling on the beach look legit.

While I pressed my face into his delicious-smelling neck, he wound his other arm around me tighter, forcing me flat against him. Frisbee Dude was still gabbing on about something, until Todd started in with the tickling.

"Oh, you know," he was saying to Frisbee Dude as I frantically squirmed on his lap, "we're just hanging out. Ha ha, you're so ticklish, puppy." His fingers tiptoed over my ribs. "Uh-uh, baby, no getting away from me." He laughed merrily, his hand clamping my face in place.

Yes, I understood that Todd was putting on a show to make Frisbee Dude feel intrusive and thus leave us alone, but it obviously wasn't working, and I was laughing so hard I couldn't breathe. Tickling and the sound of rushing waves were *not* a good combination for me.

"Stop, Todd!" I squealed. "Stop. *Stop!*" I attempted to twist and arch my vulnerable, crumpling body away from him. I was sure Frisbee Dude was getting an eyeful.

"Puppy, puppy, hold still." Both his arms were around my back now, leaving me able to hook my chin over his shoulder. "You're so squirmy. Remember last time when you laughed so hard you—" He broke off, chuckling hysterically at some made-up memory. He dipped his chin, and I could feel his breath on my shoulder. My limbs went instantly weak; I was at his mercy.

"Uh, yeah, I'll catch ya later, man," Frisbee Dude muttered, probably red with embarrassment to be front row center to our PDA.

A few seconds later, Todd's grip loosened some. We were both breathing hard and fast from our playful struggle, but neither of us moved away from each other.

"Puppy?" I finally whispered.

Todd snickered. "I was winging it."

"Nice going."

"I told you I'd do better next time." He patted me gently on the back, his long fingers brushing against the skin at my neck.

"Did you have to go overboard with the tickling?" I pulled back to face him but didn't get off his lap. Oh, no, no dummy here. "That was very dangerous." I smiled at him through the darkening sky. "I have a history of laughing till the pipes burst, so to speak."

A look of mock horror crossed his face as he glanced down at his lap. "Do we need to go back in the water?"

"No, no, I'm all good," I said as I climbed off, a bit begrudgingly, to sit on the sand. After a content sigh, I wiped the remnants of happy tears from the corner of my eyes. "What a chill day. My life is usually more like a hard day's night." I chuckled, combing my fingers through my hair—it was finally dry, thanks to the wind. "But not today. Today's been the best day I've had in longer than I can remember. I think I've laughed more than I did all last year." I sniffed and glanced at Todd. "Thank you for that."

"For the record, I've had a pretty okay time, too."

I tipped my chin, watching the sun lower behind a thin layer of clouds. "Ah, endless rain," I whispered, leveling my face to stare out at the water, "in a paper cup—"

"Okay, forgive me for asking," Todd cut in, "but what is it with you and the Beatles? That's about the tenth time you've quoted their lyrics in conversation today."

"I know. Sorry. I hardly notice when I do it anymore. It drives my family crazy when I call my hair 'Arthur' or refer to things as 'dead grotty.'"

"Grotty?"

"Grotesque," I explained. "That's Beatles lingo."

Todd scooted back, leaning against the rock behind him. "So you're a fan."

"Fan." I scoffed under my breath. "That doesn't even begin to describe it."

"That's pretty odd for someone our age."

"So says the Sinatra enthusiast."

"Fair enough," he said after a chuckle. "I'll tell you my story later. You first."

I re-crossed my legs, bent forward, and dumped a scoop of sand over Todd's feet. "It's not much of a story."

"Go on," he coaxed. "Remember, we're past all respect and dignity."

"Okay." I smiled at a memory and rolled my eyes. "When I was sixteen, my father agreed to help me buy my first car. He'd match whatever amount I had, which was eight hundred dollars. The only thing I could afford was this junked out eighty-six Chevy Nova. It had a decent engine and it ran fine, but practically everything else was broken."

"And . . . ?"

"And when I bought the car, their blue greatest hits was stuck in the tape deck." I shrugged. "That's it, really. I was a goner. After that, nearly every extra cent I earned went toward building my Beatles collection. I'm an absolute junkie."

Todd steepled his fingers under his chin. "And the puzzle pieces are fitting together." He looked to the side, following a pair of kids with inner tubes running past us, splashing into the dark blue water.

"Please," I whispered, twirling a loose strand of my crispy hair around one finger, "tell me something embarrassing about you now. No dignity, remember?"

His bottom lip was pushed out, his eyes up and to the left. "I've got nothing," he admitted apologetically. "Sorry. And I lost all dignity hours ago. Tempting you with ambrosia from the sea, showering you with gifts to keep you around." He flicked the brim of the straw hat sitting at my side. "And let's not forget how I shamelessly mauled you a few minutes ago."

The way he was smiling made me want to maul him back one better, but I was not about to make *this* conversation all about me. "Okay then." I folded my arms. "Tell me something about you that you don't share freely."

Todd squinted, in deep thought, his fist at his cheek, index finger tapping his temple. "All right, but this isn't something that *I* know for a fact, but I have it on very good authority. Several authorities. It's as good as factual."

"That's acceptable," I confirmed, leaning against the rock behind me.

"I *know* . . ." he began, leaning in a little closer. But then he paused and looked at me, I mean *really* looked at me, directly in the eyes, until his gaze dropped to my mouth for just a flash of a second.

My heart skipped.

"I know," he repeated, his green eyes staring into mine again, "that I'm the world's best kisser."

I didn't know how much time went by before I realized my jaw muscles had gone slack and my mouth was hanging open like a goldfish. Likewise, some part of me knew my eyes were going dry from staring into space.

"Blink," I heard Todd say, sounding like he was at the other end of a tunnel, "if you can hear me."

Obediently, I blinked and coughed into the crook of my elbow. "*What* was *that*?" I sputtered in between gasps, eyes watering. I held up one finger, letting him know I wasn't finished. "How do you *do* that with your eyes?"

"Huh?"

"You did the same thing this morning when I was leaving your store. All that Sinatra talk. You were *staring* at me — at my *face*. You did the same thing with Chandler. You shot a single look at him, and he was completely at your mercy. How do you do that?"

Todd shrugged, not quite grinning. "It's a gift. I've always been able to isolate and tame in times of peril." He raised his right hand. "But I swear to you, I use my power for good."

I shook my head and laughed. "You better be careful with

that. Some girls would *not* take a tempting gaze like that lying down."

Todd's half grin stretched into a full smile. "I'll consider that fair warning, Abby."

When I returned his smile, I didn't care if he could see I was blushing.

"Honestly, though." He grew more serious. "That *moment* you were leaving my store, I could've been less obvious about it, but I was trying to get a better look at you." He leaned in, studying my face through the twilight. "I always thought you had blue eyes."

I automatically looked down. The moment was gone. "They're just gray," I mumbled.

"Don't," Todd entreated. "Please don't do that."

The insistence in his voice drew my gaze back up to him.

"And they're not *just* gray," he contradicted. "They're sky and smoke, like a whirlpool of clouds. I've never seen anything like them. To quote John Lennon, you're like the girl with kaleidoscope eyes."

Of all the things to say!

As my breathing became shallow, I felt myself leaning forward. Ready for a free fall.

Then Todd did the worst thing possible. He pulled back and looked at his watch.

Seriously?

"I think I should be getting you home." He seemed to be studying his watch for longer than necessary. "I don't want your posse out hunting for you."

I couldn't move at first, stunned by the wave of disappointment that hit me in the face. "You're probably right," I managed to say. But I didn't mean it.

As I watched Todd pat the sand around himself, making sure we hadn't dropped anything, I couldn't help thinking just how complicated my life really was. I didn't know what tomorrow would bring. Would I still be around? Would my cover be blown? Would I see him again? In one day we'd gone from being total strangers to . . . something else. We had shared things, personal things. We'd laughed together; I'd almost cried. The mere memory of the way he held my foot earlier was making me hot under the collar.

The thought of not seeing him ever again sent a different kind of ache through me. It left me reluctant to get to my feet or even move, reluctant to put an end to the day.

"I know an easy way back to the Square," Todd said, standing up, brushing sand off the front of his shirt. "I'll walk you to your bike, maybe throw it in the back of my truck, if you're too tuckered out to ride home."

"Har-har."

Our shoes were at the end of the boardwalk where we'd left them hours before. I didn't put mine on for our jaunt back, preferring to remain barefoot.

"On second thought," Todd said as I followed him up the stairs, "there's bound to still be a pretty big crowd at the Square. We should probably take a different way." He looked at me over his shoulder. "It's not exactly a short cut. Is that okay?"

"Sure," I answered casually, while deep down I was mildly ecstatic to be with him for a little while longer.

When we reached the bottom of the stairs, he stopped walking and turned to me. "Also . . ." He ran a hand through his hair. "There's one more thing I want to show you."

chapter 10

"THE FOOL ON THE HILL"

With Lindsey and Steve busy checking and double-checking on their pseudo-sleeping boys, I took a cool shower, unwillingly rinsing off the hot sun and salty water of my enchanted day. I couldn't help winking at my reflection as I towel dried my hair. It was the first time in months I'd been able to take a good look in the mirror without seeing a stranger.

Also, for the first time in months, I couldn't wait for tomorrow.

During the day, my cheeks and shoulders had turned a soft pink, tan lines crisscrossing my feet and ankles from my sandal straps. I felt pretty and feminine, as if my entire body were glowing from the inside, humming like a beehive.

After crawling into some silky pajamas, I wandered downstairs to the dark kitchen and grabbed a green apple from a bowl. In the spacious living room, the ceiling fan was *tick-tick-tick*ing ten feet above my head, swirling cool air. I stretched out on the leather couch and ate my dinner.

As I stared at the ceiling, fantasies ran through my head. I imagined a tall, dark man on the deck of a sailboat, out on the open sea, the wind blowing through his hair, rustling his clothes. I saw myself leaning off the starboard bow watching the sunset in a sailor's cap and long braids. He would toss me a rope, and together we'd hoist the mainsail. In my dream, I didn't know where that breeze was taking us, but I hoped it was worlds away.

I yelped when something tugged my big toe.

"Hey." Lindsey grinned at me, and I grinned back. "You were just singing." She took my apple core. "What were you thinking about?" She walked into the kitchen, and I heard the beginning sounds of bedtime-snack cleanup.

"Nothing," I called to her. "Just daydreaming. 'Strawberry Fields' and all that." I picked at the light blue piping along the cuffs of my pajamas. "Need any help in there?" I offered over the sounds of dishwater splashing, silverware clinking, and cabinet doors closing.

"Steve's doing the rest," she answered as she returned to the living room. I sat up when she sat down in one of the armchairs. "I make food; he cleans up. That's our deal. It takes him a while some nights, but he always gets to it." She leaned over and picked up some coloring books from the floor. "These are little John-John's favorites." She ran her fingers over the scarred picture on the cover. "He loves firetrucks."

"That's sweet."

"Charlie prefers dogs," she added, opening one of the coloring books and flipping through its pages. "So where have you been all day? And with whom?" Apparently, my loving sister was in her savage journalistic mode.

When my answer didn't come right away, she looked up, wearing a shifty smile. I couldn't stop myself from smiling back, lowering my eyes demurely.

"Wow, he must really be something."

"How do you know it's a *he*?"

"Ha!" She tossed the book aside. "Because I know *you*."

What was the point in beating around the bush? Besides, way too much time had passed since Lindsey and I shared any kind of conversation like this. I couldn't help smiling again, suddenly more than willing to girl talk into the night.

"So, you know that funny little store across the Square from Sundog Books?"

"Which one?"

"The one with those weird European surfing posters in the windows?"

Lindsey squinted then nodded.

"There was this . . . I mean . . . I met a guy there."

My sister had to think for a minute. Then her jaw dropped.

"*Abby*, are you talking about *Chandler*?" she shrieked. "Did you spend all day with that *kid*? He's sixteen years old!"

"Eighteen last month," I corrected, "but no, calm down. Do you know Todd, the owner?"

Lindsey pondered for another second, agog expression unchanged. "Todd Camford?"

"Maybe," I hedged. "I don't know his last name, actually."

Lindsey finally unclenched. Then a slow grin spread across her face. "Tall? Dark? Gorgeous?"

"Check, check, check." I grinned in return.

She sprang to the couch, right in my face. "Were you with him all day?"

"Pretty much." I smiled at the thought, my hands patting at leftover tummy butterflies. "I left here just after nine and rode your bike into Seaside. He was at his store, and we just . . . sort of . . ."

"Oh! This is too cool. Twelve hours? That's the equivalent of four dates. Abby, you've been on *four dates* with Todd Camford." She sounded very impressed. "I heard he used to be a Navy Seal."

"Marine sharpshooter," I was all too pleased to correct.

Lindsey's eyes bugged out. "Are you serious? Shut the f-front door."

"I know. Why is anything military-related such a turn on?"

She chuckled sarcastically, moving back to her chair. "Umm, maybe because that means he's all rugged and focused and . . . he knows how to *operate* a *weapon*."

"Lindsey, jeez," I said faintly, looking over my shoulder

for prying four-year-old ears. Instead, her husband Steve padded down the stairs. He was wearing his reading glasses on top of his head like women use their sunglasses to hold back the front of their hair. He looked, actually, quite silly. I shot Lindsey a sympathetic glance and could see a laugh spasm building behind her sealed lips.

"Where are the kitchen towels?" Steve asked sullenly.

"In the kitchen, hon," Lindsey replied, winking at me. "What happened?"

"John tipped a glass of water all over his bed."

Lindsey moved to stand up.

"Don't worry," her husband said, sitting her back down. "I got it." He disappeared into the kitchen.

"Todd Camford . . ." Lindsey repeated. then lowered her voice. "I wouldn't kick *him* out of bed for eating crackers." She gave me another wink. "Did you get a look at his chest?"

"Easy, Lindsey," I said. "You're too old for him."

"Never too old to look." She lifted her chin. "Hey, Steve!" she called toward the kitchen. "Guess who my little sis was with today." She didn't give Steve the chance to venture a guess. "Todd Camford from the surf shop on the Square where you got your wetsuit."

Steve made some neutral grunt reply from the kitchen.

Lindsey turned back to me with an even bigger grin across her pretty face. "Todd Camford and you?" She pursed her lips. "Major explosion."

I didn't know whether to agree or disagree, or even what her comment implied, but I went on to tell her about my day. She felt it necessary to relay all of what I said to Steve when he moved back and forth from the kitchen to the boys' bedroom or to his den or to the back deck or out to his car. I was surprised the whole population of Seagrove Beach didn't know about my four-date day.

"There's this row of trees with little pink blossoms," I said as my story neared its end. "I think Todd called them redbuds."

My sister was meditative, narrowing her eyes, insisting on picturing the exact route where Todd and I had walked by moonlight from the beach back to Modica.

"He made it his personal crusade to point out everything pink, just to torture me."

"Because of the Moulin Rouge ad? Huh. Funny." She nodded approvingly and lifted her chin. "He's funny, honey!"

Steve replied with another noncommittal grunt.

I continued my story. "Around the corner, there's that street lined with oaks and sycamores and willows with the long branches that touch the ground and with shallow roots breaking through the cracks in the sidewalk."

Lindsey sat wide-eyed, staring at me, elbows on knees, chin in hands.

"He offered his arm because, you know, I kept tripping over the roots in my bare feet." I lifted a coquettish grin. "It was *almost* unintentional."

"Nice one."

"When I stopped to look up at the moon through some branches, I pulled his arm, and the rest of him, over."

"I'll bet you did—"

"Linz, babe, stop interrupting her," Steve implored from his place on the rosewood rocking chair in the corner of the room, *Sports Illustrated* turned upside down on his lap. "We don't need your commentary, Ryan Seacrest."

Lindsey made the motion of locking her lips and throwing away the key.

"Go on, Abby," Steve said, sounding more like Oprah.

"When I asked Todd what kind of tree we were standing under, he had that *look* in his eyes." I addressed Steve. "You know *that look*?"

"Yes," Steve and Lindsey answered in unison.

"Todd told me the tree is called a Kissing Willow."

It was dead quiet.

Until Lindsey sucked in a breath. "You're kidding. What did you say?" My sister was leaning so far forward she was practically in my lap.

"After that, there wasn't much talking going on. We were kind of . . . at it for a while."

Lindsey sighed.

I looked down at my lap, unable to make my huge, ridiculous smile go away. I was remembering that tender, almost anguished and relieved look in Todd's eyes when he'd finally pulled me in; how he kissed me once, drew back to look me in the eyes, and then cupped a hand behind my head. For whatever reason, it had been the most romantic moment I could remember.

After that, the next hour was a blur. Although I did recall, at one point, privately confirming that Todd was indeed the world's best kisser.

While I was sampling a taste of his neck, Todd murmured softly in my ear, saying that he'd been wanting to do this all day. I explained to him, in my own special way, that he'd fought back for far too long.

I kept my eyes away from Lindsey's expectant face, unable to share with her any further details of where my mouth had gone next and what Todd's hands had done.

"And?" Lindsey's impatient prompt startled me back to the present. She was leaning forward again, pushing her blond hair away from her face. "What happened next?"

"Umm . . ." I rubbed my lips together, recalling perfectly how Todd had tasted both salty and sweet. "He apologized, actually."

"For what?" Steve asked.

"He said he *had* to kiss me because of the legend." As the pair of them stared blankly at me, I wished I'd kept that part of the story to myself. It was just too cute. "Yeah, well." I took a deep breath. "Todd was telling me some story about how every maiden who passes under that tree has to get a kiss or she'll die a heartbroken spinster, but, uh, I probably wasn't giving him much of a chance to speak." My cheeks prickled with a blush.

Lindsey sat back and sighed like Lady Juliet leaning over her balcony.

"I asked him if he was making the story up, but he said he wasn't, that it had something to do with Ponce de Leon and the Fountain of Youth."

"What?" asked Lindsey, perplexed.

I shrugged and grinned wider.

"Did he drive you back here?"

"He offered, though I told him I wanted to ride my bike to work off the key lime pie. But he was so cute. He was all worried that I'd get lost in the dark. He wouldn't let go of my handlebars."

"I'll bet he wouldn't," Steve said, laughing like a proud frat brother.

"As I was coasting away, I asked him if he's working tomorrow. He said he is, but only in the morning, because in the afternoon he has a date with a singer."

Lindsey, deadpan: "Marry him."

L.A.-based Mustang Sally, the band renowned for back-to-back platinum albums and sold-out tours, is shockingly out of the spotlight this summer. Plans to regroup at the studio in September have set the entertainment press on fire, wondering what kind of musical gem will come out of the notable break. If the next album is anything close to its predecessors, the whole world is in for a mega-treat.

"Satellite," the must-hear song that opens their fourth album, continues to dig its melodic claws into your heart and refuses to release throughout the nearly five-minute joint. The highly anticipated follow-up to the previous year's fantastic pop cheese *Nice Going,* their album *Losin' Myself* was anything but lost. With a combination of piano-led melodies, roaring guitar riffs, plus peach of a singer Abigail Kelly's irresistibly all-American fusion of sass versus vulnerability, the album is an incessantly catchy guilty pop pleasure. With its hook-crazy, techo-lite beats and super slick power ballads, it confidently displays yet another example of why Mustang Sally is indeed the "something-for-everyone" band to beat.

In that battle, however, this band has already prevailed, winning public as well as critical plaudits en masse, beginning with their ten-fold platinum début, *Mustang Sally*. Four albums later, they are still seemingly enduring and unaffected. The hyper-catchy ex-college-coed Kelly takes her listener on a wild ride through the brazenly bubblegum electric track of "I Shoulda Saw Love" to the slightly broader palette of the pop-dance pastel "Stupid 4 U." Frankly, we can't get enough of the lyrically trivial as she strains her debutant purr into a Billie Holiday-esque plea that comes across as both ridiculous and wonderful. The difference between obscurity and overexposure is found within Kelly's own throat.

Legitimizing a one-time minor garage band, guitarist Hal Richardson, bassist Jordan McPhee, and drummer Kiyoshi Sukuki are anything but minor characters in this story. Richardson's juicy guitar licks are straight from the school of Jimmy Paige, McPhee's slap-and-pop method eerily mirrors the likes of Flea and John Paul Jones, while Sukuki, the obvious rule-breaker of the bunch, could easily go toe-to-toe with idol Keith Moon. Kelly stands by her band, living the sunny pop life, while the boys take care of essential rock 'n roll business.

"The new record will be highly stylized," Axeman Richardson reports. We hope he's right. The past albums never mockingly descended into self-parody. "When I Look at You" (a duet with Kelly's ex-squeeze, Miles Carlisle) has a definite sense of economy and speculation, while "Satellite" is a cathartic pillow for the singer and her listener to cry on. Their last album rounds out with the aesthetically potent "Minor Keys," a wistful gem in which Kelly chooses music over a lover.

chapter 11

"AND YOUR BIRD CAN SING"

"I'm leaving now!" I called out as I climbed aboard the red beach cruiser. "I don't know how long I'll be gone." Lifting my feet, I coasted down the driveway and into the street. "Probably not too long," I added under my breath, almost as an afterthought.

"Wait!" Lindsey shot from the front door. I hit the brakes. She flew in front of me, one hand in a wet lime-green rubber glove. "Where are you going?" she panted, blocking my way.

I squinted past her shoulder and then down at the ground, looking everywhere but at her eyes. "Into Seaside," I said, feeling my stomach tighten. "I have a date to keep, remember?"

Lindsey didn't reply at first, but she finally exhaled a confused, "Oh." Her tone made me look at her. Deep concern mixed with disappointment on her face.

And I knew that she knew.

I gripped the handlebars. "So I guess you heard me on the phone earlier."

Lindsey nodded once. I sighed, squeezing the handlebars.

It was another hot day, hotter than yesterday, but I'd sufficiently cooled off, having swum for two lovely hours with my nephews. We'd spent the rest of the early afternoon making and sampling homemade snow cones, while Lindsey ran errands.

And then "Helter Skelter."

"What are you going to do?" Lindsey asked.

"I'm not sure. He wants me back in L.A. tomorrow. That's why he called."

"I know," she admitted. "I heard you taking. And then . . ." She paused, moving to properly look me in the eyes. "I heard you crying."

I dropped my chin. "I wasn't crying."

A white truck screeched its brakes as it rounded the corner and found my sister and me standing in the middle of the street. We moved off to the sidewalk.

"So? What did Max say? Did he guilt you into doing something again?"

"No," I said slowly, feeling defensive. "He was nice on the phone, actually."

Lindsey chuckled—heavy sarcasm. "Naturally. He's nice to you when he wants something. Even I know that." She sat down on the curb, shading her eyes from the sun with one gloved hand. "What did you tell him?"

"I didn't tell him anything." I kicked at a bike pedal, making it twirl around and around under my foot. "I don't really have a choice, though."

"Of course you have a choice!" Her sudden exclamation made me flinch. "You're not his little puppet. You can do what you want."

I closed my eyes. Not this again.

"It's his sick little game." Lindsey shook my front tire. "Max is manipulating you; he does it all the time. You're the only one who doesn't see it."

I opened my eyes, only to stare down at my hands twisting around the handlebars. My knuckles were turning white. I let my gaze wander over her shoulder to her tidy front yard. *Suburban paradise*, I thought, a little resentfully.

"You have no idea what it's like for me now—"

She cut in with: "Because you don't talk to me anymore."

I opened my mouth, but nothing came out.

"This is unsolicited advice, Abby, but you need to fix your life or figure out something else to do."

"Something *else*?" I echoed back, unbelievingly. "This *is* my life. *This*." I waved down to myself for some reason. "This is the way it is. He needs me in L.A. If I don't go, if I don't do what he wants, it affects everyone." In the back of my mind, I couldn't believe I had to defend Max Salinger so zealously. He was the person who started everything, who gave me everything. The band wouldn't be where we were today without him. Even Lindsey knew that. "If they need me there, I have to be there. If *I'm* not working, the guys in the band can't work. We're a team. I owe them."

"You don't owe anyone." Lindsey stared at me, her expression unrelenting. "Now, *sit down*."

Surrendering to her "request," I swung one leg over the bike and let my foot fall onto the sidewalk. I slumped down on the curb next to her.

"I just miss you, sis. So much." Lindsey's voice was normal at first, but the aggression quickly returned. "You've been away from Max for only *three days*. You're supposed to be here all summer. You never get a break. I'm sure that's a big part of your problem."

I shot her my most withering glare.

"You know," she rephrased, "why you've been so out of it lately."

I bit my lip, turned away, and sat motionless on the sandy street corner, knowing there was no way I could explain to her—or to anybody, for that matter—how things were.

Yes, I was sure part of my "problem" was my job. But that was the bearable part of my nightmare, the part I could handle.

"You need to make some changes," Lindsey said, placing a hand on my arm.

I tossed another scornful glance her way, but she ignored it.

"For starters, you have to learn to tell Max no."

"Please," I mumbled, looking out at the street. "I don't need a lecture." I ran my fingers over my eyebrows, seeking relief from a new headache.

She went on as if I hadn't spoken. "And, stop beating yourself up over Christian. You know it wasn't your fault that . . ."

She went on talking, but I made myself zone out: Abby's Defense Mechanism 101. My entire consciousness was in another place now, inside my head, away from whatever my sister was saying. It was dark and tumultuous where I went, but it was far away. I didn't want to keep forcing myself inside, but there was nowhere else to go.

Despite this effort, I was suddenly thinking about Christian, about the last night I'd seen him, a year ago. The band had been leaving for London the next morning for a few quick shows. Christian wouldn't be coming with me that time like he usually did. I didn't like traveling without him; I felt safer and happier when my big brother was around. He was my anchor.

I remembered the airport-bound limo picking me up at five in the morning, after I'd fallen asleep on the couch waiting for Christian to return home with my takeout veggie burger—the midnight snack he'd volunteered to fetch after I whined and begged him for an hour.

Other than that, I had very little memory of that trip abroad. I couldn't even remember how I'd heard the news the next day—heard about what happened back home the night before, when I'd been dead asleep and didn't hear the sirens a few miles down the Pacific Coast Highway.

"Don't you know that by now . . ." Some of what Lindsey said sifted through my barricade, but her voice was distant and muffled. "Why will you never talk to me about what happened?"

I couldn't move. Couldn't breathe. I was being held under water, a riptide pushing, undertow pulling, and the only voice I could understand was telling me to relax and breathe, to give in.

But I was choking.

"We can't change what happened." I felt her stroking the back of my hair, like I was some needy lap cat. "Maybe you should call Mom and Dad."

"I can't!" I snapped, wiggling her hand off my hair.

Lindsey sat back, knowing she'd struck a nerve. "Then promise you'll stay here for the summer, where I can feed you and clean you and make sure you sleep."

"You don't have to take care of me, Lindsey. I don't need anyone."

"You let Christian take care of you."

My spine stiffened. "I don't want to talk about that."

Lindsey's expression morphed from blank to sad to defeated.

For a few seconds, I almost relaxed, thinking I was off the hook, but she shook her head and set her jaw. "No, Abby. It's been a year. Let's talk about it."

But I'd already told her I couldn't. I wouldn't.

Our mutual, stubborn, nearly identical silence seemed to stretch on forever as we stared at each other.

Lindsey was first to break the standoff. "Well?"

"Well what?"

She narrowed her eyes, daring me.

I huffed. "What do you want me to say?"

"I want you to tell me what happened that night."

"You know what happened." I growled. "You saw the police report. You read the tabloids." I yanked out a cluster of grass by the roots and tossed it into the street.

"No, Abby. I want *you* to tell me."

I looked away, blinking into the wind. "I can't," I whispered, wrapping a rope of my hair around one finger. "It's the middle of the day. We're out in the front yard. Cars are driving by. It doesn't feel right."

"Something like this will never feel right. I've heard every excuse in the book from you. So come on. I'll start, okay?"

I shrugged indifferently, but my lips were sealed shut. I was not budging.

For some reason, Lindsey took this as a sign to press on. "Late that night," she said, "Christian went to the deli down the street, just like he had on a hundred other nights."

I felt a familiar snaky rope slithering inside my throat. I tried, but I couldn't swallow it.

"And he didn't come back." She waited several seconds. "Because . . ."

"Because?" I echoed sarcastically. "Because he got *shot* and *died*, Lindsey! *Jeez!*" My throat was closing up, anaphylactic shock, deathly allergic to the topic of my brother's death and how he would still be here, if not for me. "What else do you want me to say?"

"Just that." Her words came out methodically. "Four men held up the deli, and one of them shot Christian. In no way could you have stopped that, Abby." She reached out and touched my arm gently. "We all love him. We all miss him. The funeral—"

This was all I could take. "I *said* I can't talk about it." My voice came out cruel and angry.

Lindsey flinched, her expression showing the hurt I'd inflicted.

But I didn't care. This conversation could not go on. It was bad enough that I wanted to peel off my skin every time I thought about it, but to *talk* about it? Impossible. After a year, I was well aware of my punishment, and it was a livable sentence—like a brand burned on my soul, something that would always be there, a constant reminder of the horrible thing I did, how my selfishness damaged our family forever.

No matter what anyone said, I knew it was my fault. And the only way I could figure out how to make up for it was to be a success—to make it worth it. Somehow.

That feeling was something I never admitted to anyone. Not even to Dr. Robert.

"I'll go back to L.A. like Max wants." I had to force my voice to sound resolved. "I'll work hard so you won't have to worry about me. No one will worry about me, okay?" When I stood up, my legs felt like jelly.

"You're hiding behind your job. That's another of your problems."

I ignored her. One battle at a time. "Max knows what's best for me and for the group. He's the boss."

"He's your manager," Lindsey corrected. "*You* pay *him*. You're *his* boss."

I crossed my arms. "You know what I mean."

I stared past Lindsey, allowing myself once more to remember back to the day Christian died. It was a Friday. Or rather, it was a Friday when I found out he had died; it had taken hours for the message to reach me. By then, we were stuck in London—bad weather, every airport closed.

I missed my brother's funeral because of work. When we returned to L.A., I'd been sent straight to the studio to record "Satellite" and the rest of the album. Broken, grieving, and probably in shock, I'd been in no condition to be at work, let alone to cut our next single. But Max thought it best that I get right back on the Mustang Sally roller coaster—no time for mourning, no time for thinking, no standing, no screaming, hands and legs inside the car at all times.

I wanted to burst into tears, to tell Lindsey how unbearable everything had become, but I shut down instead. Telling her wouldn't help.

"Well." She sighed. "*I* want you to stay here. For the whole summer." Her hair was blowing in the breeze around her neck as she stood and turned toward the house. She seemed more angry than hurt now. And ya know what? I was totally fine with that.

"Would you do me one favor?" she asked. "Say good-bye to Todd."

My stomach took an unsuspected nose-dive, remembering what I had to say to him, what I *must* say to him. And I was totally dreading it.

"I was just on my way into town," I said, straddling the bike.

Lindsey shook her head. "I mean *really* tell him good-bye. Properly. After last night, don't lead him on." She paused thoughtfully. "You still don't understand how people perceive you. You're different. You're a huge star. You know that, don't you?"

I bit down on my raw cheeks. "I hate when you talk to me like I'm a circus freak."

"We live in a small community; I run into the guy practically every other day." She broke off and started pulling at the end of her ponytail. "You might not be aware of this, but Todd's been here only about five months. I don't know much about him, but you can't help picking up tidbits, living in a place like this year-round. The girls and I—"

"Lindsey, I have no intention of listening to gossip. I have to live in that world every day," I reminded her bitterly. "Why can't you people mind your own business?"

"I'm sorry, but *that* is how *this* world works." She spread her hands. "Someone moves into town during the off season and we discuss it. It wasn't like we were printing a story in a tabloid; we were *talking*."

"Same thing."

"Just hear me out."

I huffed and folded my arms, balancing the bike between my legs.

"A few months before Todd moved to Seaside, he broke off his engagement."

I didn't know what I was expecting my sister to inform me of, but it wasn't that.

"I guess," she added, "the wedding was only days away."

Of course I couldn't help feeling for Todd. But bygone mistakes didn't scare me, especially when they happened to better a person's character. We all had relationship baggage. I knew I did. And I was the last person who should judge anybody by the choices he made in the past. Besides, I was leaving, anyway. Right?

My stomach fell again. "How *shocking*," I jabbed, even though I felt pressure behind my eyes. "But hardly front-page material." Yes, I wondered about the details, but not at the expense of letting Lindsey divulge the secret she was holding. I loathed gossip. She knew it, and she knew why.

"Just go easy on the guy. I suppose he's been in his mourning period all this time. And *you* . . ." She paused for effect, her voice morphing into an accusing tone. "*You* might be the first girl he's shown interest in since his breakup. I've seen what you're capable of doing to guys, *any* guys. They're drawn to you; they can't help it. That boyfriend from back home is *still* totally obsessed."

I rolled my eyes.

Lindsey took a step toward me. "And Miles, Mister Sexiest Man Alive, was in the magazines for months after you dumped him, wrapped around your little finger. I saw him on *Letterman* a while back, talking about you. And don't pretend that new song of theirs isn't about you. The girl in the video could be your twin."

"Idiot," I mumbled as I dropped my gaze to stare at my feet, at the bike pedals, and then at the sandy asphalt.

Then, for just a moment, when I lifted my chin to face the afternoon breeze, I let my mind go, thinking of yesterday, of last night. I closed my eyes, imagining what today might bring, and tomorrow . . . if I could only let it. Fingering the ends of my hair like a paintbrush, I ran a fistful of it along my cheek. "I don't think it's fair for you to compare Todd to David or that idiot Miles."

"What makes him different?"

I exhaled deeply and slowly, while flashes of my most current, delicious daydream sent heat through my body, only to settle in my stomach as a dull ache. "I don't know," I said. But of course I knew. I had been thinking about Todd all morning, counting the minutes until I would see him again.

And then that call from Max terminated any other plan.

"Absolutely everything," I responded. I was smiling now, but it made my face throb like the mother of all sinus attacks. "I like him, Lindsey. Ha! *Like*. That doesn't even come close. I know it's totally crazy to say this after only one day, but . . ." I lowered my voice, as if my words might make it all the way to Max's office in California. "I've never felt this way about anyone. Never. We got along so well. He's funny and smart, and when he looked at me . . ." My voice choked, the lining of my throat growing thick. I rubbed my hand across my face. "Am I supposed to walk away? Just like that?"

Lindsey didn't respond, but I was actually asking her this time. I really wanted an answer, because I suddenly didn't have one.

"Well," she finally offered, "like I said, it's your decision. Always has been. Nothing's impossible."

Great. Thanks.

"I wouldn't worry about impressing Todd," she continued as she walked backward across her front yard toward the house. "I'm sure he was blown away by you. He's probably at home right now thanking his lucky stars."

I let out a sigh. "I'm the lucky one," I whispered.

Big, long-winged, hairy bats were flapping around in my stomach as I rode up to the curb in front of Todd's Tackle. I leaned my bike against a pole and pushed open the heavy glass door.

Gong!

When I entered, two customers were leaving—women who looked to be in their mid-twenties, armed with several large shopping bags. They were giggling their heads off like a pair of teenagers, while glancing back into the store at something. Or someone.

"He's, like, so way *hot*," one of them said, kind of swoonily.

"Totally," the other agreed.

Neither of them noticed me when we skirted past each other.

Todd was at the counter bent over a laptop. The big smile that stretched across his face when he saw me sent those bats in my stomach into a tizzy.

"I was afraid you weren't going to show," he said, gesturing to the clock on the wall that read half past two.

"You know women!" My enthusiasm felt forced, leaving a bitter taste in my mouth.

From his expression, I could see Todd sensed something was off. "Sometimes I do," he said as he met me in the middle of the store. He was summer vacation personified, his blue golf shirt open at the throat, giving me a little peek at some lovely chest hair. I tried not to over-grin, knowing I could report this information back to Lindsey. She did love a nice chest.

Looking closer, it was evident his Diesel shorts and shirt probably cost a cool hundred bucks apiece. Yes, he was dressed down, but with more style than a Kennedy on vacation.

Self-consciously I put my hands in the back pockets of the same shorts I'd worn yesterday, fresh out of the washer and dryer. "My manager called," I said to his open collar. "They want me back in L.A. Now."

I held my breath, studying his expression, waiting for a reaction.

He *seemed* disappointed, and I wondered if he was painfully dying a thousand deaths inside but refusing to show it, like me. I was ready for him to burst into a rage and demand that I stay.

"Oh." He shifted his weight. "That's a real shame."

I blinked, staring into his eyes, feeling all kinds of disappointed.

We stood in silence for a few moments. Todd then glanced away and I looked down at my feet. I'd painted my toenails DayGlo orange a few hours ago. The optimistic color seemed to be mocking me now.

This is not *fair*, I thought, grinding my back teeth so I wouldn't cry or something equally humiliating. *It's too soon. I need more time, much more time, but I just can't take it. And since Todd doesn't seem to care . . .*

"Yeah, well," I said as I gazed across the room at nothing,

"I'm calling Max tonight with my final answer, so, I guess we should just . . ."

Todd's head snapped to attention, his bright green eyes boring into mine, going wide and then narrow. "You have a choice?"

His question threw me. "Well, technically, none of us have to be back till September."

Todd flew behind the counter and pulled out a sign: GONE FISHIN'. He hung it on the inside of the front window. "Let's go," he commanded, towing me out by the elbow and locking the door behind us.

"But I told you—"

I could see his jaw set under his skin. "When would you have to leave?"

"Tomorrow morning."

"So that gives me"—he looked at the face on his cell—"fifteen hours."

"To do what?"

He looked up at me. And smiled.

chapter 12

"I'LL FOLLOW THE SUN"

"Yesterday you mentioned you used to dance."

I nodded, wondering what Todd was getting at.

"The bio on your website says you got your start in musical theater."

We were strolling again, just like yesterday, except this time Todd wasn't as tranquil. There was an urgency to today, like he had a definite agenda in mind, though I could also tell he was trying hard to keep the atmosphere casual.

Apparently we were both in restrained-panic mode.

"My website?" I lifted my eyebrows. Todd grinned like the cat that had swallowed the canary. "Is that what you've been doing all day? Hard at work surfing the Internet? You'll never sell beach towels that way."

"Skeptic."

We turned a corner, ambling through the neighborhood with the shallow tree roots—the setting of last night's kiss. Despite what the responsible side of my brain said, in my heart, all Todd needed to do was hold me under our shady Kissing Willow or touch my face, kiss my neck, and just maybe . . .

But he didn't. We walked under the long and leafy branches without either of us saying a word about last night.

"I danced ballet till I was fifteen," I explained as we neared the footpath that led to the beach. "Which was really good for me." My arms automatically moved into the *Vaganova grande pose*: one arm out to the side, the other above my head, both curved elegantly, fingers forming an oval.

"Nice," Todd said, observing my stance with an air of appreciation.

I immediately broke my pose. "Even as a kid, I needed an outlet. Ballet takes a lot of discipline and concentration."

"I can imagine." He smirked. "All those pink tights and hair glitter must be brutal."

I grabbed him by the arm and pulled him back. "Hey, tough guy. You try cramming your swollen and blistered feet into a pair of pointe shoes, spend hours spinning, making jumps, landing, and then stopping every few minutes to wipe the floor so you won't slip on your own blood."

Todd cringed.

I let him go and smiled lightly. "My instructor was quite the slave driver. I suppose that's where I get my"—I cleared my throat—"my unique work ethic."

"What happened with that?"

The toes on my right foot involuntarily pointed as my leg slid to the side, itching to stretch myself into a perfect *arabesque en avant*. "My audition for Juilliard didn't go well," I said instead, relaxing my foot, feeling leftover disappointment from years ago. "Their official explanation was that my proportions weren't right, that my legs were too long."

Todd looked down at the legs poking out of my shorts. "These old things?" He swatted my knee. "How preposterous."

"I had a growth spurt," I explained. "Happens to everyone. I knew I was too tall for my age, but I was devastated and angry at the world for giving me this incredible passion and *almost* the body for it."

Todd looked thoughtful, his green eyes full of unasked questions. Instead of asking them, though, he said, "That's pretty intense logic for a teenager."

"Mmm." I shrugged. "I guess I learned to take my lumps at an early age. After ballet, I decided to go out for plays at school."

"You were the lead in *Brigadoon*."

I stared at him for a second and then rolled my eyes. "Google actually got that one right. Theater was another good way to get me comfortable onstage. It's lucky I've always had great choreographers and directors. Unless I know where to go, I'm helplessly clumsy."

"Impossible." Todd laughed. "I don't live in a cave, Abby. I *have* seen you perform."

"That's exactly what I mean. I can learn a routine, execute it perfectly, then walk behind the curtain, trip over a chair, and knock down the entire set. Splat. Dead bodies."

He probably assumed I was exaggerating, because he laughed again.

Up ahead, directly in our path, a group of about eight teenagers was gathered in a circle, inconsiderately blocking the entire sidewalk. The boys were showing off their surfboards; the girls were posturing and posing.

The worst.

I barely had time to gasp before every muscle in my body clamped down and went into petrifaction mode.

One lone Frisbee dude on the beach was one thing, but a swarm of autograph seekers could easily escalate into pandemonium. It had happened to me so many times. *Please, not today.*

The split second after my reaction, I felt Todd grab my arm.

"This way," he directed under his breath, swiftly guiding us around a different corner, leading me down a narrow alley between two stores.

My heart hammered behind my ears when we stopped, sheltered between a pair of turquoise Dumpsters.

"Are you okay?" he asked, leveling his face to mine so we were eye to eye.

I swallowed, surprised at how startled I still felt. I knew my face was drained of color, because it suddenly felt ice cold.

Todd watched me, his expression a little alarmed at whatever he was seeing. Slowly I peeked over my shoulder; no one had followed us.

"Here," he said, pointing through the alley. "This is a short cut, anyway." He took my arm, prompting me to walk. As we started off, he looked over his own shoulder as those kids sauntered loudly past the mouth of the alley, oblivious to us. Something like annoyed suspicion flashed in his eyes, but then his expression changed into something more hostile, mirroring looks I'd seen on Shugger when I was under siege.

Armored car is right. I exhaled again, feeling very looked-after.

"Sounds like yours was pretty different than my high school experience." Todd spoke conversationally as we fled the scene. "We traveled." His hand was still gripping my elbow. "I was the habitual new kid for most of my life, always having to leave my friends just when I made some. But my family is close and we stuck together, so it wasn't all bad."

"Where did you go to high school?" I asked, more than happy to think about something other than crazy fans or the sick feeling in my stomach whenever I thought about leaving tomorrow.

"It was in San Sebastian, actually."

My eyes moved up and to the left, picturing a detailed map of southern Europe.

"I graduated early and they have a different academic system than here in the States," he said.

My mind flipped through the geography book in my head. *Between Spain and France. The Pyrenees. Spain's port resort, beaches and hills. Hemingway wrote about it.*

Todd went on. "I was only seventeen at graduation. Barely eighteen when I entered Annapolis. I was luckier than my sisters, though. Jessica attended three schools, her last year."

I groaned sympathetically. "I would've hated that."

"She did," Todd confirmed as we cut through a parking lot behind Town Square.

"So, how'd you do in school?" I asked. A gust of summery

wind hit us head on. "You must've done pretty well, for Annapolis to take you."

"Tolerably, but like I said, it was a different system."

"Ha! Mister Modest," I joked, wrangling my hair that blew in the wind. "You were valedictorian of your high school, weren't you?"

"No," he said. "There's no such thing in Europe. But I was asked to give the commencement speech at graduation. They were probably just indulging my American heritage, though."

I stopped in my tracks, holding the ends of my hair in two pigtails. "Are you serious?"

Todd looked back at me. He seemed confused by my question.

"*You* gave the commencement speech for San Sebastian?" I let this information roll around in my head for a second. "What do they speak there, Spanish?"

"Mostly. A type of Spanish called *Castellano*." The way he pronounced the word made my stomach do a somersault. "But a small percentage still speaks Basque. I gave my speech in Basque."

"Of course you did." I snorted. "Is there anything you *can't* do?"

"Plenty," he replied, deadpan.

I lifted my chin and let out a sarcastic chuckle. "Over achiever!"

He gave me a sideways glance. "You're one to talk."

I blinked a few times, wide-eyed.

Now *he* was hooting with sarcasm, actually slapping his thigh. "Correct me if I'm wrong here, but isn't it *you* who retired from competitive ballet at fifteen and then just happened to find yourself succeeding in one of the most cutthroat businesses around? And let's not forget your photographic memory and—"

"Well *you*." I cut him off. "You're just, ya know . . ." I was trying to sound accusatory, but the way he was grinning made me lose my thought. "You're all . . . *perfect*."

Todd frowned at me, but a moment later, he brushed it

off with a chuckle. "Naw. I'm just as flawed and depraved as any other hot-blooded man." He looked me in the eyes, all intense and beseeching. "Stick around long enough, and I promise you'll find that out."

The singing from my pocket started up, disturbing us again. I exhaled, annoyed at the never-ending parade of interruptions. "*You* answer it," I said, passing Todd my musical cell.

He stared at it for a second then put it to his ear. "Abby's phone."

I snickered at his authoritative tone.

He narrowed his eyes, looking confused as he listened. "Hello? Is anyone—" He flinched, holding the phone away from his head. I heard Molly's screechy voice. She was freaking out. "Umm, maybe you should . . ." He handed the phone back.

"Molly." I laughed. "Hellooo. I'm right here."

"Abby? Crikey!" She panted. "Whadoyou . . . Howthee . . . Whowas—" Her panic suddenly dropped off. "Oohhh . . . Was that *him*, then?"

I smiled. "Mm-hmm."

"Put him back on."

Clearing my throat first, I passed the phone over.

"Hello, again." Todd listened for a few seconds. "Hmm, that's very—" She cut him off. "Oh, yeah, I agree. Yes, well, but I don't think that's something—" Cut off again. He laughed. "Oh, uh." His eyebrows pulled together. "Let me think— Leo— Yes, that's right. How did—" More laughing. "I do. Perfectly. Right. Yes, and, uh, *ciao* to you, too."

He ran his fingers through his hair and passed the phone back. "She wants you now."

"Okay, Molly." I spoke down the line. "This is the last time you'll be calling today. You can say exactly three words to me, so make them good."

Molly didn't hesitate. "You're marrying him."

♪

We crept along the side of Cherry Pie Place, just like yesterday. But this time, all the windows and window shades were wide open, a shiny black Range Rover sat in the driveway, and a blue-and-white-striped awning was pitched over the back patio. The scent of a very recent steak cooked on a grill made me worry.

"Todd," I whispered, "someone's home."

"Shhh—stay close to me." He took my hand and pulled until I was right at his back, practically hugging him from behind. "Just in case." He somehow managed to smell even better than yesterday.

That same dog barked at us through the fence. Todd stopped and slid his fingers through the space between the boards, letting the dog sniff his hand. After a friendly nose pat, we continued in silence until we reached the end of the boardwalk.

"Feel like swimming?" Todd smiled, eyeing me. "You're certainly dressed for it again."

"I don't think so." I squinted at him. "I've already been in. I think my hair's had all the salt water it can handle."

Four or five groups of sunbathers were out on the beach, but evidently no one belonging to the white house behind us. A dark-haired young woman stretched out on an orange beach chair waved to Todd. He waved back but tried to mask it from me by running his fingers through his hair.

"Who's your *friend*?" I asked, hoping I sounded more teasing than jealous.

"Becky," he said with a shrug, looking the other way. "Or Becca. I don't really know."

Sure.

We kicked off our shoes and walked out to the short breakers, where fewer people were around. The dazzling blue water was shallow and as flat as glass, one of those postcard days the "Redneck Riviera" is famous for.

I waded out until the water was almost up to my knees, stinging a tiny scrape on my shin inflicted by little John-John earlier that day. Todd remained behind me, sitting on the damp sand.

When a boat pulling a skier sped by, I waved my hands over my head. The driver waved back and honked the horn. Behind them, a pair of gray pelicans dove in the water. One came up with a yellow striped fish hanging halfway out of its beak. I laughed and turned around. Todd was shading his eyes with both hands. I walked to where he sat, my body blocking the sun from his face. "Why are you just sitting here?"

"Why not?"

"The water feels great." I splashed him at little. "Don't you ever swim?"

He yawned, covering his mouth with the back of his hand. "I swam this morning before the sun was up."

"Alone?" Ha-ha. Just checking.

He nodded.

"You must not have slept for very long."

He looked out at the water. "I didn't sleep at all, actually."

"Bad heartburn?"

He squinted up at me, giving me an accusatory look, as if his not sleeping was somehow *my* fault. "It was something like heartburn."

My stomach made a happy little flip, so I plopped down on the watery sand right next to him. We sat shoulder to shoulder, our legs out in front of us, toes teasing the spraying waves.

"I have pretty bad insomnia," I said. "I have for years. Nightmares, too, sometimes." I stretched my arms above my head. "But not last night. I slept like a baby."

"I'm glad. You must've really needed it."

A flock of seagulls were off to the left of us, picking and scavenging at the scraps of a leftover picnic. A little boy with a stick ran into the flock, scattering the birds. Todd was watching the seagulls squeaking and squawking as they flew over the water. I was watching him.

Almost automatically, I reached out and touched his cheek with my pinkie, right below his dimple. "You got a little sunburned yesterday," I pointed out, moving my hand up to finger a strand of his hair. His eyes slowly closed. "Todd?" I whispered.

"Hmmm?"

I sighed and bit my lip. "I don't *want* to leave tomorrow, but—"

He turned his face my way, not having very far to lean in, and kissed me once, sweet and slow—a breeze off the ocean—almost like he was asking permission. He opened his eyes to look at me.

Permission granted, Lieutenant.

When we kissed again, it was totally different. He scooted closer, his warm hands on either side of my neck. The pressure of his fingers under my hair was solid and strong, yet always gentle. When his lips parted, I got dizzy, like he might positively absorb me. For a second I feared I might be swooning like those silly ladies in Jane Austen novels.

"That was rude of me to interrupt," he whispered, his lips on the corner of my mouth. "But I'm not about to make this decision easy for you."

How he managed to string together so many coherent words was beyond me; I couldn't even remember what day it was. His fingers combed through my hair, and I caught a flash of his green eyes as they flickered open.

Before I had time to reply to his faux apology, his left arm had me around the waist and his right hand clamped under my knees, swinging me around so my legs draped across his lap. After I exhaled a surprised gasp, my lips crashed against his again. He pulled me against him tight; I could feel his heart racing in time with mine.

"Relax," he whispered on my cheek. "I'm not the one who's leaving."

That's when I noticed my grip around his neck was probably a little too tight. I did relax, but I didn't slow down.

The tide came in, shallow waves bubbled over our feet, as all the while screaming skyrockets blasted off around my head. Mental Fourth of July!

"Abby." Todd's voice was hushed as he drew away, our foreheads touching. "I've been doing some thinking."

"I don't like the sound of that."

"Shut up, please." He chuckled. "I'm trying to say something important, and you're not . . ." He reached back to unlock my hands from his neck. "You're *not* making it easy for me."

My hands were suddenly on my lap and Todd was looking away.

Uh-oh. I sat back.

"I don't want to be a confusion to you," he began half-heartedly, his emerald eyes following a pair of jet-skiers spinning doughnuts. "You said yesterday that your life is complicated. I don't want to add to that. I know how important you are to your people. I know they want you back. But I have to admit something while I still have the chance." He didn't go on right away and I waited as he stared down at the sand. "I thought about you all night," he continued. "I feel like a teenager with a crush I can't shake." When he looked up, my heart pounded expectantly. "I didn't think I could feel that way again. After only one day, Abby."

"I know," I said. He pretty much just summed up how I'd been feeling, too. Totally crazy.

"If you stay," he continued, "starting something would be far too easy. I'm halfway there." He didn't go on, but paused to draw a pattern in the sand with one finger. "Last night I was even planning things we could do together over the summer." He laughed softly, but it didn't touch his eyes. "Can you imagine?"

I could.

When he looked at me, his crooked smile shattered my heart. "So I think the prudent thing would be if we just . . ." He sliced his hand through the air in a slow, cutting motion. "Stop."

Before I had the chance to fully take that in, a sharp shock of pain shot through me. The top half of my body jolted forward.

"What's wrong?" Todd asked. He looked horrified. "Are you sick?"

I wasn't sure yet. All I knew was—it hurt. "I don't know," I gasped, looking at my feet in the wet sand where the acute pain originated. It was a ginormous orange crab, claw clamped on my big toe.

And I screamed bloody murder—*"Get it off! Get it off!!"*—as I hysterically kicked both legs out in front of me.

Todd grabbed my flailing limbs. "Stop moving!" he shouted over my hysterics. "She'll fix deeper if you try to shake her off." His grip on me tightened like an iron clamp. "Hold *still,* Abby. Now!"

Fearing that he'd resort to punching me out to get me to comply, I yielded.

He pinned down my legs with one hand, quickly prying the claws open with the other, and then he tossed the cruel crustacean down the beach all in a matter of seconds. Panting in time, we silently watched as it disappeared into the water.

"Are you okay?" he asked. His hand was dripping with blood.

"Is that mine or yours?" I gulped, staring at the small pools of crimson against the white sand.

"Both, I think."

The line of the horizon tilted to the side, and my head felt like it weighed a thousand pounds. I found it weird how the waves sounded fainter, yet the whooshing wind seemed louder than ever.

"Hey, look at me. Look. At. Me."

I pushed my focus toward the voice.

Todd was staring at my face, looking anxious. He rolled his eyes. "Okay, let's go."

I felt my body leaving the sand as he picked me up, cradling me to his chest. I closed my eyes—half in pain, half in immense, delicious, womanly pleasure—while he began walking us away from the water.

"Are you taking me to your store?" I asked, trying to ignore the pulsating throbs in my foot.

"I live closer."

"Isn't the Square across the—"

"Hush!" he snapped, shifting my weight in his arms. "If you're really injured, act like it."

"I *am*." I opened my eyes. "But where—"

"Yes, Abby, the Square is across the street." His grip around me changed; yeah, it was definitely more like a hug now. "But I live right here."

"Right where?"

He was heading straight toward the white house with the blue-striped awning.

chapter 13

"ACT NATURALLY"

Todd carried me all the way up the boardwalk stairs, through the wooden gate that separated the beach from his backyard, under that striped awning, past a gas grill, and up to the sliding glass door of Cherry Pie Place, the black lab padding beside us the whole way.

With his hands otherwise occupied, I slid open the door.

"Welcome to *chez* Camford. Sammy, *here*." The first part was offered to me as Todd knelt down to semi-gently deposit me on a leather couch. The second comment was to the frisky pooch licking the side of his face in an affectionate homecoming. Todd snickered and stroked its head, murmuring his own greeting. I never thought I would be jealous of a pet.

"Sam!" Todd chirped in excitement to his dog, who, in turn, froze and tilted its ears, watching its master intently. Todd cocked his head about an inch. "Shark!" The dog turned and bounded through the open sliding glass door. Todd stood up and shut the door behind him.

"You didn't have to put him out."

"Yes, I did," Todd said, wiping off the side of his face with a grin. "Otherwise, you'd be next to get the tongue bath. And Sam's a she."

"Sam?" I asked, leaning forward to look at the dog through the glass. She appeared to be chasing a butterfly in a circle.

"Sammy," Todd corrected. "As in Davis Junior."

I sat back and laughed. "You're kidding."

After a shrug, Todd dashed out of the room through a swinging door. I heard him opening and closing drawers in another part of the house.

Thanks to the lab barking gleefully in the backyard, my first impression was that Todd's home was a happy one. My second was that it smelled exactly like him, which gave me a sudden swoony feeling.

I pulled my foot onto my lap, stretching my shirt out to wrap my mangled toe in the bottom of it, so as not to get blood all over his nice furniture. After a few deep breaths, deciding that I was *not* going to bleed to death, I investigated my surroundings from where I sat.

The living room was tall and wide, and because of all the open windows, full of moving air. A row of dark, six-inch rafters sliced across the high white ceiling. The floors were creamy taupe Corinthian tile with a large blue, brown, and black rug spread across the middle.

His place screamed bachelor pad, but also European simplicity. Looking down, I noticed the couch I was sitting on: tall back, long, and with soft padded cushions in black leather and silver legs. It smelled expensive.

In front of me sat a rectangular coffee table, rich and marbly. Three long, shallow drawers ran its full width, reminiscent of something that might have been full of treasure maps on a pirate ship.

Still gripping my foot, I leaned back against comfy cushions, wedging myself between two. To my left, the room was lined with pale oak shelves, some with books, others with pictures in frames, trophies, and further evidence of an exciting life. For a brief moment, I envisioned how nicely some of my Mustang Sally awards might look on one of the empty shelves.

Silly Abby. I smiled to myself. *Always jumping ahead.*

To my right, a complicated-looking sound system with both a turntable and an iPod dock filled a corner of the room. The shelf beside it held a stack of vinyl record albums.

A red punching bag dangled from the low ceiling on the other side of the room, right in front of a large picture window. On the adjacent wall hung an Annapolis pennant and a framed *Robin and the 7 Hoods* vintage movie poster autographed by the entire Rat Pack, including Sinatra. Positioned just above the mantel, displayed like a piece of fine art, was a massive plasma TV.

Boys, I thought with a sigh. *They do love their toys.*

Straight in front of me was the highlight of the room: the view of the Gulf through floor-to-ceiling windows and a set of tall French doors.

Over my shoulder was the doorway through which my host had disappeared. The door was still swinging. His house was a lovely space. I wondered why he didn't tell me he lived there yesterday.

Finally he reappeared, carrying a large bowl of water and a first-aid kit, with a white towel draped over his shoulder. He knelt down. "This will hurt you more than it hurts me," he cautioned. "But don't worry, I'm a professional beach-towel salesman." Before I could squirm away, he dunked my wounded foot in the murky, steaming-hot water.

The pain was instantaneous. Yelping, I jerked my foot out, splashing both of us, as well as the carpet and couch.

"Don't make me get rough," Todd warned, holding me down by the shoulders. "Just relax, Abby, okay?" The slow sound of his voice was soothing and a bit hypnotic. "Relax." His hands slid from my shoulders, down my arms. He leaned forward, one hand carefully picking up my hurt foot. His other went gliding down the back of my calf. When I inhaled jaggedly, he cocked an eyebrow.

I was pretty much putty in his hands as he gazed up at me like he was positioning us for something more than just a kiss. If I hadn't been in so much pain, it would've been *quite* the turn-on . . . him kneeling at my feet, being both gentle and bossy.

"Ready?" he asked. His expression turned concerned, maybe wondering if my stillness was a sign that I was going into shock.

I took in a breath and nodded.

As he re-submerged my foot, I let my body absorb the pain, concentrating on some complicated yoga breaths that weren't doing crap. I stared up at the ceiling, while below me, Todd worked his Dr. Feelgood magic.

"So, why all the sneaking around?" I asked in an effort to stop grinding my teeth. "This house is gorgeous and right on the beach."

He didn't say anything at first, still tending to my wound. Finally, after a shrug, he said, "I've lived here six months and never brought a woman home—a *date*, I mean. You're the first."

"Oh." Maybe Todd was more private than I thought. And I'd practically forced my way in here. After all, he couldn't have just left me down on the beach with a crab hanging off my big toe. "Sorry." I started inching my foot out of his hands, but Todd took a hold of my leg.

"Don't," he said, lifting his chin to look up at me. "I'm very happy that you're here, Abby." When he smiled, I felt myself relaxing into my seat again.

"Thanks. So am I." I smiled back. "So, tell me about this place."

"What do you want to know?" He enfolded my slightly less throbbing foot in the towel.

"Is it yours?"

"That's kind of a long story."

I got the feeling he didn't want to talk about it, but since it was evident I wasn't going anywhere, he sat back, readjusting the towel.

"My father's always been into real estate. He owns properties all over. One was this house."

"Was?" I asked, because he seemed to have emphasized that word.

"Six months ago I bought it, along with the store in town, lock, stock, and barrel."

Wow, I thought, staring at the top of his bent head. *Todd's a . . . grown up.*

"I thought you said your family grows olives."

"Olive oil," he corrected. "That's my mother's side." He unfolded the towel, exposing my toe to the fresh air. It stung. I winced.

"Olive oil from Sicily," I repeated through my teeth, trying hard not to whimper. "How very *Godfather*. You don't plan to whack me for a cannoli, do you?"

Todd chuckled while applying some kind of creamy, soothing ointment to my toe.

"That's how you ended up here?"

"More or less. Turned out Manhattan high finance wasn't for me. Among other things," he tagged on, expertly wrapping my toe in white gauze. "Now, every morning I see the sunrise through my window, walk to work in shorts, and know I hit the jackpot." He tucked the frayed end of the gauze. "It's not as lavish as my family's other houses, but after traveling for the majority of my life, I'm grateful I have a place to hang my hat." He looked down, bandaging his own injured hand now. "You know, a real home."

"I know exactly what you mean."

Slowly he lifted his chin. "Yes," he said, "I guess we have *that* in common, too."

The way he was looking at me, filling the small space between us, did something to the oxygen flow to my brain. My chest felt hot, and I couldn't seem to breathe normally. Sure, I'd lost some blood, but I think the new light-headedness was due more to the atmosphere around that couch—hot, hazy, and swirly, just like yesterday, right before I dived into the water to extinguish my raging hormones. There was no body of water around now, but I didn't feel like extinguishing anything, anyway.

Todd shifted an inch closer, making my pulse go ticking up the backs of my legs.

Right then, right that second, the things I'd been ruminating about, pushing around in my stupid brain, and essentially obsessing over for two days faded into nothing. Finally I knew exactly what I wanted.

Then I heard the song, reminding me that I would never get exactly what I wanted.

chapter 14

"DON'T PASS ME BY"

"Helter Skelter."

I yanked the phone from my pocket and glared at its face, wishing for once that I was having a nightmare.

"*Max.*" The word came out like a strangled, whispered scream. "No-no-*nooo*!" I howled over the song, hating the sound of John Lennon's voice for the first time in my life.

Suddenly my palm was empty, and Todd was staring at my singing cell in his hand. He seemed to be pondering something, maybe whether to answer it himself or smash it to smithereens. A second later, with a side-winding pitch, my phone disappeared. I heard plastic crack when it made contact with the hallway floor.

I stared at him, a bit indignant at first, but then it was forgotten. "I *swear*!" I yelled at the ceiling. "Can't I have one day of peace? The whole thing was supposed to be a fun-filled gig for a few months, and I'd have cool stories to tell around the sorority house. I did *not* sign up for this!"

"Are you okay?" Todd asked.

I shut my eyes and clenched my fists, fighting to get a grip on my emotions as the deluge of anger built. But the dam broke.

"Ha ha ha." I laughed manically. "Am I okay? You're asking if I'm okay? *What the hell!*"

Todd stared.

"No, I am *not* okay. I am the furthest thing *possible* from okay." I stood up, winced in pain, and hobbled away from the sofa on my aching foot. "The four of us, we started out as regular kids, just musicians having fun. But do you think anybody understands that?" I felt Todd's eyes following me as I paced around the room.

"I just fell into this," I went on, pent-up rage bursting out. "My summer job that year was at a recording studio. *Seriously?* It was practically an accident it even happened. I sang for the studio owner one day to help with his new equipment—just messing around, the first song I thought of. My brother's favorite." I looked at Todd pointedly, but his confused expression was unchanged. "Two months later it was a done deal. Lights, camera, action!" I propped myself against a bookshelf, knocking over a few picture frames in the process.

"I thought Max Salinger discovered you." The calm curiosity in Todd's voice sounded so out of place. "He saw your picture and—"

"Not even *close*."

I was losing it again, so I tried to breathe steadily and calmly, to relax the way Dr. Robert had coached me. But it wasn't working. "That *man* is a control freak. I don't know what happened. He used to listen to me, used to care about what I thought. Now I can't wear a dress to an event or change my hair without his endorsement." I was hearing Lindsey's words. "Can't I make a single decision on my own? Can't I? Huh?"

Todd stepped toward me but froze as "Helter Skelter" warbled anew from down the hall. His eyes held on mine, perhaps gauging what my next insane reaction was going to be. I was sure I didn't disappoint.

"It's *suffocating*!" I shrieked over the song, pressing my hand against my mouth, bending in half.

"He's a Svengali," Todd said from across the room. "Salinger. Isn't he?"

I looked at him.

"Wanting everyone under his thumb."

My hand remained at my mouth, and I nodded.

"I've experienced his type in business before." Todd thought for a moment. "So then, why don't you just ... just —"

"What?" I interrupted. "Fire him? Quit?"

Todd shut his mouth.

"That's what everyone says. 'Just quit, Abby. It's *so* easy.' But I can't. This is my livelihood. It's what I do." I turned away so he wouldn't see my quivering bottom lip. "Singing ... performing ..." My voice dropped to a tearful whisper. "It's what I *know* I was put on this earth to do — I feel it in my blood. I love it so much that it kills me inside." My voice dropped even lower. "And sometimes ... I hate it. Do you know how that feels?"

Todd said nothing.

"Why doesn't anyone understand?" I stomped once, making my brain shift gears. "You think Max saw my picture, and *that's* what he liked?" I unleashed another sarcastic cackle. "Don't get me started on pictures. We're four of the biggest nerds you'll ever meet."

"Why don't you come sit down?" Todd reseated himself as an example and motioned to my previous spot on the couch.

I shook my head, resting my sore foot on its heel.

"How about some water?" he asked.

I thought for a moment and then nodded, feeling calmer at the suggestion.

Todd passed through the swinging door, then returned with two chilled water bottles. "Well," he began again, "you certainly don't look like a nerd on your *Losin' Myself* cover."

"I wouldn't put too much stock in pictures," I mumbled, staring at my bandaged foot. "I warned you about that yesterday. You've no idea how much fussing with makeup, camera angles, and lighting is involved in pictures." I took a drink, little drops dribbling off my chin like I was a nursing calf. I wiped them away with the heel of my hand. "Those journalists are always going on and on about 'Abigail Kelly's *fresh* face, her *naturally* sun-kissed skin.' Ha! Do you have any idea how many moisturizers and bronzers and blushes I have to wear to get that *natural* glow? Seriously, any girl can look good through a soft-focus lens under twenty colored lights with grease smeared all over her body."

I hobbled to the corner of the room with the red punching bag. "Probably sounds naïve, but I didn't think anything from the *Losin' Myself* photo shoot would end up somewhere." I dropped my water bottle and took one hard punch at the bag. "That outfit I had to wear." I wound up for another swing. "I was completely *mortified* by it." My voice was getting higher and more labored. "My *grandparents* saw those pictures, and I looked like a *prostitute!*"

I attacked the bag for a while, swimming in adrenaline. "That album cover?" I panted. "Just so you know, major doctoring went into making me look like that. I was practically a cartoon." I stopped to breathe, shaking my hands in pain. "Whose thighs are that taut? Whose complexion is that flawless? Reality, please!"

"I hate to remind you, Abby," Todd's voice seemed distant, "but I think you're rather adorable right now; even yesterday, soaking wet with seaweed in your hair. You weren't wearing makeup *then*, were you?"

The point seemed irrelevant, so I took another hard swing at the red bag. Pain on the heels of pain, I was suddenly thinking of something else, something worse than a few retouched pictures. No matter how hard I pushed it down, the vilest of memories always broke surface last, like a screaming, breeching torpedo. Even though I tried to stop them, I felt the words coming up.

"And then my *b-brother.*" My strained voice cracked on the last word. Pulling in my chin, I beat on that bag—one-two, one-two, one-two—until my arms ached. Gasping for air, I stopped and hugged it, hung off it, burying my face in its leather. I knew a fresh tidal wave of mental pain was heading my way. Instead of paddling for shore, I let it crash over me, flailing in the chaos of the memory.

"It was so awful," I said weakly, limping toward the French doors. "Shugger wasn't at my house that night. I can't remember why. So Christian went out to the deli alone." I reached up, touching the window with one finger. "There was one other customer there during the holdup, a pregnant woman. Christian tried to help her, but those four—" I cut off, swallowed, then stared through the glass, focusing on a single gray cloud. "There were four of them and just one of him. Four against one." My voice broke as I turned around. "One of them pulled a gun. How fair is that?"

Todd slowly rose to his feet. He looked confused at first, but then something seemed to occur to him. "This was a year ago?" he asked, taking a few cautious steps forward.

I felt myself nodding, my stomach in a bundle of knots.

He shook his head and exhaled, an anguished expression in his eyes. "I . . . forgot about that. I read it; the story was all over the Internet back then, but I didn't make the connection." He was standing right in front of me now. "Your brother was—"

The loud, screechy, unintelligible sound that ripped from my throat silenced him before he could say the name aloud.

"Oh, Abby." His expression broke as he reached out to me. But I recoiled.

"I can't." I backed away. "I can't talk about it anymore, okay?"

"Okay."

My eyes suddenly flooded with tears that I couldn't blink away; I hadn't cried about Christian since the day I found out he died. I whipped around, my blurry gaze searching for a way out of the room. I didn't feel my torn-up toe anymore. I didn't feel anything as I headed for the sliding glass door. If I could block out the memory, push the monster back down, I'd be okay. I'd survive. I just needed to hold on until I was safely out the door, and then I'd be alone to—

"Hey." Todd's voice came from over my shoulder.

I turned around.

Looking almost indifferent, he was leaning against the arm of the couch. "If you want . . ." With one finger, he gestured to his chest. "You can tell me about it." His voice was practically a whisper. "Abby, you can talk to me."

I felt tears flowing down my quivering chin, but I could not do what he suggested.

"I'm no expert, but it might help."

I took a breath, held it, and then blew it out. I did it again and again. Minutes ticked by.

Todd's expression was impassive as he circled the couch and sat down. "I'll be hanging out over here if you need anything," he said.

Lindsey and Molly and the shrink I'd been guilted into seeing back in L.A. had all requested the same thing of me. *To talk.* But never once had I felt it was okay to speak of Christian and what happened that night.

So why, then, was my jaw voluntarily unclenching now? For the first time in a year.

"I . . . I shouldn't have sent him out that night!" I practically screamed, knowing that this confession had been building up for months. "It was late, and he was so tired, but I didn't care, 'cause I was hungry, and . . . I knew he'd go if I whined enough. He was just so great that way." The nerves behind my eyes throbbed and my dry throat ached. But I pushed on.

"While he was at the deli, I fell asleep on the couch. I didn't mean to—I swear. And . . . I didn't know . . . it . . . *happened*. He was only a few miles from home, right down the road. There were sirens, ambulances." I shuddered, feeling like I was about to be sick. "I didn't hear them."

While blankly staring at pictures on the wall, I rambled on, speaking of how my team had flown to London early the next morning. "When Max told me what had happened, it was too late; we couldn't leave. The fog, the stupid London fog. We were stuck there for days. I couldn't get to my family, get back to Christian in time." My watery voice broke. "I know it's my fault he's gone. It tore my family apart, and I can't forgive myself."

With every labored inhale, my heart throbbed painfully inside my ribcage, like it was about to detonate. But I'd finally said it, purged those secret feelings and fears . . . to a stranger, a stranger I happened to be irresistibly drawn to. "What in the world would he think of me now?"

Nervously, I looked at him.

To my horror, Todd's face was white, drawn tight, like he was in actual physical pain.

I turned my head and slammed my eyes shut, feeling a brand new stab of regret. I knew nothing would be the same between us now that he knew the truth. Not that I blamed him. I should have left his house right then, before I contaminated anything.

When I opened my eyes again, I was surprised to find Todd directly in front of me, blocking my way to the door. His expression was still pained as we stared at each other. After a long moment, he took a step toward me and unfolded his arms, wide open.

Almost in a faint, I fell forward, not taking the time to figure out how he knew this was what I needed. Not space, not psychotherapy, not a triple cocktail. Just this.

His strong arms wrapped around me, holding me up while my hands were pinned in front of my chest, fingernails digging into my palms. The tears really came then, fresh and hot. He rocked us back and forth. The louder my sobs, the tighter he squeezed.

This guy, this *man* I'd known for two short days, who named his dog after a member of the Rat Pack, whose sisters nicknamed him Pockets, who'd been lost in the Andes for eighteen hours, who loved Frank Sinatra, Dr Pepper, and the Marines, he was the only person who allowed me to unload one suitcase of personal baggage, one corner of repressed feelings—all with no judgment and no blame. Nothing but his calming presence.

For some reason, it was enough.

After a while, Todd's grip around me relaxed, forcing me to make a conscious effort to stand on my own.

"I miss him," I choked out. "So much. I know I shouldn't feel this way, but I can't stop. It never stops!"

Before I got the chance to break down again, Todd pulled us to the couch, offering Kleenex and sitting in patient silence beside me until I composed myself.

Then I talked—probably pretty incoherently—about my parents, my brother, my job. Molly, Hal, Max. Todd didn't say much; mostly he just offered somber nods and dry tissues, and the occasional wisecrack that made me laugh.

Out the window, the afternoon sun hung low, suspended between high noon and twilight, a deep yellow yo-yo on a blue canvas.

"Can I ask you something?" Todd said.

I sniveled, wiping my eyes.

"Do you really think your parents blame you?"

My throat constricted—that strangling snake.

"Yes," I replied. But then I heard Lindsey's voice again. "Well, maybe not *blame*." Even as I said it, though, I knew it wasn't completely true. "Doesn't matter—I blame myself, and I feel too guilty to be around them. It's been a year." I looked at Todd through my wet lashes, a Kleenexed hand covering my mouth. "Does that make me a horrible person?"

One side of his mouth pulled back compassionately. "Of course not. We all have reasons for what we do and how we react. No one is allowed to tell us how to feel."

Another sob vibrated from my core. "Thank you," I managed to whisper.

We sat side by side in companionable silence, only the sounds of birds and waves and wind through the open windows. Another hour later found us in his kitchen. Todd built a sandwich while I balanced on a barstool. I was force-fed half the sandwich and a glass of milk, explaining that I was looking rather half starved and homeless.

While I chewed, I took the time to compartmentalize

my feelings again, to pick them apart, tuck them back into their corners, dealing with grief the best way I knew how. I'd mastered that trick from years of practice. It may have been a false calm, but by the time I finished eating, I felt much better.

When we returned to the living room, that yellow yo-yo in the sky hung lower. I nestled onto the couch while Todd sat on the coffee table across from me. He held my sore foot on his lap, picking at the gauze contemplatively.

"I'm sorry I ruined our day," I offered. "Not what you signed up for, right?"

Todd exhaled a chuckle inside his throat and gently squeezed my foot before setting it on the coffee table. Wordlessly he moved to the spot next to me. Despite the earlier drama, the moment our shoulders touched, warmth gushed into my chest. It was almost like I was lounging in a dentist's chair, inhaling that wonderful, deadening gas, dulling my senses, calming frayed nerves.

Todd pulled my focus when he leaned forward, elbows on his knees. I could hear him breathing, see his back muscles expanding and contracting. I breathed along with him, which relaxed me further, and I settled against the couch.

"I know I've been stuck in my head the last hour," I said to the short hairs on the back of his neck, "but what have *you* been thinking about?"

He exhaled before sitting back. "Nothing much." He sat back. "I'll tell you some other time." There was a quick flash of a smile before he turned away.

My heart wrenched as I studied his profile. He seemed to be frowning—that brooding, pensive frown . . . with those lips. And I was lost in my own mind, thinking of our kiss on the beach, our kiss last night. How I loved the way I felt when he was near, when he smiled at me, looked at me, laughed with me, talked with me. Could he make me feel that way every day, I wondered?

A buzzing from Todd's pocket interrupted my pleasant reflections. He pulled out his cell, inspected the number, silenced it, and tossed it on the coffee table. "Anyhoo," he said blankly. "Where was I?"

"We weren't talking."

From across the room, his house phone rang. "We'll let voice mail pick up," he suggested. "It'll be my mother."

Really . . .

"*Ciao, mio caro*," came the smooth tones of a sophisticated Italian accent.

"She'll be reminding me to call my sister. It's her birthday."

"I'm just phoning, dah-ling," the accent continued, "to remind you to wish little Nichola *buon compleanno.*"

"I called Nikki this morning," Todd commentated over his mother, "and sent a Strip-o-Gram to her law office."

"Such a good brother." I dabbed at the moist parts of my face with a new tissue.

"Give us a call when you can."

"We spoke last night," Todd said, shrugging.

"I'll give your love to *Papà.* Oh, and let us know how it goes with that new girl you mentioned last night. Did you see her today?"

Todd chuckled tensely.

"I hope you cleaned your house, and that you didn't wear that awful shirt with the—"

Todd flew off the couch, swearing as he lunged for the phone. "*Sta zitta,*" he hissed, attempting to drown out the voice mail.

chapter 15

"ALL TOGETHER NOW"

"*Pronto, Ma.*" His voice was stressed as he spoke into the receiver. "*Come stai?*"

The rest of their cryptic conversation continued in Italian. I recognized a couple of words but was clueless of their context, because Todd was speaking so quickly. His eyes moved to me a few times, flashes of a smile. After he hung up, he stood by the phone, one hand at the back of his neck.

"Sorry," he offered when he returned, looking slightly scarlet. He sat on the coffee table. "My father's been across the pond for a week. She's lonely."

I loved that he was blushing; it helped me feel a little less insecure about my similar tendency.

"That's sweet," I said, wondering if my eyelashes had really just fluttered.

"There's blood on your shirt." He tugged at the clothing in question. "You look like you've just murdered someone. Let me give you one of mine to change into."

He made a move to stand, but something in my expression kept him seated. For another few moments, it was quiet.

Never had I felt so comfortable being with someone in silence, just feeling how my heart beat inside my chest, knowing he was near.

Suddenly, Todd slapped his hands on his knees, and I jumped about a foot.

"Okay," he said in a nervously tense voice that made him even sexier, "I'm afraid I'm going to have to talk now. What I need from you, Abby, is to please just sit here." He reached out, forcing my shoulders back into the couch. "And let me say a few things. No interruptions. Okay?"

"I can't leave anyway." I smiled, flexing my damaged foot.

Todd chuckled lightly, eyes rolling to heaven. But then, it was like his entire demeanor changed. First, his spine lengthened and straightened, and then his shoulders squared, all while an unmistakable expression of conviction took over his face. He wasn't joking around anymore. Lieutenant Camford, USMC, in the flesh.

Oh, baby.

"A few months ago, I made a conscious decision to take more chances in life, not to fall back on that safe bet. I'm a Marine at heart. I deliberate strategically; that's how my brain works." He exhaled and leaned back a bit. *At ease.* "But while speaking on more tender subjects, you should also know I can sometimes be longwinded. I apologize for that in advance."

I was about to speak, but he lifted a hand, probably sensing that I was going to say something inappropriately sarcastic to lighten the atmosphere.

"Abby. I really like you," he stated, locking eyes with me. "And when I say you, I mean *you*, not Abigail Kelly the rock star."

"I'm hardly a rock star," I mumbled.

"I like what you're about," he resumed. "I like what you laugh at, what you cry at, what's important to you." My bones were beginning to feel all ribbony at his words. He tilted his head to the side, noticing my new expression. "The way you smile with your whole self. Like right now."

I couldn't help grinning, though a bit self-consciously.

He cleared his throat and adjusted my bandaged foot. "I told you to keep this elevated."

After another moment, he sighed loudly, as though frustrated about something. "I never knew I could have so much in common with someone like you. Yesterday was one of the most refreshing days I've spent with a woman in quite a long time. Lately my dating experiences haven't been very positive." His focus seemed a little strained as he looked away. The clock above the mantel ticked. "Like I was saying down on the beach, we've known each other only two days—barely enough time to start anything." He was lacing and unlacing his fingers between his knees. "That being said, I have no qualms at telling you that I have a feeling about this. About you and me."

I swallowed, trying not to melt into a puddle.

"I hope I'm not taking my delicate male braggadocio into my hands when I assume that you have a feeling about me, too?" He hesitated.

I nodded.

"Good." He nodded in return, with a smile. "Because I think we've got something here." His index finger made a little motion, pointing to me and then to himself. "I know we're still pretty young, so it's only fair to warn you."

The way he was grinning at me made his warning seem more like a delicious challenge.

"I *am* looking for someone, Abby. Someone to be on equal footing with, someone to balance me." He stopped again to chuckle at something private. "It's pretty amazing that we understand each other so well. On some level, I feel like I already *know* you."

I wanted to tell him I felt exactly the same way. I wanted to say *something*, but I knew he wasn't finished.

"I see the drive and commitment in you. You're loyal to a fault, and your passion for life shows in everything. That's incredibly attractive to me." He turned to look out the window. "Last night, you said you laughed more with me than you had in a year." His lips smiled but his eyes did not, as if he were thinking about something else. "You don't know how good it makes me feel that I can do that for you."

He didn't go on right away, perhaps running the complexity of our scenario through his business-school brain one last time.

"You're interesting, Abby, and inspiring, and . . . well, I suppose that's all I have to say." He shrugged. "I just thought you should know how I feel before this goes any further."

He slapped his hands on his knees again, which was probably a signal for me to start talking. But I had nothing ready. Nothing, at least, as lyrical or poignant as his words had been. I'd grown lazy, too, used to having my responses written out for me, singing what was placed before me as my answers to the world's questions.

"Interesting and inspiring?" I couldn't help repeating. "Is that what you were mulling about over the last hour?"

"Maybe."

I laughed quietly, tucking some hair behind my ears. I may not have had a speech prepared, but there was one thing I *was* sure of, and the man sitting across from me should have been aware of at least that much.

"I want to stay here," I began. "I do. More than just about anything."

Todd didn't so much as blink at first, but then he exhaled and dropped his chin. When he looked up, he was wearing a relieved expression. For the first time that day, he looked truly calm.

"But," I quickly added, "I suppose it's my turn to say my just-so-it's-out-there stuff."

"Please." He leaned back. "I'm all ears."

As I took a moment, my gaze moved to the window. Gray clouds were blowing in from the west. It looked like rain was coming, which only meant the streets and air would be clean and refreshed in a matter of minutes. The great thing about tropical climates was that bad weather hits, but the effects usually *improve* conditions.

I wondered if the same could be said for people.

There was something more I needed to get off my chest. And I was totally dreading it. From miles away thunder rolled, as did the pit of my stomach when I began to speak. "Todd," I said, looking down at my lap, already feeling ashamed, "if you want me to stay because you'll get your picture in the paper, it's not worth it. Being around me is more of a hassle than anything. Believe me." When I looked up, he flinched, his brows angled.

I knew it was an unfair thing to suggest, because there wasn't a bone in my body that believed Todd wanted fifteen minutes of fame out of me, but that kind of thing had happened before. More than once.

I ran one hand across my eyes, forcing myself to go on. "It's just . . . nowadays, I don't always know who my real friends are. I don't know who wants me because of *me* or because of who I am." I stared at the wall across from me, my voice growing louder. "It really, really sucks. Now it's nearly impossible for me to trust any—"

He cut me off by sweeping his hand through the air, rising to his feet, and grumbling in a foreign language that was unfamiliar to me. It wasn't too difficult, however, to recognize the universal tone of swearing.

"I don't mean *you*, necessarily," I amended. "I'm—"

"Just . . . give me a minute, please?" he muttered. I couldn't see his face, but his voice was strangled as he made his way to the red punching bag in the corner. He stood in front of it, staring, and then he took a few swift jabs. A few more. Soon he was whacking away at the thing like Mohammad Ali.

"Todd?"

"One more set."

I gasped, hoping his bloodthirsty tone wasn't directed at me. I sat still, a silent countdown going on in my head.

Finally, exactly twelve pummels later, he stopped. I was nearly blown away when he turned to me with a little smirk twisting his lips. "I've got this temper thing," he said, scratching his ear with the back of his hand. "Which I'm working on." He gave the bag a gentle tap. "Huh. A few months ago I would've torn this thing from the hook and smashed it through a window." His smile flattened as he exhaled. "I'm sorry—that had nothing to do with you. Something about what you said."

"I'm sorry I said anything."

"Don't be." He reached one hand behind his neck, kneading the muscles. "There were similar problems with my last relationship. We were engaged, and she . . ." He trailed off, his shoulders slumping an inch.

I, on the other hand, leaned forward. I was curious to hear about his ex, of course, but more so, I felt compassion for this man I'd just met but who I felt I already knew as well as anybody.

While he rubbed the back of his neck with one hand, I noticed how his stare sank to a lower point out the window, like he was reliving something unpleasant. And suddenly, it took everything in me not to run into his arms and promise that everything would be all right, promise that his ex—whoever she was, that *greedy woman*, that *evil cow*—would never hurt him again if I had anything to say about it.

Almost as an answer to my undeclared promise, Todd spoke. "I know it's not fair to drag baggage from past relationships into new ones." Deep creases lined his forehead. "But my memory serves me far too well. That's in my nature, too."

"What do you mean?" I asked.

"My family," he said, looking away, "has quite a bit of money. Some people enjoy taking advantage of that. I've been used before, too."

I blinked, finally understanding. More importantly, relating.

"So I perfectly understand why you have to protect yourself." He turned back to me. "We both do. And yeah, it sucks."

So we were in agreement. Fabulous.

I looked away to stare at his bookshelf, forcing myself to read a plaque he had received from some entrepreneur group. Next to it was a framed document with the United States Marine Corps seal at the top.

After a minute I said, "There're some other things we have to talk about."

Todd nodded. "I know."

"But why don't we wait till you calm down some more?" I grinned, enjoying how our roles had reversed.

Todd grinned back, if only for a second. "I am perfectly calm, Abby," he stated, but the vein popped out on his neck told a different story. He lifted his bandaged hand, noting his bright red knuckles. "Maybe I overdid it a bit."

"This is just as new for me as it is for you," I explained.

Todd held my gaze, his injured hand dropping to his side.

"We have to make up the rules as we go."

"Rules. Right." Some more foreign swearing went on as he took another hard punch at the bag. I guess he wasn't as calm as he'd proclaimed. "This whole thing really does suck," he said. "I wasn't expecting to like you so much." He shot me a playful glare. "It's really irritating."

"Thanks." I tried not to laugh. "You irritate me, too."

Todd finally smiled, a deep, genuine one, all the way to his bright green eyes. Seeing it made the bonfire flare in my chest. I fought to stifle it. Now was not the time for unpredictable female hormones . . . no matter how helpful they may be.

I pushed on before losing my nerve. "Even if I stay here all summer, I'll have to leave eventually—in September. You have a house here, a business, and Sammy. Your life is *here*, not there."

His smile dropped.

"I know," he said through gritted teeth. "I've been thinking about that." He made a fist, ready to take one last whack at the bag, but he looked at his bandaged fingers, grimaced, and flicked the bag with his other hand.

"It's only three months."

"I can count," he replied with a half grin.

We both chuckled, but it faded quickly.

"So I'm guessing the time for all hedging has passed?" he asked.

I snorted at his major understatement.

"Okay. What's the plan?"

I sighed and moved my gaze out the French doors, considering potential reactions to the new plan I had in mind. For starters, Lindsey would be thrilled, but she'd shower me with *I told you so*'s. Max would be pissed, even though he'd *claimed* it was totally up to me whether I went to work that summer. Everyone else, I realized, would manage just fine without me for three months.

And then there was Todd. My stomach did a backward flip when I looked at his hopeful yet dread-filled expression. A summer fling had never been my style. But my heart started racing with excitement at the very idea.

"Come on, Abby." Todd was the picture of ease now, strolling toward me. "Time is of the essence here. No pressure intended, of course, but I'd like to know if you'll be around this weekend. The Village Green amphitheater is showing *Dumb and Dumber* on the big screen Saturday night. As of now, I'm dateless."

"Tempting," I said, rubbing my eyes with the heels of my hands.

Todd sat on the coffee table next to my wrapped foot. His expression had changed. It hadn't ended as a literal frown, but it was a different kind of smile, a smile with a specific emotion behind it: pity.

Don't worry about it, Abby, his wordless expression screamed at me. *If this isn't what you really want, you're off the hook.*

That was just it, though. I didn't intend to be let off any hook. This *was* what I wanted.

And for the first time in five years, I was taking it.

"Essentially, I'm a greedy man," Todd said, wearing that same sympathetic smile, "but I want you to be happy. If leaving tomorrow will make you happy—"

I placed one finger over his mouth. "It won't," I murmured, allowing myself to touch the lovely creation before me. A part of me needed to make sure he wasn't some cruel ghost of my imagination, taunting me with something I couldn't have.

His eyes were closed, waiting. I tilted my head, slowly taking in every detail of his face.

And suddenly, something remarkable happened, like a switch turned on deep inside my chest. Instead of wanting to make out, to have a summer fling . . . I wanted to fall in love.

Todd turned his face, kissing the center of my hand.

"I will absolutely hate myself," I whispered, trying to keep my voice steady, "if I leave." Todd opened one eye, looking a little surprised.

I smiled. "So with your permission, Lieutenant Camford, I have decided to stay."

He blinked a few times, still unbelieving. "Really?"

As an answer, I pulled him in, inhaling his smell, tasting every corner of his mouth. His hands slid around my back, pulling me to the edge of the couch. When our faces drew apart a million years later, we were both breathing hard.

"You're sure?"

"I decided an hour ago." I curled the front of his hair around one finger. "But you wouldn't shut up. *Sometimes* longwinded?"

He turned his face, laughing into my hair. "I wax poetic maybe once a year," he explained. "You evidently bring out the Byron in me." He abruptly released his grip and leaned back, his hands bracing his weight behind him. "But you've made a very wise decision, because quite frankly, Miss Kelly, if you were to leave tomorrow, I'd be forced to hunt you down like a caveman and drag you back by your hair." One side of his mouth pulled back. "And I always win."

I leaned forward, but he lifted a hand to stop me. "There's one more thing I've been meaning to tell you all day."

"What is it?" I asked impatiently, not able to keep from staring at his mouth.

He took his time, drawing in a slow inhale and then letting it out just as slowly. "You," he finally whispered, running a finger across my chin, "absolutely take my breath away."

It was right then that I knew, down to my curling toes and thumping heart, that I had made the correct decision, maybe the most correct decision ever to be made in the history of decision-making. I reached for him, torn between wanting to stare into his incredible green eyes and an almost painful desire to kiss him.

Naturally, we kissed. And kissed.

Long after the sun had set, I pushed back my tangled hair, rubbed my swollen lips together, and stood up on very wobbly legs.

"Where do you think you're going?" he asked, reaching for my waist. "You said you were staying."

"I believe your earlier Babe Ruth imitation broke my cell."

He grinned up at me, running a hand through his equally mussed hair.

"Max might want to hear the news right away," I explained. And then, at the risk of sounding totally cliché, I kind of got lost in Todd's eyes for a moment, visualizing the rest of the summer: sunny days relaxing on the beach with a paperback novel. Moonlight swims. Evenings curled together on that very couch, catching up on the last four seasons of *One Tree Hill*. Or with no TV on at all.

I dropped my chin, feeling Todd pull me down.

"May I use your phone to call California?"

ABIGAIL KELLY:
SWEETER THAN SUGAR

As she strolled up center stage and plucked a microphone from the stand, the entire venue crackled with feedback. The place then went silent.

"Oops." Abigail Kelly giggled into the only mike that seemed to be working. "My bad."

While the techs behind her labored to get the sound back up, Kelly stood under the spotlight, treating the crowd to an a capella rendition of "Hey Jude."

In a typical day in the life of a world-famous pop music icon, Abigail Kelly gave Paris fans another reason why she's so straight-from-the-heavens charming, so talented, and so darn likable.

It's her ability to just go with it.

"I have no idea what's coming next," she told Paris's TrèsSweet last week at an after-concert press event. "What we're doing now is working so well, and the guys and I are having a blast, so why change a thing?"

After a string of number-one hits that don't seem to end, Mustang Sally's lead singer is still all about the fun. She enchanted fellow party attendees with her behind-the-scene stories of being the only female on a tour bus full of men, reminding us of Gwen Stefani's similar plight with No Doubt a decade ago.

For someone who hasn't seemed to touch earth in five years, Kelly also appears quite normal.

"Oh, sweet!" she exclaimed after digging through the contents of the swag bag that every guest received. "I scored BB cream!" She held it up to the light. "And it's Dior."

How can you help but love a girl—someone who's graced more magazine covers this year than Oprah—who still gets excited over makeup?

chapter 16

"EIGHT DAYS A WEEK"

I was sitting cross-legged, feeling cramped despite the slightly oversized first-class seat. My feet were asleep, which was probably what snapped me awake. When my eyes fluttered open, I saw Todd staring out the window at the pearly early morning sky. One hand was at his chin, the latest courtroom crime novel turned upside-down on his lap, a finger marking its place.

Watching his profile, I could see the faint two-inch scar that ran from the corner of his mouth to just above his chin, the result of a boating accident when he was twelve. He coughed into his fist and there was that dimple, set deep into his cheek. I closed my eyes, knowing the mere sight of that simple indent in his skin could get me quite worked up.

Even though my feet were painfully deprived of circulation, I didn't move, so as not to disturb him. As we flew through an air pocket, the plane dipped and corrected. I felt Todd move closer. He knew I hated flying. He knew a lot about me, actually.

I sneaked open one eye to see him changing the time on his watch, preparing for life on the West Coast. Definitely the end of summer.

I exhaled. It seemed like only yesterday I'd made that phone call from Todd's couch to Max's office.

When I'd assumed Max would be merely pissed off, I hadn't known the half of it.

"What the hell, babe?" he'd bellowed. "What are we supposed to do now?"

Not my problem, ass hat, I'd wanted to say, but didn't. Of course. After listening to ten minutes of his yelling, I told him I would see him in September. Then I dropped Todd's phone to the floor and climbed in his lap.

Our summer couldn't have gone better. I'd been destressed and deliciously lazy in a way I hadn't been since I was a little kid. I read twelve trashy novels, kept a journal, and even started a sketchbook. Lindsey read somewhere that drawing was a healthy form of non-aggressive therapy. I didn't know about *that*, but I sketched all summer, if just to appease her.

Todd and I had one argument. He started it, but I assumed most of the blame. I was being passive-aggressive instead of honest. At the time, the summer was almost over and I was afraid of leaving, so I lashed out. *Real* mature. It wasn't the highpoint of our time together, both of us angry and worried, saying things we didn't mean. But we apologized afterward, and we both meant it. Sometimes those kinds of things can actually draw two people closer together, if they're lucky. We were lucky.

I watched him turn a page of his book and scowl at whatever he'd just read. A moment later he nodded and chuckled under his breath. Whatever the problem was, he had thought it out and dismissed it. That was another thing we had in common—we were both ambitious and yet found immense pleasure in simple things.

He coughed again, and I couldn't stand my numbing appendages for another second, so I wrenched my feet out from under me, wincing as the flow of blood shot pinpricks up my legs. I reached up and rang the bell for a flight attendant.

"What do you need?" Todd asked, dog-earing the page he was reading.

"I'm parched. How soon do we land?"

"About four hours."

"Four?" I straightened up, having that recurring panic about boarding the wrong plane, falling asleep, and waking up in a bathtub full of ice cubes in Mongolia, half my organs gone.

"You were asleep for a grand total of ten minutes."

I moaned as he passed me his Dr Pepper. "Crap. I planned on sleeping through the entire flight." I swirled the ice around inside the glass and took a sip of the chilled brown liquid. "After last night, I thought we'd both be zonked out."

Todd stretched his arms out in front of him and cracked his neck. "You were the one who stayed up all night packing, not me." His index finger traced a circle over my knee through the hole in my jeans.

"You could've stayed up with me," I said. "Like we did last week."

Todd looked at me and grinned, and we both recalled the night we were awake until the sun came up, just lying around, talking. Well, mostly just talking. All summer we could gab for hours and laugh until one of us busted a gut. But we could also sit, speaking only when I needed him to pass me that cupcake I couldn't reach or when he asked me to turn up the volume on the ballgame.

I smiled at him. We really were an amazing fit.

"I still can't believe we're doing this," I said, rubbing my shoulder against his. He lifted a quick flash of a smile. "You're not nervous, are you?"

"I'm not nervous." He gave my nose a peck. "I'm happy."

The band was scheduled to record our next album at Studio Universe in Los Angeles from September to December. Per my instructions, upon our touchdown at LAX, Molly would have my Malibu house ready for me, and only me.

We'd discussed it, but no, Todd and I would not be living together. It wasn't my style, and Hollywood hadn't warped me so much as to make me forget that. Neither of us would have ever been considered libertines, but we certainly weren't monks, either. I simply wasn't willing to rush into anything and make the same mistakes I'd made in the past. My relationship with that idiot Miles was almost purely physical. We never talked, and then we ended up having screaming matches that rivaled Ike and Tina Turner. Ending up like that with Todd was painfully unthinkable, so if it meant that for a while I made us behave like a couple of fifteen year olds with purity rings, then so be it.

Plus, I knew Todd's background. His parents were extremely conservative, almost to the point of being old fashioned, which I happened to find charming. Todd would have rather moved into a hotel than live with me in sin.

Back in Seaside, when I would innocently fall asleep on his couch, the evening always ended with me being scooped up and taken home.

"Puppy," his deep and dreamy nighttime voice would whisper, his fingers tickling various parts of my body. "Last call. You don't have to go home, but you can't stay here."

Lindsey and Steve had gotten used to the tall, green-eyed man showing up on their doorstep in the middle of the night with me, half conscious, propped up against his side or completely cataleptic in his arms.

At the beginning of the summer, it had been mostly just the two of us, but after a few weeks, Todd deemed it "safe" enough for me to meet his local buddies. Even Frisbee Dude. They were great guys who probably resented me for stealing away their surfing pal. After their initial reactions, à la Chandler, the guys got used to me, and I was mostly hassled with questions about how well I knew Taylor Swift and could I give them Emma Stone's cell phone number. Todd also kept in touch with his college alums and Marine brothers-at-arms; they drifted in and out over the summer, dragging him off to cave dive and deep sea fish and climb random tall things while I happily napped on the beach—or in his bed, when he wasn't looking.

"Will you be working as soon as tomorrow?" Todd asked as our flight attendant loaded us up with water, more Dr Pepper, honey roasted peanuts, and a warm chocolate chip cookie the size of a dinner plate. I declined mine, knowing full well that the eight and a half pounds I'd packed on over the summer would have to come off once Max took one look.

"I think so," I replied. "Nathan sent some of the new material a few weeks ago." I reached for my brown-and-gold Gucci carry-on under my seat. "I haven't even looked at them yet. They could be in Swahili, for all I know." I tore open a large FedEx envelope, laying the hundred-some-odd pages of sheet music on the pull-down table in front of me.

Todd's eyes went wide and then glazed over. "It looks like Swahili to me."

"Music's a snap," I said, speed reading through the first song, hearing notes in my head. It was mid-tempo, low register, and something of an ode to a certain frozen dessert, reminding me of George Harrison's "Savoy Truffle," his precious ditty devoted entirely to the contents of a box of chocolates. As Todd read over my shoulder, I added, "You're the one who's fluent in four languages at last count."

"You're memorizing those, aren't you?" Todd asked when I flipped a page, barely glancing at it, though its picture in my brain remained intact.

I tapped the side of my head. "I wouldn't survive without this baby."

"Are you actually expected to sing the word *consternate?*" he asked, pointing to the sheet of a fast-tempo number about a girl meeting a boy for a date on the moon. "You should do more songs like 'Intimate Strangers.' One of my favorites."

I balked in surprise. "Really?"

He nodded, flipping through some more pages. "It's joyful and sentimental without sounding like a torch song. The lyrics are pretty clever."

I smiled. We hadn't talked about my career very much; in fact, Todd was the showoff when it came to singing along to

the stereo. His gyrating Mick Jagger was spot on, only to be
bested by his croony Sinatra.

"I really like that song, too," I confessed, staring at his
lowered eyes. "I changed it up a little during one of the takes,
and we kept it that way."

He looked at me. "Which part?"

"I kind of tweaked the last verse so it was relevant. I
thought my fans would be more interested in a happily
ever after, rather than a song about a one-night stand, so I
changed the end. Writers hate when singers do that." I rolled
my eyes. "But even something as small as a few lines or the
phrasing . . . When I can change something, I feel like the
song becomes mine, and I'm sharing a piece of my soul."

Todd lifted a slow smile and leaned his face close to mine.
"You really are so talented, Abby," he said.

I felt myself blushing.

With a different smile, he added, "Despite those blasphemous, kitschy pop concertos of 'E-mail My Love' and 'Drive-
through Crush.'"

"The kids in Korea love those."

"Shame on you." He touched my chin with one finger.
"And for someone who worships the Beatles."

Despite the blasphemous kitsch, I was proud of one
thing. Unlike many of my professional peers, I seldom used
"melisma." Translated: I *did not* over-sing. I clung onto the
melody of a song with both hands, sustaining my notes,
holding them close to me. It was important to control and
protect, to use crescendo or vibrato only when fitting.

Simplicity, less is more, was my motto. At the beginning,
I'd practiced incessantly to convert my singing voice into a
mere extension of my speaking voice. I studied dynamics and
heeded my vocal coaches, all while relying on what can only
come through instinct. Once I got the hang of it, singing with
a mood came naturally. Without realizing it, my unconventional dichotomy of techniques was perfect for singing into a
solo microphone, which is all about the subtlety of breathing
and phrasing.

No doubt about it, I preferred performing live. No studio tricks, no reverb or pitch control. Pulled apart, just the mike and me. Despite a career of running around stage in the frantic pop-singer-sprint, when it came to recording, I was a crooner . . . just like Frank Sinatra.

"How long does it take you to record one song?" Todd asked, holding a piece of sheet music close to his face as if that might help him decipher the unknown "language."

"Depends," I replied as we sailed over the clouds. "Some artists are allowed to punch in their songs one note at a time, but if you know what you're listening for, you can totally tell. So many records use a single take for each time through the chorus; they add layovers to make it sound different, but it's the same exact version over and over. Totally cheating. Must be like a vacation," I muttered, scanning through the next few pages. "Max prefers me to record the whole song straight through, no stopping. In theory, I agree with that approach. I create a mood when I sing. I'm a performer. I'm better if it's all in one take. But"—I couldn't help sighing—"it's pretty brutal on the musician, standing in one place for hours at a time, trying to sing through a four-minute song perfectly in one try."

"Sounds frustrating," Todd said just as the Fasten Seat-belts sign illuminated. The airplane bounced through some choppy air.

"I guess," I replied, adjusting the buckle around my hips, "I'm just suddenly very aware of what's coming."

"Pretty bad?"

The plane shook some more, almost as an answer to his question. I nodded, closing my eyes, attempting to mentally calm the turbulent skies while picturing my happy place. *That white, sugary beach behind Todd's house. Inside our private little Stonehenge. Twilight. Blue and pink swirling clouds.* I exhaled, steadily, purposefully. *We're sitting on a large bamboo mat playing a game of Twenty-one. No wind. No cameras. We're eating cheese and crackers and key lime pie.* I knew if I concentrated hard enough, I could paint that scene in my mind, stroke by stroke, like a Rembrandt.

"In your opinion, what makes a good producer?" Todd had gotten very good at distracting me when needed. He was a regular Molly.

I opened my eyes to see him reading a different piece of music. Before replying, I wracked my brain for an answer he'd understand. "Someone who lets me be myself," I said, my stomach turning pukey as the plane jerked again. "Someone who also allows me a little fun."

"Does that make a difference?"

I took a drink of water, swishing it around in my mouth before swallowing. "A huge difference. Recording's not really about the band or even the singer, but about making the song sound good. It's a group effort. Great producers will do anything to make that happen. I'm really lucky to have Max and Nate." I stared past him out the window, feeling a little claustrophobic. "It's less stressful when I'm allowed to have some fun along the way, though that rarely happens these days. It's all work."

"Rough business. Um, you're doing it again."

"Doing what?"

"Wrapping your hair around your finger like a tourniquet."

I lowered my hand and pumped my fist, restoring circulation.

"You do that when you're nervous or stressed. I noticed it our first day together. You standing in the middle of my store in those tatty cutoff jeans, twirling your hair like a sexy little psychopath."

"I happen to like those cutoffs."

His attention must have moved to where mine was fixed, on the stack of music set before me. "I'm putting this away." He seized the pile and shoved it back in its envelope.

I didn't object the way I probably should have, but instead took the opportunity to grab him by the cheeks and kiss him as much as deemed appropriate while sheltered behind the privacy of the First Class curtain. It was my little way of saying "Thank you for keeping me sane." I couldn't see them, but I knew camera phones were going off all around us.

Countless pictures of Todd and me had found their way onto the glossy pages of the tab rags that summer, or so I heard—I hadn't looked. The possibility of a few more didn't matter right then, not while I was wrestling with my seat belt, trying to climb into Todd's seat with him.

"How do you feel about being on YouTube?" I whispered as I playfully bit his bottom lip.

He pulled away. Mr. Todd Camford was not a big fan of making out in public. But as I'd explained to him on our third day, anytime we were together while not behind closed doors, we would be "in public." That was something he'd have to get used to . . . if he wanted me. And he wanted me.

"You don't keep up with much in the world, do you?" Todd said.

"Not since I bequeathed my busted-up cell to you three months ago." I fluttered my lashes. "And then that rotten Molly had to send me a new one. Life was so much better without all that hassle." I slid my hand up his arm, inside his T-shirt sleeve at the bicep.

"Yes, I know," Todd said, his eyes flickering disapprovingly at my hand under his shirt. "Molly's been calling me all summer, keeping us aware whenever anything new is posted."

My hand froze. "Posted?"

"Oh, baby." He grinned, playfully patronizing. "We're on YouTube all the time."

"Seriously?" I sat up straight. "You are, too?"

Todd nodded gravely. "My parents seem to think *I'm* the celebrity. They don't keep up with entertainment trends, but my sisters tell them everything." He smiled and kissed my forehead, my cheek, my chin, probably thinking he needed to apologize for his parents' lack of coolness.

I hadn't yet met Colonel and Mrs. Camford in person, but at that moment, I fell in love with them. "Thanks," I whispered. "Thank you for being such a good sport about all this. It's a ridiculous way to live, I know."

He chuckled softly, his arm tightening around me. "I think you're kind of worth it. You gave up your summer to stay with me." He brushed the tip of his nose over mine. "Now, this is the least I can do for you."

I kissed him again, long and passionately, not caring a hoot if we'd be on the Internet later that day.

"Cool it," Todd whispered, even as he ran his hand up the inside of *my* sleeve.

Once the plane stopped its rocking and rolling, an informal queue of passengers began to form behind our seats. "I hate to bother you," one young woman said to me, smiling, a gap between her teeth. She presented the back of her boarding pass along with a pen.

I took them with a smile. "What's your name?" I asked and signed my best wishes.

"Just to warn you," I began again to Todd after the line of autograph seekers died down, "life in the studio's no picnic. Max is, well, you know."

"I can't wait to meet him." Todd was rubbing his hands together like a magician ready to pull a rabbit out of a hat. "I've been doing a lot of studying up on him."

"Really?"

He leaned back and crossed his arms. "Fascinating specimen of ego. The man's a master businessman. Did you know that in the nineties, he basically reinvented global representation, how entertainment contracts are negotiated today?"

"No," I replied honestly. Maybe it was a bit narcissistic of me, but I always found it surprising to be reminded that Max Salinger had a career before managing Mustang Sally.

Todd tapped his chin. "He wrote a book about management when he was only thirty, and did you know . . ."

The way Todd was talking about Max surprised me. And he looked, well, impressed. "They should bottle him to study at Harvard," he continued. "Students could learn a lot. I know I could." After a chuckle, his expression darkened. "His *tactics*, however . . ." The sentence trailed off.

"What?" I asked, wanting him to finish his thought.

Todd shifted, uncrossing his arms. "Well, some things you've told me, he sounds like a typical type A, obsessive workaholic." He shook his head an inch and looked down. "In my opinion, that's not the best way to deal with people who need support." When he looked up, I recognized the expression that crossed his face as worry.

Over the past three months, I'd become something of a master at reading Todd's face. The throbbing vein on his forehead meant concern. The crinkly lines shooting out from the sides of his eyes were mischief. I was about to get kissed really, really good when the tips of his ears got red. When he pressed his lips together until they resembled two straight lines: anger.

"It's a good thing I'm completely prepared," I said, feeling like I needed to reassure him, even though I knew darned well there was no real way to feel even halfway prepared for what was in store for us.

Todd opened his mouth, probably about to dispute my statement by pointing out that among other things, I hadn't bothered to learn any new songs over the summer.

"Completely prepared," he said with a kind smile instead, realizing that was exactly what I needed to hear.

chapter 17

"WITH A LITTLE HELP FROM MY FRIENDS"

After three months of relative peace and quiet, my cell exploded with calls and texts the moment our plane touched down.

"All yours," Todd said, passing it to me.

"Is it too late for me to go to clown college?" I asked, staring down at my phone.

The first call was Molly, reminding us that she and the car were waiting in front of the airport. She called right back—Shugger was meeting us directly outside the security checkpoint.

"I don't know why she doesn't just text," I complained. As the plane taxied down the runway, I listened to three months' worth of messages, deleting most of them after the second word. Nothing like a tidy voice-mail inbox.

"Looks like vacation's officially over," Todd said, glancing at the cell as he handed me my carry-on. I unzipped the side pocket, pulling out slate shadow, charcoal liner, and black mascara.

"Sorry," I said after painting on some quick smoky eyes. "There's a lot for me to catch up on."

"It's fine," he replied, gathering some of our things from the overhead bin. "Anything I can do?"

"I'm afraid not. But it should quiet down once we make it to the car." After slicking on some cherry-red lips, I sighed and looked up at him.

He did a double take. "Wow."

"What?"

His green eyes crinkled mischievously. "You look . . ." He tilted his head to the side. "You're *her* now, aren't you?" His first two fingers made air quotes. "Abigail Kelly."

"In the flesh." I beamed, puckering my glossy red lips. "And all the crapola that comes with her."

Todd ruffled the top of my head. This casual touch not only sent a familiar sizzle down my spine, but it also filled me with a comfort I'd grown used to.

"The airport's always crazy," I continued into my compact, touching up the purposefully smudgy makeup. "You're welcome to keep a distance from Shugger and me if you want." I snapped my mirror shut and tucked it away. "Actually, I wouldn't blame you if you made a run for it back to Florida right now."

"Now that you mention it . . ."

I grabbed his arm. "Don't make me hurt you, Marine."

"Relax," he soothed, his thumb rubbing the inside of my elbow.

Suddenly it was *me* who longed to make a run for it, to hop aboard the next returning flight back to his home, his beach, his store, his wonderful world.

But *my* world was calling now. "There'll be a lot of people," I said, tucking my hair behind one ear.

"Obviously."

"Shugger's likely to grab me before we even see him. He's sneaky that way, despite his size. You'll recognize him; he looks like Chuck D, but bigger, and he always wears white."

Todd nodded.

"Oh, and he calls me 'Sally.'"

"I know, Abby."

"It's like an inside joke that's barely funny."

"I know, Abby. You told me all that."

"Oh." I nodded and smiled at him. "There'll be questions, too. About you. *Apparently*, your picture's been everywhere. Pretty tough to lay low, but we can try."

"Whatever you think is best," Todd said, pulling me into the aisle. "Like I told you last night, this is *your* turf. Until I get my feet wet, you're completely in charge of me."

"Oooh, I like that." I kissed his cheek, rubbing off my lipstick mark afterward. "Stay close to me. When Shugger separates us, it's okay." I took his hand as we climbed the ramp that led to the gate.

When we rounded the last bend, I could hear it.

"Todd," I said out of the corner of my mouth, "don't freak out."

"Don't . . . ?"

"When Molly called last, she told me our arrival time had been leaked."

"Leaked?"

"Yeah." I grasped his hand tighter, for *his* benefit. "So just—don't freak out."

"Why would I fr . . ."

Usually the cool, macho Marine officer, Todd actually flinched when we exited into the terminal. The noise from outside security seemed exceptionally loud today, and growing louder the closer we got.

"You're not scared?" he asked as we stepped off the escalator.

I slid on my sunglasses. "Dah-ling," I replied, doing my best impersonation of his mother's accent, "I am much too petrified to be scared."

He turned a shade of green.

"Don't worry." I squeezed his arm tight. "Allow me to be *your* armored car for a change."

Todd stopped walking and held me at his side.. I stood at his side. "I think . . ." He hesitated, looking down at me. "I think I might need to kiss you first. Do you mind?"

More than willing, I complied, allowing pedestrian traffic

to pass us by. As our respective fingers linked around each other's, I felt like we were a real team, poised to face the horrible, hairy beast of Show Biz together.

"Ahhh. Thank you," he breathed, taking a deep inhale of the side of my neck when we were finished.

"*Prego*," I whispered, properly rolling my *r*.

In response, Todd moaned one of his throaty growls, making me want another five minutes to pull him into a dark corner and finish that kiss.

People were waiting for me, though. There were always people waiting. So instead, I plastered on a smile and chirped, "Ready?"

Todd stood up straight, shoulders squared. "Lead the way."

The ear-splitting roars were like white noise to me as we passed the last security exit. Shugger immediately seized me on one side, while another bodyguard popped up on the other.

"Flamingo's landed," Shugger reported into a headset.

The excited mob was barely being held at bay by the troop of airport rent-a-cops and flimsy barricades. Signs welcoming me home were peppered throughout the throng. Cameras flashed, questions were shouted. Everyone was cheering.

"Sally," Shugger's low voice boomed out. His muscled, protective arm around me gave an affectionate squeeze. He seemed bigger after all these months, or maybe I'd forgotten what a mountain of a man he was. It wasn't every day you see a six-foot-four, three-hundred-pound black man dressed in impeccable head-to-toe white linen. Well, maybe in Miami you do.

After properly assessing that I was okay, my burly bodyguard's round, toffee-colored eyes moved to Todd. "So, this is him?"

"Shugg!" I got right in his huge face. "Do *not* embarrass me."

Shugger chuckled and then pursed his lips, pointing his chin toward Todd. "How's it going, son?"

Todd attempted to formally introduce himself, but most of it was lost to the other noise. The two men shook hands across me while I waved and blew kisses to the screaming crowd.

Shugg let go of me for a quick second and laid one large hand on Todd's shoulder. "Ya ready for this?"

Todd forced a smile, but his eyes revealed bewilderment, lights and flashes reflecting between every blink.

Shugger laughed. "You'll get used to it. Don't worry, Shugger Daddy's got ya."

Shugg handed off my purse to the other bodyguard, who slipped it into a larger bag.

"Y'all set?"

We nodded.

"A'ight. Let's bounce."

With me sandwiched between my two huge escorts, we began our rapid escape through the sea of people like some demented scene à la *A Hard Day's Night*, girls shrieking, fans crying, pushing, pulling, fighting their way to gain a glimpse. From the lobby, past baggage claim, to the car took all of five minutes, yet somehow we managed to lose Todd along the way. I was practically hurled into the back seat, and then Shugger disappeared.

"Welcome home." Molly beamed at me as the limo door slammed shut.

"Hi!" I grinned.

"Hi, yourself." Her white teeth gleamed. "Now get over here."

She grabbed me, and after planting a kiss on each of my cheeks, sat back against the seat, her chestnut hair long and silky and as straight as a razor, falling just along the corners of her brown eyes. She was all legs, cheekbones to die for, and a smile that made the angels weep and the men follow behind her with their tongues hanging out. Her nose had a microscopic bump—probably the sole reason why her modeling career never shot off the way it should have.

Lucky for me, Molly also had the disposition of a girl's best friend as well as the work ethic of a coalminer. I somehow felt more organized just from sitting across from her.

"So, get to it then," Molly said through her heavy accent, looking like a young Victoria Beckham while sounding like The Artful Dodger. "Where's the yummy bloke?" She wore a hungry grin on her bow lips.

"There, somewhere," I replied, pointing out the tinted window. "Shugg went to find him."

"Bloody 'ell, Abby," she chided disapprovingly. "You lost him already?"

"You know me. Can't keep a man."

She flipped her hair. "I'm dying to get a look at him."

"You've seen Todd," I said, remembering what I'd heard about the magazine pictures. Then I remembered what Todd had said on the plane. "You've been calling and texting him, too, right? On *my* cell?"

Molly pulled an innocent face. "*You* never bother with it anymore, so I reckon *someone* should care."

I grinned, letting her off the hook.

Molly grinned, too, easing farther back in her seat. "Well, you look ripping," she said, folding her arms. "Nice skin, killer tan. Just fab."

"I'm not even wearing blush. Didn't use mascara all summer till this morning."

She nodded in approval. "How was the flight?"

"Fine." I couldn't help observing the sparkling tennis bracelet around her wrist. I adjusted the priceless homemade seashell necklace that hung inside my shirt. "I didn't sleep." I broke off to yawn. "But it was fine."

Molly snickered. "Doll, you never sleep. Oh, plans have changed," she added, her fingers swishing across her iPad. "Max wants us at Studio Universe straightaway."

"I just landed. Or doesn't he realize I was on the other end of America this morning?"

Molly said nothing, just shot me the same look we'd been

exchanging for five years. Without a word, we could communicate volumes. And at that moment we were in total agreement that Max Salinger was being utterly unreasonable, and there was nothing we could do about it.

I slumped back on the hard leather seat, knowing it was useless to argue. Molly kept me on my schedule flawlessly. Sometimes she was much too excellent at her job.

"What time is it, anyway?" I wondered absentmindedly.

"Half past nine." She glanced at me over the top of the tortoise-shell glasses perched on the tip of her nose.

"Oy vey," I moaned. "It's going to be a very long day." I closed my eyes, my fingers mechanically twirling a strand of hair. "What are we waiting for?"

"For your paramour."

"Oh, him. He's probably been abducted."

Silence fell as Molly stared at me. "There's a mob out there. You're not worried about him?" She leaned forward, looking concerned but also like she wasn't sure what to do next.

When I clapped a hand over my mouth, she was probably ready for me to start freaking out in a mad panic. But instead, I buckled in half and burst out laughing.

"Crikey, Abby."

When I blinked up at her through my tears, Molly looked positively *gob smacked*, as she would have said, like she hadn't witnessed me laughing in a year.

Maybe she hadn't.

"Heaven help the person who tries to mob him." I doubled over. "He'll probably restrain them in a sleeper hold."

"No worries," Molly said, still sounding shocked. "Shugg'll find Captain America. Hopefully before he gets arrested."

I hooted again, sending Molly into a giggling fit.

"Ya know, they've been asking me about him. Those bleeding tab rags," she elaborated, motioning out the window. "Jord and the boys, too. Max as well. Bloody cheek." She crinkled her nose. "They seem to think I'd have the big scoop about everything, but I disclosed nothing."

"I'm taking him on the red carpet next Sunday. It'll all be out soon."

Molly looked up from her iPad, all concern. "Oh, luv," she began. "Could be a major mistake. Ya think he's game?"

I peered out the window at the shutterbugs. Still no sign of Shugg or Todd. "He says he's willing to jump in with both feet, if that's what I want."

"The boy's got guts, yeah? I'll give him that."

"It was *his* idea to come to L.A., you know."

Molly farther arched her already arched eyebrows, finally putting her tablet on the seat.

"Before last week, we wouldn't even talk about the end of the summer, like totally ignoring the subject would stop it from barreling right toward us." I perched my elbow on the armrest. "He knew I wanted him to come, but I couldn't ask. Yesterday morning when I was in the middle of packing up my bedroom, he sprang it on me."

Molly's eyes opened wide.

I gazed toward the tinted window, smiling, remembering how Todd—after informing me of his decision—had immediately threatened to change his mind when I started doing that hysterical laughing/crying/shrieking thing girls do so well.

"It was such a relief," I continued. "The last few weeks, I felt sad and sick whenever I thought about leaving." I glanced at my assistant, who was smiling back at me. "So even though I *might have* planted the seed"—ha-ha—"*he* made the ultimate decision. Even left Sammy and his surf shop in the hands of his eighteen-year-old sales clerk."

"Who's Sammy?"

"His dog. The sweetest dog. Todd's going back for her later, maybe after Christmas." I reached up, activating satellite radio. The back seat of the limo filled with Top 40 music. "I love this song, don't you? Makes me get *down*." I was singing along, bobbing my head, hands up. "Yeeah-yeeah!"

Again, Molly gaped like she was seeing a stranger. "Right blimey." She folded her arms. "You 'ave changed. Full of beans, you is." When she allowed her grammar to slip like that, I knew she was flustered.

"He's *gorgeous*, by the way." She crossed her ten feet of legs under a summery cotton skirt. "Real posh."

I had no idea what she meant, but I took it as a compliment for Todd, just the same.

"So, uh." She stared down at her cell phone. "How is the . . . ?" She purposely let her voice trail off, leaving me a fill in the blank. When she looked up, she cocked one eyebrow to add an explanation point.

"We haven't—" I began, but then decided against further explanation.

Molly pushed her glossed-up lips into a pout and twisted them to the side, displaying her confusion. "No way."

I kept my eyes wide and steady.

"Okay." She seemed to be thinking about something else while decoding my expression. "I'm sorry, but . . . how do you *survive*?"

Shifting in my seat, I was about to issue a lecture about how Todd and I were not animals, but I gave up. "I do yoga," I admitted, "and chew a lot of ice."

"What about him?"

"He boxes." I scratched my cheek. "Quite a lot lately."

"Sexy beast." Molly grinned. "Well, ya have more will-power than me."

"It has little to do with willpower," I admitted, suddenly preoccupied by my nails. "Most of the time."

I could have further admitted that there had been plenty of times that I wanted to jump Todd's bones, like when I caught him watching me playing the piano, or when he'd just finished a workout. Those moments were becoming more frequent. But still, I wanted to wait for the right time, the right night.

"Oh!" Molly exclaimed, pulling my mind away from images of Todd's glistening boxing body. "*Oh, oh, oh*!" She looked like she'd accidentally discovered the correct answer on *The Price is Right*. "I can see it now." She cocked her head to one side. "Yeah. I *thought* you looked different."

"I look different?" I asked, concerned, running my fingers through my hair. Sure, the roots had grown out some, and sure, maybe I'd gained a little weight, but had I changed enough to merit such an outburst?

Molly leaned toward me and whipped off her glasses like a saucy reporter. "Why, Abigail Kelly, you're disgustingly in love with him, aren't you? Admit it!"

The fact that I was grinning like I had a hanger caught in my mouth was probably confirmation enough. "Disgustingly," I verified.

She pointed one condemning, French-manicured finger at me. "Right. I knew this was a new face."

"What do you mean?"

"Doll, it's me." She rolled her eyes. "I've seen you through David and that idiot Miles and all those other rubbish blokes. I've seen it all." She reached across the aisle and touched my chin with a finger. "But I've never seen *this* face."

I looked down, feeling the tingling of an oncoming blush.

Molly sat back and laughed. "Go on then, what was with that frantic voice mail you left me last week? You were in hysterics, swearing you were never speaking to him again."

"Oh, that," I mumbled, blushing for a different reason. "There was an . . . incident." I stared down, picking at my nails again. "Todd made me watch Shark Week."

"And?"

"And nothing. It was *upsetting*."

Molly cackled uncontrollably, holding her hand out to my face. "Abby, oh, Abby. You need major therapy."

I sighed. "Tell me about it."

"So anyway," she began, calming herself, "his rental place is right down the PCH from you, just like you asked. I sent the address to your phone. I take it you'll be on your own, not needing me to come over like usual after the studio?" She eyed me. "He'll get you all tucked in and what not?"

"I believe we'll have everything under control."

"Ahh, of course." She smoothed the front of her skirt. "So do tell, the 'I love you' scene; that's my second favorite part of a new relationship. I must hear every teeny tiny detail."

"Well, technically ..." I went back to my nails. "We haven't said it yet. Not in so many words."

"Wha?" Molly sat up like she'd been electrocuted. "Why ever not?"

I shrugged, through sharing for the time being.

Molly looked thoughtful for a moment, slouched, and folded her arms in front of her. "Well, it's not like the boy won't bloody well know it every bloody time he sees you." She glared as my grin expanded. "I can't even *look* at you; it's quite nauseating." She muttered for a while, her heavy accent sounding like a foreign language. "Bloody conventional American. Alpaca farmer."

Her rant was cut short when she lifted her buzzing cell, reading something on the face. "Jeez ..." she muttered.

"What's wrong?"

"That idiot Miles is tweeting about you again."

My upper lip curled. "Me? Why?"

"Halloo. Because he's a bloody idiot!" We both cracked up. "Apparently the boy is *finally* getting over you."

I lifted my eyebrows—it was about time.

"Rumor has it his latest song is called 'Life's a Bitch and So Are You.'"

"Classy." I rolled my eyes.

"Oh, and get this. He's taken to wearing *guy*-liner."

"What an idiot."

"Duh."

We screamed with laughter until the limo door flew open. Knowing what was coming, I jumped next to Molly as Todd and Shugger dove into the empty seats across from us. Sweating and panting, Shugger banged his fist three times on the glass partition, and the long car pulled away from the curb, leaving behind the hounding mob to eat our dust.

Molly and I stared at the two men, watching them catch their breath.

"Looks like the secret's out," Shugger said between pants, his gold front tooth flashing when he grinned. He elbowed Todd. "You got a brave one here, Sally."

"So, something happened, honey?" I asked Todd, trying not to smile. Then I blinked, noting his expression. "What happened? Are you okay?" I crawled across the aisle, wedging myself between him and Shugg.

"Sure. Fine," he clipped with strained composure.

Shugger burst out laughing, deep and jovial, as he moved across to the open seat next to Molly. "When I found him, he was surrounded by peeps shoutin' questions and what not. Twenny mikes in his face. Shudda heard 'em all."

"Did they hurt you?" I asked, genuinely concerned.

"No. Why?"

I put my hand on his chest. His heart was racing. "It gets out of hand sometimes," I muttered, suddenly angry with myself. "Sorry. That was stupid of me. I should've been more careful. Some armored car I turned out to be."

"I told ya." Shugger punched Todd's arm good-naturedly. "We call the airport *baptism by fire*." My gigantic security detail cracked up like a little kid until there were tears in his eyes. Then he pulled off his Bluetooth headset and mopped the side of his bald head with a hanky.

"What were they asking you?" I questioned Todd.

"I couldn't tell, at first," he replied, rhythmically patting my hand that was pressed against his heart, "but I think it was about me—*us*, I mean. How'd they know I'd be with you?"

The other three of us howled in unison. Shugger and Molly bumped fists.

"We got too used to Seaside where no one bothered us," I explained over the others' laughter.

"Oh." Todd nodded and then added nonchalantly, "One of them asked me if you were pregnant."

All laugher in the car was suddenly cut short.

Todd opened his mouth, but seemed to have fallen speechless.

Shugger cleared his throat and folded his arms, displaying two huge biceps.

"She's *not*," Todd threw into the silence.

Shugger cracked his knuckles with his thumbs.

"Hey, she's not, man." Todd lifted his right hand. "*Believe* me."

Shugger's chuckle broke the tension. "Chill, bro." He patted Todd on the shoulder. "It's all good under the hood." He turned and glared at me. "You'd tell me if you were, Sally. Right?"

I nodded, suppressing a smile. If he only knew how very *non*pregnant I was.

Shugg chuckled again and pulled out his cell, coordinating our entrance into the studio.

I felt Todd slowly exhale. I glanced at Molly.

"Sexy beast," she mouthed.

I turned to Todd. "By the way, I have to go into the studio this morning after all. Max wants to meet." When I looked at Molly, she was still grinning. "But we can go home first, right?"

She narrowed her suede brown eyes.

I moaned, whacking my head against the seat.

"Prat," Molly muttered under her breath.

I nodded concurringly.

Forty-five minutes later, the car pulled to a stop outside a black glass high-rise, home to Studio Universe. Our motley crew hopped out at the back entrance, and the limo pulled around to the underground parking lot.

"I don't know how long we'll be here," I said to Todd as we entered the building through an unadorned gray door. "Hopefully not too long."

Molly was cough-laughing into her fist, which wasn't a good sign.

"It'll probably be just Max and maybe a few techs," I further explained, trying to ignore Molly's subtle cough attack.

We stepped inside an elevator mirrored on all four walls. It smelled of cigarette smoke, carpet cleaner, and Windex.

While checking my makeup in the mirror one last time, I caught a glimpse of Todd's reflection. "Easy, honey." I rubbed his arm. "I promise they won't jump on you all at once."

As the two mirrored doors peeled apart, I realized that what I'd just promised Todd was *not* going to happen was exactly what was about to happen.

chapter 18

"MAXWELL'S SILVER HAMMER"

Hal, Jord, and Yosh were hanging out in the vestibule. Hal was holding court, doing his über-loud cackle/talk, probably trying to tell one of his stories that only he finds pound-on-the-floor hysterical. The noise quickly died out when they all turned to see our foursome stepping out of the elevator.

"*There* she *is*!" Hal exclaimed, twisting the guitar strapped across his shoulders to point at me. "The grand duchess." One set of his fingers tiptoed up the strings while the other strummed a tune.

Hal bore a striking resemblance to Calvin, sans Hobbes, especially that morning, with his spiky, orange-tipped hair sticking straight up. I hated to think of how many tubes of mega-hold gel had to die to get Hal's hair that tall.

His comic book resemblance was shattered when he released the neck of his guitar and flicked the ashes of his cigarette into the drinking fountain.

"Put that out, you cretin," I ordered, commencing our sibling-like banter.

Hal grinned and took a drag. "Huh. I *own* this place, duchess."

"You're disgusting. You were supposed to quit smoking this summer. It was the one thing you promised." I crossed the room toward my band mates, feeling the need to mother them after being away so long.

"He tried," said Yosh with an uneven smile.

"Not hard enough," I replied, slapping him a high-five greeting.

Yosh's bleached and feathered hair fell over his thin black eyes. His name, Kiyoshi, meant *quiet* in Japanese. As the drummer and archetypical loudmouth of Mustang Sally, Yosh was anything but quiet.

"We knew Hal'd fall off the wagon once the playoffs started." Yosh sneered, twirling a drumstick and then pointing it in Hal's direction. "The Giants are *trash* this year, dude." He turned his drumstick to me. "Come closer, duchess, give us a hug." He continued his request à la *The Partridge Family*: "I think I love you, duchess," he sang with outstretched arms, "so what am I so afraid of?"

"Please, Yosh," I whined, covering my ears. "Non-singing drummers were invented for a reason." The other guys laughed. "And *you*," I said, glaring at Hal. "I hope you won't be lighting up around me." I coughed dramatically. "You know those things are killer on me pipes."

"Ha!" This came from Jordan as he rose from an armchair. The thick, metal chain that connected his belt to his wallet jingled like Christmas bells. "We voted while you were off frolicking in the ocean and decided your voice needs a change." He chuckled, rolling the sleeves of his black AC/DC T-shirt over his shoulder, exposing a new set of Tribal tattoos. "Maybe a little secondhand smoke will lower you two octaves."

"There is no smoking in California," I protested.

"Precisely why I'm out here." Hal stomped his black Chuck Taylors on the floor and snubbed out his cigarette on the rubber soul of one. "This is Cherokee territory."

"Bloody imbeciles," Molly muttered from behind me.

"What was that you were just playing?" I asked Hal, reaching out to pluck at a string. "One of your own? It was nice."

"Hands off the merchandise, duchess."

"Speaking of . . ." Yosh grinned.

And I was suddenly yanked into the middle of a tight group huddle. While locked inside the smothering bear hug, I was overwhelmed by the combination of cigarette smoke on Hal's clothes, Yosh's cologne, and a hint of Turtle Wax, which meant Jord had lovingly polished his restored yellow Camaro lately. The constant undertone smell on all three surfer boys was piña colada–scented sex wax from their surfboards that never seemed to wash off.

When our hug was over and I could breathe again, I turned around. "Guys. *This* is *Todd*." I pointed to him with both hands in a "tah-dah" fashion. Of course they'd already "met" Todd over the phone, but this was the first official face-to-face.

"You'll be seeing him around," I added, "but don't get jealous. He promises he won't break up the band."

"First one of you to call me *Yoko*," Todd warned as he stepped up, "is a dead man."

Shugger chuckled while Molly gave me a very approving nod. "Sexy beast," she mouthed again.

"The man knows about your Beatles fixation," Hal said, ruffling the top of my head, "and can still stand to be around you?" He gave Todd an endorsing nod. "Righteous, dude. We'll commiserate later."

Todd returned Hal's nod. "As promised."

Hal gave me a sideways glance, snickered, and walked away.

Oh boy, they're already friends.

After the initial and expected interrogations, the guys paraded single file toward the studio door, performing some noisy, bizarre game of Follow the Leader. Shugger followed behind them, attempting to trip up Yosh, who was last in line.

I turned to Todd. "Sorry." I laughed, my fingers covering my mouth. "I didn't think they'd be here yet."

"They're funny." He sounded surprised. "It's like witnessing characters in a comic book come to life. We'll get along fine," he assured me with a smile.

I leaned in and gave him a hug.

Molly cleared her throat. "Sorry, Abby, but they're waiting for you." She left us, crossing through the threshold behind the guys.

"I have a feeling I'm not going to like this." Todd gave a mock grin that showed his bottom teeth.

I stood on my toes, linked my fingers behind his neck, and kissed him, lingering on his bottom lip. "I have a feeling you're going to *hate* this."

He nuzzled his face in my hair. "Do you remember that first day back in June, before we walked to Modica to get you a tuna sandwich?"

"Turkey," I corrected, pulling myself closer to him, "with Swiss and sprouts. Bob was out of tuna."

"Right." He smiled, dotingly. "I don't know if you noticed at the time, but I took a moment before offering to walk you back."

"I did notice," I confessed, lowering to flat feet. I remembered that moment like it was yesterday. "What was that about?"

"It was decision time," Todd explained, looking past me. "I saw it in my head. And I pretty much knew if I went with you then, one day I'd be standing right here."

I wrapped my arms around him even tighter. We rocked back and forth in the middle of the empty lobby of Studio Universe—unfamiliar territory for Todd, extremely familiar for me. Standing there, swaying in his arms, it felt like I could handle anything. When I looked up at his face, the tips of his ears were red. I closed my eyes and waited.

"We're burning daylight, babe," boomed a deep voice from behind us.

I was sure Todd felt my body go stiff in his arms. Like a pair of teenagers caught exchanging goodnights on the porch, we immediately stepped apart, turning toward the voice.

Max Salinger, framed in the threshold, held the glass door open with one foot. His six-two, two-hundred-fifty-pound physique took up most of the doorframe. Expressionless, he held an unlit Cuban between his teeth, a BlackBerry in one hand. He was dressed in his customary razor-pressed black trousers and hundred-dollar, plain white short-sleeved shirt.

He took out the cigar and rolled it between his fingers. "You rested and ready?" he asked, then looked me up and down with a not-so-discreet smirk. "You've put on a little." The smirk grew. "We'll have to fix that, pronto."

"I missed you, too, Max," I said, narrowing my eyes into a playful glare. I'd just taken a risk: it would either piss him off or break the ice.

Max glared back and grunted.

I held my breath, not knowing yet if that was good or bad.

After another moment, he put the cigar back in his mouth. "Smartass," he said and grinned.

I exhaled, feeling Todd's hand take mine, helping me pull it together.

Max thrust his fingers through his short and slicked-back brown hair. It looked darker than usual, and I wondered if he was attempting to blend in the flecks of silver that started showing up last year. When I'd first met him, I thought he had a little Baldwin brother in him; he was a good-looking man, very intelligent and majorly charismatic. He was still all those things now, but he'd also become less patient with me. We argued more, too, not that arguing with him made a difference; I seldom won.

"So." Max's attention shifted to Todd. "This is him?"

I took a quick glance at Todd. In the past three months, he'd witnessed me surrounded by a sudden crowd of fans in Panama City, and he'd even spoken briefly with Tom Hanks when he called my cell to talk about a show he would be producing next year. But I had never seen Todd actually star struck.

Until now.

"Yes," I said, giving Todd's hand a squeeze. "Max, this is Todd Camford."

Todd ran his thumb along my palm before he dropped

it and stepped up to Max. Right up to him. No fear. Once a Marine, always a Marine. "How do you do?" he said and extended his hand to my manager. "It's nice to finally meet you, sir."

"Sir?" Max repeated with obvious amusement. "Hey." He looked at me. "I like this one." The two shook hands and Max slapped Todd on the back. "I hear you run your own store back home."

"Yes, sir," Todd answered.

Max took out his cigar. "How old are you?"

"Twenty-eight, sir."

Max looked down and chuckled. "Now look, drop that *sir* thing, understand? Makes me feel like an old man." He glanced at me with a weary expression. "No comment from the peanut gallery," he warned. "Call me Max." He slapped Todd on the back again.

"Sure thing." Todd nodded. "Max."

Max looked at me and rolled his eyes. "All right, play time's over." He pushed the door open wider. "Time to work, babe."

Today's plan was for Hal and the guys to lay some tracks with the second unit engineers while Max, Nathan, and I spent the next several hours behind closed doors. Our goal for meeting was to listen to fifty submitted demos and narrow down to twelve. From day one, I'd always been involved in this process, although recently, if contrary to Max's vote, my opinion was moot. Almost as if the whole thing didn't concern me.

Todd was also included in our gathering. Surprisingly enough, Max didn't argue with my request.

We were arranged in a scattered half circle in a small rehearsal room. Nate, floppy-haired, neurotic, producer extraordinaire, sat in one corner, controlling the music and giving a brief introduction to each song. Max sat in another corner, his long legs stretched out in front of him. Occasionally he tapped on a laptop. He was also taking a lot of phone calls, which slowed our progress.

Todd was separated, inconspicuously, behind us. Whenever I craned my neck over my shoulder to look at him, he was either tapping on his own laptop or his eyes were fixed on Max. He didn't speak the entire time.

Between Nate and Max there seemed to be an undercurrent of a tense little debate; therefore, my opinion was asked for even less than usual. Groggy from travel, I didn't have much to add anyway, so I nodded a lot and agreed with whatever Max said, while listing names of candy bars in my head alphabetically.

Before I knew it, Max leaned back in his chair and called it a day. I was a little stunned; it had been only four hours. Max must have been taking it easy on me after all.

When I stood to stretch, I noticed Todd hadn't moved. He was staring in Max's direction. I waved my hand in front of his face.

"Hey," he said, blinking up at me. "Doing okay?"

"Good enough," I answered.

"You didn't say much." He stood, glancing at something over my shoulder.

"I don't really have to."

When we stepped out into the hall, Molly was there, arm extended, thrusting a toothbrush and toothpaste in my face. I took them gratefully. "Your bags are home," she informed me. "So are yours," she said to Todd. "Well, then . . ." She winked at me and turned away.

"I don't pay her enough," I said as I watched her walking toward Jordan at the end of the hall. He looked severely crumpled and in serious need of a haircut. Molly would no doubt take care of that issue, too.

After brushing my teeth in the ladies room, I returned to the lobby to grab Todd and hit the road. He was standing by the elevator, chatting with Max. They were both smiling, and Max had his hand on Todd's shoulder. The relief and happiness

I felt from simply looking at them made me smile in turn. All my worrying that Max would have something against Todd, just because of his existence, was all for nothing.

Max, who apparently just said something extremely hilarious, started howling with laughter, but Todd only stared at him, wearing a befuddled, polite smile.

As I neared them, one of the engineers nabbed me, prattling on about vacation spots in Florida. I didn't want to be all diva-rude, so I "hmm'ed" and nodded while eavesdropping on the other conversation across from me.

"What do you think it is about her?" Max asked Todd once he stopped laughing at his own joke, which probably had something to do with a girl from Nantucket.

Todd was holding a few business cards while entering something in his phone. "I can't put my finger on it," he answered, "but—"

"But," Max interrupted, "I bet you *did* put your finger on it. Didn't ya, kid?"

Todd's eyes slowly moved up to Max.

Uh-oh. I knew that expression ... just like that day back in Florida when we'd nearly stumbled into a pack of teenagers. Seeing Todd like that made my neck break out in a sweat. I was about to spring from my one-sided conversation and place myself between the two men, when Max shook Todd's shoulder.

"Heh-heh. I'm just messing with ya, sport." He chuckled and looked away.

"To answer your question," my insightful boyfriend amended, pulling back Max's attention, "from the little I've learned, I believe it's something you have or you don't have." Todd's gaze left Max, and he noticed me watching. His tense expression melted. "And Abby has it." He shot me a tiny smile.

"In spades," Max tagged on, turning to look at me. "She sure is a long, cool drink of water."

Todd's eyes didn't waver from me, but his brows pulled together, jaw clenched. He was about to say something. Or worse, *do* something.

Oh, crap.

I needed to excuse myself—right now—before their little pow-wow had Todd losing his temper and going Rocky Balboa all over my manager's face.

Max chuckled again, giving Todd another shake of the shoulder. "I'll see you kids tomorrow, bright and early."

Molly came up behind me. "Are my cars at home?" I asked her, relieved that the tension was broken.

"The Mercedes is usually kept here in the underground lot," she said, pulling a pen out of her hair, "but it's being detailed. The Porsche and convertible are in your garage. I'm still driving the Mini Coop, if that's okay." She waited for my approval. I didn't know why she bothered asking; she had been driving the Mini since the day I bought it. I didn't care. She loved it. I should've just given it to her. "None of your others are here," she added.

"Fine." Max sighed. "Our car will drive you home." He turned toward his office. "Grand to meet ya, fella," he threw in Todd's general direction.

"I'll see you tomorrow," Todd replied. But Max was already gone.

chapter 19

"OH! DARLING"

"What food do you have here?" I asked.

"None," Todd responded.

"What? Why?"

"Because I walked through the front door for the first time an hour ago. I haven't shopped, have you?"

I groaned dramatically and rolled to the other side of the couch.

After the forty-two-mile drive to Malibu, I'd given Todd a lightning-fast tour of my house—there wasn't much to see, of course. I stripped off my jewelry and heels, and we hiked a quarter mile up the beach to Todd's new digs.

I liked his house. It was smaller than mine, but had a more open floor plan. My six-bedroom, seven-bath Mediterranean-inspired whatever was ridiculously huge. His living room featured wall-to-wall windows, facing west. The view out the French glass doors was fantastic, miles of blue water and blue sky. Beach, beach, beach.

The sofa I was flopped across sat in the middle of the room. Its design was interesting and modern. It sat low, with two spongy black cushions, white arms and base, and an array of gray and blue pillows that had lined the back before I kicked them to the floor.

My unpolished toes curled around the wool Berber carpeting that ran the length of the room, mixed tufts of brown, tan, and green that matched everything in the room.

On the walls that were not made of glass, there was an eclectic variety of hangings: bamboo runners, brightly colored abstracts, and more than one clock.

I propped my feet on the large, rectangular leather ottoman in the same espresso shade that marbled through the carpet. With my eyes closed, I listened to Todd unpacking in the other room. I tried to trick my brain into thinking we were at his house back in Seaside.

"Are you hungry?" Todd asked. He made his way from the master bedroom to the kitchen. "I'll run out to the store later. I noticed one a few miles down the highway."

My eyes flew open. "No!" I said as my stomach muscles tightened.

Not that store! That's where . . . I shut out the thought, forcing my attention up to the gorgeous crown molding. Luckily the sick feeling passed a few moments later.

"I mean, didn't Molly stock the fridge?" I asked, turning around to rest my chin on the top of the couch. "She didn't have to, but I was hoping."

Todd opened the refrigerator. "She did." He knelt down to explore the inventory. "Excellent. Barbeque pulled pork from Rib and Loin." He removed a bag from the shelf. "How did it get here?"

"I may have mentioned to her that it's your favorite."

"No doubt you did." He turned to flash his teeth at me. "But what I mean is, how did she get it here all the way from Tennessee in one day?"

"She probably had it flown in by special delivery."

Todd nodded at my explanation.

"I'm looking forward to it after how much you raved about it all summer," I added.

He lifted the lid of one Styrofoam container, inhaled its contents—sighing in ecstasy—then replaced the lid and returned the bag to the shelf.

"We're not eating it tonight?"

"Patience," he said. "It'll taste even better tomorrow."

"Mmm, can't wait."

His smile twisted into something roguish. "There's nothing like a good-looking woman who smells like ribs. Er—wait a second." The edge to his voice made me sit up. "What is *your* putrescent soy milk doing in *my* refrigerator?" He slammed the door closed and turned to me, green eyes squinting in mock disgust.

I rolled off the couch and walked to the kitchen "Oh. Hmm." I scratched my chin. "I guess Molly *assumes* I'll be over here a lot, although she might've asked you for a food list. What kind of assistant is she? She probably bought what she thinks all men— *Todd*!"

I found myself being yanked forward into a hug.

"Has anyone told you that you talk too much?" he whispered against my cheek.

"Really, Lieutenant Camford . . ." I moaned breathlessly. "You're supposed to be an officer and a gentleman."

Methodically he swept the hair off my shoulder and ran his mouth down the side of my neck. My body shuddered as I breathed him in. He pulled back, but only to move up the other side. His hands slid down my ribs and his thumbs hooked through my belt loops, pulling me closer. My back arched automatically when his mouth stopped on the hollow behind my ear.

"Thank you for inviting me here."

"Sure," I managed to say while I exhaled, gripping the back of his head.

"This is the best it's ever been for me, Abby," he murmured into my hair. "The best." He kissed my ear. Slowly. "This." He kissed it again. "I hope you understand that."

"Yes," I whispered, not really understanding anything.

Todd pulled back, leveling our faces. "Do you?" he asked intently.

Then we crashed together, like two dehydrated hikers finding an oasis in each other's mouths. He tasted sweet and clean like Juicy Fruit gum at first. Then he tasted like Todd, like everything I loved.

"The best," he repeated softly, his nose skimming the length of my cheek. I grabbed his face—*he* was talking too much now.

We free-fell for a while.

The pressure of his lips changed, went firm for just a second, and then intentionally weaker. After a lovely sigh, he bent his head over my shoulder, breathing hard and fast. Once again we had successfully rendered each other breathless.

"By the way," he said, stepping back and twirling me out of his arms with a sexy little dance, "who chose all this? The furniture and everything."

I reached out for him, comically grabbing the empty air in front of me.

"Yes, I agree, probably Molly," he suggested, answering his own question.

"I wasn't finished with you yet," I complained, clutching the counter to steady my wobbly legs.

Todd's lips twisted; he probably noticed I was incapacitated. He didn't know the half of it.

I pressed both hands against my racing heart, shooting him an accusatory glare. "You know I can't *handle* when you do that."

"Oh, yeah?" He grinned steadily. It did something to the base of my stomach.

"This is a warning, Todd Camford. That shirt of yours *can* be torn off."

"Relax, Abby, you'll survive. Have some ice." He chuckled good-naturedly, strolling past me toward the living room. "You wish," he added with a wink, tucking in his shirt.

Exhaling long and slowly, I stared after him. *The silly boy, he has no idea.*

I leaned over the sink, sipping a glass of cold water, contemplating gnawing on a chunk of glacier to cool myself down, or maybe standing inside an industrial freezer. A few minutes later, I found Todd at the open French doors, gazing out at the Pacific.

"Sometimes in the morning the water is so blue it almost matches the sky," I said. "It's like watching a moving picture of sapphires."

"You love it here," he surmised as a cool breeze off the ocean blew into the room. Turning to me, he added, "And I love—" He cut off. My heart pounded as we gazed at each other, that unspoken phrase hanging in the air.

"Me, too," I whispered. Even my hand holding the glass of ice water started to feel hot.

Todd's eyelids drooped as he released a slow sigh that ended in a growl. "*Bella mio*," he purred in an exaggerated Italian accent, eyeing me like a jaguar about to pounce.

"Stop." I pressed one hand out. "Back away."

"Don't be so dramatic." He rubbed an index finger up my arm. "I just want to kiss you again. Come here."

"Kiss?" I pulled my hand away, with probably just a bit of dramatic flair. "You call that thing you do a *kiss*? Ha!" I pointed at the area in front of the fridge where he'd attacked me only a few minutes ago.

He tilted his head and frowned in confusion.

"Todd Camford." I pressed the cool glass against my cheek. "I swear to you, I will lose all rational control if we keep kissing like *that*. Are you prepared for that eventuality?"

"Fine," he said, rolling his eyes. "Lightweight." He turned from me to face the room, while I felt a tiny bead of sweat trickle down my neck.

"So, back to the subject." He waved his hand around. "Who did all this? I'm leasing the house, but I know it didn't come furnished." He pointed to a framed picture of a sunset. Too much turquoise. "It's all a bit girly, not really me."

"Save whatever you like; we'll return the rest," I suggested. "I'm pretty sure Molly organized the decorating, so she'll see about the returns." I finished my water and set the glass down. "I know what you mean. You saw my house earlier. It's so empty you'd never know I've lived there for so long. The place was crammed full of stuff when Christian was alive."

I had no idea why I just said that. I hadn't meant to; it just popped in my head then popped out of my mouth. And suddenly, the room started to spin.

My flashbacks had become more frequent lately. They'd started in hardcore about a week ago; being back in California was obviously an additional trigger. Panicked at being discovered, I darted my eyes to Todd, but he didn't seem to have noticed anything out of the ordinary. Which was a relief. I didn't want him to know how derailed I'd been feeling lately.

I cleared my throat, trying to swallow the lump that was always there when I thought about my brother.

"All his things are gone now," I pressed on conversationally, needing to make myself busy. I moved to the mantel, straightening the already straight mahogany clock. I attempted to swallow the lump again, but it was still there, bigger now. Was it growing? I tried to distract myself by speaking, but the subject wouldn't leave my mind.

"After it happened, Molly used to come over all the time, probably every day." I adjusted the clock another half inch and wiped one finger across its face. It left a sweaty smear. "When I couldn't function on my own." My voice dropped to a whisper. "When I'd wake up screaming from another nightmare."

As I turned around, Todd was standing by the open French doors, staring at me. He looked like he was holding his breath. I was holding mine, too, waiting for my subconscious to push the painful memory away. Sometimes it took a while. I dropped my chin, trying to forget that Todd was watching.

A minute later, I felt his hands on my shoulders.

"I'm okay. Really, it's nothing. I'm totally fine."

He eased me in, planting my head against his chest. His hands rubbed slow circles over my back. Exhaling, I felt like I was trying to release something stuck inside. but I couldn't get it out.

"I've got you, sweetheart," Todd murmured, stroking my hair.

I closed my eyes, nodding, trusting.

"It'll be all right," he added under his breath. "I know it will."

♪

While Todd went to finish unpacking in his bedroom, I wandered into the kitchen. Like the living room, its western walls were floor-to-ceiling windows and glass doors, displaying the same beautiful view. I stood for a moment, leaning against the island that divided the stove from the sink area.

During the previous three months in Florida, whenever I'd been at home, Lindsey had taken care of the family meal preparations. When I'd been with Todd, which was most hours of the day, he'd used his patio grill or we ordered from Modica.

I ran my palms over the smooth, cool countertops. *It's my turn to cook*, I decided with a grin.

I didn't know how Molly had done it, but the kitchen was fully stocked. Not only that, but all the shiny stainless-steel appliances appeared to be brand new. If I'd been any kind of cook, that kitchen would have been a culinary dream.

However . . .

"You okay in there?" Todd called out the second time the smoke alarm started shrieking.

"Just peachy," I called back, fanning a potholder through the air under the alarm. "I *so suck* at this," I muttered, dumping the pan of whatever I'd just burned to a crisp into the sink. Dishes were piling up.

Twenty minutes had gone by and I had already exhausted my entire repertoire of menu ideas, burning and/or drowning everything I attempted. Beyond frustrated, I planted my hands on my hips, brushing the hair off my face with my elbow.

That's when I noticed Todd leaning against the doorframe.

"We're having cold cereal for dinner," I stated. "Which

would you prefer, Kashi or Cap'n Crunch with Crunch Berries? You have both."

Todd exhaled loudly in pretend pity. "We're much too young to die." He made his way into the smoky kitchen, snatching the dishtowel off my shoulder and draping it over his own, a sort of passing of the torch.

"If you insist," I agreed, more than happy to hand over the reins until I learned how to boil water without turning his beach house into a pile of ashes.

A second later, two petite steaks appeared on the counter. Todd was bent over, adjusting the flame of the range. "That's the very last of this kind of food for me," I reminded him as I headed for the living room to open more doors and windows, fanning the billowing smoke to follow me out. "You saw Max's expression today. Diet starts tomorrow."

"We'll have to make the most of tonight, then."

I heard something heavy drop on the kitchen counter.

"You know I love it when you eat like a pig."

"Flattery will get you everywhere," I called, dragging from the hall closet a large portable fan to help the smoke along its way outside. "You haven't told me yet. What did you think of today?" I searched the north wall for an electrical outlet. "At the studio."

"It was . . . interesting." Impeccably polite as usual.

I switched on the fan, and the room began clearing of smoke. "Oh, yes," I said as I joined him in the kitchen, "we are a very *interesting* bunch." I stood right behind him, watching him peel a potato. "The band, they act like thirteen year olds most of the time." I snatched a baby carrot from an open bag on the counter. "But," I said, crunching, "when they're serious for two seconds, there're no other musicians I'd rather work with."

Todd stopped peeling and turned his chin toward me. "That's quite a compliment coming from you. You should tell them."

"Why would they care?" I reached for another carrot.

Todd flicked my hand and then returned to his work.

"Abby," he began a moment later, "you're so blind some-times. There's been no one like you in twenty years. Even your critics agree. You're this generation's Britney, Madonna, and the Beatles rolled up in one."

"You don't have to say that," I joked. "I'll give you my autograph if you ask me nicely." I hopped onto the counter, taking a more comfortable seat to observe him cooking. He was looking intense and focused, making me feel all kinds of hungry.

"I'm being serious. Just because *you* choose not to read the trades doesn't mean *I* don't."

My stomach dropped. "Don't believe the hype," I muttered, knocking my heels against the cabinet doors below me.

"It's not hype." The expression in his green eyes looked a little weary. "It's statistics. You're on the short list as one of the most influential people in the country." He stared down at the pile of potato peels before him. "Higher even than the president."

"I actually *did* hear about that." I knocked my heels harder, rattling around whatever items were inside the cabinet.

"Pass me that spatula, would you?" He pointed his chin to a bunch of red-handled kitchen utensils nestled in a gray ceramic pot behind the toaster. I stretched out across the cold granite countertop, my fingers fumbling to grab the spatula without spilling the entire contents. I latched onto it with two fingers and lifted it out of the pot. When I sat up to hand the utensil to Todd, he wasn't chopping anymore.

"Here." I waved it under his nose.

"Thank you," he said, taking it from me, but then he let it drop onto the cutting board. "You seem to have trustworthy people on your team." With his eyes lowered, his dark lashes shielded whatever expression he wore.

"I do. They're top notch. Best in the business, or so I'm told."

Todd nodded, though probably not fooled by my ill-in-formed reply. "You have an accountant, a financial manager, someone who handles your money?" He still wasn't looking at me, probably embarrassed by the subject.

"Yes," I replied, sliding off the counter. "*And* a lawyer." I scooted myself between his body and the cutting board, forcing him to look at me. "I own my house free and clear. An apartment on the Upper West Side, too. Six cars." I bit my lip. "Seven, actually. And the band is sole owner of Studio Universe, including every piece of equipment."

"Okay, okay." Todd rolled his eyes. "I get it." And with that, we let the subject drop. "So what's on for tomorrow?" He washed his hands at the sink.

"Molly can sync the schedule to your cell's calendar," I suggested, swiping another carrot off the cutting board. "I never look at it. Might give me a coronary." I froze my face into an open-mouthed gasp, hands at my throat.

"Drama queen."

"I'm not due at the studio till eleven. That's about all I know."

Todd shut off the water. "Good. You can sleep late."

"I wish," I muttered. "Dirk the Drill Sergeant will be pounding on my door at eight, armed with his evil gym bag of free weights, tape measures, and other torturous devices. Then we're running on the beach."

"You? Running?" A smirk colored his voice. "This I have to see."

I tried to ignore his dig and the dread of the upcoming workouts. "I *believe*, because of the red carpet next Sunday, we should have most of the nights off." I scratched my chin. "That is, if tomorrow's plans don't change."

Right on cue, a phone rang. "I didn't realize I have a land line," Todd said as he breezed by me, turning down the flame on the stove as he passed.

In the living room, a black cordless phone sat beside a table lamp. "Hello? Ah, yes. Sure. Hold on, please." He spun around, the phone pointing in my direction. "It's for you."

I pressed my fingertips to my chest and squealed, *"Me?"* like I'd just won a prize.

"Is your cell dead again?" he whispered in a lecturing tone.

I shrugged, reaching for his phone.

It was Molly. Our conversation was very short. Tomorrow's plans had changed.

Dirk would be on my doorstep at six in the morning. Yes, vacation was definitely over.

PRESS RELEASE

LOS ANGELES, CA—After being out of the spotlight for three months, singing sensation Abigail Kelly (of Mustang Sally fame) held a small press conference today. Neither Kelly nor Kelly's publicist would offer any information about the alleged boyfriend, Todd Camford, that Kelly had been seen with all summer while vacationing in Florida and who has lately been spotted with her around town and at Hollywood's Studio Universe. Kelly's publicist issued the statement that Kelly and her band are now in the studio working on their fifth album, and that Kelly is surrounded by good friends.

chapter 20

"I'M LOOKING THROUGH YOU"

"What did he do to your voice?" Todd asked.

We were hugging the Pacific Coast Highway just northwest of Santa Monica on our way back to Malibu. The Indian summer night air was still warm, even at midnight, and the convertible top was down.

"It didn't sound like you when he finished with it." Todd shifted gears. "He made you sound . . . synthesized."

I laid my head back on the seat, looking up at the twinkling stars breaking through the thin layer of overcast. The smell of the briny, salty ocean air was pungent, and I could almost feel the tide twenty feet below, pulling us down.

"Too much reverb on the vocal," I answered, tranquilly. "It's just that style of track. Pretty funky, right?"

Todd didn't answer, but stared straight ahead.

"Some songs are like that," I added. "Max was just messing around, using pitch control."

"Is that what it's called? Moving your voice up and down like a computer?"

I nodded. "It was just a scratch vocal. We'll do the master later on."

Todd mumbled something I didn't quite catch, but he sounded peeved.

"Want to try that Greek restaurant tomorrow night?" I asked, moving our conversation to something lighter. We'd been back in L.A. a full week. It was a grueling experience, getting used to everything again. And I was sure it had been extra tough on Todd, who was dealing with everything for the first time.

When he didn't respond to my question, I went on. "It's got to be better than the sushi we had at lunch today, right?"

Finally he turned to me with a grin.

"Seriously?" I paused for effect. "Japanese and Polish fusion?"

Todd cracked up. "That was the worst wasabi I have ever tasted, and I've been around."

We laughed for a minute, talking about other things we'd done the past week. Of course it had been mostly work, but I was also trying to show Todd a good time. Los Angeles could be a magical place. Whenever I got a ten-minute respite in recording, he would grab me, and we would dash out to this tiny garden behind the studio. A manmade creek ran through the middle. We always kicked off our shoes first and stood on the shallow bank, but that was usually all we had time for. When we got around to splashing each other, my cell would be ringing.

"So," he said after a few minutes, "I take it Max is producing this whole album?"

"He and Nate both this time. They want to get back to the roots of our first record, more straight pop." I covered my mouth to yawn. "Or something like that."

In my peripheral vision, I saw Todd shaking his head.

"You've got good ideas, Abby. I'm there every day. I see it. You should speak up more often."

I just looked at him.

"If you're interested in *my* opinion," he muttered, with a touch of sarcasm.

Okay . . .

He was wearing that expression again, the one I'd seen a few times that week. His bright eyes appeared unusually dark, his lips pressed together.

"It's *your* name that's out there," he continued, fighting for volume over the highway, "so why don't you sing the way you want to? The way you sound your best. When you're recording, I hear what you're trying to do." He looked at me, half of his face in shadow. "You should make people listen to your opinions instead of letting them blow you off every time you speak."

I recognized the strain in Todd's voice, and I understood his frustration. I'd so been there.

"I can't," I said.

"Why?"

"Because . . ." I cleared my throat. "If I had *my* way, the whole album would end up sounding like one long *Abby-sings-the-Beatles* song."

Todd chuckled. I took it as encouraging.

"Despite what you think, I'm not all that creative. I *need* producers to guide me." I patted my mouth, covering another uncontrollable yawn. "Don't worry. Max knows what he's doing."

Something seemed to change in the air, and I knew instantly I had said the wrong thing. My eyes flickered to Todd's face to catch his reaction. The half of it that wasn't shrouded in shadow appeared just as dark.

"Don't put your blinders back on," he said, his hands tightening around the steering wheel. He shifted and revved the engine. The car jerked forward. "Despite what you continue to believe, this is *your* band; you're the leader. Do what you have to do."

I didn't know what to say, so I chose not to speak. He sat silently as well, which was probably for the best at the moment. Admittedly, Todd had a temper, but he was also the most in-control person I knew. Only a few times had I seen his composure slip.

His composure was slipping now.

"Don't you realize how you behave when you don't get your way?" He shook his head, staring out at the road. "You clam up; you shut down; you let everyone walk all over you."

His upper lip curled. He looked a little disgusted, disgusted at *me*. "To say that's a terribly unattractive quality in you is an understatement."

My mouth fell open, but I didn't know what to say.

"Why do you let him do that?"

"Who?"

"Max," Todd snapped. When he turned to look at me, I flinched at his angry, disappointed, confused expression. "Stand up to him. Speak up if you want him to respect you. Be brave. Every day, I have to watch you be reduced to a timorous, pandering pushover."

Me, mouth hanging open, stunned by his words. Even if he were right, he had no idea how much that hurt.

Of course I knew my behavior changed when I was recording. The pressure was almost unbearable at times. And Max had become the last person to show sympathy. When we worked, he was all work. So I got out of his way. This reaction was a learned behavior, perfected over the course of five years. I was sure it had gotten worse since Christian, my original armored car, wasn't with me anymore.

At the thought of my brother, hot, sharp tears stung my eyes.

"Timorous?" I repeated, not bothering to conceal the hurt in my voice. "Pandering?"

Todd shot me an impatient look.

"It's called *survival mode*, Todd, and you know why."

He shook his head. "No. That's crap, Abby, an excuse."

His comment knocked the air out of me.

"I don't buy it anymore," his harsh voice continued. "If you're not happy, then do something; if you need help, ask for it."

The rest of his chewing-me-out session had to wait so he could concentrate on whipping the car around a tight turn, much faster than necessary. I gripped the sides of my seat. My fuming driver's eyes were set in a hard, flat glare; it didn't look like he was watching the road at all.

"What's *wrong* with you?" I gasped after he shifted into fifth, rocketing the car forward. "You're driving like a maniac. Slow down!"

He did, eventually, pulling off the highway onto the gravel shoulder. He shifted to neutral and wrenched on the parking brake.

I tore off my seat belt. "*What* is your *problem*?" I hissed, jerking open my door and nearly falling out. "*My* problem?" he replied sarcastically, cutting the engine.

"You've been like this for days." I slammed the door. "Why are you so pissed?"

"Because I'm pissed at you, Abby. You're pissing me off."

"Why?"

He didn't move.

"Well, now *you're* pissing *me* off!"

Todd sat motionless behind the wheel of the convertible, still facing me. His brow was wrinkled, displaying a mixture of anger and fatigue.

"Are you going to tell me what's going on?" I insisted, "or were you simply going to drive us off a freaking cliff?"

"This isn't—" He stopped himself by running his hand across his mouth, but I thought I heard an angry and muffled, "working."

His head was bowed now, his finger and thumb running back and forth along the bones under his eyes. "Get in the car," he said coolly. "Before someone runs you over."

But I wasn't about to move.

A moment later, his head snapped up when a car appeared in the other lane. Its headlights hit Todd's face, and I could see the hard glare in his eyes was gone. He looked plain worn out.

My muscles unclenched, relieved that we weren't yelling anymore.

"I'm serious." His right hand was on the headrest of the passenger seat. "Get in the car."

"Not with you driving like that," I complained. My voice was softening, following his suit.

"I'm sorry." There was a touch of desperation in his voice. "It won't happen again." He reached over and opened my door from the inside. "Now, *please*."

My feet were moving before my brain could process the request.

"Seat belt, please," he instructed as he stared straight ahead into the night. After firing up the ignition, he tapped the gas, revving the engine just enough until I looked at him. He lifted a teeny smile.

At a very safe and responsible velocity, we drove in silence. Todd turned on the radio to a sports station. The Giants lost to the Dodgers in eleven innings. Hal would be fit to be tied tomorrow. I stared out the windshield, chewing on my thumbnail.

"I'm just looking out for you." Todd switched off the radio. "You know that, right?" His face was still twisted with emotion. Both of his hands were wound around the steering wheel, but he let his right hand fall. It found my left hand. I could feel tension surging through his body.

"That was really stupid of me." His voice was almost a whisper. "And very unkind, those things I said. Please forgive me for losing my temper. It's not, well, it's not you." He shook his head an inch and sighed, sounding a little defeated. "I don't know what I'm supposed to do."

"About what?"

He didn't answer, but the way his gaze shifted made it seem that his thoughts had veered in a different direction. "I hope you'll be patient with me." He curled his fingers tighter around mine. "This is harder than I thought it would be."

"It'll get better. I promise. It's a shock for everyone at the beginning."

"I guess." He nodded. "It's just, sometimes I don't understand why . . ." He trailed off.

I sat quietly with his hand in my lap, waiting for him to relax. It took only a few minutes that time. We were improving.

♪

"Okay, Abby," Nate's enthusiastic voice spilled through my headphones, "let's run through it again. And . . . we're rolling."

Through the thick glass that separated the control room from the recording booth, I saw both Nate and Todd. Max's throne of a swivel chair was empty; he was letting Nate take lead on this one. Nate was concentrating on the flat computer screen in front of him, or *screens*, I should say—there were four, one on a laptop and three others in a sort of uneven cluster. Todd sat forward in his chair, elbows on the edge of the long mixing board. His attention was constantly moving from me to Nate's screens to his own laptop. He nodded to me every once in a while, which was all the communication we shared.

Every so often, Nate would grin, lean over to him, and they'd have a short conversation that I couldn't hear. It always ended in laughter or even a friendly guy punch. Other times, Max appeared behind Todd, said something to him, and walked away. From what I could make out, Max's comments seldom warranted a response, because Todd's replies were always brief.

When I finished that take, I stood still, staring at Nate through the glass, hoping against hope we wouldn't have to run it again. Twelve times at any song was usually my limit. Anything beyond that came across too rehearsed, and we would have to move on, unfinished. Max hated that.

I exhaled slowly, reminding myself that recording was a balancing act. And unfortunately, most of the time I sported the poise of a monkey in a tutu.

While waiting for Nate's decision, my mouth stretched open in a yawn, making my eyes water. My impatient glance moved to Todd, who was also yawning. Our gazes locked, and we grinned at each other through the glass, the pair of us mutually extra sleepy. Unbeknownst to the rest of the recording party, Todd and I had been up until four in the morning the night before, having much to discuss after his botched attempt at *Thelma and Louise*-ing us off the Pacific Coast Highway.

Todd's attention was suddenly pulled to whatever Nate was pointing at on the computer screen. Nate started laughing and so did Todd. I picked up a pencil, continuing the cluster

of hearts I'd been doodling on the corners of my sheet music.
I hadn't had to consult my notes for hours. Todd was right; I
did have a photographic memory.

"Perfect." Nathan's voice came through my headphones.
"We got it."

"Okay, babe."

I looked up, hearing the new voice. Max was leaning over
Nathan to speak through the talk mike. "Close the lid on tonight. Get your tail outta here. I gotta work with the guys."

Not requiring a second invitation, I peeled off my ear-
phones and slid into my heels. After I made my way down
the hall, I found Todd and Hal chatting in a corner outside
the control room. Colorful stickers with logos like IN-N-OUT
BURGERS, WHILE MY GUITAR GENTLY WEEPS, BODY GLOVE,
and RON JON'S SURF SHOP covered Hal's scarred, scuffed, and
well-loved guitar case. Always a little too protective, Hal was
hugging his instrument in his arms.

"Finished yet, duchess?" he asked with a playful smirk,
knocking his shoulder against me.

"Yes, your royal highness," I replied. I looked at Todd.
"His *real* name is Henry Beaumont Charles Xavier Rich-
ardson the fourth," I explained. I then turned back to Hal.
"He hates it." I stuck out my tongue at the king.

"Shut your cake hole, Abby."

"Temperamental musician," I complained jokingly.
"Moody little boy."

Hal growled and turned to Todd. "Would you look the
other way so I can smack your girlfriend upside the head?"

Todd lifted his hands. "Keep me out of this."

"Jealous much?" I said to Hal, fluttering my eyelashes at
him.

I was surprised when Hal's cheeks went red. Maybe it
wasn't such a good idea to tease him. If he did have a little
crush on me, like Lindsey said, then that was just mean.

"You better get in there." I pointed toward the studio.
"Max was saying he wants more button on the kick before
the mix down."

After one last glare, Hal knocked my shoulder and stomped off around the corner. If there was one thing he really loathed, it was being told how to play his guitar. He never voiced it, but Max drove him berserk. I still enjoyed pushing Hal's buttons when I could.

Todd was shutting down his laptop and gathering some books from a tall, round table in the corner of the lobby.

"If you keep this up," I said, gesturing to his computer, "you're going to know more about producing than Nate."

Todd looked up. "And Max?" he said with a wink.

"Todd Camford, L.A.'s newest impresario! Are you ready to see your name in lights?"

He narrowed his eyes. "Hilarious."

Hearing Max's voice behind me, I whispered, "Let's make a run for it before he changes his mind." I motioned subtly at Max through the open doorway.

Todd looked surprised. "Are you done for the whole day?"

"Because of the red carpet tomorrow," I confirmed, leaning on the couch shoved against the wall. "I've been starving myself to fit into that stupid dress." I planted my hands on my hips. "But I've had the last fitting, so all bets are off. Shall we go back to your place and scramble something?"

Todd grinned and slid a hand around my waist.

"I bet you're bored stiff in there," I said as we walked past the control room. "You've been sitting in that same chair for more than a week."

"Nope," he replied. I was relieved to hear joy in his voice again. "Just yesterday I was sitting in *that* chair." He pointed at the short, blue-cushioned armchair that sat directly before the glass. "Front row, center. Best seat in the house." As he looked at me, my heart went all gooey.

Just then, Nathan rounded the corner, trudging directly toward us. His left arm was full of brightly colored manila folders, while his right hand pressed a cell phone to his ear. Luckily he stopped just before crashing into us.

"Oh, hey," he said, looking a little startled to see us

standing there. His brown hair was floppier than usual, giving Hugh Grant a run for his money.

"You all right?" Todd asked him.

"Oh, sure. Good deal, good deal." He turned on his heel, always a little too neurotic. "Just work stuff." He took three steps toward his office and stopped. "Hey, Abby?"

"Yeah?"

"I was wondering, during that final take of 'On the Rocks . . .'" His head pointed toward the recording booth. "Why did you take those extra rests at the verse before the bridge?" He took a step toward me. "You did it that way only the last time through."

I shrugged. "Didn't it work?"

He snorted. "Of *course* it did. It was really genius. I just want to know what made you change your phrasing at the last minute."

I pushed out my bottom lip, pensively. "Well, I'd been thinking about it during the other takes, wondering how it would sound. It made sense to me. I don't know, I just . . . felt it."

Nate raised a smile, and then he glanced at Todd. "I told you, man," he said. "I told you she was good. Complete natural."

A noisy group of six or seven office workers marched past us, separating Todd and me from Nate. After they passed, Nate was still standing at the doorway, one hand on the knob. "By the way, *what* is she still doing here?" He was speaking to Todd while pointing at me.

I caught a quick flash of unspoken understanding in both men's eyes.

"I'm taking her home right this second," Todd assured him in a fatherly voice.

I could see that he and Nate were becoming good friends. Ten or so twelve-hour days could do that to two guys. Plus, on a personal note, I obviously considered Todd to be irresistible. I hoped it was only a matter of time before even Max Salinger succumbed to Todd's charms.

"Good deal." Nathan nodded in approval before opening the door. "Hey," he said to Todd, "good luck on the carpet, man."

Todd cleared his throat and slid his hands in his pockets, looking a little embarrassed. "Thanks. Any advice?"

Nate scoffed. "Not from me. I don't do those industry shindigs." He nodded at me. "Strictly A-list celebs."

"A-list?" I chuckled. "I'm just there to hobnob and get autographs. Hey, do you think I'll finally meet Paul McCartney this year?"

Todd and Nate groaned in unison.

chapter 21

"LONG TALL SALLY"

Mustang Sally was not up for an award, but we were presenting one. When wrapped in the right packaging, and if all the planets were aligned, red-carpet events could be pretty cool.

On the upside, dressing up for one night wasn't so bad. Red carpets meant meeting with Jillian, my stylist, to sort through the designer endorsements shooting down the pipe. At every RC event, I was asked the same question, "Who are you wearing?" a zillion times, as my small army dragged me from one interview to the next. I always made sure I was well informed about each article of clothing and jewelry attached to my body.

On the downside, red carpets made for excruciatingly long evenings, the sleazy paparazzi came out in full-force, and if the RC was in Los Angeles, the sky was either pouring down rain or the air was a hundred degrees. Or both.

"Mwah! Mwah! You look beautiful, Abigail. You look like a million bucks! Love *the dress!"*

Ironically, those same bloodsuckers chewed you up and spat you out the next day, replaying *ad nauseam* that split second you'd scratched your nose or adjusted your underwire. The majority of my morning-after reviews were kind if not over the top. At least I had *that*. I knew of a few A-list women who sank into dark depression and even resorted to unnecessary surgeries after an RC snafu.

That particular Sunday evening, I was more nervous for Todd, it being his first industry event as well as our public debut. I could hold my own against those press jackals, but Todd was brand new to the hype, and it wasn't exactly his scene. Although not even A-list celebs could hold a candle to him in his vintage Armani tux, snowy-white French-cuffed shirt, black silk tie, and gold cufflinks.

Eat your heart out, Sinatra.

I squeezed Todd's hand between both of mine when our car stood next in line at the throat of the red-carpet drop-off point.

He looked at me, his eyes big and green, surprisingly serene.

I guess I'm more nervous than he is, I thought, still wringing his hand.

Despite how neither of us cared about such things, Todd and I surely appeared a gorgeously smashing couple that night. My hair was piled high in shimmering ringlets, with long golden tresses tumbling down my back, bouncing when I moved. My black silk, beaded, slit-up-to-here, cut-down-to-there had been designed specially for me. A major rush job, since my measurements had altered slightly over the summer.

My free hand moved to my wrist and then my neck, re-checking the borrowed baubles, lest we forget to mention the Fort Knox–worth of crown jewels that had been lent to me for the occasion. Throat, wrists, fingers, ears—all important areas of skin—screamed Harry Winston, Cartier, and Tiffany's. Exhibiting that much ice in public was an unnerving feeling, but it was all part of the game.

"Have you ever been to Buenos Aires?" I asked Todd, attempting to divert him from staring out the window at the flashing lights and chaos.

He turned to me but didn't answer.

"Because," I continued, feeling a twinge of nerves, "the crowds there are the absolute worst. It's like every single citizen is a pop music fanatic. Insane. We always have to hire extra security."

"Huh," Todd replied distractedly.

"Have you been there?" I asked again.

He nodded once.

"When?"

"Several years back." He was looking down, winding a cufflink.

"Vacation?"

He shook his head, one corner of his mouth pulling back. It wasn't like Todd to be purposefully evasive. He had me fascinated.

"What was the occasion?"

He took a quick glance at the driver in the front seat of the limo and then back at me. "Work," he said with a slow blink.

Hmm, I thought as I watched him watching me. If it had been several years ago, his work wouldn't have been his surf shop. "So the New York firm you worked for sent you to Argentina? Why?"

"It was before grad school, Abby."

"Before that?" I said, thinking aloud. "But weren't you still in the Marines? What work were you—"

"I was sent to Buenos Aires to follow a terrorist back to Iraq and then shoot him through the heart at thirteen hundred feet."

I gaped.

Todd smiled. "And now," he said as my car door was being pulled open, "a little Hollywood pressure seems like nothing." He brushed his lapel. "I think we're on."

"Abigail! Abigail!" The crowd roared when Todd and I stepped out of the black stretch limo and onto the scarlet runner.

"Couldn't we just make out in the car all night instead?" I whispered to him. "I'll let you get to third base. Twice."

He chuckled and grabbed my hand. "After"

First we had to slowly pass by the seemingly never-ending wall of cameras. We smiled and waved, then Todd stepped back while I made a few thousand or so requested turns as cameras flashed. By the time we reached the first interview stop, I could tell where all eyes were focused. And they were not on me. Designer-ensconced women were a dime a dozen in this town. Elegant, sophisticated, debonair gentlemen, however—who made a tuxedo look like second skin—were a rare breed. Cary Grant, George Clooney, Todd Camford.

Standing next to Todd, I was secondary, which I graciously welcomed.

"Who are you wearing?" was our first question.

Shocker.

I offered up the necessary information, but I doubt anyone was listening.

"You must be *the* Todd Camford the whole entertainment world is buzzing about." She gleamed a toothy smile, shoving the mike under Todd's nose. Her imitation Chanel Number Five was gagging me.

"Yes, this is Todd," I answered for him, but she didn't even look my way.

"Your first time at this three-ring circus?" she asked him, nearly bubbling over with gusto.

"Yes, it is," Todd said with a modest, dignified air. The enchanting smile he gave her managed to make even *my* heart flutter.

The woman actually giggled. "That's a sharp-looking monkey suit," observed our friendly press hyena once she regained composure. "Who are *you* wearing?"

"An-gel-lee-no," Todd pronounced down into the mike, carefully articulating every syllable. I felt his open hand on the small of my back, delicate, overly cautious, and careful not to snag my dress. "He's that very prolific, esoteric Greek designer," Todd further explained.

"Ah, *yes*." Our interviewer beamed, somehow showing at least fifty front teeth. "*Love* him. He's absolutely *fabulous. Love* his fall line."

Almost like we'd planned it, Todd and I both tilted our heads and smiled at her, charmingly, artificially. Todd's fingers pressed into my back as tooth lady returned our simpering smiles. She was completely oblivious to the fact that Todd had invented said "prolific, esoteric Greek designer" on the fly.

"Nicely done," I whispered as Molly dragged us to the next interview station.

"You were right," he whispered back. "This is painfully brainless."

"Just keep smiling," I sing-songed through my teeth as we approached the interviewer.

"*Mwah! Mwah!*" Et cetera, et cetera.

We were offered the same compliments, asked the same questions, and Todd had a different answer for the origin of his tuxedo every time. By the end of our carpet walk, he had the makings of a bruise on his bicep from my pinching him to keep myself from laughing. That evening, while hanging off Todd's right arm, was the first occasion when I really did feel like we belonged in the spotlight. We totally killed that carpet.

Hal, Jord, and Yosh joined Todd and me at the last stop. The clicking of cameras sounded like hummingbirds as the five of us, arms around one another, posed for final pictures before we ducked into the venue.

The balance of the evening went pretty much as expected: unearned awards, lengthy speeches thanking everyone from Allah to "my dog who ran away when I was five," and the occasional drunken and inappropriate political protest. Lovely.

We sat three rows back, just left of center. It seemed like the television cameras swung to catch our reactions more times than necessary. I blamed the chiseled, Hollywood-like features of my dashing date for that.

The band and I were due backstage to prepare for our

award presentation after the act currently onstage was finished performing. The house lights were low, only a lone spotlight shining on center stage.

"My time soon," I whispered into Todd's ear. "I have to sneak out while the lights are down."

"I know," he replied, watching the singer onstage.

"You did really well tonight," I said then waited with anticipation as his handsome profile slowly turned to me.

"You, too," he said, lifting one eyebrow. "And you didn't trip once."

I groaned. "The night is still young."

A bright rainbow of colored lights illuminated the stage as a thin curtain peeled back. A full orchestra was dramatically revealed behind the solo performer. The music swelled, filling the concert hall with raw, electric energy. Todd's eyes moved back to the stage, engulfed in the moment. I was happy he was enjoying himself. I'd worried he would be bored.

Too soon, it was time for me to go. The house lights were dimmed and I made my move to slink past the two road blocks that were Todd's legs and out into the side aisle. As I took my first step, I fell across his lap. "Fire in the hole, Lieutenant," I hissed. "My shoe came off." He held me by the waist, and I bent in half. "I can't, ugh, reach . . . it."

While trying to ignore the snickering coming from the row behind us, I twisted and turned, bum un-elegantly in the air, trying to find my blasted heel. I could feel Todd shaking, attempting to control his laughter. Not helpful. "Oh, Abby," he snickered, "I like you."

"Shyeah," I mumbled, deadpan, as I slithered clear of his seat, one four-inch slingback in my hand. I grabbed Todd's shoulder as I slid on the shoe.

His sudden tight grip on my wrist startled me. He was holding me at his side, unyieldingly.

"What's wrong?" I asked, leaning down.

But he didn't speak; only a tiny smile sat on his lips. His fingers stroked my palm.

I tilted my head, wondering what was going on. Before I

could ask again, his smile suddenly changed—it swept up his face and into his eyes, radiance practically shooting out the tips of his hair. My heart pitter-pattered inside my chest just like it had that first day in Seaside.

"What is it?" I asked.

His only answer was a new smile, one I'd never seen before.

I touched his face, wishing I had the time to drop into his lap and make the world go away.

Todd's grip tightened as his mouth opened. "I . . ." he began, his eyes sparkling like gemstones in the darkness. Then his new smile shifted into the pulled-back grin I loved so much. "You look very beautiful tonight, if I hadn't mentioned it yet," he whispered, softly jiggling my hand inside his.

"Thanks," I replied, smoothing his tie. "So do you."

He lifted his chin, pointing behind me. "They're waiting for you." I turned my face just in time to see the three heads of the other members of Mustang Sally inconspicuously disappear behind the heavy red velvet curtain that obscured the exit behind me.

Todd halfway rose out of his seat as the arm that held my hand gently persuaded me toward the exit. "Knock 'em dead, Abby," he whispered.

chapter 22

"Twist and Shout"

"**S**hake your tail feather," Todd whispered impatiently. "Shugger and Molly are here."

I looked up from where I was lying on the rug, my bare feet up on the leather ottoman. For the past ten minutes, Hal and I had been conference-called into a morning radio program broadcasting out of Dallas. Even when we had no new album or concert to promote, we were still promoting.

"Time's up," Todd said, pointing to his watch.

"Thirty seconds," I mouthed.

"You need shoes."

"Which ones?" I asked, the phone away from my mouth.

"Irrelevant. Whatever you were wearing yesterday. Those . . . whatever . . . *strappy* things."

"Jimmy Choos?"

He looked at me blankly.

"Black alligator, with the silver straps." I pointed to a location under his couch.

Our first month in California was almost at an end. I was working fulltime, and Todd was doing his best to keep me on track, shouldering some of Molly's herculean task.

"Sally." The low, rumbling request made me lift my chin so I was looking at Shugger upside down, standing

in the open doorway. His enormous lips were pressed together with annoyance while the rest of his face showed no
emotion.

I immediately sat up and terminated my part of the call.
"Yes, I really have to go now. Hal will take it from here.
Byeee!" I tossed the phone on the couch. "Oh, hi there," I
said innocently, beaming up at my huge bodyguard.

A growl rumbled from deep inside his throat. His face remained humorless as he pointed one thick, accusing finger
at Todd.

"Hey man," Todd said, raising his hands like he was surrendering to the cops. "*You* try getting a woman off the phone."

Shugg growled again as we paraded past him out to the
car. He hated being late.

The limo pulled away from the curb. "Got the bags?" Molly
asked.

I looked at Todd, and he nodded.

"Bloody right of Max to put you up downtown tonight,"
she went on, tapping violently on her iPad. She was in a state.
"Although I don't know what the bloody use will be. He told
me it's to be an all-nighter at the studio for everyone, because of the string of your bleeding personal appearances
today."

"It's a nice gesture," I said, lowering sunglasses over my
eyes, "at least to *offer* us the Hotel Roosevelt." I looked at
Todd. He was staring out the window at the passing scenery.
One of his hands was at his chin and the other rested on the
seat between us, barely touching my leg.

He blinked slowly and breathed slowly, like he was truly
relaxed. The hand at his chin moved up and his fingers
ran through the side of his hair. It was uncharacteristically
mussed; dark strands poked up in back like a cowlick.

I drank him in, all the things I liked, all the things I loved,
all the things I wanted, suddenly wanted more than anything
else in the entire world.

Strange. Nothing new and nothing major, but something
about the way he looked right then caused a smoldering

volcano to erupt in my mid-region. With my next breath, that thick heat flowed up to my chest. I felt flushed and feverish as I looked down at my arms that were covered in goose bumps. The car rolled over a pothole. Our shoulders knocked, and I thought my pounding heart was about to beat right out of my chest.

It was right there and then, in the company of Molly and Shugger on our way into L.A. for a costume fitting, that my decision was made. It was time.

And I figured Todd should know about it, too, since it involved him.

Now, how shall I put this?

I reached over to Todd's arm. "I've always wanted to stay at the Roosevelt," I said to him.

Nice beginning, Abby. Subtle. My fingers ran light circles along the inside of his elbow, up his forearm, to just inside the sleeve of his shirt.

"Maybe," I said, my voice softer, "we'll get finished with work early enough tonight to check out the Gable and Lombard honeymoon suite."

He was still staring out the window, apparently needing another hint.

"I hear they sprinkle the king-size bed with rose petals. Did I ever tell you how much I love rose petals, Todd, and king-size beds?" My hand slid down to the curve of his elbow and squeezed.

Slowly, Todd turned from the window. His expression was puzzled at first as he focused on my face, probably trying to read my eyes behind the dark glasses.

I flipped them up to hold the front of my hair back, giving him a better look at me.

He blinked a few times once he was able to decode what my expression was screaming at him.

"Oh," he said. It almost looked like he gulped. "Is that so?"

I nodded once.

Grinning, he took my hand off his elbow, sandwiching it between his two hands. He was blushing a little, which made me feel even crazier for him. I leaned over and gave him a kiss, nuzzling my nose to his cheek afterwards.

"You might've waited to inform me of this till we were alone," he said quietly, still allowing me to cuddle.

"We *are* alone." Then I remembered that Molly and Shugger were sitting in the backseat with us, but I didn't move away. "This is as alone as we'll ever be in broad daylight."

Almost as an acceptance of this fact, Todd kissed me back. This was not his usual M.O., so I took full advantage of his lapse in judgment.

"*Ughh*."

My eyes fluttered open at the sound.

Across the short aisle from us, Molly's arms were crossed, a definite pout on her lips. "Geh a *room,* why don' 'cha?" she grumbled, letting her Eliza Doolittle slip out.

"That's the general idea, Molly," I replied.

Todd moved his face away from me and pressed his fingertips on my collarbone, forcing me back to my seat. "Control yourself," he implored in a whisper before turning his face away. Under his breath he added, "But only until tonight."

My heart jumped to my throat, the pit of my stomach burned, my arms and legs prickled and tingled—sensory-overload—while Todd's gaze was directed out the window as before, playing it cool.

A moment later, however, he burst out laughing. "Little Miss Subtle." He grinned at me, wrapping his arm around my shoulders, scooting me over.

A warning growl vibrated from the other side of the limo. "Err, ya'll'll be gettin' *two* rooms, Sally," Shugger snarled, narrowing his eyes. "Or I'll—"

"*Shugg*," Molly hissed. "Give it a rest already."

About a million hours later, after two interviews, three fittings, lunch with a reporter, and one stop at an inner city elementary school, the four of us arrived at Studio Universe—time for me to start my *real* job. After chatting with some record execs in the lobby, we stepped into the elevator.

Simultaneously, all of our cells started ringing. Molly answered hers but got no reception. The second the elevator doors opened, I knew something was wrong, and I could hear Max's voice from down the hall.

His back was to us when we entered the recording studio. As soon as he heard us come in, he turned around. "Our future *ex*–technical engineer has managed to crash the whole system," he said, pushing a hand through his dark hair.

I looked past his shoulder to find a pale-faced twenty-something guy with a phone plastered to the side of his head, frantically clicking a mouse while staring at a black, ominously blank computer screen.

Max glared down at the guy. "He *promises* it will be up and running by ten a.m. tomorrow." Then Max looked at me with an expression of tired frustration. "Nothing for you to do here, babe. I guess you're off until then."

"What?" I said, not so much because I hadn't heard him, but more because I couldn't *believe* what I heard. "I'm off?" I repeated slowly. "For sixteen hours?"

Max nodded and then turned his back to continue barking at the poor tech guy.

I shot a look at Todd; his eyes were wide, staring back at me. We were thinking the same thing.

"Sixteen hours," I whispered in a rush. "At the Roosevelt."

The gaze between us was electric.

Todd sprang into action. "I'll get the car keys—"

"I'll grab my purse."

We shot in opposite directions, not wanting to waste even a minute.

"Where's the . . . and my . . ."

"Your overnight bags are still in the limo," Molly said to me, answering my unfinished questions. "I'll have them sent over. You're already registered; just check in at the desk under Todd's name. And *you*," she grabbed my arm as I was about to rush by, "are the luckiest sucker I have ever met."

I looked past her at Todd, who was holding the elevator

door open with his foot, one enthusiastic hand beckoning me over. "Don't I know it," I said with a grin.

Molly let go of my arm. "See you tomorrow. Do *not* be late."

"I won't!" I called over my shoulder as I practically sprinted toward the waiting elevator. When I made it inside, Todd stepped back, and the doors sealed.

We stood side by side, looking straight ahead. I was breathing hard from my wind sprint, and my breath was the only sound as we began our descent.

After a second, Todd bumped his shoulder against mine.

"Hi," I said.

"Hi," he echoed, looking down at me. His green eyes held an excitement I'd never seen before. When I turned to him, I lost my breath for a whole new reason.

The next thing I knew, my back was pressed against the wall, the emergency phone digging into my spine. Who knows how far we would've gotten had the elevator not stopped a few floors down. We broke apart and were standing shoulder to shoulder again when the doors opened and some hipster doofus in a rumpled suit stepped in. Todd nodded a greeting at him and then straightened his shirt that I didn't even remember untucking.

I dropped my eyes, trying so hard not to laugh. I didn't let go of his hand until we reached my Mercedes in the underground parking lot.

"Please say you know a shortcut," I pleaded, fastening my seat belt, much too far away from him.

Todd revved the engine. "Hold on, baby."

I whooped as he pealed out.

Before I knew it, we made a right on North Highland Avenue, a left onto Hollywood Boulevard, and then that historic, glorious HOTEL ROOSEVELT sign came into view, all lit up like a beacon in neon pink.

Todd practically threw the car keys at the valet guy, not giving the ever-present paparazzi a chance to realize it was us before we were safely inside the lobby. The bleach-blond desk clerk smiled. Todd was about to toss her his entire wallet before he had the presence of mind to simply pull out his driver's license. One weird look when I explained that we had no luggage and two keycards later, we were on our way to the penthouse.

"Good thing this VIP elevator isn't glass," I gasped after Todd grabbed me around the waist.

"What elevator?" he murmured, burying his face in my neck.

My heart was pounding against his, when finally that blessed bell dinged and we hit the twelfth floor.

"The key," Todd whispered, breathing hard.

I gave him a puzzled look.

"Where is our room key, Abby?"

"You're holding it," I said, pointing to the torn and slightly bent paper envelope in his hand.

He exhaled a relieved chuckle.

I stood behind him, pressed against his back, while he attempted to insert the keycard. It took him three tries before the light turned green.

"Wait," he said, holding open the door for me. "Your bag isn't here yet. Is that okay?"

I smiled up at him. "What exactly will I need?"

In answer, he grabbed me in a hug, lifted me off my feet, and kicked the door shut behind us.

Todd stayed behind at the hotel the next morning, claiming that he wanted to take advantage of their gym and Olympic-sized pool, though he was sound asleep when I left at nine thirty. Still bathed in afterglow, it was nearly impossible for me to concentrate on anything while I drove back to the studio. I missed my exit twice.

Molly was standing outside the elevator when I stepped

off. "Max is waiting," she said, handing me a tall to-go cup of something steamy and lemony.

I flipped up my sunglasses. "Thanks," I said, taking a sip.

She grabbed my jacket and purse. "Band has been here an hour."

"I'm not late, am I?" I asked on our way to Max's office.

"No," Molly replied, "but you know Max. He thinks we're already way behind schedule because of last night."

I nodded and took another drink.

"Speaking of . . ." She let the sentence fade out.

"Yeah?"

She linked an arm through mine. "So?"

"So what?"

"*So.*" Molly yanked at my arm, impatiently. "In the rooms at the Roosevelt, do they really have solid gold flecks in the crown molding?"

"Molly." I sighed, glancing at her. "I swear under federal oath, I couldn't tell you what color carpet was on the floor. Or if there even *was* a floor."

Molly patted my arm. "Atta girl."

chapter 23

"I SHOULD HAVE KNOWN BETTER"

Molly was right. Things were pretty tense all day because of the time we had lost. But whenever my eyes met Todd's through the glass and he gave me the innocent grin that I now recognized as the complete opposite of innocent, I knew it had been worth it.

Almost everyone else was allowed to go home around two a.m. The few of us left scattered. Max disappeared into his office. Todd was going to drive back to Malibu; no reason for him to hang around and fall asleep in a chair. Nate left to ride down the elevator with him and grab something out of his car.

While all this activity was going on, I was promised a thirty-minute break to rest my eyes and voice until the other two were ready to continue recording.

The stiff vinyl couch in the kitchen wasn't exactly a king sized bed covered with rose petals, but it would do for a catnap. In all of ninety seconds, I lost consciousness. The low buzzing of the refrigerator was a perfect lullaby.

I had a nice dream for a change. I saw Todd's face, fuzzy at first, but then perfectly clear, which only pulled me deeper into my dream. I thought I was remembering parts of last night, but then the scene changed.

"Why don't you do something?" Todd was saying to me. His dream voice was hushed but earnest. *"You have to do something, before it's too late."*

My dream arms struggled to reach out, but a part of me knew they were pinned beneath my sleeping body.

"Try, Abby. You have to try harder. Now," dream Todd implored, *"because there's nothing I can do for you. This is all, and it's not enough."*

Then he simply floated away.

Bam!

My eyes flew open.

Something must have crashed somewhere down the long maze of hallways. Its echo made me catch my breath. I laid still and tense, listening. There were only murmurs now, low and stifled. Slowly I sat up and rubbed my eyes, thinking I must have dreamed the crash. The kitchen was dark except for the red-and-white Coke machine glowing in the far corner.

Slam!

I knew it was real that time, so I swung my legs off the couch and edged toward the door.

Murmurs reverberated through the dark, empty halls, coming at me from all directions. I neared the lighted control and recording rooms, and the murmurs became voices and then the voices became people.

"It's because of *me* these kids are as rich and famous as they are." I heard Max before I could see him as I paused at the open door.

"When were you going to tell them?" a demanding voice growled.

I froze when I realized it was Todd.

"When were you going to tell *her*? Tell her what you did."

I'd never heard Todd sound so angry before, or Max for that matter, especially at each other. Todd looked up to Max like we all kind of did. Only three days ago, the two of them went golfing while I had a photo shoot. Todd came back singing Max's praises.

What could have changed since then? What could have

changed since Todd left to ride down the elevator with Nate twenty minutes ago?

"That's not your concern." Max's growl made me jump.

I pressed my back against the wall by the door, afraid to even breathe.

"I promised Abby I would do anything to make her happy, but *this* is intolerable. After *this*, I will *not* look the other way."

"Don't tell me how to run my business, kid."

"Deceit comes second nature to you, Salinger—"

"This has nothing to do with you."

"She's the best thing that ever happened to your career."

"Every inch the means to an end."

All I could hear after that was a bunch of mumbling. I edged myself closer, straining to hear.

Max let out a sarcastic chuckle at whatever Todd had just said. "It actually worked out perfectly," Max continued. "Now if I can just find a way to make her less of a pain in the—"

"Shut your damn mouth," Todd snarled.

More mumbling.

I moved closer, but blood whooshed behind my ears, distorting every sound.

"It's because she trusts you," I heard Todd say, slightly calmer. "Completely. Even though you know she has no reason to trust you now. She needs *guidance* from you, not *criticism*."

"That's not my job, sport."

"She was getting stronger over the summer, and healthy. Now she's sick and stressed out again, and exhausted. She starves herself. I'm sure you've noticed that."

No reply.

"Do you even care?"

No reply.

"She deserves to know about this, about what really happened back then, so she can make her own decision. Are you going to tell her?"

Silence.

"Then I will."

"Go ahead." Max chuckled, sarcastically, dismissively. I knew the tone. "You're too late, but go ahead."

As I turned toward the door, I saw two shadows moving under the florescent lights. The larger was motionless, probably leaning against the wall. The other was pacing.

"I don't know what you think will happen," Max's voice said, more curbed this time, "but there's nothing you can do. Don't think I haven't planned for this; it's been years. You're not the first, you know. She'll never choose you over—"

"*Stronzo*!" Todd growled the Italian curse word and then continued swearing as he moved away. By his breathing, I knew he was struggling to get a grip before whatever he had to say next.

"Look, Max." In Todd's voice there was a pleading tone behind the calm. "I'm in love with this girl. Don't do this to her."

I gasped softly and stared at the shadow on the white wall across from me.

Todd had finally said it. I knew I should have felt something at the announcement, something wonderful and glorious and glowing. I should have burst through the door, pounced on him and declared, "I love you, too," but I stared at his shadow and felt only dread. I wondered why.

"Forget it, kid," Max snapped.

Ahh, yes. *That's* why.

"I'm going to marry her," Todd snapped back. It almost sounded like a threat.

All was quiet again. Too quiet. The taller shadow came off the wall, bending in the light, moving toward the other shadow.

"That will never, ever happen. I will not allow it. Do you understand?"

Todd's angry, measured voice growled back. "What're you gonna do about it?"

The other shadow moved forward now—there was about to be a head-on collision.

A sickening thought crossed my mind. I had witnessed Todd physically lose his temper before, nearly pulverizing an innocent punching bag. Despite the sheer material size of my manager, I was fairly sure Todd could have dismembered Max in a matter of minutes with nothing more than his military-trained bare hands.

Without another thought, I flung myself around the corner.

The two men were practically nose to nose. It was *Tombstone*, an old-fashioned showdown between the white hat and the black hat. But which was which?

"What's going on?" My voice shook as I stood in the doorway. Upon seeing me, both men stepped away from each other. "Hey," I looked at Todd. "What's wrong?"

He said nothing. His face was a mask of fury. I barely recognized him.

Max moved to the far side of the room, his head bent over the keyboard. He looked annoyed, but otherwise composed.

I folded my arms. "Will somebody say something?"

Max didn't so much as acknowledge my presence.

Todd's eyes flickered to me. In them was a mixture of weary and absolutely livid.

I took a step toward him. "Tell me, please," I whispered. "Why are you so . . ."

He shut his eyes, jaw clenching.

I was starting to feel genuinely panicked from the tense silence.

Finally Todd let out a sigh. "I need to leave here," he said tightly. "Now—" He broke off, his jaw still set. "I'll see you at home." He gave me one quick, narrow glance as he breezed by, leaving the studio.

I stood, baffled.

"Did you hear me? Come on, babe." The voice came from behind, though it seemed far away. It startled me, and I jumped. "I said, let's get back to work."

"What just happened?" My eyes stared into the empty space where Todd had disappeared behind the elevator doors. How long ago was that? It felt like hours. "What were you arguing about?"

"Hey!" Max barked.

I jumped again and whirled around.

His face was grave, a little frightening, and beads of perspiration dotted his hairline. "We've still got work to do tonight, babe. Stop wasting time."

My scrutiny slid off Max's face and down to the floor. I was replaying what he'd just said. Yes, I heard his words, but I couldn't comprehend their meanings.

"Are you just gonna stand there like an idiot?" he said.

I felt myself nodding faintly, confused.

Max's face slowly became less taut. He sighed, looking exasperated now. "You're not gonna be any good to me tonight, are you?"

I shook my head, understanding his words that time.

"Okay. Go, but I want you back here first thing—"

I didn't wait to hear any more.

"First thing!" He called after me when I grabbed my purse and dashed out the door.

chapter 24

"TICKET TO RIDE"

The stupid elevator was taking too long. I pressed and pressed the down button until the tip of my finger turned red.

"Come on," I hissed through gritted teeth. "Come *on*."

Finally a *ding* announced the elevator arrival. The doors opened. Todd wasn't inside, but I didn't really expect him to be. I couldn't push the lobby button fast enough. The mirrored doors closed and the car silently dropped without stopping until it hit the ground level.

The lobby was empty and dim except for the emergency track lights running along the walls. I flew to the main entrance, pushing open the two sets of heavy glass doors.

The hot night air hit me like a slap; the Santa Ana winds whisked through the palm trees, rustling the dark blue awning that tented the entrance. Even for a Sunday night, the sidewalks were packed. The night clubs were just closing up, kicking their patrons out after last call. Music from the bar next door bounced and echoed down the street, the ground pulsating under my feet.

I yelled for Todd, but even if he were still there, there was no way he could hear me. The line at the curb to catch a taxi was short. I'd probably just missed him. I pulled my cell from my bag, jabbing at speed dial number one. It rang once, straight to voice mail. I ended the call and then spun in a circle, not sure what to do next.

"You lost, sunshine?" A woman in a short black dress was leaning against the side of the building behind me, her fingers flicking ashes off the end of a long cigarette. "Are you alone?" she asked, fluffing the back of her curly red hair and then taking a long drag.

"No!" I gasped over the noise of the crowd. "I'm just looking for—"

"He went that a-way." Her red-tipped finger pointed up the street. She lifted her shoulders, smiled, and then pulled another drag. "Looked like he was in a hurry."

"Why did he . . ." I asked aloud, ignoring her. Then it occurred to me. "I need a car."

Without another thought, I swam my way through the bodies on the street, attempting to get to the parking lot behind the building. I heard a few people calling my name, fans recognizing me, but I kept stroking forward.

"Hey!" the woman in the black dress called out to me. I peered back while still moving ahead. "Maybe you should just let him go."

This comment made me hesitate for a second, half of my brain wanting to tell her that she had no idea what she was talking about, while the other half wondered if she was right.

When I was ten minutes from Malibu, he finally answered his cell.

"Hello, Abby." His voice sounded calm, which surprised me.

"Todd!" I gasped, insanely frantic. "Where are you?"

The line was silent, and then I heard him exhale. "I'm at my house. Would you please come here before you go home?"

"Of course. Are you okay?"

Again, he didn't answer right away. "I'll see you soon."

After crashing through the front door, I saw the top of his head. He was sitting in the middle of the couch, bent forward, elbows on his knees. Relieved at the serene picture, I blew an exhale out of my rounded lips and stepped into the living room.

As I passed the kitchen, the aroma of turkey bacon from the breakfast he had fried while I was on the phone with Dallas early that morning still lingered in the air. I approached him from behind and touched his shoulder.

"I'm sorry I lost my cool back there," he said. "Inexcusable. Again."

"Don't worry."

"Did he tell you why?" Todd's green eyes were unreadable as he watched me walk around to the front of the couch.

"He didn't tell me anything. I left right after you."

Todd looked away and sighed, running his thumb and fingers over his eyebrows. When I sat down beside him, he immediately stood and walked to the French doors. He unlatched the lock and opened both doors wide. The sky and ocean were black; the wind howled ominously in the darkness. He was standing with his back to me, raking his fingers through his hair and then rubbing the back of his neck.

"Do you have a headache?" I asked. "Can I get you something?"

He dropped his hand. "It'll pass."

The instant he turned around to me, I realized the calmness I *thought* I'd seen upon entering the room had actually been a façade. His arms were hanging at his sides, his hands curled into fists, his muscles pulled tight. Extreme stress covered every inch of his frame. I hated seeing him like that.

"What . . . ?" I began gingerly as I stood up from the couch, taking small, careful steps toward him. "What were you arguing about?"

His eyes narrowed, as if he were searching for some kind of answer on my face. "Different things," he replied vaguely.

"Like what?"

"I've been trying to decide how or *what—*" He stopped there. His eyes drifted from my face to the empty space beside me. Then his lips sealed together.

"Whatever it is," I said, placing myself directly in his line of vision, "I can handle it."

"Can you?" Something about his skeptical, almost cynical tone made my chest feel hollow.

"I'm a big girl," I assured him, forcing myself to stand a little straighter as proof.

But there was no smile on Todd's face. Instead, he paced one complete lap around the room before finally sitting down. "I need to ask you something. It's not an actual question, though." He looked up at me. When I didn't move, he patted the spot on the couch next to him.

I sat. "What is it?"

After a hesitation, he said, "I just need to know something, and please, be honest."

"Always." My voice cracked, for some reason.

He bent forward, like when I'd first come in, focusing on his hands. "Would you quit?" he said.

"Quit what?"

His eyes made their way up, looking straight ahead but not at me. "Singing," he clarified, his voice low. "Would you quit singing if I asked you to?" Finally he looked at me. I'd never seen this expression. Doubt, maybe? "Your career," he added.

I backed away an inch. "Why?"

"I just need to know."

"Todd, these last few weeks have been extra stressful, but ..."

"That's not—"

"It'll get better," I cut in.

He shook his head and looked down again.

"The record will be finished next month. We'll get a break then. Probably. And Max will—"

He lifted his gaze to me, his emerald eyes cold.

"Whatever you two were fighting about, I'm sure it will blow over." My voice was weak and shaky, totally unconvincing, even to myself. "Right?"

His eyes looked deep into mine, searching, as before. After a minute, he reached over and took my hand. It was the first time he had touched me all night. He squeezed my fingers, his skin so warm, reheating mine. I was beginning to feel calmer as his intense expression melted away.

"Thank you for answering honestly," he said a moment later. "It makes things easier." His lips were tight, but they bent at the edges into a flat smile.

I smiled back, a little unsure. "I'm sorry this is such a nightmare for you."

"It isn't really," he said.

I bumped his shoulder, trying to be playful. "You know I can't just *quit*," I said, exhaling a little laugh to lighten the mood.

Todd's eyebrows pulled together ever so slightly.

"It's not like I can wake up one morning and decide to hop on a plane and take a trip or whatever."

"I know," he agreed, "but I can."

"Oh." I blinked. "Well, yeah." I blinked again. Several times. "I guess you can." It hadn't escaped my notice how worn out he looked, how completely stressed.

A little vacation away from all of this madness might do him a world of good.

"Todd." I smiled, feeling relieved by the simple solution. "That's a great idea."

He sat back, looking surprised by my answer. "I'm glad you feel that way, because I'm leaving tonight."

My smile dropped, but I tried to remain calm as I gaped at Todd, who was staring intently at something on the rug between his feet.

"I totally get it that you need a break," I said after a moment, "but why right this second? Isn't that a little drastic?"

He didn't look at me.

"I mean, believe me, I know this is all psycho-insane if you're not used to it." I tried to laugh but couldn't quite get there. "I *have* to take it, but you don't."

When he looked at me, he still wasn't smiling, so I smiled for the both of us and went on, feigning support. What else could I do?

"I suppose I'll have to find *some* way to be the *cool, supportive* girlfriend, but just don't stay away too long. Okay?" I was growing nervous at his silence. "Say hi to Chandler for me, and Lindsey, and Steve, and, uhh, Sammy. And bring me back one of those tie-dyed shirts that came in last month. Oh, and a jar of red currant—"

I stopped cold, responding to Todd squeezing my hand like a vise grip. His jaw was clenched, his face pale. And then, just as he turned from me, his eyes snapped shut.

That was when I realized, much too late, that I was getting it all wrong.

"I'm sorry," was all I heard. I think he repeated it several times, but I couldn't be sure.

The next thing I knew, his hand had vanished from mine, and he was gone from the living room. The hot Santa Ana winds blew, knocking the French doors against the wall.

"Todd?" I exhaled, not really sure how long I'd been sitting there alone. I heard him in the bedroom. Stumbling through the doorway, I first noticed his half-packed suitcase lying open on the bed, dresser drawers ajar. I felt a wave of panic.

"You don't have to do this," I said toward the open closet. "You don't have to . . ." I choked out the next word, a little disbelievingly, "go."

"Yes, I do." Todd's even-toned voice came from deep inside his closet. He had already decided.

"Why?" I asked when he reappeared.

But he didn't answer.

"Is this because of Max?"

Todd's eyes flashed to mine and then back to his packing.

"Whatever you two were fighting about, tell me. I can fix it."

"No, you can't fix it, Abby, and I can't fix it, either. It's something I wish I didn't even *know*. Apparently, it doesn't matter. Just promise me that you'll stay close to the guys—Nate and

Hal especially. They're better friends than you realize. Molly, too. Promise me."

Incredulous, I shook my head. "What are you talking about?"

He bent over to close his suitcase, zipped the sides, and then straightened up. But his eyes didn't seem to be focused. "You're not a green kid who doesn't know anything," he went on, shoving items into the smaller pockets of his suitcase. "You know enough, and you need to take care of yourself, do the right thing. You need to *deal* with this mess of yours, because I can't do it for you, and I can't be here like this."

My brain couldn't move fast enough to decipher the string of orders shooting out of his mouth.

"You're not a puppet on a string." His voice was even louder. "So don't let Salinger—"

"Stop yelling at me, Todd. *Please!*"

He blinked and turned to look at me, at what must have been my baffled, terrified expression.

"Ah. You see? This is *exactly why*." He dropped his chin. "Since that night on the side of the highway, I promised myself I would never again lose my temper. But tonight." He looked up, his green eyes were thin and piercing, staring at something off to the side. "You have no idea what I wanted to do to him after what I found out."

"Found out *what*?" My heart pounded in my throat. "What happened?"

Ignoring my questions, he pushed his first suitcase onto the floor and then brought out his other empty one from the closet. He unzipped it and flipped the top open.

A second wave of panic struck. "Will you *please* stop packing for two seconds and *talk* to me?"

He stood very still and then looked up. He seemed confused—surprised even, that I was standing there.

He let out a little sigh and lifted a hand, inviting me to him.

I was there in three running steps.

His strong arms wrapped around my body, only they weren't as tight as I required at the moment. I would have gladly allowed him to squeeze the life out of me if that meant he wouldn't leave. I pressed the side of my face against his chest and pulled myself as tight to him as I could. His hands were moving over my back, my shoulders, in my hair. Then he kissed me, hard. His grip was rough and forceful, almost desperate, as he pulled me up off the floor. Raging and conflicting emotions stormed through me, making my muscles go tight, then weak. I fought back the urge to cry as I held onto him with everything I had.

I didn't want to breathe, didn't want to break the connection. But much too soon, his mouth pulled away. My feet touched ground, and his hands slid down my arms, stopping on my elbows.

I leaned in again, but he held me away.

His broken expression turned my stomach to liquid.

"I'm sorry it's happening like this," he whispered, not quite looking at me. He was breathing hard, but quietly, trying not to let it show.

My focus was glued to the beloved face before me that was rigid and surly with emotion. "Have you been miserable the whole time?" I asked, wretched at what the answer might be.

"I'm not leaving because I'm miserable."

"Then *why*?" I pleaded, panic making me shake.

Although his eyes were still pained, he smiled gently. "Honestly? You honestly don't know?"

I opened my mouth to reply but could only shake my head.

Todd didn't speak for a moment, either. For some reason, he was editing himself. I knew by his countenance that he was struggling with his words. I wanted to help him—to reach out, touch him, hold him, but he was standing a good three feet away now, his arms folded against his body. His nonverbal signal rang loud and clear: he wanted me to stay away.

"Abby, you are the most beautiful, amazing, alive person I've ever met. I feel so lucky to know you."

I sensed a "But" coming next, and I didn't think I could take it.

"But . . ."

I inhaled, but my lungs couldn't seem to find enough air.

"But," he repeated, "my being here isn't helping you. I see that now. You've got some things to take care of. Things I can't help you with. Things in the way."

I shook my head, hoping to rattle loose some understanding. "What things?"

Todd sighed and walked to the window. "I can't be in a relationship like this," he said, his hand rubbing the back of his neck as he looked out into the dark night. "There isn't room for three."

"Three?" I asked, even more confused. "Do you mean Max?"

Todd didn't reply, but his expression was confirmation enough.

"Are you serious?" I grabbed his arm. "Todd, I *swear*, there's never been anything between Max and me."

"That's not what I mean," he said, stepping back. "I don't like who you are when you're with him, Abby."

My stomach clamped; there was no arguing with that point.

"I can't sit back and watch the way he treats you. Not anymore."

"It's not . . . that bad."

"Yes, it is." His voice was firm. "It might seem okay to you, but it's not. And there're other things now."

I stared at him, waiting for him to complete the thought. When he didn't, my hands flew into the air. "So tell me."

He looked me in the eyes. "Don't trust him."

But that was it.

"Todd." I almost laughed. "You can't order me not to trust my manager but not tell me why."

He put a hand to his chest. "I'm asking you to trust me."

I could only stare at him, completely dumbfounded by his doubletalk.

Without another word, he walked back to the bed and zipped the last suitcase shut. The sound hit my spine like nails on a chalkboard, causing me to react in the worst possible way.

"So is this how it works with you? The first sign of trouble and you cut out?" My biting, irrational words spat out like poisoned darts. "Is this how it was with your old fiancée?"

He stopped zipping and faced me. "This is absolutely nothing like that," he replied, his jaw tight. "This is me, Abby, doing the only thing I can think of to not completely destroy the most important relationship of my life. Please let me do this."

We stood in silence, at a perfect impasse.

He was finished. Part of me knew to let him go, but just as he skirted past me on his way out of the bedroom, I remembered something. "I heard what you told Max," I uttered very quietly.

He stopped and turned back. "What did you hear?" The way his eyes didn't meet mine, but moved down and then from left to right made me wonder if he was searching his memory to recall the conversation.

I took a step toward him. "You said that you love me."

Todd sighed, and for some reason he looked extremely relieved by my answer. "Oh." He nodded. "Well, you knew that already, of course." His lips twitched, one corner beginning to turn into that lovely grin that always managed to turn my insides absolutely mushy. My heart thumped almost painfully, and the taste of our last kiss clung to my lips, so unfinished.

I took another step toward him, with more confidence this time, until I was standing only one arm's length away from him. "You also told him you're going to marry me."

I wasn't sure what I assumed his reaction would be, but what happened next was utterly unexpected.

Right before my eyes, Todd's countenance changed. The relieved expression he had been wearing only seconds earlier was swept away—blank at first, then replaced with something like . . . indifference. He squared his shoulders and leveled his chin, his eyes vacant yet determined.

I couldn't read his expression any longer. He was wearing his warrior face—the one that revealed absolutely nothing, the one that sometimes scared me.

I'd struck a nerve, without even meaning to.

He tried to move around me. "I have to go," he said, as if I hadn't spoken.

"Take me with you," I whispered in a panic.

He stood still and then turned to look me dead in the eyes. "No, Abby."

It was a sucker punch. My entire body flinched from it. But I pushed through the stunning pain. "Stay tonight." My begging voice trembled. I reached out and placed my hand on his stomach, grabbing a fistful of his shirt. "I need you. Please." I ignored the desperation in my tone as my other hand took a hold of him, wringing the front of his shirt between my hands, barely conscious that I was un-tucking it. My hands slid inside his shirt to his waistband. "Stay with me tonight. Stay."

"Abby." His voice shook. When his blank expression broke, it became the picture of anguish. "Abby . . . don't do this."

I knew he was fighting it, but I couldn't stop myself from sliding my hands around his middle. His bare skin was warm against mine, and I felt his core tremble at my touch. He whispered my name again, the same anguish behind the word.

When I reached up to kiss him, he grabbed me.

Once more, my feet came off the floor. I wrapped them around his back, hooking my ankles. My foot knocked against an open dresser drawer when Todd spun us around, taking us back into the bedroom. The next moment, gravity changed, and my head hit the pillows. I didn't even have time to breathe before his mouth was covering mine again, hot and sweet. Then he moved to my neck, my throat, searching and hungry. We moaned simultaneously. When he rolled us over, I felt his hands slide under my shirt, tracing up my spine, stopping right in the middle. He pressed his palms flat, burning all the way to my core.

I tried to speak his name, but was cut off by another fiery kiss. He rolled us again so we were on our sides. I took hold of the bottom of his shirt, wanting to tear it off just to get it out of my way. As it was about to clear the top of his chest, the kissing stopped.

His hands were no longer on my back, but they moved to each of my cheeks, holding my face back, away from him. "Abby." He was panting. "Stop."

I opened my eyes, stunned and confused.

"I'm leaving." There was a deep notch forming between his eyes. "If we do this now, you'll hate yourself." He swallowed and lowered his gaze. "And you'll hate me."

I couldn't speak, couldn't move.

The next moment, Todd was removing my hands from his body. "And I wouldn't be able to live with myself." When he rose to a sitting position, he pulled me up, too, tugging down the front of my shirt to cover what he had uncovered. I could see that his face was pained and embarrassed, but other than that, I couldn't seem to focus on anything.

"I'm leaving," he repeated, but it sounded more like he was trying to convince himself and not me.

Before I could collect my thoughts, he was on his feet, readjusting his own tangled clothing. "I'm sorry," the back of his head said, and then he disappeared through the door.

I slid to the edge of the bed, but I couldn't move any farther; it was like the room was going fuzzy around the edges, inching in to the center like a window frosting over in winter. I heard him close and latch the French doors. Some part of my brain realized I was in shock.

Take me with you, I repeated to myself.

You'll hate me, I heard in reply.

A staccato horn honked from outside. *Taxi*, I supposed, from somewhere inside my psyche.

I heard the front door open then close.

Another punch, over and over, trying to wake me up.

"Wait!" I called out, stumbling and then falling onto the floor.

chapter 25

"BABY'S IN BLACK"

"I'm staying here, okay?" Molly asked.

I must have shaken my head.

"Please, Abby." She sniffed. Her voice sounded watery. "Abby, please."

Blankly, numbly, I stared past her and into my front yard. The leaves were starting to turn—yellows, oranges, and reds before a crystal blue backdrop. Malibu was exceptionally cheerful in the late fall, under any other circumstances.

"I didn't mean to do it. You know I didn't." She sounded a little hysterical for some reason. "But . . . but I knew Max was about to go majorly mental on you, so I *tried*. I was trying to help!"

Puzzled, I moved my eyes back to her. Molly's expression was frantic and broken. Had something happened? I didn't know, because I couldn't think, couldn't remember. I didn't let myself.

"You know I would never do that to you. Ever. Except . . ." She lifted a hand, reaching out like she wanted to touch something on my cheek.

That was when I remembered what had happened earlier that day. She was right. I'd totally lost it, came unhinged. And in front of everyone. I moved my own hand up to my cheek, flinching in pain at the touch and the memory.

Molly flinched, too. "Abby. Abby, I'm so sorry."

I stood in front of her, not able to recall what I'd done to deserve the slap, although I was sure I had. Had I shrieked at someone? Punched an intern? Or simply checked out, walking dead? I did recall that afterward, everyone else in the control room had gone back to their tasks. Show's over. Nothing to see here. Molly had driven me home, though, and her eyes, when she finally managed to look at me, had been bloodshot—matching mine, probably.

It was settled then, I decided, as I stared past her at my wrought-iron gate. I would not allow myself to emote, especially at the expense of Molly, someone who was only trying to hold me together while watching me fall apart all over again. She had practically moved in with me after Christian died. This time, however, I was cognizant enough at least to *attempt* not to drag anyone else down. I didn't wish to have any witnesses for part two of my personal unraveling.

If memory served me correctly, the numbness would be along soon enough. I could wait for it. Throwing myself utterly into my job had worked before. I supposed I had *that* much to look forward to.

Molly was crying now, because she knew I couldn't cry, which is what friends do. I loved her for it, even though I couldn't express it. All I could do was push her away, tears streaming down her cheeks as she stepped backward off the porch and into the light October rain.

Because I am Abigail Kelly: superstar.

In the past few weeks, I had worked the red carpets, lost eight more pounds, met with Habitat for Humanity, recorded five of my older songs in Spanish, and shot a jeans ad for The Gap.

No arguing, no drama. Not a blip in the radar.

I was a marvelous faker, about as stable as a house of cards on a windy day.

Not until I got home at night, locked the door, and closed

the blinds did I choose to feel. Feeling was not my friend. Feeling brought pain. Pain brought memories. Memories brought more pain. I was stuck in the cycle of my own creation.

The danger that accompanied falling into a self-inflicted stupor—keeping everything subterranean—was that every once in a while the volatile fault lines would shift and expand, and then the quake would leave me straddling my own San Andreas Fault, one foot on either side. Which was probably why Molly had been forced to slap me out of whatever state I'd been in. As I heard her drive away, my shame was insurmountable. But shame had to wait its turn.

After Molly left, I sat on the floor in the middle of my living room and stared out the window at the darkening sky. This was a common routine, although more than once I caught myself staring at a wall or watching a candle flicker out, eyes burning from not blinking, waiting for the night to be over.

He'd called once, the day after he left. I hardly recognized his voice. He wanted to make sure I'd made it in to work. After that, my calls went straight to his voice mail. I stopped calling after two weeks. I stopped hoping after three.

Funny how one thing could set off another, and another—the irrepressible domino effect, reopening old, sloppily stitched-up wounds that never quite healed, everything I fought so maniacally to keep under control, to desperately squelch. All of those hungry monsters were crawling to the surface again, tearing out the stitches.

So it was back to the necessary separation of my life: peas not touching the meat, meat not touching the potatoes, potatoes not touching the salad.

Once again, fooling the world.

"I'm coming to town," Lindsey announced.

"When?"

"Next weekend. Just me. Steve's taking the boys to park

hop in Orlando." Lindsey made a gagging sound over the phone. "I hate Disney World."

"Mmm," I replied.

"So? How's it going?"

"Fine. Really busy. Lots going on. It's an exciting time."

I was getting pretty good at the twice-weekly phone calls from Florida. Lindsey's voice still reeked of skepticism but had thankfully lost its anxiety after a month. I started racking my brain for conversational topics when I knew she would be calling the next day.

My knees were bent and pressing into my chest as I sat wedged in the corner of my ivory couch. "Max thinks I should go blonder," I offered, as I absentmindedly began tugging and wrapping a hunk of hair around one finger. "He's thinking Marilyn Monroe meets Gwen Stefani. Might go well with the new record. It's got a retro Hollywood vibe to it."

"How does it sound?" Lindsey asked.

"Uhhh . . ." I had to think fast, because although I'd been singing those songs for two months, for the life of me, right then I couldn't remember a single track.

"It's no *Sergeant Pepper*," I finally said, "but it's good."

"I'm interested to hear it."

So am I . . .

I was relieved; my sister didn't seem to be in a particularly nosy mood that day. Those "other" conversations sucked the most. She seemed to be in the mood only for a chat. Molly had also stopped looking at me like I was in some kind of full body cast. It seemed like things were finally getting back to normal. If by normal you mean comically tragic.

"*People* mag did a cool spread on you this week," Lindsey said. "Two pages, and the pictures are nice. The article is about your philanthropy in New Orleans. I hope it's true." She laughed.

"Believe what you want," I replied. *You always do, anyway.* I cringed, not liking how snarky my thoughts had become. Lindsey didn't deserve it, but I couldn't help myself.

"Can I ask you something?" she said.

"Hmm."

"Why do you sing?"

"Because I suck at science."

My sarcasm had sharpened over the past few weeks, and my old chum, cynicism, was back with a flare. At least that was definitive proof that I was still alive.

"No," Lindsey said, without as much as a chuckle. She wasn't humoring me after all. So this wasn't a social call like I'd thought. My stomach felt tight and hollow. "I mean," she continued, "why do you sing for a living?"

"Beats tap dancing."

Her frustrated sigh was audible through the phone. I put a hand over my eyes, wishing I could hide my shame.

"Does it make you happy?"

"It used to—" I cut away, knowing I'd slipped up. When I had taken her call five minutes earlier, I had no intention of being open about anything. I was not about to get trapped into saying something I'd regret. Thus began my backpedaling. "Is there a reason you ask?" I said, my apathetic mask securely in place.

My sister didn't answer for a moment. I heard voices in the background. She was probably fussing with her boys or building an eighteen-layer cake or knitting a sweater with one hand or any of her other perfect Super Mommy tasks.

"I was just wondering," she continued. "You seem willing to give up a lot for it."

"Everybody has to make a living," I offered, unwilling to allow the conversation to go where she wanted it to. "I haven't won the lottery yet."

"Okay," Lindsey said after another sigh. "I can see you're not in the mood."

I didn't reply, eager to be off the phone. I had things to do, after all, like getting back to my busy hour of staring at the wall.

"But Abby, I want you to listen very carefully." Her voice was different, stronger, almost defiant, which worried me.

"As your older sister, I am permitted certain privileges, re-sponsibilities, and inalienable rights."

Uh-oh.

"And there are a few things I need to say to you."

I waited, blinking and flinching like I knew a line drive was about to rocket directly at me.

"Are you listening?"

I swallowed hard, disinclined to risk another sarcastic remark. "I'm listening, Lindsey," I replied, trying to hide the consternation in my voice. I continued looping the hair around my finger, tighter now. The painful pounding at the tip of my finger made the aching in the other parts of my body seem less noticeable.

Before I had time to lift up my mental baseball mitt, Lind-sey's line drive smacked me right in the face. "Abby, Christian was murdered, and you think that was your fault."

The new pain hit like a brain freeze. I couldn't breathe.

"You feel too ashamed to even *talk* to Mom and Dad about it," she went on. "And because of all your misdirected, gratuitous guilt, you put everyone else's needs before your own, because you're terrified of disappointing anyone, to the point of making yourself sick. You're petrified of the man who runs your career, and by some *crazy miracle,* someone good comes into your life who's willing—"

"Stop!" My voice echoed through the empty house like I was in a cave.

But I had no follow-up. I just needed her to stop.

"You lost him," Lindsey said in a small voice.

"I didn't *lose* anything, Lindsey. He *left* me. There's a very distinct difference."

Weird. I heard the words exiting my mouth, but I didn't know where they came from. Words, or even thoughts like those, had been hidden for weeks, stuffed back in some dark region in my mind—bright yellow caution tape blocking the entrance. Danger: Do Not Enter.

I felt embarrassed that my face was flaming red, even though no one was around to see it. I hadn't planned on this.

I wasn't prepared. For the most part, Lindsey had respected my unspoken decree of silence about this topic. Now here it was. Here *they* were. She managed to level five taboo accusations at me in one fell swoop.

"I just think," she said, "I think there are some things you need to take care of, and you need to do the right thing."

Her words set my teeth on edge, hearing his exact words from the night he left. My heart pounded in my ears. It was exhausting.

"Are you still assuming we—"

I cut her off. "Why did you just say that?" My voice sounded like a growl. I didn't mean for it to come out that way, but I couldn't control it.

"Say what?" my sister asked apologetically.

I didn't answer her.

"Talk to me."

"I don't know *why* you keep trying to get me to talk about things." My words came out in a rush. "It never helps. Don't you think I know I'm pathetic? Is that what you want to hear? Yes, he's gone forever, and it was inextricably *my fault*. Yes, I am wretched to my nucleuses about it every minute of every day." I was suddenly not sure which man I was talking about. My throat constricted, the familiar snake.

"Why does this keep happening to me?" It was a rhetorical question. I'm not even sure where it came from.

"Abby." Lindsey's voice surprised me, even though it sounded calm and patient. "I'm your sister, and I love you very much, but the choices you make . . ." She trailed off, like it should've been evident what she was leaving out. "This isn't like you. This isn't how you used to be. First, the way you're dealing with Christian, and now Todd."

My fingers grabbed and squeezed the front of my hair at the roots. A part of me knew what was about to fall out of my mouth. It was easier to comment on *his* name instead of the other. "He never gave me a reason that night," I said, leaning forward, attempting to quash the knot in my stomach. "Not one that made sense. He was pissed at Max, but so what? One minute he was telling Max he was going to marry me, and the next minute he was gone. Oh, but not before telling me that my life is a mess, and that he couldn't handle being with me anymore. Did you know *that*, Lindsey?"

"I know what you told me." She waited. "And I know what Todd told me."

My fist released its grip and I sat ramrod straight. "He talked to you about it?"

"After some major coercion on my part."

"You've seen him?"

"This is a small town."

The room around me felt like it was tilting to one side, like I was in a "fun house" purposely built on a hill. I hung onto the arm of the couch.

"What did he—"

"You're right," Lindsey cut in. "Todd did tell me your life is a mess, and he did tell me that he couldn't be with you anymore, not the way you are now, the way you let Max walk all over you."

I slammed my eyes shut, seeing bright white lightning behind my lids and then darkness.

Lindsey went on, determined to cause even more agony. "He's not stupid, Abby. Do you think he didn't notice your manic mood swings, how you're light and happy, and then you totally zone out into some dark funk at the drop of a hat? Do you think that's normal? You suppress everything, total denial, total self-indulgence. How do you think it made him feel when he saw you self-destructing like that? Do you think it was easy for him to watch you, knowing there was nothing he could do? Can you blame him for cutting out? He's got his stuff together. He's independent, ready to move his life to the next level, and he wanted you—"

"Stop it, Lindsey!" I shouted. "Just stop!"

What was I supposed to do with that information? There was no more space in my chopped-up brain. Didn't I already have enough ghosts?

"I'm not self-destructing," I argued feebly, once I could manage that much. "I'm—"

"Yes, you are," my sister interrupted without a beat. "Answer me this: are you sleeping?"

"No," I replied, indignantly. "But—"

"Are you eating?"

I didn't answer.

She went on. "Are you taking vitamins? Going for walks? Making time for yourself?" She paused. "You were doing those things last summer, getting better, and now—"

"I cannot have this conversation with you," I cut in. "I *won't*." My voice cracked. I knew how hopeless I sounded. "It doesn't matter. What's done is done. *Let It Be. Ob-la-di.* All's well the ends—"

"You forced him," Lindsey said, cutting off my lame string of clichés.

I scrubbed my eyes with the back of my hand, smearing mascara everywhere.

"You forced him to make an impossible decision. Do you think he *wanted* to leave? He was ready to change his world for you, but you couldn't do the same."

I dropped my face into my hand. Lindsey didn't speak. She was probably waiting for me to cry, but I couldn't cry. Crying meant that I was allowing myself to feel. It wasn't time to feel.

"I better go," I muttered before she circled back to that other name. "I have to work out. Dirk'll be here any minute." She tried to speak, but I cut her off. "Thanks for calling. I'll see you next week."

chapter 26

"NOWHERE MAN"

Hal was flipping through last month's *Rolling Stone*. His hair poked out from the bottom of a black baseball cap like blades of orange grass. Watching him was entertaining, a distraction. After my conversation with Lindsey the day before, I was in dire need of a stellar distraction.

I leaned my hip against the doorframe, observing as he periodically laughed at something he was reading, other times he literally snarled. When he started hissing profanities at the magazine, I knew he was about to slam it on the table.

"And so is your old *lady*." The magazine landed with a *bang*. "Stupid lowlife tone-deaf elitist."

"No need to break the furniture," I said from the open doorway of the kitchen.

Hal swiveled around. "Duchess!" His voice was loud enough that the whole Studio Universe probably heard him. He rose to his feet, opening his arms to me. Well, he opened one arm. The other was pinned to his chest in a blue sling, results of a skateboarding accident from a few days before.

Sling or no sling, Hal's hugs always felt good. He was thin as a rail, but he was cuddly. I allowed myself to enjoy the physical contact while trying hard not to breathe in too much of the secondhand smoke trapped in his shirt.

"I don't know why you read that stuff," I said. "It always ticks you off."

"Stupid reviewer's an effin' hack," he muttered, his eyes narrowing as they aimed like two laser beams at the magazine. "Rippin' on the Foo Fighters like that. Who *does* that?"

"You're such a tough guy," I teased.

Hal looked at me and tilted his head. "How ya doing?"

"Fine!" I lied. It was second nature now. "Never better!" I smiled, feeling like a jack-o-lantern: ghoulish, unnatural grin, insides entirely scooped out.

He still had his one good hand on my shoulder. His callused fingers found some skin and pinched.

"*Ouch*," I squeaked.

"What size are you these days?" he asked, pinching me again.

"Size four, soaking wet," I replied, knowing this was surely a lie, too. The skinny jeans I was wearing, that I'd bought just a month before, that had originally hugged my curves in all the right places, were hanging on me like a pair of hobo trousers.

"You're wasting away to nothing." His fingers went to tickle my waist, but the second after he touched me, his fingers froze, then recoiled.

I felt actual physical pain when I saw the shocked expression on Hal's usually carefree face. "Duchess?" He spoke cautiously. "You're skin and bones."

If I'd had anything in my system, I might've puked it out. "I've been working out a lot," I offered as I took a retreating step backward. "I've got a photo shoot next week. You know the camera adds ten pounds."

I turned from him, walked to the refrigerator, and opened the door. As I stared blankly at the contents, I racked my brain, trying to think of the last time I had eaten a proper meal. "Mmm, leftover Chinese." I leaned in to give the illusion that I was interested. "Is this Nate's?" I closed the door and pulled open the freezer.

Hal didn't reply, and when I turned around, the shock on

his face had calmed into worry. I recognized the merging of expressions—I'd seen it on Lindsey the day I showed up at her house back in June.

"Good thing I've got the glam squad," I said, turning back to the freezer, letting the arctic air waft around my face. "They can make even *me* look human on a day like today. Ha ha ha." My fingers clung around the handle. My face was starting to burn from the cold.

"Hey," Hal said from behind me.

I wasn't willing to turn around yet, to confront what was coming next. I was just so tired.

"Hey," Hal repeated, his voice closer than before. "I know I act kinda stupid some of the time."

I let loose an ironic chuckle that burned my throat on the way out.

"Okay, okay," he said after his own chuckle, "I know I act *really* stupid *all* the time, but . . ." His hand was on my shoulder. "We're *simpatico*, you and me. We're . . . connected."

Something in his voice made me close the freezer and turn around.

Hal's blue eyes were warm and kind, his mouth set in a compassionate frown. No anxiety and no pity. Hal had grown up.

Sometimes I forgot. I'd forgotten he was really a man, a whole year older than me, in fact. Despite his leaning toward annoying the crap out of me, he had always cared. I knew I owed him so much. So much more than I was giving him now. I winced inwardly, feeling a fresh wave of guilt.

"I'm your friend," he went on, his hand on my shoulder, "and I can listen. Maybe I can even help. And, you know . . ." He looked down, smiling to himself. "Well, I'm sure you know how I've always felt—"

"I just need to sleep," I interrupted smoothly, rudely, offering this as a legitimate excuse.

Hal dropped his hand and stared at me.

I quickly added, "But you know how it goes. There's no sleep in this business if you want to make it big." My cheeks hurt as I lifted another jack-o-lantern grin. I immediately felt ridiculous. Hal was only trying to help. There was no excuse to belittle his sentiments because I couldn't stand to feel any real emotion.

I hung my head, staring at my feet, ashamed on so many levels.

After this, I knew Hal wouldn't stick around. He would sense that I was not about to budge an inch, that the brick wall guarding the fortress was well intact. He would tiptoe out the door, careful that his feet didn't crunch the layer of eggshells that followed me around. He would leave me alone to wallow, just as everyone else had learned to do.

But instead, Hal laughed his normal, wonderful, infectious laugh, his head thrown back, his mouth wide open.

"Hoo hoo ha ha, duchess!" he howled. "Big?" He hooted again. "You wanna be big?"

I stared at him.

"Have you been living in a friggin' cave? We already *are* big." He punched my bicep. I stumbled back. "We're bigger than anyone!"

"That's . . . what we wanted," I said, rubbing my arm. "Right?"

Hal laughed a minute longer and then pushed out his bottom lip and shook his head. "We three guys, we got what we wanted a long time ago. We got to play the Super Bowl." His smile widened. "That's as big as it gets for punks like us."

"I'm glad for you," I replied sincerely.

Hal said nothing, just watched me in silence.

After a few moments, I felt the itch to flee. So I made a move toward the exit.

"But what we *didn't* know was that we'd get big at *your* expense, Abigail."

Hearing Hal call me by my real name stopped me in my tracks. A lump formed in my throat as I turned around.

"From day one," he continued, leaning on a corner of the kitchen table, "we knew this business was no place for a nice girl like you, someone who actually feels things and has principles." He smiled. "But you're just so effin' talented, and instead of finishing college or having babies, you've let us ride your star for all these years." His smile suddenly dropped, like he was thinking of something else. "I can speak for the rest of the guys and say how sorry we are. Very sorry, about so many things." His gazed dropped to his shuffling feet. He looked more remorseful than I'd ever seen him.

"What so many things?" I asked.

Hal lifted his chin. His face had gone a little pale, but his cheeks were red. He actually looked embarrassed about something. I'd never seen that expression on him, either, but a quick moment later, he shot me one of his easy grins. "For one thing, we all liked the guy. We were hoping he was your ticket outta here."

Oh no. Not Hal, too.

Hal walked toward me. I stood frozen in place, wishing I could jump out the window before he said anything more. "Hal—"

"He thought you hung the moon, Abby." His good hand reached out and held onto the back of my neck, squeezing me. "Just seeing him around here, the two of you together, sometimes it made me a little jealous. Stupid, I know." He looked away to chuckle at something private. "And you . . ."

I blinked when our foreheads touched.

"When he was here, I'd never seen anything like it. You sparkled. You went from stately little duchess to delirious swan princess whenever you looked at him, whenever he walked in the room. The look in your eyes, and in his eyes, it was like you were both hearing the same song."

"I forgot how poetic you can be," I said, even as all his sympathetic words bounced off my chest like bullets to Superman.

Hal let go of my neck, and I took a step back.

"He wanted to marry you."

I bit down on the inside of my cheeks and looked away.

"He told me," Hal pressed, as if I didn't believe him. "He told me the second he knew you were ready, he was dragging your butt away from this crapola. We were all sitting around waiting for it."

I took another retreating step as hot blood throbbed and pounded through the artery in my neck. It felt like my whole head was on fire. I wrapped my arms around my middle, breathing slowly, fighting, fighting, consciously trying *not* to give myself a brain aneurysm.

"Then *poof!* He was gone." Hal paused, perhaps waiting for me to reply, but I had gotten so used to letting people talk. So I stood tongue-tied, hugging myself so tightly that my ribs bowed.

"He's a great guy, Abby. He was good for you. I don't know; maybe the timing wasn't right."

"I couldn't find a better man to get dumped by? Is that what you're saying?"

Hal's eyebrows bent. "Sometimes," he muttered quietly, "I just don't get you."

But I barely heard him. My mind had drifted away. I was picturing a man standing in a doorway, the last time I had seen him. That picture was only one of the images I carried around with me, jabbing at my insides like a prickly cactus. I swallowed this every day, over and over, knowing full well that I was slashing away at my soul.

The man I was picturing was only part of the pain. My brain understood this. I knew I was not well, but I also felt trapped. I was like a functioning alcoholic terrified of rehab. Part of me knew I wasn't miraculously going to be happy when this record was finished, or at the end of that tour, or when I bought my next flashy car. That same part of me knew that if I wanted to be fixed, I had to do it myself and stop waiting.

Another part of me, though, couldn't do it, couldn't face it. Because I was weak.

My attention was pulled back when Hal snapped his head to the side, glancing toward the open doorway. We both heard the sound of Max summoning us back to work.

As I turned to leave, Hal's one good hand grabbed me by the arm. "Listen, you knucklehead." He hissed the words in a soft rush. "Do *not* let Max the Tool scare you or push you around. You hear me? He's always done it to us, but don't let him do it to you—not anymore. You're better than this; you're *bigger* than this." He squeezed my arm, hard. It brought tears to my eyes and a yelp to my throat. "I know you think you can't deal with all the crap that's happened, and with your bro, but you can. I know you can." He squeezed me again.

A silent sob hung in my chest.

"You can do it, Abby. But just do it already, okay, kid?"

His kind yet stern eyes held me a moment longer. I could almost feel his positive energy sizzling through the air, working its way to me. I craved it, badly, but he let go of my arm, grinned, and strolled toward the door.

"You just say the word, duchess." His voice was cheerful again. "And I'll call in the cavalry."

As I stared after him, stifling that sob, I knew it was not the cavalry I needed. But what I did need scared the beejee-bees out of me.

The curtain in the entryway pulled back an inch, then I heard locks and deadbolts being released. Just as the door was opening, my insides liquefied. I suddenly wondered if my decision was a terrible, terrible mistake—showing up here in the middle of the night, unannounced. Perhaps unwanted.

Perhaps unwanted . . .

But the second I saw the face before me, I knew, down to my toes, that I had finally made the right decision.

"Abby?" came the voice I couldn't stop thinking about.

And then my heart, even after so much time, started tapping in my chest.

chapter 27

"FIXING A HOLE"

"What are you—"

That was all I heard. Her arms reached out, and the next thing I knew, she was hugging me. She smelled just the way I remembered, just like she always smelled, like baked goods and Mary Kay face moisturizer. My arms were weak and heavy, but I lifted them to hug her back, linking my fingers behind her.

"Hi, Mom," I whispered, my voice thick.

She squeezed me tighter, and I released a slow, deep exhale, trying to drive out the stale, poisonous air that had been trapped in my body far too long.

"Oh, honey," she said, over and over.

I could tell she was crying. I sucked in my lips, biting down hard, squeezing my eyelids together to keep it all in.

When she finally released me and I could see her more clearly under the Tiffany porch light, I was blown away. Even at one in the morning in her pink nightgown and slippers, the woman was gorgeous, classy. She was Lauren Bacall, frozen in time.

"I'm sorry it's so late."

"Oh." She shook her head, dusting tears off her cheekbones

with the back of a finger. "Nonsense." We stood for a moment, awkward. "Come in."

I crossed through the threshold of the house where I had grown up.

As soon as the front door shut behind us, she was calling up the stairs to my father. I heard some rustling and a screech that sounded like he'd stepped on the cat's tail.

"What is it, Kathleen?" he said. He lumbered down the stairs, rubbing one eye with a fist.

Swallowing hard, I stared toward my dad, worry and guilt coming back. After all this time, after what I had done, the damage I'd inflicted on our family, I had no idea what his reaction would be. Dad had adored Christian, his only son. They had a special bond no one else understood, and I took it away. I swallowed again, bracing myself for the worst, resigned to face the blame in person.

Upon seeing me, Dad froze in mid-step, squinted, and protruded his neck to take a better look without his glasses.

I held my breath.

"Oh my goodness," Dad finally said. His handsome and round, sleepy face turned red, and his hazel eyes glassed over with moisture. "Oh my goodness," he repeated, almost inaudibly this time, because his bottom lip was quivering. "Oh, my baby."

"Daddy!" I croaked.

And finally I broke down crying.

"Wonderful . . . wonderful!" was all I could understand as he swept me into him, holding me—I'd almost call it smothering, but his embrace was too safe, too completely welcomed to be called anything but Home.

I felt my face contorting hideously in the way faces hideously contort while engaged in hysterical sobs. I pressed my wet cheek against Dad's shoulder. Both of our bodies shook as we blubbered in unison. Then another voice joined in, and our soggy duet became a trio, Mom bawling right along with us, her arms wrapping around, holding us together.

And somehow, I felt a miniscule, yet very real, un-clenching of my heart.

♪

"More bacon, sweets?"

"Mmm!" I replied, pushing my plate toward my mother, still chewing. "More pancakes, too, please."

"How did you sleep?"

"Like a log. I love that bed."

"George, turn down that racket," Mom called to my dad a couple rooms over. After his breakfast, he'd set out to install a new system of Bose speakers in his study. She looked down, shaking her head with a knowing smile. Dad wasn't the greatest at reading directions.

After taking a deep drink of orange juice, I leaned back in my chair, my gaze moving around the kitchen. "I love the new wallpaper in here," I offered. "You always wanted gold flowers. When did you do this?"

"Oh," Mom replied, pouring a swirl of pancake batter on the sizzling griddle, "about a year and a half ago."

I held my breath while doing the mental math. My eyes burned with more tears as I pushed the last bite around my plate.

A few weeks ago, Molly had asked me if I wanted to visit Dr. Robert to get back on the happy pills. I didn't want pills, though. I ditched my Zoloft the third day I was in Florida. It was like I hadn't needed them anymore, like I'd been cured, even though I had been far from it. Maybe last summer had been nothing but a bandage and not what I really needed to fix my gaping wound of denial.

I quickly glanced at my mother, then down at my plate. "Mom? I'm sorry it's been so long."

"We're just glad you're home," she said. "We've missed you."

"It's only been a little over a year," I offered, feeling my cheeks burn. I stared down at my plate.

"We've missed you for much longer than that."

"I know." I crossed my legs under the table, my top foot twitching. "I've been, uhh, busy."

"I know." Mom smiled. "Oh, your phone was making all kinds of obscene noises earlier this morning." She gestured to my charging cell on the counter.

I grabbed it and read its face. "Molly," I said, looking at my list of missed calls and messages.

"Nothing important, I hope." Mom sounded nervous. We both knew I might be summoned back to L.A. at a moment's notice.

"Probably not. She sent an e-mail. She usually sends a couple a day, just touching base."

"What did she say?"

I read through the message, to myself first, just in case there was anything inappropriate for a mother's ears.

I hate when my brain doesn't work, which is most of the time. When I'm not doing, you know, work stuff for you, ppl think I'm shy, but it's just that I can't spew out everything my mind thinks bc 1) ppl will think I'm an idiot, and 2) I don't want to get funny looks. Or maybe that goes w/ ppl thinking I'm an idiot. And then when I do say something, ppl are like, "Wow, you talked." Bloody ppl. Hope you're having a great time with your 'rents.

Safe enough, so I read it aloud.

"She's a good friend," Mom surmised.

"The best."

Molly was the best, the way she took care of my disaster of a life so selflessly. Yes, she was my employee, but we were friends, the best of friends. I knew my pain had been her pain.

"Have you spoken to Lindsey lately?" Mom asked.

Absentmindedly, I started straightening my utensils at the sides of my plate. "She calls every week. She came to visit while Steve took the boys to Orlando."

"That's right. She mentioned that." Mom stared down at the sizzling griddle. "It was probably a good thing."

"Probably," I agreed, lifting up my juice glass and wiping the bottom with a gold-and-orange cloth napkin. "Although I was so busy. Max didn't—"

"No, honey," Mom interrupted. "I mean it was probably a good thing for *her* to take a vacation."

"Why?" I asked, then took another sip of juice.

"Well, you know, with all that mess last spring."

I set down my glass. "What do you mean?"

My mother looked at me. Her lips were parted and the confused expression in her eyes gave away the fact that she assumed I was privy to information that I wasn't.

I dropped my palms on the table. "What's going on with Lindsey, Mom?" I asked, feeling a panicky tickle in my stomach. "Is she sick? Are the boys hurt?"

"No, no, it's nothing like that." She paused to flip the pancakes. They looked perfect: golden brown, just like the perfect pancakes Lindsey had made for me over the summer. But pretty much everything Lindsey did was perfect. "Well, I thought you already knew," Mom finally admitted. "I assumed she told you about it over the summer."

"Told me *what*?" The panic in my stomach was now crawling up my throat like spiders.

"It was complicated, you know. She and Steve were having problems."

"What?" The word came out in a croak.

"It's all fine now," she said, waving her hand dismissively and then running it through her hair. "And it has been for more than seven months. When she moved out for a while—"

"Wait a minute." I cut her off, standing up from the table, the chair behind me nearly toppling backward. "Are you telling me that Lindsey left Steve?"

The lines on Mom's face were still and blank, but I could see her eyes, and she didn't have to say another word. The confirmation was there.

I let out a moan of confusion. "Uh, when? For how long?" I asked, slumping into my chair.

"Over a year ago. It was after your brother died, and ..." She let her voice fade out. "You were out on tour. In Amsterdam, I believe. Didn't she go see you there?"

"Yes, but . . ." I stared down. The pancakes, bacon, and orange juice were churning in my stomach like a runaway blender. "But ... " I shook my head. "I was with her all summer, living in her house. Why didn't she tell me about it? Why did she leave her family? Her ... *children*?"

"I really don't know the specifics, but the way she put it afterward . . ." Mom flipped the pancakes onto a plate and turned off the griddle. "She said she was feeling selfish and discouraged." She took the empty mixing bowl to the sink and rinsed it under the water.

"Discouraged about what?" I asked, my eyes narrowing into a baffled squint.

"About her marriage, being a good wife to Steve, being a good mother."

"Mom, that's crazy. Lindsey is the best mother ever. She's Martha Stewart and Florence Nightingale in the body of a Victoria's Secret model."

My mother turned to me. "That's an unrealistic combination." Her next words came slowly and methodically. "No person like that exists."

"But," I began, still feeling blindsided, "she's always seemed so satisfied and together, like her life is totally . . . perfect." I mumbled the last word.

"No one's life is perfect, Abigail," my mother offered as she loaded breakfast dishes into the dishwasher. "Your sister was very lucky the situation turned out the way it did." She paused thoughtfully then returned to the breakfast bar. "And I think with what she and Steve learned from the separation, their relationship is even stronger now. She's much more content, genuinely happy."

My mother placed two fluffy pancakes on my plate then pushed it across the table to me.

I stared down at them. No appetite. "Why didn't Lindsey tell me?" I wondered aloud as. my hands gripped the edge of the table. "Why, when she was going through such a devastating time in her life, didn't she confide in me, her own sister?"

Mom leaned against the counter, watching me in silence.

"Why didn't she tell what was happening and how she was feeling? Maybe I could've helped. At the very least I could've listened. She should have talked to me."

That was when reality hit like a ton of bricks. Lindsey hadn't shared with me, just like I hadn't shared with her. Last year, I'd chosen to slip into an emotional coma to deal with our brother's death, while my sister's solution burned her out, trying to make everything perfect, and then giving up. We both failed, hurting those we love along the way, without meaning to, without realizing it at the time.

My chin dropped to my chest. Tears for my sister, whom I loved more than my own life, gushed from my eyes like a deluge. I cupped my face, sobbing over my uneaten seconds.

"Mom?" I choked out. When I looked at her, at her face, I saw what the last year and a half had done to her. After Christian died, I'd cut my parents out of my life because I had been too selfish to think of anything but my own guilt. Making it, in a way, as if they'd lost two children.

"Mom?" I repeated. It was a cry for help that time.

In an instant, she was in the chair next to me.

"I'm sorry, Mom," I sobbed. "I'm sorry I cut out like that. It was terrible, selfish. I'm so sorry!"

"Oh, honey." Mom's voice was soothing. "I know, I know. We each fell apart in our own ways." Her long, slender fingers curled around my wrist. "But it's going to be okay." I could smell her scented hand lotion.

"We're going to stick together from now on. Aren't we?"

My tears were still flowing, but I also nodded.

"And I think," Mom continued as she scooted her chair closer, "after all we've gone through, each of us will be stronger, ready to handle choices in the future. You think?"

When I couldn't answer, her fingers found my face between my hands. She gently lifted my chin like I was a little girl again. "This life is a learning process, my precious, most precious Abigail. And the trick is . . ." She paused, tiny teardrops clinging to the corners of her blue eyes. "The most important thing . . . is to love each other, and ourselves, and find what makes us truly happy."

I sniffled and nodded, wanting all of those more than anything.

"Maybe that's music for you," she added, "or maybe not." She smiled as a single tear trickled down her cheek. "But once you find your happiness, don't let it go."

chapter 28

"SHE'S LEAVING HOME"

"How's the old salt mine? Another day another dollar?"

I couldn't help laughing at how my father always treated my career like any other. His same questions might have been asked of a lawyer or a waitress. I curled my feet underneath me, sinking deeper into the comfy leather armchair.

"Busy," I said, offering him my flat, routine answer.

Dad glanced up from the foldout instruction booklet he was reading and eyed me.

"Well, honestly, it's been pretty miserable the past few months." I offered a weak chuckle, like the misery was simply par for the course. "I practically had to sign my name in blood to come see you for twenty-four hours on a weekend."

My father's study had looked the same since I was a kid. He'd designed the room himself when he and Mom built the house. He loved the dark, wooden paneling of all four walls, the plush, coffee-colored carpeting, with the rich mahogany and leather furniture. We all referred to his room as "the cave," because it got so dark and spooky with the heavy brown curtains pulled over the windows, blocking out the relentless Arizona sun, even now, in late October.

I took a sip from the warm mug of chamomile tea I was cradling between my hands and watched my dad working to install his new speakers.

"Do you need some help?" I asked, knowing full well that my involvement would inevitably make matters worse.

"I'll get it," Dad insisted as he carefully dumped the contents of a white box onto his desk. "Your uncle Richard promised these are the simplest things to mount." Methodically he sifted through a pile of plugs and wires. "Aha!" he exclaimed. "*This* goes *here*."

Despite his crippling inability to read a roadmap, Dad was sharp as a tack, and it wasn't long before he was adjusting the volume on his new sound system. I was very proud of my father. He worked so hard to provide a comfortable life for his family. A few years ago, when I got the first of my really big paychecks, I offered to buy my parents a new house in Los Angeles so they could be closer to Christian and me. I wondered why, at the time, but neither of them was interested. Dad claimed he was much too young to retire from his marketing agency, and Mom had her little group of lady friends, plus her job at the museum.

But as I sat there, sinking deeper and deeper into the cozy armchair in "the cave," smelling meatloaf baking in the oven, seeing the framed family portrait from ten years ago hanging on the wall behind Dad's desk, I perfectly understood why they never desired to leave the comfort and warmth of home for some fancy dwelling in Orange County.

And suddenly, my life under its current regime felt horribly irrelevant.

"Wait," I requested, leaning forward, "go back to that last one."

Dad turned to me with a smile. "You know Sinatra?" He pushed the button to skip back a track on the CD he was scanning through. "When did this transformation take place? I thought you were solely interested in that Charlie McCarthy kid and his Slug Bugs."

I forced a polite laugh at the old family joke at my expense. "It's *Paul McCartney*, Dad," I corrected warmly. "The *Beatles*? Ever heard of them?"

Dad chuckled and adjusted the volume of the music spilling through his new speakers. I rested my head against the back of the chair, closed my eyes, and listened. The song had become familiar to me the previous summer, and it was painting a picture in my head, allowing memories to roll out like a movie.

After a while, the nerve endings in my face informed my brain that I was smiling, although I couldn't believe such a thing was remotely possible, given the circumstances—the circumstances of my listening to the favorite song of a person I was attempting not to think about every two seconds.

Deal with it, Abby. Deal. Deal. Deal . . .

"He first recorded this in nineteen forty-nine," I said as I opened my eyes.

My father was leaning back in his chair, his feet propped up on his desk.

"Then again when he was in his sixties. Of course, the vocals are superior in the early version, but I prefer the later cut. He'd lived longer, and the lyrics meant more then. He was emoting."

"Spoken like a true Sinatraphyte." Dad smiled. "I'm impressed." He took a sip from his own steaming mug. "Surprised, but impressed. Where did this new appreciation come from?"

I shrugged evasively, nervous and a little reluctant to dive into the subject. Dad was watching me, however, waiting for an answer to the simple question.

"For four months I hung around someone who worships the Rat Pack," I said, willing my croaky voice to sound noncroaky. "I guess some of it rubbed off."

Dad didn't miss a beat. "Linz told us about him."

My heart started to thud, but Dad's kind eyes were gazing at me from across the room.

"Todd," he said, as if he were speaking any other name. "Right?"

I felt myself nod. Then I let the words slide off my tongue with zero obstruction. "Todd Camford." Speaking his name aloud made something inside me tickle, just like that June morning before I'd pedaled Lindsey's big, stupid bike into Seaside. "Sinatra's his favorite," I added a moment later, my voice hopelessly thick. "Dino," I said, clearing my throat, "post–Jerry Lewis runs a close second."

"He has excellent taste," Dad confirmed. "Care to tell me what happened back in September?"

Wow. Not even a preamble.

I exhaled, my gaze leaving him to study the texture of the brown curtains. They were moving a little from an over-head vent, making them look like a fountain of cascading dark chocolate. "I'm still not sure," I admitted, shifting in my seat. "He and Max had this major blow out one night, and then he left. Something happened that made him stop loving me."

I coughed and my hands suddenly felt freezing cold, even though they were curled around a warm mug.

"That's not the story I heard."

I looked at Dad, feeling my face scrunch in confusion.

"Lindsey." He lifted an eyebrow. "You know how she likes to talk. She made it sound like you chose your career over him." He took a drink from his cup. "Didn't sound like he stopped loving you at all. Sounds like he left *because* he loves you, but he couldn't help you. Was that it?"

"Lindsey's worse than a paparazzo," I muttered, but I couldn't stop myself from crawling way back into the part of my brain behind the yellow caution tape, pulling forward more memories. I shivered. My whole body ached like I had the flu.

"The press sure loved him," my father's chipper voice went on, pulling me away from my thoughts.

My skin felt so cold that I didn't realize my palms were sweating. The mug slipped between my hands.

"Your mother and I read more about *him* than about *you* a few months back. They say he's from Portugal. Is that accurate?"

I took a deep breath and faced him. "He's American, Dad. I warned you never to believe what's printed in that trash. And since when do you and Mom read the tabloids?"

"We've always kept tabs on you. Of course, we've had to work harder at it without your brother."

After he said this, I waited to see his expected reaction, but there wasn't one glint of blame or judgment behind his light eyes, which surprised me.

"He kept us up to date on everything. Where you were, where you'd be, when you'd be on television. He was our personal Abigail Kelly PR machine." His tender expression never wavered. His eyes moved up to the ceiling and then to the old family portrait behind his desk. "He sure loved his time with you."

My throat was closing up, that old strangling serpent. "You don't have to say that, Dad," I whispered, as another feeling quickly moved in. I recognized that the Niagara Falls of tears was coming. "Christian," I managed to choke out, "should've stayed at his job instead of dropping his career, his law degree, his *entire life* to ride around in some lame tour bus with me so I wouldn't be lonely." I exhaled, forcing out all the air from my lungs. "He'd probably be a partner by now, and maybe married with a family of his own."

I closed my eyes, pinching back the oncoming torrent, one last vain attempt at false bravado. When I opened them a moment later, my father was shaking his head.

"Your brother didn't give up anything, Abby. He absolutely loved it; he was so proud of you. He told us so, every time we spoke."

My trembling fingers curled tighter around the mug in my hands, its cloudy liquid splashing over the rim and onto my jeans.

"Dad." I inhaled with a gasp. "I'm so sorry for what happened. I'm so sorry I took Christian." I hung my head, finally saying to him what I needed to say. Burning tears seeped through my pinched eyelids.

"Oh, honey." I heard Dad stand up from his chair and walk around the desk to me. "We're all sorry. We all miss him. It was the worst kind of tragedy a parent could imagine." He sat on the arm of my chair. "But not for a minute, not for a split second, did we ever, *ever* blame you."

I felt his hand on my shoulder. He held it there for a moment and then softly shook me. "None of it was your fault. It wasn't his fault, either. It just happened. Abby." He shook my shoulder again, and I sobbed even harder. "It wasn't your fault. You loved him." His next words came succinctly. "It. Wasn't. Your. Fault."

From the very beginning, Lindsey had said those same words to me, over and over. So had Molly and Hal, and Todd even, all of my friends who cared about me. Probably my parents would have, too, if I'd given them the chance back then. They'd all begged me to believe them, but I just couldn't consider the concept. I had been too wrapped up in my own selfish suffering.

Until now.

Somewhere deep inside, I knew it was true. Christian's dying had not been my fault. He had been taken from us— *taken*—and there had been absolutely nothing I could have done to stop it. My mind already knew this, but it felt brand new to my heart, and I was finally able to grab hold of it.

Tears were coming faster, pouring down my cheeks, down my throat, soaking into the neck of my shirt.

"I love you, Abby," the tender voice of my father said as he patted my shoulder. "And I know it's been the hardest for you. But it's time to let it go, baby."

Sniffling, nodding, I fought to reply. My mouth was open, but only strange, incoherent noises were coming out. Through soggy lashes, I looked up at him. "I know," I finally managed to articulate between fits of sobs. "This is me, Dad. Letting it go."

Dad pressed his lips together, smiling approvingly. "That's been stuck inside of you for a long time, hasn't it?"

"I've screwed up so many things," I whimpered after I calmed down. "I just . . . I wish I could get a do-over on my life, change *everything*. I wish I could go back."

"No," Dad said, the tone of his voice reminding me of all the times he had offered me advice over the years. "You can't go back to fix what's wrong today. You can only go forward." He leaned over and kissed the top of my head. "Go forward, Abby."

—FROM THE *BRITISH SUN*—

ABBY CAUGHT IN SEXY LOVE SCANDAL!

What on earth is up with Abigail Kelly these days? We're so glad you asked. Sources say when she was on holiday in Miami last month, current boy-toy T.C. was nowhere to be seen. Have they finally split?

Surely you jest!

When asked about the conspicuous absence of the hunky American, sources close to Abby implied she was sick to the back teeth of his boring, laid-back style.

"We're just two different kinds of people," Abby disclosed to a close friend. "Sometimes a girl just needs a bit of a break from it all."

Miss Mustang was spotted at all the hottest clubs in South Beach, getting down and dirty with the local lads. Something's fishy, methinks. Time to get your feet on the ground, princess.

chapter 29

"ALL YOU NEED IS LOVE"

After reading the same paragraph four times, I reached for my homemade bookmark, the long, thin piece of paper with my growing bucket list running down the center. Checkmarks, underlines, asterisks, and exclamation points highlighted various items. After replacing it, I closed the book, drumming my fingers over its brown-and-white cover. Dad had lent me his copy of *The 7 Habits of Highly Effective People* when I was visiting. I'd read it twice in three days, taking special notice of the passages he highlighted and the notes he had written in the margins. My favorite chapters were the ones about finding a proper balance in life and how to become proactive—two habits I desired yet was currently lacking.

I slid the book into my bag, noticing that my phone was blinking with a new message. Molly. I sighed, smiling. She was only one room away. After I read it, I turned off my phone and pulled a small yellow tube out of an inside pocket of my purse.

"What are you doing a week from Tuesday?" I asked as I applied the sweet mentholated balm, making a complete circle three times and smacking my lips. "We have the morning off."

Hal looked up from the magazine on his lap. "Sleeping in, of course."

"Think you could possibly roll out of bed and be at Club Le Deux by ten? They're opening early for me."

"What's the occasion?"

"Memorial." I smiled, allowing my gaze to drift off into the middle distance. "For Christian. You know, since I missed his last one." I felt Hal's hand on my arm. "We got a really bad Neil Diamond impersonator to perform."

When I looked at Hal, he was smiling, too.

"It's gonna be a rockin' party. Will you come?"

"Hells yeah." He kicked the side of my chair. "Wouldn't miss it, duchess."

I exhaled, mentally checking off another item on my list. After a few minutes passed in silence, I asked, "Have you written anything lately?"

Framed portraits of the stars from this TV network's past and current sit-coms plastered the walls. Between them were flat screens showing the live feed of the late-night talk show we were about to perform on.

Hal hesitated at first, his eyes moving from me to the closed door behind us. Yes, we were alone in the greenroom, but not for long. "I write every day, duchess," he finally said. "Pretty soon I'll need to add another wing onto the house to hold all my notebooks."

"Or you could get a place of your own," I suggested.

Hal snorted and wandered toward the craft service table.

"I'd love to hear some of your songs," I said. But Hal only gave me a look from across the table.

"That one you wrote a few years ago about graduation." I thought for a moment. "Something *Nation*."

"'Dirtbag Nation,'" he corrected, his mouth full of Ritz crackers.

"And I love that one about the girl you met in Central Park, that one you sang to us on the bus."

"'Beatrice Cries.'"

"That's it. It was stuck in my head for days."

"Whatever, duchess." He snorted again and reached for a cube of yellow-and-white marbled cheese.

"We're not on for another twenty minutes." I joined him at the table, reaching for my own piece of cheese.

Hal eyed me skeptically when I popped it into my mouth, probably astonished to see me eating solid food.

"You've got your guitar all nice and tuned." I chewed, swallowed, and took another piece of cheese. "Would you play something for me?"

Hal looked down, perhaps deciding if I was worth sharing a part of him that was extra special.

Watching him from across the table of snacks, waiting for our time slot to perform, I felt a warm gush of gratitude in my soul for him. He'd been good to me. Not exactly like a brother, Hal was something more.

I was dying to bond with someone, anyone. Hal and I had always been close, sharing a kind of higher connection, *simpatico*, as he liked to put it. To express this, most of the time we fought like a couple of first graders. As I watched him from across the table, my heart broke a little. I had cut him off before, so unkindly, that day in the kitchen at the studio when he'd tried to tell me about his feelings. I couldn't stand to hear it at the time; I didn't want to deal with it. I couldn't handle any more change.

I looked away from him, ashamed of my past behavior. Above everything, I was Hal's friend. We needed each other, and I would do anything for him.

"I do have one I think you might like," he said. When he lifted his chin, he grinned, not needing any further coaxing.

I returned his infectious smile.

Then the two of us, tucked away behind closed doors, shared a secret.

While softly strumming his guitar, Hal sang to me his latest effort. It was a simple song about strength, about loss, about miracles, about it never being too late, and about how some things were simply meant to be, no matter how many times you screwed up. It was like hearing out loud the hopes of my heart.

My breathing slowed and my body sank into the stiff, red wingback. I knew I was crying. And I welcomed the emotion.

Hal's song had a minimal yet beautiful melody and something of a bluesy hook because, after all, it was Hal.

I was moved, I was touched, but mostly I was impressed.

"Wow," I said after he finished. "That was really *good.*" The word was not nearly sufficient enough.

My band mate shrugged.

"You should record it." I leaned forward, wiping my eyes with the backs of my fingers.

"Yeah, right," he said, resting his elbows on his Gibson acoustic. He sounded grateful, but also defeated. "Someday, maybe."

I shook my head. "Seriously. It gave me chills." I showed him my arm covered in goose bumps. "This is way better than anything out there right now." I rubbed my arms. "Better than the crap we've done lately."

"Of course it is," he agreed, his orange hair falling across his forehead. He was smiling, but regret showed on his face at the same time. Seeing it made my heart ache on his behalf.

"Why don't you record it?" I suggested.

"I'm no singer, duchess."

"You've got a great singing voice. You just never get to use it."

He rolled his eyes, but blushed just a bit. "Anyway, I wrote it for a woman's voice."

I bit my thumbnail. "Maybe Max will let *us* do it." Before the words were completely out of my mouth, we both knew that was an impossibility. Max handpicked every song. Sure, he used Nathan's perfect ear and killer instincts as a sounding board, but Max had ultimate say. We also knew that Max wouldn't give anything of Hal's a fair shake, just because.

For the first time, I understood that Hal and the rest of the group felt just as trapped as I did.

I stood up to pace, automatically returning to the food. "There must be something we can do." I took a handful of M&Ms and poured them into my open mouth like a rainbow. Hal watched me the way he used to do when I'd first joined the band. He was looking to me for a solution. But I didn't have one. Yet.

"This is a hit song, Hal," I said. "You know it and I know it. It needs to be out there for high school kids to make-out to at prom."

"Classy."

"Aren't I?"

We laughed. It sounded like music.

More than almost anything, I wanted someone in our group to have some kind of personal triumph. It might not be me. And that was okay.

"There are a hundred other chick singers out there besides me," I continued, nibbling on a green bell-pepper stick. "Why don't you make a demo to send around? Exactly the way you did it just now. Anyone would kill to sing on the demo for you."

"Naw," Hal said with a wave. He stared into his empty guitar case. "Anyway, it needs a piano accompaniment instead of guitar."

"You play piano."

"The bridge needs work."

"Shut up, Hal!" I insisted. "The song is freaking perfect."

He snapped shut his case and looked down at the tips of his callused fingers. We were losing momentum here.

"Well . . . what if . . ." I paused to wet my lips, getting an excited tickle in my stomach as I created a plan. "What if *I* sing it? Yeah, yeah. *I'll* make the demo."

Hal looked up; his expression seemed confused.

"I'd love to!" I rushed over and knelt at his feet. "Oh, please, please, please. Please let me."

He chuckled, but it lasted only a second. Then he shook his head and stood up. "Uh-uh, Abby. No way. If Max the Tool found out, he'd go freakin' ape all over you."

"And on you," I added.

"Not me," Hal corrected. "Seriously, the man don't give two squirts about me, but if he found out you were squandering away your talent on drivel, he'd tear you a new one."

Suddenly, that made me fuming mad. "I don't *care* about *Max*." I jumped to my feet, punching a hard fist into my palm as I paced the room. "I want to *do* something. I *need* to do something. I need to do this for you, Hal." I spun around to him. "Please let me."

"Better keep your voice down," he cautioned, eyeing the closed door over my shoulder. We both knew who was right behind it.

I groaned at his lack of motivation, then walked to stand in front of one of the monitors, my arms folded tight across my chest. The guest on the interview couch was some kind of zookeeper. He had a green parrot thing perched on one shoulder while stroking a brown-and-orange baby tiger in his lap.

"We're on soon," Hal informed me from behind. "Where's Molly?"

"With Jord, watching the show from backstage," I answered, still studying the screen. The zookeeper was now feeding kibble to a llama. "This . . ." I pointed to the screen, "is the dumbest thing in the entire world. All of this." Hal was watching me, his guitar in his arms. "I mean it. If having all this success still means we can't do what we want, or have what we want . . ." I threw my hands in the air. "What are we doing, Hal, and why?"

Just then, the door of the greenroom swung open and Max crossed the threshold. The sudden tension accompanying him felt like the calm before an explosion. "Four minutes, babe," he warned, surveying the room, not focusing on anything in particular. "No!" he boomed, swatting the inside of his hand with a rolled up piece of paper. He turned his back to us. "No, the negotiations are final. Five years, no less. And yes, just the one, that's the new deal."

Max was talking into his Bluetooth. Hal and I shared a

look and a shrug; we could never follow Max's one-sided conversations. "I said non-negotiable," Max snarled as he turned back around.

Someone's panties are in a wad, I thought, maybe a bit unsympathetically.

"No, no. Not the other three—" That was when he seemed to notice me. "You're wearing that?" His eyes moved down my outfit. "This is not what we discussed. It's awful. Totally unacceptable."

At first I couldn't tell if he was talking on his phone or not.

"Did you even bother looking in the mirror this morning?" He pointed the rolled up paper at me.

I was a little stunned, and I automatically inspected what I was wearing. It was a tailored brown cotton tank, black low-rise trousers, and tall brown suede boots. Casual-classic and completely modest. For a change, I felt comfortable in my clothes. Plus, the whole outfit was brand new, a little shopping spree I'd treated myself to.

For the record, no, I *hadn't* bothered to look in the mirror that morning.

"Is that all you brought with you?"

"Umm, yeah," I replied.

"Where is . . . she? Where's that other girl?"

"Molly?" I asked, puzzled.

Max shook his head briskly. "No-no, that other one. Hair and makeup, stylist."

"Jillian?"

"Whatever."

"She's not coming. I told her I could do this kind of thing myself from now on."

Max's face turned gray and then red. "You did what?" he hissed. "Who exactly told you that you could do that?"

I grimaced at the harshness of his words. Max's scrutinizing eyes gave me the once-over again, making me feel like I needed another shower.

"At least knot the bottom of your shirt in the back so the front is tight." He stared directly at my chest, clinically.

"Give the people at home something to look at." He glanced at his watch. "It's time." He gave me one last scowl before stomping out of the room.

Numb from shock, I touched my hands to the sides of my shirt, my fingers obediently curling around the bottom hem.

"Don't even *think* about it," Hal said from behind me.

I turned around.

"You look great, just the way you are. And if Max the Tool—"

The bumper music started playing on set, announcing the pause for a commercial break. We were on in three minutes.

I uncurled my fingers and smoothed out the bottom of my shirt. "Thanks," I said, wishing I could run over and hug him and explain how special he was to me. Instead I walked toward the door that led to the set.

"Hey, Abby?"

I stopped so he could catch up. "Yeah?"

"Are you happy?"

His question made me blink. "Happy? Yes," I answered after a beat. And I was, comparatively.

Hal tilted his head as if examining me. "Yeah. Happy's one thing, but it's time to get the rapture back. Where's your rapture, girl?" He made a fist and gently knocked my chin. "Let's get you that rapture, shall we?"

As he walked ahead of me, I felt on the verge of tears. When he turned back again, he was grinning. "Oh, and that favor you were asking for earlier. If you still want to, well, I'd be effin' honored."

chapter 30

"FREE AS A BIRD"

I adjusted the cracked and battered, dilapidated headphones over my ears and gave Hal a nod. His steady piano intro began the rhythm track.

It was going to be another late night, crammed in a makeshift recording studio that Hal, Jord, and Yosh had built in the guestroom of the house they shared high in the Hollywood Hills.

At *those* late-night sessions, I was an enthusiastic participant.

"You sure you wanna do this?" Hal kept asking me. He didn't have to. I was sure.

"Level the mike, duchess."

I did.

"Recede more, just a bit."

I stepped back an inch.

The microphone was vintage. I recognized it as a Neumann U47 condenser mike, probably fifty years old. It matched the rest of the equipment in the small recording booth. Hal was a sensitive artist. He liked antiques, objects with history.

"Sugar-plum fairy, sugar-plum fairy," I counted off into the mike. "Too much feedback." I licked my lips.

"Watch your vowels," Hal instructed.

"It's not like she's never done this before." Jord snickered, cradling his Fender bass like a lover.

"Yeah, Hal," Yosh chimed in from behind his drum set. "Stop being such a *Max*!"

The three of us hooted with laughter.

"Shut it," Hal snapped from behind the window of the homemade control booth. "I need a level."

Jordan ran his fingers up the scales.

"Sample Test Track," Hal spoke into the talk mike, giving our recording a verbal title. He pointed at Yosh, who cracked his drumsticks together three times as the count off.

Singing was a pleasure in that cozy home studio. It was as comfortable as being in my car, my favorite "stage." There was no pressure there, and no egos. We were allowing ourselves to relish in the creativity—something none of us got to do much of anymore. Plus, Hal's studio was much tidier, much more streamlined than I was used to. Rather than a huge control room with wall-to-wall soundboards, mixing consoles, monitor speakers, and equipment racks like at SU, Hal had one computer. All his mixing was done with a keyboard and mouse. "Mixing in a box," he called it.

As I began my part, the sound vibrations left me, bounced off the carpeted walls, and then back onto me in a very familiar way. I closed my eyes, feeling the lyrics, concentrating on my phrasing. The heels of my hands pressed against my diaphragm for control. Gradually my right hand moved up to my heart, pressing in. It remained there.

It wasn't the notes I was visualizing behind closed eyes. With Hal's poignant lyrics percolating through my mind, I saw a face—fuzzy and distant at first, but there. With my mind recently liberated from other past issues, I was forced to confront what was left. I pictured our story as motivation while I sang.

Perhaps not my brightest idea.

"Sorry, guys," I apologized, wiping my wet cheeks with the back of my wrist. We were forced to stop more than a few times when my voice cracked like Peter Brady's. No one complained, though. In fact, they all seemed to expect it. "Can we start again?" I shook my hands out. "I'm ready."

Even though it was only a demo, I wished I'd been performing better for Hal, wished I had my full vocal arsenal behind me. But I was too shredded. Not sad exactly, just emoting . . . with every part of my soul. Finally. For too long, my emotions had been delicately balanced under my top layer of skin, but recently they had all burst out. I hoped this gush of raw, embarrassingly honest sentiments would make up for my lack of perfect pitch and somehow translate into beautiful music.

Perhaps taking my emotional response as a cue, or perhaps relying on his instincts as a budding producer, Hal slowed our song down, scaled it back, stripped it naked, to just the mike and me, a little piano, some understated percussion, and Jord's bass line like gentle thunder. Hal surprised us all by adding his own voice as the harmony backup. Stunning. I also added my own touches, changing some of the phrasings and lyrics when I thought it might work better. Hal welcomed my changes and suggestions. The four of us pooled everything we had into molding our piece of art.

As I looked around the room at my guys, I was flooded with every positive emotion. When I wasn't crying my eyes out, the four of us were all smiles, knowing we were experiencing something magical. It was coming together, nothing like any of our Mustang Sally pieces. This recording was something different, something special, our group effort.

It was joy.

Love.

Rapture.

I scooted to the edge of my stool and sat up straight, flexing my diaphragm in preparation for our next run through. I caught Hal grinning at me through the glass. I beamed back, realizing that this was the one thing I could do for my guys; it was what I could give. Finally, it was enough.

Two nights of sneaking off after our regular day's work

and we finished the demo. Hal gave it the working title "Indian Summer." The words of the title didn't actually appear anywhere in the song, like Bob Dylan's "Rainy Day Woman #5," which has neither a rainy day nor a woman #5, and Billy Joel's "Summer, Highland Falls," which speaks neither of season nor location. Hal was artistic and poetic. And it showed, even in the title, which was written across the front of the white CD in Hal's unique script. Below it were three sets of Japanese characters.

We stood alone in their kitchen on our last night of recording.

"Jord and I get co-producer credit," Yosh explained. "He gave you co-writer's credit, too. Did you know that?"

"What?" I stared down at the CD. "He didn't have to do that."

"This was really good for him," Yosh continued thoughtfully, his newly dyed black hair falling over his dark eyes. "For years we've been trying to convince him to send his stuff around."

All I could do was smile, dusting off some leftover tears. "I wish I could've . . . done it . . . better." My throat started closing up again.

"You sang your face off, Abby," Yosh said in a rare moment of warmth, which made me gulp another sob.

Hal walked through the door. "What's with all the waterworks, lady? You keep crying, and you're gonna drown." He chuckled and opened the fridge.

"This has been so great, you guys," I managed to choke out.

"Oh, no!" Yosh yelped, backing away from me like I was contagious. "The dam's about to break." He spun a one-eighty and comically exited the room.

"You okay?" Hal asked, eyeing me.

"Rapturous," I said.

Hal laughed.

"Out of everything I've ever done since I started this whole thing," I further explained, steadying my breaths, "I've never been more proud of any piece of work. This was worth it."

Hal cracked open a can of Red Bull and took a long drink.

I pressed the CD to my chest, feeling my heart beating against it. "'Indian Summer' truly is a labor of love."

Hal took another swill. "*Love* is right," he agreed, tossing the empty can into the trash. After a belch, he wiped his mouth with the back of his hand. "It's a love song, duchess, and it's about you." He propped one hand leisurely on the counter and grinned at me, a strange grin, a polarizing grin. "I wrote it *for you*."

"You . . . did?" I squeaked, trying to smile. My stomach made a weird little flutter—could have been love, could have been nerves, could have been dread. I honestly didn't know. I did know that I wasn't ready for things to change. I "loved" Hal, but . . .

He was looking hard at me . . . gazing, kind of.

"I'm sure you figured it out from the lyrics," he said, grinning modestly. "I'm not very good at hiding feelings in songs." He straightened up and took a few slow steps toward me.

I stood with my back pressed against a kitchen chair.

"The other guys know and, well, I thought it was pretty obvious by the way you sang it tonight." His eyes locked on mine, zeroing in, causing my fingers and toes to turn cold. "You know, you're flawless when it comes to interpreting lyrics. I'm constantly amazed by the directions you go in and the lyrics you changed." He chuckled softly. "It's like we're totally riding the same wave." He was standing right in front of me now. The top center of his orange hair was gelled into a tall faux hawk. I wished I could've laughed at how funny he looked, but I was afraid to move.

"You're always dead-on," he added, "and you killed this one tonight. I know you were feeling it; I know you're feeling it now." His finger flicked at the CD case I was holding. "How could you *not* know? So obvious. The song's about you, duchess." He took a beat. "And Todd."

"Oh." I blinked, staring at him in confusion. "But I . . . thought—"

Hal's soft chuckle cut me off. "What? That I was into you?" he finished.

I nodded once as my lower lip jutted out. Hot tears of embarrassment burned behind my eyes. I felt ashamed all over again.

"That's ancient history, duchess." Hal reached out, laying a hand on my shoulder. "It was over a long time ago."

"I'm sorry," I whimpered, my voice choking with a sob. "I didn't mean to hurt . . ."

"I know." Hal chuckled again. "After a while, I knew the best thing I could do for you was to play the hell out of my guitar."

"You're my best friend, Hal." I sobbed in joy, throwing myself into his arms.

"Hey, now." He pulled back and tapped my chin with his fist. "Get a grip, duchess; I said the song's about Todd, not me." He leaned against the table at my side. "Now, tell me how much you love it."

"Hal." I sniffled, staring down at the CD in my hands. "It's so amazing." I pressed the disc to my heart, wishing it could've inserted into a slit in my chest like a jukebox, so it would always be with me. "I don't know what to say."

"You don't have to say anything." He grinned. "I'm the official head writer around here, okay?"

More tears spilled out of my eyes as I nodded over and over.

"Now give us a hug," he demanded, "and we'll call it even."

Satellite radio was set on classical music while I drove northwest to Malibu that night. At the late hour it seemed only fitting that all the pieces were Baroque. Bach's "Concerto for Two Violins" was playing—vibrant, cheerful, but also calming, almost spiritual. My Mercedes glided up the PCH, practically on autopilot, until I pulled through the wrought-iron gate.

I was still humming Bach's complicated melody when I unlocked my front door. I stepped inside, bolted the door behind me, and dropped my purse and keys on the floor in the empty entryway. The sound echoed.

Still need to get an end table, I thought as I switched on the living room lights. I'd never really noticed before, but the room was very bright, very open, and very empty. The clean, white walls were bare. The solitary ivory sofa off to one side was the only stick of furniture.

I stood in the middle of the room and slowly spun around, examining the sheer nakedness. I knew there wouldn't be much more to see in any of the other rooms, either. I smiled, remembering Christian's stupid exercise equipment, his massive kicked-up stereo system that had taken up one full wall of our family room, and his entertainment center that had taken up another wall. We were—well, *he* was going to build a new state-of-the-art media room upstairs. But he never got to.

All that stuff is gone, I thought, chewing my lip. *There's nothing left of his, not a hint that he ever lived here.* I leaned against the corner of the couch, wondering where it all went. I still couldn't remember much about those first months after he died, and that realization hurt a little. Molly had probably given everything to Goodwill. or perhaps she auctioned it off on eBay and earned a little extra cash for herself.

Tilting my chin up, I cupped my hands around my mouth. "Hellooo," I called aloud and then stopped to snort a laugh. "Echo . . . echooo . . . echoooooo."

I dropped my hands, grinning for a new reason. Since Hal's demo was now done, I suddenly had the perfect idea for what the next balancing-my-life step would be.

chapter 31

"GOLDEN SLUMBERS"

Some kind of New Age music was piping through the PA system when I swung open the front door and stepped inside.

Not wanting to make a federal case about it, I had told only Molly, mainly because I needed her to look up an address for me of one that would still be open this late, which was what brought me there, all the way to Venice Beach at eleven o'clock at night.

Few other customers were there as I strolled up and down the aisles, fingering the paintbrushes, canvases, charcoals, and other curious art materials. The store was a little daunting, honestly; a lot of time had passed since I'd employed this part of my brain.

A twenty-something guy with an unkempt blond ponytail sat behind the front counter. I approached him, finally admitting to myself—despite my fervent desire for ambiguity—that I required assistance.

After clearing my throat a few times to no avail, I asked him, "What do you suggest for beginners?"

He was wearing a navy blue painter's smock, smeared and speckled with a rainbow of colors. If he'd had a crazier ponytail or an ounce of facial hair, he might have looked more like the mad-genius artist he was trying so hard to portray. "Depends," he replied without looking up.

"On what?"

He casually flipped a page of the art magazine he was reading. "On what you gonna do."

I didn't reply, wondering if there was some secret pass-word I needed to utter before I'd be graced with coherent information.

"So, what is it?" the guy asked, evidently irritated at the interruption so near to closing time. He flipped another page. "Drawing?" he prompted after an aggravated sigh. "Painting? Pottery?" Finally he looked up at me in annoyance. "Decou ... page ..."

His voice faded out as his jaw went slack, while his brown eyes grew wide like the centers of Van Gogh's sunflowers.

I coughed awkwardly. "Umm, painting, I guess," I offered, chewing on the inside of my cheek. "I took some art seminars in college. I liked painting the most."

The guy just stared at me from across the counter.

It wasn't *his* fault, per se, but I so detested being gawked at like some indentured two-headed pygmy at a sideshow. It made that scared and submissive part of me long to run for the tall grass, to hide from the world behind another mask. But I wouldn't do that anymore.

"Is there a book that will teach me?" I offered again.

The clerk blinked once.

I exhaled through puckered lips, a little frustrated. Then an idea came to me. It was a dirty trick, of course, but I had a feeling it would work. I leaned toward the counter, slowly. Another trick I learned from Molly. One spaghetti strap of my tank top slid down my shoulder, just so.

"Oh," I said, hopefully kind of sulkily. "Well, maybe ..." I hesitated, allowing a strand of my hair to tumble over my shoulder and then across one side of my face. I slowly brushed it aside with a finger. "Do you happen to offer classes here?" I displayed the most enticing, sparkly, superstar smile I could muster.

This finally woke him.

"Uhh, yes, *yes*. We *do* offer classes." He nodded and panted as he spoke. "But, oh," his smile dropped, "not for beginning painting. Right now we have advanced ceramics on Mondays." His backbone seemed to grow straighter. "I teach it."

I laughed, leaning away from him, fixing my shirt, crossing my arms in front of me. "I think I'd better stick to painting. How about a book?"

"Oh yeah, we have books. *Lots* of book. *Loads* of books!" The guy actually leaped over the counter, ushering me to the aisle devoted to painting. "Here's an amazing one." He handed me a copy of *Painting with Your Inner Id*.

"Something more basic, maybe," I suggested as I scanned the shelves. "Looks like I'll be teaching myself."

"Okay, okay" he said, nodding over and over. "Try this—it's the best." He handed me a tall, thin softback. "It's a tutorial manual, step by step. You'll be a Picasso in no time."

An hour later, I left the store with three bags full of art and painting supplies, after signing only four autographs. Not too shabby for midnight on a Thursday. I also had my helpful cashier's phone number in the back pocket of my jeans.

Maybe because I'd spent the previous two nights wide awake at Hal's place, or maybe because of the adrenaline racing through my veins, I ended up spending the entire night filling up Christian's once-empty and forsaken bedroom with brightly colored paint jars, easels, paper, canvases, and an array of brushes and art books. I covered its bare and lonely walls with inspirational prints from the Masters: *The Starry Night* by Van Gogh, Renoir's *La Grenouillère*, *Water Lilies* by Monet, and my favorite: Degas's *Dancers at the Bar*, all while blasting a mixed CD of golden crooners I'd locked in a bottom drawer months before.

I am Abigail Kelly, Renaissance woman.

A few hours later, I was sitting on the floor of my new home art studio, smoothing out that homemade bookmark with my long list, now wrinkled and with permanent fold marks. For weeks I'd carried it with me everywhere I went.

Grinning, I made a check mark beside one more item. My home—along with my soul—was crawling back to life.

Next, I painted. I painted every night for a week. I was not very good. I stank, perhaps. But at the beginning, it wasn't about being good, it was about *doing* something, *finding* something, and *unlocking* something.

Those late nights, after the duties of my day job were complete, I rushed home, eager to work my new craft, losing myself in the shapes of a bowl of fruit, with horribly disproportional apples. With only the sound of the ocean seeping through the open windows, those stolen moments were cathartic for me, and peaceful, allowing my heart to expand and my understanding to increase.

There was something quite magical and wonderful that happened in a room when it was just you and a blank piece of painter's canvas. You were forced to dig deep. You learned to find yourself and what you were really made of—warts and all.

Things were becoming clearer. I knew what I wanted, but you can't always get what you want, or so another classic British rock band once said.

I stopped in the middle of a brush stroke and stared out the open windows into the dark night. I wondered, *So then, what is to be Abigail Kelly's next move?* Celebrity conventional wisdom told me to hit the party circuit, get a tattoo, shave my head, fire my staff, develop a dysfunctional eating disorder and/or a trendy little addiction to painkillers, visit the Dalai Lama—or in my case, jet to India to sit with the maharishi—all while dating a string of high-profile celebs like Chris Hemsworth and Rob Pattinson.

To be perfectly honest, at different hours of different days, one or more of those suggestions sounded pretty darned great.

On night number six, after a few hours of painting, I fell asleep on the small sofa in the corner of my art studio. And I dreamed.

It was different from my dreams in the past when he'd come to visit me. His hair had never been the correct shade in any of my dreams; that night it was even lighter. His face was aglow, his body also—which was new, too—like he was being lit on all sides by a heavenly crew of lighting techs.

Floating before me, he extended one iridescent hand. I watched myself reach out and take it. I felt nothing between my fingers, like he really was a ghost.

He grinned—the same grin from when we were kids and he teased me incessantly, or when we were in high school and he leaned on the horn until I made it to the parking lot, or when he stood in the wings, watching me onstage, beaming like the proudest brother on earth.

"Go forward, Abby," Christian said to me.

I thought I felt him touch me that time. Maybe he squeezed my arm. Actually . . . it felt more like he knuckle-punched me on the bicep—his trademark big-brother punishment.

"Or I'll tell Dad." He smirked, jokingly, radiantly. "Ya little brat."

I woke up bathed in refreshing tears, happier than I'd ever been.

♪

The last weekend in November, Lindsey came into town again. At my request.

When she'd visited me a few weeks before, while Steve and the boys were at Disney World, there wasn't much for her to do; we still weren't really speaking.

This visit was different. We talked about everything. Her secondary undertaking was to help me pick out a new couch. It wasn't the most popular color of the season, but I insisted on brown. "I want to feel like I'm in Dad's cave," I described. "You know, comforting, with big fluffy pillows." I turned the page of the Pottery Barn catalog we were flipping through as the two of us laid belly down in the middle of my naked living room. Other decorating magazines and catalogs were strewn around us.

"I want some cool chairs, too. One has to be red. And a coffee table." I rolled onto my knees, animated, using my hands to explain. "And one of those groovy leather cocktail ottomans."

Lindsey lifted her chin and looked up at me. She had tears in her eyes.

♪

Max was in meetings the next afternoon, so the band had time off. Hal volunteered to tag along with my sister and me on our shopping spree. He was absolutely adamant about hand-picking my new TV, which was fine by me. I couldn't tell a back-projection thingamabob from a digital-resolution-whatever.

"Now's not the time to be frugal, duchess," Hal said after he playfully jabbed an elbow into my ribs. We were standing before a never-ending wall of screens. "If you're gonna do it, do it right." He pointed at one screen. It was enormous. I was overwhelmed. "Seventy-inch plasma, ten-eighty-P, anti-glare, surround-sound compatible."

"I have no idea what language you just spoke, Hal."

"It's a totally sweet system." His eyes lowered as he pushed buttons on the long, black remote.

I snatched it from him. "Which channel is Lifetime?"

"You're *such* a *chick*." He gagged, grabbing the remote back from me and flipping through channels. "This is full HD." He stopped on a channel showing a football game. "It's like actually being there." He sighed, eyes glazing over.

"If I buy this thing, will you promise to come over and have a movie slumber party with me?" I asked, taking my own jab at his ribs. "We can watch *Star Wars*."

He turned to me. "Which one?"

I thought for a moment. "The first one?"

"The first one made or *Episode One*?"

"Hal." I patted his shoulder. "We really need to get you a girl."

His eyes narrowed to slits. He was probably about to un-leash a very fitting comeback, when his cell rang. He pulled it out, examining the Caller ID.

"Yeah," he said to me, holding out one finger. "Gotta take this, dear." He backed up and took a few steps away. "Talk to me," I heard him say as he rounded a corner.

I turned back to the wall of screens, staring up, still quite overwhelmed.

Hal returned only moments later. He was grinning.

"What?"

"Ohhh ..." He was trying hard *not* to smile now. "Nothing." He lifted his hand, waving two fingers to the sales clerk who stood off to the side. The startled young man approached. "The lady has made her decision," Hal said and nodded at me.

I rolled my eyes at the ceremony.

"Uhh, Abby?" Lindsey came up behind us. "I think maybe we need to call security."

I followed her pointed finger to see out the front windows of the electronics store. My stomach dropped, as did my smile. I felt Hal step right behind me.

A huge crowd of people gathered outside to watch me picking out a freaking TV.

"Ridiculous," I muttered. My gaze moved to my sister. "I'm so sorry." I turned to Hal. "Should we call Shugger?"

"Hell, no," he answered, attempting to draw himself up to his full five feet nine inches of height. He puffed out his chest. "It's high time us little people learn how to take care of ourselves, right?"

I nodded uncertainly.

He took ahold of my hand and reached forward and took Lindsey's. "Allow me to show you ladies a little trick I learned from the drummer of Hybrid Theory." The three of us were walking now. "We slip out the back."

Lindsey returned to Florida the next day. With her help, we'd bought enough furniture and things to fill the living room. But she left it up to me to do the actual arranging and decorating. A few weeks later, I found myself gazing around at the finished product.

I'm glad I went with the contrasting browns and blues, I thought as I stood just outside the room, flipping on and off the switch of my new table lamp. It instantly brightened the space, while also painting a sort of rainbow halo around the colorful glass shade.

I stepped into the room. The couch in the center was a rich café, fat and cushy, with extra deep down-filled cushions. It was just plain luxurious. It matched the rectangular ottoman that doubled as a footrest and coffee table. Three tall cinnamon candles sat in the middle on a funky little pottery tray. Flanking the sofa was an arm chair with azure and cognac stripes, and on the other side was a glossy mahogany end table, where the glowing Tiffany lamp sat. Lindsey had insisted that I get colored throw pillows to offset the dark furniture. I fought it at first, but then went with antique blue and bright turquoise. I sighed contently. The room was pretty, soothing yet energetic.

Off to the left side of the sofa, I reclined on the red chaise longue. It was the one piece of furniture that didn't match the others, but it was quickly becoming my favorite. I allowed my eyes to flutter closed while I stretched out comfortably.

Maybe it's my favorite chair because it has the best view of my favorite wall.

This thought made me open my eyes. They fixed on the ceiling first then slowly moved down to the wall in question. I sat up . . . and smiled.

The charcoal drawing of the horse catches the eye first, I considered, *but then I immediately go right to the oil abstract with the yellow and red squares*. I snickered. *My comically pitiful attempt at Picasso*. I linked my fingers behind my head, admiring the homemade art gallery.

Furniture was one thing, but until a few days ago, what my home hadn't had was a personal touch. Inspired, I'd sifted through my twenty or so finished products, chose my favorite few—the ones that didn't scream out "first grader finger painting—and had them framed.

I looked down at my fingers. There was blue paint under my nails. I smiled again, hunkering down as my eyes moved from frame to frame.

And then they stopped.

I always saved this particular painting for last. I'd debated hanging it up at all, but it was so beautiful, my masterpiece. It was a watercolor landscape, and my first attempt to paint from memory and not model: white sand, blue water, swirling gray sky, and the back of a dark-haired man sitting on the beach.

chapter 32

"CARRY THAT WEIGHT"

" I dunno, Abby. You're quite certain, then?"

I swiveled around on the bar stool to give Molly a playful glare. She was eyeing my reflection in the bathroom mirror, looking petrified. But I wasn't. I knew what I was doing.

Before I swiveled back around, I slapped the handle end of the scissors into her open palm.

"Cut it."

I was fully prepared for Max to throw a hissy fit. But I was not expecting the string of expletives that flew out of his mouth when he saw me the next day.

"*What* in the—" was the first semi-complete sentence I could make out once his serious swearing concluded.

"It was time for a change," I explained, dropping my purse into the empty chair beside Max in the control room.

Nathan's eyes bugged out as he stared at me through the thick glass of the sound booth.

"It looks more natural this way," I said.

"Natural?" Max repeated the word like it was in a foreign language.

"Brunette is the new blond," I further reported, "and short is in." I ran my fingers up the back of my new chocolatey cut, flipping and twirling the short, pixie-like ends, sweeping wispy bangs to one side of my forehead.

Max's face was growing progressively redder. "Who . . . who did this to you?"

Discreetly I flicked my gaze toward Molly. Her tall, willowy figure was frozen like a statue in the far corner of the room. One hand was at her face, nervously pulling her lip.

"*I* did," I said to Max, indignant. Out of the corner of my eye I saw Molly's posture relax.

Max stood up. "You had *no right!*" His voice was much stronger than I thought was necessary. "No right to do a stupid thing like that."

"No right?" I repeated slowly, as if I were the one translating a foreign language now.

Max exhaled loudly. "We're not arguing about this, babe."

"Exactly," I said with a roll of my eyes. "This is a ridiculous conversation. It's *my* hair."

His eyes narrowed and held on me for a second, as if he were trying to figure out what game I was playing. Then his gaze ran across my face, brazenly scrutinizing me, forcing upon me that need-to-shower feeling.

"It looks *terrible*," he muttered over his shoulder as he returned to his chair. "What's done is done, but you're never to do an idiotic thing like that again. Do you understand me?"

Unsure how to reply, I said nothing. Surely I couldn't promise such a thing, right? Chopping off my hair had been the right thing to do, a personal statement of change. It had nothing to do with Max. I did it for me.

I looked through the glass for a little help, but Nathan was gone, and Molly hadn't stirred from her place in the corner.

"I'm sorry," she mouthed, her pretty face flushing with fear.

I shook my head briskly, not about to let her take any of the blame. It had been *my* idea to cut and color. And it had been a *brilliant* idea.

"Holy crap!"

I turned to see Hal standing in the doorway.

"Whatja *do* to yourself, duchess?" His arms reached out, Frankenstein-style, as he advanced toward my head. "It's all gone," he whined while his fingers fiddled in my hair like a mama gorilla to her baby. His hands moved to my cheeks to tilt my face up. "I like it," he said, nodding approvingly.

"Brings out all that gray in her eyes, doesn't it?" Nathan inserted as he walked through the door. "She always wanted to look like Ringo." A teensy smile of acquiescence played on his lips. "Good deal," he whispered.

Max huffed.

"Naw," Hal said to Nate, wagging one finger in the air. "She looks like the chick from that TV show. You know," he snapped his fingers, "*that* one."

"Exactly!" Nate exclaimed. They both stared at me, grinning and nodding.

"Yeah." Hal sighed wistfully, "that chick's a major hottie."

"Guys." Molly walked to me. "Leave her be." She swept my mussed up pixie cut back into place. "So fab." She winked.

"If the beauty parlor talk is over," Max interjected, "we have work to do." He looked at me, lifting one mocking eyebrow. "Unless there is something else you feel you need to share?"

"Actually, there is," I blurted out.

The room went dead quiet.

Max spun around in his chair, arms folded, mockingly taken aback. "Oh?"

I swallowed, wetting my suddenly dry throat, fingering my list in my pocket. "I know the album is almost finished." I gestured to the large wipe board hanging on the far wall, our recording schedule scribbled on it. "Once it is, I'm taking a break. A vacation."

"You just took one."

"That was three months ago. I'd like to spend Christmas with my family for a change."

No one in the room moved, except for Max, who was shaking his head.

"No way you're leaving," he said, matter-of-factly. "The promotional circuit starts in two weeks. That covers the next two months. The album release date is in March. We'll be touring into next year."

I looked from Max to Nathan for corroboration, or maybe I was just hoping for a little support, but Nate was staring down, blinking at his shoes. I glanced at Hal. His face was pale, his mouth turned in a frown.

"Oh," I said, feeling deflated after doing the math in my head. "Maybe I can take a day or two, or—"

"Maybe." Max swiveled back to the console. "And maybe the year after that you can have a little vacation." He turned to the other three standing behind me. "The rest of you," he snapped, "out of here." His eyes shifted back to me. "We're working alone tonight."

Nathan's lips parted, ready to jump in and say something. I braced myself, grateful that someone was finally going to stick up for me, but instead, he sealed them together again.

My stomach sank.

When I looked at Hal, his cheeks were burning red, his bright eyes equally incensed.

As he went to take a step toward Max's turned back, Nathan grabbed his arm, pulling him away. "Don't," I heard Nate mutter under his breath, making Hal's intense expression dissolve.

The whole interchange took only a few seconds—totally unnoticed by Max, who was barking at someone on the phone.

Nathan was still yanking Hal's arm. "We'll catch ya later, Abby," he said, leading Hal toward the door through which Molly had obediently exited a moment earlier.

Thoroughly puzzled, I waved good-bye, watching them disappear. While I stared through the empty doorway, suddenly ill at ease to be left alone with Max, my stomach plunged again.

I was pouring a stream of golden honey into the Styrofoam cup that was balanced between my knees. The lemony water was steaming hot. I cleared my throat a few times and swallowed hard, but this didn't help, either.

Phlegm? Allergies? Throat nodules? Who knew?

"I think I need to rest my voice." I closed the cap on the honey bear and licked my finger.

There was nothing in return to my comment, only silence. I held the lemony honey water to my lips, inhaling the steam. I sneaked a glance at Max and rolled my eyes.

It wasn't an oddity for him to ignore me; I'd grown accustomed to it lately. But instead of the way I normally zoned out while I waited for him to get around to acknowledging me, I caught myself glaring at the back of his head. It was getting really late, but not late enough, it would seem, for him to dismiss me of his own accord.

I blew a puff of steam away. "Also," I droned on, even though I knew I wasn't being listened to, "I'd really like to go home and finish my tree."

Max's attention was fixed on the various computer screens in front of him. Over and over, he was replaying one section of a song. I was so used to the constant sound of my singing voice, it was annoying background noise, like the hum of the A/C or noisy traffic on the 101.

"What's that, babe?" Max finally said, inattentively, without looking at me.

"My tree," I repeated to his profile. "I'm painting a redwood tree. I've been talking about it for four days."

There was another long stretch of silence. I crossed and then uncrossed my legs, irritated with the feeling that I was talking to myself.

Max and I were working on a charming little ditty called "Nothing on Me." We'd completed it weeks ago, but Max had recently become unsatisfied by the original recording, claiming that the new album was in dire need of more urban-sounding tracks—"urban" meaning "overtly sexual," in my opinion. I didn't agree with this sudden veering of style, but nobody asked me, and I hadn't spoken up.

For no particular reason, or maybe for a million reasons, I felt myself glowering at the side of Max's face, my foot tapping impatiently. I knew I was playing with fire, but something inside wasn't willing to work under those circumstances anymore, the way he snubbed my ideas and pushed me around. I felt like it might be time to push back.

Maybe it was my sassy new haircut.

"I want to finish painting my tree," I repeated for a third time.

"Listen," Max snapped.

I jumped, spilling hot water on my jeans.

His face was halfway turned in my direction now, while his attention remained glued on the screen. "You need to *stop* all that. I don't want you up half the night wasting your energy on some stupid hobby." He clicked the mouse, adjusting something on the program he was running. "It's costing us every day you show up tired and distracted like this."

"Cut me some slack, jack," I muttered into my fist. This unexpected burst of pluck surprised even me. It made me snicker quietly, but afterward, I was a little afraid to make any sudden movements.

I heard his chair squeak, and I knew Max was looking at me, although *glaring* was probably a more accurate term, what with the prickly feeling shooting up the back of my neck.

Success! I had finally said something to win Max's complete attention.

For one instant, however, while he stared daggers at me, I wished I could take it back, to go back. But not this time.

Go forward, Abby.

When I looked up, his tight and pale lips were pushed out. And I'd been right: he was big-time glaring.

"What'd you just say to me?"

Halfheartedly, I plastered on an apologetic smile. "You're

absolutely right, Max," I agreed. "I *am* tired." I took a few sips of my hot drink. "Just like you said. Don't you think we need more balance around here? I was reading the other day about—"

"Look," he snapped irritably, but then he sighed loudly and rubbed the back of his neck. His expression turned calm. "Come on, babe." His voice was calm, too, and patient. "We've got a lot to do tonight." He knew I was about to interrupt, because he lifted a hand. "I know, I know. Yes, it's late and you're tired, but if we work together, we'll get this done and it'll be gold." He leaned toward me. "We could do with some gold now, know what I mean? Maybe we'll go out and celebrate properly afterward. Any place you like. Sound good, kiddo?"

There was a twinkle in Max's eyes, the same twinkle I remembered from when we first started working together. Lindsey insisted this was how he manipulated me, how he was generous and empathetic until he talked me into something I didn't want to do. I had never really noticed before, but Max Salinger was kind of a snake.

"You with me, babe?" He smiled, his voice smooth like silk. "We're so close to wrapping this thing up. Just a couple more hours."

I stared at Max's face while biting the inside of my cheek. This wasn't going as planned. Not that I'd "planned" anything, but I had made some mental notes of things I'd like to express if the opportunity presented itself. My recorded voice grew louder as Max worked his editing magic.

I blocked out the bothersome sound and turned my back on him. "I'm burned out, Max; that's why I need a vacation," I said over my own voice.

"Already decided. Not gonna happen."

"Fine," I said, choosing to let him win that battle. When I swiveled back around, I could clearly make out that he was smirking, like he *knew* he'd won, like he knew he could get me to do anything he wanted. Was this some kind of game? Was my life a joke to him?

"We need to focus on the future now," Max said, back to business.

I sat rigid in my chair, my toes curling in anger. "Yes. The future," I agreed under my breath.

"We need to finish this record. The first single's 'Lonely Boy.' That's set in stone. Our people will leak it, and then the video shoot's next week. We're in New York for that."

"New York." Steam from my cup started to warm my face.

"Ronald Blain's directing."

I was only halfway listening, chewing on the rim of my cup.

"He's got some radical ideas. We'll play up the French burlesque vibe. Very macabre and obvious. We're talking *Moulin Rouge* meets *True Blood*. I see you in stiletto thigh highs, fishnets, and strips of torn leather, maybe a dagger or a whip."

His words shook me awake. "Seriously, Max? That's disgusting. No way!" I downed the rest of my hot drink in two gulps, my sore throat burning. "There's no way I'm wearing anything like that."

He leaned back in his chair, looking amused by my outburst. "That's funny," he said, lifting his eyebrows. "You say that like you think you have a choice."

Was he serious?

The door leading out into the hallway was propped ajar. A window in the vestibule hung open a crack. I heard glass shatter somewhere outside on the street and then a distant siren wailed. It was an eerie sound, empty and unsettling, adding to the alarm bells ringing in my head. "I do have a choice," I said tentatively.

Don't I? Of course I do!

I pushed back from the console, forcing my voice to sound steady. "And I won't let you talk to me like that." My legs shook a little when I stood up, my scalded throat going dry. "It's disrespectful, and . . . I deserve better."

Max turned away from me—and laughed.

"This isn't funny." The sound of my wobbly voice made me cringe. If I started crying now, I'd lose all credibility. "Don't laugh at me."

But Max didn't stop.

"I've always done everything you wanted," I said, pacing backward a few steps. "You know I have."

He wasn't laughing anymore, but his smug grin was back in place.

"I've sacrificed and alienated people I love. I ended up pushing away the most important person in my life because I was—"

"Oh, I get it," Max cut in. "This little tantrum is about that guy?" He folded his arms across his chest.

"Todd," I corrected as I frowned down at him, my voice ragged with emotion. "His name is *Todd*, Max. And I love him."

Now . . . I hadn't planned to say those words out loud, and never to Max Salinger. But they'd come so effortlessly, so honestly. "I love him," I repeated. It had floated out as a whisper, but I felt my lips stretching into a giddy grin. "And I don't care why he left or where he went. I don't care if it takes the rest of my life; I'm going to find him and marry him." The prospect made my heart beat hard and my grin stretch across my face.

"Pshaw," Max scoffed. "I did what I could to keep that whole thing away from the press. You'll thank me later, babe. I spun it our way. It was the right thing for us."

My smile went limp.

"I will admit, though," he added, "this one lasted longer than I thought. But once he got here, I knew it was a matter of time."

"Excuse me?"

He chuckled to himself, waving me off. "Nothing, babe. Forget it. Just trust me, I was doing us all a favor."

I huffed dubiously, confused and frustrated.

Max studied me for a moment, then chuckled again, like he'd figured something out. "Oh, I get it. You're hard up." A corner of his mouth pulled back into a sardonic smile. "Tell ya what. I'll make a call and get Miles Carlisle to fly out for a visit. Will that cool your engines?"

My top lip curled in disgust. "Miles?" I said, swallowing a sour blob in my throat. "Max, why on earth would you think I would ever want that idiot Miles again? He's a prick, and *gah!* An *idiot*! Don't you know he cheated on me in front of the whole world?"

Max pressed his lips together, trying not to laugh. "I'm just saying, if it's only some . . ." He cleared his throat. "Extra-curricular recreation you're after, I'll bring him back, for a couple weeks even. No strings, no prob. Like before. Maybe *that* can be your vacation."

I looked at him, struck dumb. Literally.

"No?" Max said, correctly appraising my state of disgust. "Fine. He was the only one who boosted your career, but whatever." His focus was pulled to my purse hanging off the chair; my phone inside was singing with an incoming call. "Shut that thing off."

Hastily I reached inside, silencing the ringer. "It's only Hal," I said, knowing his ring tone.

Max made a face. "Thrilled that's almost over," he muttered.

"Are you mad at Hal or something?"

He made the same face. "Not worth the energy, none of them. When we take you solo—" He stopped himself and coughed distractedly.

After rewinding what he'd just said, I lifted my eyebrows. "There's something you're not telling me." After I spoke, I nearly laughed. *Such* an understatement.

"No," Max said. "We're done talking, babe." He pointed at me and then toward the mike on the other side of the glass. "Time's up." He swiveled to the computer—discussion over. "Back to work. Now."

Slowly yet obediently, I rotated around.

A split second later, something made me stop, something like a little prickle at a memory, an itching of so many un-answered questions. "Max?" I said, staring at the florescent green exit sign above the door.

He sighed. "Yeah?"

"What did you and Todd argue about?"

When I turned around, Max was looking sideways at me with an odd expression.

"He wouldn't say, and he left that night. What happened?"

"It was nothing," Max answered gruffly. "I told you."

"No, you didn't. You didn't tell me anything."

Max turned back to the computer. "Not tonight, babe. We've got work to do."

"I want to know." I folded my arms like a pouting child. "I have the right—"

"Hey!" he barked. "I don't know where all this attitude is coming from, but I don't like it, and I won't have it." He stood up, taking a long stride toward me. "First, the ridiculous obsession with painting, and now *this*." He reached out and flicked the ends of my short hair.

I jerked my head away.

"All these crazy things you've been doing lately. People around here think you've lost it."

"Tell me what you fought about," I insisted. My mind was a heat-seeking missile now.

Max's eyes remained glaring down at me.

I glared right on back.

"He was getting too close, that's all," Max finally offered, his meaty fingers thrusting through his hair. "Asking too many questions, just like the others, like that *sister* of yours. Questions that were none of his business. So I warned him to back off or else."

"That doesn't make any sense," I said, blinking. "What questions?"

He sat down, swiveling away from me.

I planted my feet firmer on the floor beneath me, stabilizing my stance. "Tell me what questions Todd was asking you," I demanded.

"It . . . it was nothing, babe," he said dismissively, but his voice was colored with deceit. I could tell he was hiding something important. "He got all bent out of shape about, well, you know, about what happened with your brother."

"What about Christian?"

"*Damn it!*" Max's growl made my heart thud like two football players crashing into each other. "Won't you ever shut up about it? No one cares about your little dramas."

His words made me flinch. But I'd come too far. I couldn't back down now.

So I closed my eyes and shut out the world, thinking first of my happy place and then praying for some kind of divine intervention to help me understand. Ideally, I would have preferred an earthquake or a bolt of lightning or even a nice flood. But what I settled for was a tiny voice.

Abby, you need to do the right thing.

The words came crystal clear, as if from little Jiminy Cricket perched on my shoulder, whispering in my ear. My thoughts were able to focus again, and my eyes popped open. With muscles clenched, I narrowed my eyes. I wasn't going anywhere.

Max huffed sarcastically at my altered expression. "Okay. Fine. You wanna know? You want me to spell it out for you?"

I nodded firmly.

"He heard about what happened in London. Nate must've told him that last night; he's the only other person who knew, because *I* sure as hell didn't say anything." He pressed his lips together, apparently through speaking.

I thought for a moment, but came up with nothing. "What did Nate tell him?" I finally had to ask, my stupid brain not quite there yet. "Do you mean about why I missed Christian's funeral?"

Max didn't move, wouldn't acknowledge my comment either way.

"So what?" I folded my arms. "There were no flights out of London that night or the next day, remember? Max, you told me the airports were closed. You told me . . ."

Once it started, I couldn't stop it from coming. Once I knew, it was like I'd always known the truth about what really happened all those nights ago. The excuses, the whispers, keeping me busy, keeping me away from my phone, not letting me talk with anyone else, not even giving me time to cry when I'd found out my brother had died.

Standing there, learning the truth about my manager and his long-reaching control, I had a new kind of burning in the pit of my stomach.

The lids around Max's black eyes narrowed. He blew air out his wide and flaring nostrils like a charging bull. Even while caught in a bald-faced lie, the man was unabashed, pompous, and shamelessly proud.

I felt sick to my stomach—first at his betrayal and then at my past submission to him. "I could've flown home," I whispered, mostly to myself, a small part of me still unsure if I was on the right track. "I could've been with my family. We needed to be together." I stared at him, waiting for him to tell me I was wrong. But he only stared back. "Did you threaten Nate?" My voice was elevating to shriek level. "Is that why he didn't tell me?"

He shrugged. The smug attitude was back.

This *news*, this most recent piece of information—I felt like the revelation should have shocked me more than it had, or maybe it didn't matter. Maybe it was nothing more than the smoking gun on top of an overflowing table of evidence, showing the kind of man Max Salinger really was. I didn't blame Nate for not saying anything to me. Max had probably cowed him into silence, just to cover his own deception.

"I went onstage for you!" I said, enraged. "You knew I was sick and in shock, but you *forced* me, the day of my brother's funeral. You made me perform that night."

The sound of the distant siren from the street was coming closer, practically right below the window.

"You bet I did." He seemed almost happy to accept the accusation. "I wasn't about to lose revenue, all those ticket sales and merchandise, screw up an entire concert schedule, just for *you*." He arched one eyebrow. "Despite what you think, this is a business, babe. You're nothing but a commodity. An asset. A brand. My own personal wind-up doll that spits out money."

The image nauseated me. "Jeez, Max."

He smirked, but I was not about to show weakness.

"Come on, babe. You take things so personally." His voice was calmer now, almost kind, the way he used to be. The man was a genius with the guilt. "Get over yourself. Laugh it off, and let's move on."

"I'll laugh in a minute," I assured him, "but I need to get a few things straight first." I started counting off on my fingers. "You treat me like a piece of meat and then you lie to me. You lie to everyone."

He rolled his eyes.

"You never listen; you freak out when I make a tiny decision for myself. You're a slave-driver."

He opened his mouth to contradict, but I cut him off. "It's *midnight*, Max." I pointed at the clock to prove my statement. "I've been working since six this morning. What do you call *that*? Oh, and let's not forget how you're willing to pimp me out to Miles Carlisle."

Max chuckled.

"Shut it, Salinger," I snapped, wanting to karate chop him. "Apparently I'm going *solo* now?" When I took a step toward him, a muscle in his cheek jerked. "Do the guys know about this? Do I get a say? Or was that going to be another decision you made behind my back? *I* don't want to go solo. Do you hear me?"

He didn't answer.

I shook my head, and my eyes slid off his face to stare at the space beside him. Strange, but I actually felt relieved, almost giddy. So many things finally made sense. How *stupid* had I been? How completely *brainless*?

Things had changed. I wasn't sure when, exactly, but I knew I was different. I wasn't crazy after all! I was someone who could be trusted to make a decision, someone who wouldn't resort to sneaking behind the back of her paid employee to do what she wanted, to cut her hair, to paint a damn tree.

"I hurt my family," I pressed on, "and my friends. The man I love left, and still, I did everything you wanted and you . . . you *lied* to me? You could have gotten us out of London, even with the fog." I made myself say this last piece of the puzzle aloud, the most damning bit of evidence. "You knew Christian, Max. You . . . you liked him, right? How could you do that? How could you make me—"

"I never made you do anything. Stop playing the victim. We're all tired of it."

A little derailed, I exhaled, regrouping. I gazed methodically over the room, the place that had become my second home for the past five years. I looked at the long desk, the computers, the chairs, speakers, and shelves. Everything was out of focus, everything except a pathway out the door, which seemed to be traced in fairy lights.

"You're right." I stared down, nodding, like it was suddenly dawning on me. "You're so . . . completely right." As I lifted my chin, I felt myself smiling, practically beaming at him. "It's always been my decision. All of it." I reached over and grabbed my purse. "Just like right now."

It was a pleasure seeing his stony expression balk.

"I'm so outta here." My voice was a fusion of fortitude and resolve, sounding strange coming from a mouth that had been metaphorically gagged for so long. My smile grew when I noted how Max's smug smirk dropped when I hooked my purse over my shoulder. I spun an about face, gliding under that green exit sign.

"You're not leaving!" Max bellowed from behind me. "You're not leaving till *I* say you are."

I kept steady my forward march, steps solid and determined.

"You'd better think long and hard about what you're doing, babe!" he called out as I passed through the glass doors and into the vestibule. "There's no such thing as a graceful exit in this business!"

I pushed the down button of the elevator with a strong and steady finger.

"Don't do this, babe!" he roared, right behind me now. "Don't you leave!"

Say nothing. Just walk away. Deal with it when you're both calmer.

"Remember all the things I've done for you."

Ignore him, Abby.

"You owe me everything."

Or not.

I wheeled around, compelling myself to once more stare down the beast.

Max's bulbous, pathetic face was red, his expression livid.

"You," I hissed, jamming my finger right in his face, "are fired!"

The elevator doors opened, and I backed inside.

He stared at me, mouth ajar.

"And . . ." I tilted my head, lifting a sticky-sweet smile, "this is my studio, and I'm calling security."

Right before the elevator doors closed, I displayed a single finger.

My descent to the ground floor began. The only sounds I heard were the mechanics of the elevator, paired against my pounding heart. "By the way, Mister Salinger," I said, feeling true relief for the first time in years, "the name is *Abby*." I nodded to my reflection in the mirrored doors, feeling like I weighed as much as a feather.

Right on the heels of relief, however, my stomach made a little squeeze, knowing what I had to do next.

By the time the elevator hit the lobby floor, I'd already taken out my long To-Do list, checked off another item, and drew a thick circle around item number three. It was the only one left.

chapter 33

"THE LONG
AND WINDING ROAD"

"I hope I didn't wake you," I said, slightly winded.

Not even an hour had passed since I'd left the studio, straight down the elevator, straight to my car, and straight to the freeway. I hadn't even bothered to stop at home. "There's something I have to tell you."

"You fired him."

I blinked. "What?" I asked after I passed through airport security, hopping on one foot while I slid my shoes back on.

"Nothing, nothing," he said, sounding a little embarrassed. "Silly, duchess, I thought—"

"No, Hal, you're right."

Silence. "You fired him." He sounded disbelieving. "In, like, *person*?"

I laughed. "Right to his face. Then I flipped him off."

A girls' softball team was running past on its way down to Baggage Claim, too busy to notice me.

"Woo-hoo, duchess! You're one badass rock star. Where are you, anyway?" he asked, probably hearing my labored breathing.

"LAX," I said, looking down at my boarding pass and then up at the screen of gate postings. I might have to make a run for it.

"Oh, yeah. Of course," Hal said after a beat. "So then, what's the new plan?" he asked, but his quiet voice answered his own question: "You're leaving the group." There was another pause. "Aren't you, duchess?"

"Hal . . ."

"Uh-uh, Abby." He cut me off. "No tears. This is a celebration. Rhapsody! Don't worry; we'll be okay without you."

"But *I* won't," I said, looking down the long terminal at the gate numbers. Mine was the last on the end, so I picked up the pace. "The four of us, we're one big dysfunctional family, Hal. We'll figure out what to do next. Together. We're a team."

"Badass rock star," Hal repeated with a grin in his voice.

I laughed, hooking my purse strap over my head and shoulder. I was running now, toward my gate before the last boarding call. "Now that that's settled," I said, "who's there with you?"

"Just some of the guys. Shugg's playing Guitar Hero. Molly's around here, too, somewhere . . ." He trailed off, intentionally. "With *Jord*."

"You're kidding!" I said, agog, switching my phone to the other ear. "*My* Molly? And *Jordon*? Hooking up? Since when?"

"Ahh, that's been in the works for a while."

"Wow, I did not see that coming," I admitted with a laugh, drawing closer to my gate.

"You've had a lot on your mind." Hal's voice was comforting through the phone.

"Put her on. We have to talk."

"She's a little *busy*, Abby." He snickered. "I'll tell her to give you a shout tomorrow, 'k?"

"Okay." I skidded to a stop, nearly losing a shoe in the process. "Hal, I have to go. I'm at the gate. They're boarding."

I handed my boarding pass to the woman at the gate. "No carry-on?" she inquired. I shook my head. She smiled, examining the paper and my ID a little more closely. "Have a nice flight, Ms. Kelly."

I returned her smile and passed through the gray doors onto the ramp.

"I won't be at work tomorrow, or the next day, if . . . you know . . ."

"Well, *obviously*," Hal shot back, sarcastically.

"Would you call Nate, please?" I asked, lowering my voice as I approached the line of other passengers queuing on the Jetway, eager to take their seats. "And Jillian and—"

"It's done, duchess. You did a great thing tonight. The guys are gonna be so effin' proud. Now go. Go do what you gotta do. Don't worry about anything else right now, okay?"

"Okay." I exhaled, resting my cell against my mouth. "Thanks, Hal. I love you."

He chuckled away from the phone. "Dude, *now* she gets around to saying it." His voice dropped a notch. "Yeah, I love you, too, Abby. Good luck."

chapter 34

"OB-LA-DI, OB-LA-DA"

The sky was pouring down rain, which seemed fitting. Barricades were up, caution tape was strung from end to end, blocking all entrances.

I had never seen Seaside Town Square under construction. To me, it had become something out of a book—a fantasy place where wishes dwelled and dreams came to life. At least, that was how I'd been painting it lately.

My eyes scanned the setting through sheets of December rain. It was still too dark, too early in the morning to make out any details.

"Will you pull over here, please?" I asked the cab driver after paying him the hefty fare from Pensacola to Seaside. "Thanks for letting me talk." I gave him an extra big tip.

After splashing my way through the circular lawn in the middle of the Square, I dashed to the sidewalk and under the protection of the roof extensions that covered the shops. I passed by Ye Olde Fudge Shoppe, McGaraghan's Gardens, Scenic City Toffee Company, Modica Market, and Sundog Bookstore.

What I came to next made my stomach drop. CLOSED FOR CONSTRUCTION read a sign on the inside of the window. I cupped my hands around my eyes, peering in. It was a mess. It looked like someone had taken a sledgehammer to the walls. All the racks and tables were shoved to one side and covered with sheets; heaps of plaster and piles of broken sheetrock cluttered the middle of the floor; naked wires hung loose from the ceiling.

The muted orange of the sunrise breaking through the clouds reflected off the window. Water from the ends of my hair trickled down my neck, soaking into my shirt. I spun around, wiping my rain-drenched eyes with the back of a hand.

Then I took off running.

Through the rain I splashed, dodging puddles, leaping over sidewalk streams, losing my shoes in the mud somewhere along the way. It was the kind of running you see at the end of romantic comedies. There was always running—running toward something or someone. I was running toward both.

A woman under a red umbrella was walking her dog. A nondescript jogger in a yellow poncho trotted by. Both eyed me skeptically as I loped past them, drenched to the skin. A car honked as I crossed the street outside the designated crosswalk. I waved to it from behind me and kept running, torpedoing toward my goal.

Other than pure adrenaline, I felt something extra, like a cosmic, magnetic gravitational pull helping me along my way.

Faster now, I ran past Wandering Thoughts, A Summer Place, and all those other sugar-cookie homes that sat behind their white picket fences along the north side of the Gulf. Glimpses of wintery-gray water flashed in between the summer cottages.

Half a block away now. Finally, there it was.

But I stopped, considering—almost for the first time—what it was I was about to do.

I had been traveling for hours. I was finally there, yet I still didn't have a plan. After the FASTEN SEATBELTS sign went out, Hal and I e-mailed the entire time I was in the air, strategizing about Mustang Sally's next move. Should we totally retool the group immediately? Should we go in a brand-new direction and then burst onto the scene with a bang? Or should we regroup in a few months, giving each of us time to decompress properly? Hal and I had decided on the latter, pending what the others thought.

We'd probably have to release an independent album, because without Max—let's face it—we might be dropped from our label. Hal and I thought the guys would be thrilled about that, though; we'd all become rather disenchanted by the massive bureaucracy that came with being high-profile artists on a major label. Five years earlier, I'd willingly signed my life away to a group of businessmen in dark suits and slick smiles to live the dream of every American girl. But what if your dream came true and it was nothing like you dreamed?

After I'd landed in Pensacola, I told Hal that I'd be in touch with him either in a couple of hours or in a couple of days, depending on how this whole thing turned out.

Still a few houses away, I stood in place, breathing hard from my run, rain beating down. I bent in half, bracing myself, hands on my knees. I still couldn't catch my breath, and my insides were twisted in knots.

Foolishly, I was stalling the inevitable, fighting a gravitational pull, delaying the very reason I was there. It took effort, but slowly I straightened. I took one step forward and then another. From my angle of approach, the sun was rising directly behind the house, illuminating its silhouette in a halo of muted yellow and orange through the rain.

I was standing right before it—the place I'd been mentally re-conjuring for weeks. My chest sagged with heaviness when I noticed there was no shiny black Ranger Rover in the driveway, no blue-and-white-striped tent in the backyard. All the inside lights were off. The dim lamp above the porch flickered morosely in the breaking dawn. I allowed my dripping hand to reach out and touch the gate that swung open in the wind.

It hadn't occurred to me—nothing had occurred to me. In all my rushing and running, I hadn't thought about what to do if he wasn't there. Had I expected him to be waiting for me, lying fetal positioned on the floor, listening to "Don't Get around Much Anymore" over and over until I decided to show up?

I pressed my lips together and clenched my eyelids, my whole face scrunching—not that tears mattered much as I stood in the downpour. I lifted my chin, allowing the torrents to hit me dead on. I couldn't feel it, but I knew I was crying.

That's when I heard something.

Sniffling, I turned toward the sound. A mixture of raindrops and teardrops clung to my lashes, blurring my vision. Through the blur, I saw a figure standing stock-still in the driveway. I had to squint because I was staring directly into the hazy orange sunrise. The figure remained frozen, probably wondering why this loony, barefooted woman was loitering around the front yard at seven a.m. in the rain.

He took one step forward, then two more, almost at a rush. But then he stopped. Thinking better of it, maybe.

"What are you doing here?" the figure queried.

"I was in the neighborhood?"

"You're all wet," he observed.

"So are you."

He was beautiful standing in the morning rain, his dark hair slick and sopping. His green eyes were the same as I had been painting in my dreams. His black T-shirt clung to his body like a wetsuit.

"I think there's a storm." He held a hand out to the side like he was testing the air for rain. A moment later, he looked at me, dropped his hand, and frowned. "You're shivering."

My teeth chattered in response. "Because I think there's a storm, and they're usually accompanied by colder temperatures."

His lips twitched—an almost-smile. "Weather? How tedious. Can we skip the small talk?" His motions were cautious, his hands hid deep in his pockets. Raindrops bounced off his shoulders and the top of his head. "What happened, Abby?" Todd asked.

I sniffed a few times then looked down at my bare feet, suddenly feeling awkward, wondering where my shoes had gone. Somewhere back there in the mud.

"I flew all night," I finally said.

"Are you . . . okay?" His tone sounded anxious. Even through the rain, I noted the worry on his face. His brows were pulled together, causing a notch between his eyes. It looked like he hadn't shaved in a while.

I sniffed again and nodded, wrapping my arms around myself, feeling shivers of leftover adrenaline. "I found out what Max did in London, about Christian." Uselessly, I wiped at my eyes with the back of a hand. "And I'm sorry. I'm sorry you were put in the middle like that. I didn't know. I'm sorry."

He didn't reply right away, making me wonder if he was even interested in an apology. Or was I three hours, three days, and three months too late?

"I know," Todd finally said. His gaze held on me for a moment then moved up to the sky. He looked back at me and reached out his hand. "Here, come with me."

When I placed my hand inside his, heat shot up my arm and my fingers tingled. Instinctively, I reached out and grabbed him with my other hand, too. I needed to feel that spark again.

He led me onto the front porch. The roof sheltered us from the rain. Once we were covered, he let go of my hands, and we sat on the steps.

"Do you need anything?" he asked, sweeping back his wet hair with his fingers. "A towel?"

"I'm okay." I leaned forward and wrapped my arms around my legs, resting my chin on my knees. I hadn't noticed before, but Todd's soggy front yard looked like it was under major renovation as well. Fence posts were pulled up, leaving deep holes filled with muddy water. A pile of two-by-fours was stacked along the side of the house, mounds of dirt everywhere.

"I passed by your store," I said, trying for polite conversation. "It looks a little like London after the blitz."

He exhaled a chuckle. "I had some nervous energy to discharge. You remember how I used to be." He flashed a flicker of a sheepish grin. "But I'm working on it. I've been taking yoga."

"You?"

I couldn't help laughing. Todd laughed, too. "And my store, well, it seems like a mess now, but believe it or not, it looks a lot better today than it did a few weeks ago. My life needed a shake up."

I laughed again, mostly to myself, as I gazed out at the street in front of us. The scene was wide open, a new life, a real life. Messy, wet, and muddy, exactly the way I wanted it.

Last night, somewhere over Texas, that invisible cord that had been binding me to a warped and unhappy half life had finally snapped for good. As I was sitting next to Todd in the chilly, drizzly morning, I caught a glimpse of a brand new kind of freedom.

"I began my own shake up a while ago," I said. "It was a huge mess at first, but it's also looking a lot better today." I blew my bangs out of my eyes.

"I like your hair," Todd said with a smile in his voice. "What's left of it."

"Thanks. That was part of the shake-up. But actually . . ." I took a beat. "Actually, I wasn't just storm tracking in your neighborhood." I leaned back, crossing my muddy feet in front of me. "I came to tell you something."

Todd's eyes fixed on me in his hypnotic way. Even after months apart, it still managed to make my heart jump into my throat. We weren't touching, but the heat between us was unmistakable. It burned my insides like a campfire; every part of me wanted to grab him, but I couldn't even tell if he was happy to see me. His eyes, that weird semi-smile, his body language, were all a muddle of mixed communication.

"I was wondering when you'd get around to it," he said as he leaned back on his hands. "Why are you here?" He took in a breath. His face looked troubled, hesitant, like he was preparing himself to hear bad news.

"I was drifting along," I heard myself whisper in rhythmic cadence, "till something brought me to the sea. When I saw you, I found me."

I couldn't help noticing an air of appreciation cross Todd's face. "Nice," he said.

"Yeah, but that's not even *my* line," I admitted quietly, a little embarrassed by my lack of romantic originality, chagrined by the fact that I'd become my own worst chick flick cliché: girl running through rain to find her hero, then plagiarizing lines from a love ballad. "I stole it from a song Hal wrote."

"'Indian Summer.'" The teensiest of smiles twitched at the corner of his mouth. "It came by special delivery a few weeks back."

I blinked, wondering if he could see the millions of questions behind my eyes and further wondering if he realized my heart was in his teeth.

His tiny smile grew. "We've been in touch."

"You and Hal?"

Todd nodded.

"I hope he wasn't bothering you," I said, bewildered.

"Of course not. I always liked him. You know that." His gaze left me and moved out to the street. "In fact, when he first called, you were never mentioned, so after a while, I figured he hadn't told you. When we spoke a few weeks ago, he said he had to be quick because he was helping you pick out a TV."

"That was *you* on the phone that day?" I asked, remembering how strangely Hal had behaved after he'd taken that call at the electronics store, looking both guilty and exceptionally pleased with himself.

"We spoke for only a second then," Todd continued, "but later he managed to give me an earful about all the home decorating you'd been doing, and painting, I understand?"

I nodded.

"A few weeks before that, he mentioned you were in Tucson." He turned to me. It looked like he was holding his breath. "Did you see your parents?"

I nodded again.

Todd let out his breath. "Good, Abby," he said. "That's really good progress." His voice sounded relieved, but also a bit detached, like he was my academic advisor.

"I fired Max," I blurted.

I wasn't sure why right now was the moment I decided to broach the subject. My body responded to the new burst of adrenaline, and I sprang to my feet. "The guys and I, we're going to run the band on our own. It'll be different. Smaller, but better. Because . . ." I faced Todd, who was sitting with his arms on his knees, looking up at me. "Because I truly love it." My throat started feeling thick, full with emotion. "I forgot that for a while, but I do. It's what excites me and energizes me, and I just *love* it, more than almost anything." I looked him in the eyes and swallowed. "But that's not what I came to tell you, either."

He tilted his head to the side, wearing a worried look again.

I turned around to stare out at the rainy street. "That night you left," I quickly pressed forward before I lost momentum, "you said that ours was the most important relationship of your life. I wanted to tell you then that I felt the same way— *feel*, I mean. Feel right now." I was still standing with my back to him, unable to face whatever his troubled expression had morphed into.

That was when I felt something on my shoulders. It took me a moment to realize Todd's hands were resting on top of them. The sudden heat was a shock to my system. It burned through my wet clothes, soaked into my bloodstream, and spread warmth through my entire body.

"I love you," I said, unable to stop myself.

But nothing came in return, only the splattering of rain.

It felt like hours were ticking by. I pinched my eyes closed, feeling my heart sink. Then suddenly I was spun around; Todd's hands were on the front of my shoulders.

"What was that?" he asked, tipping his head down a bit. "I couldn't quite . . ." He paused, the side of his mouth pulling back. "Hear you." One hand left my shoulder and slid behind my neck. The feeling of his fingers on my bare skin snapped my senses to attention. Every hair on my body leaned toward the location of his touch, like a sunflower stretching toward the sun.

"Well?" he said, his eyes narrowing playfully.

"I love you, Todd," I said, properly, staring into his eyes.

The next thing I knew, his arms were around me, hugging me so tightly that my heart banged in surprise. When I managed to inhale, I took in his scent, his dizzying pheromones.

I forced myself to speak. "Todd—"

"Shh." He cut me off with a squeeze. "You had your say; now let me enjoy this." He squeezed me tighter. His mouth moved down to the side of my neck; the three-day beard tickled. I heard my blood rushing behind my ears like the Gulf at high tide.

"So?" he breathed in a whisper, his nose on my cheek. "Was that all you came here to tell me?" His nose moved in a slow circle.

"I can't rememb—"

Before I could finish, his hands moved to the sides of my face, his eyes so full of love. The way he was holding me, precious and protective, was like I was something lost. Lost, but miraculously found.

And then he kissed me, perfectly, with so much wonder and magic.

I had no words, but Todd had one. He whispered it.

The first moment I could, I threw my arms around him. The force of my enthusiastic, propelling body knocked him backward. We stumbled and fell onto the porch in a heap.

"How's the head?" I asked, taking a breath.

One side of his lovely mouth curled up as an answer.

I hovered above him; drops of rainwater from my hair dripped onto his cheeks. With another kiss, we were rolling. I heard something fall off the side of the porch and crash onto the wet cement below. We'd probably kicked over some potted plants.

"What took you so long?" I asked, my face buried in his neck.

"Ha! Me?"

"Why make us sit in the rain like that?"

He stopped kissing me and pulled back, bracing his weight on his elbows over me.

"Why did you let me keep talking a blue streak when you knew why I came?"

Todd furrowed his brows and rolled to his side. "I didn't know why you came." He passed one hand across his forehead as something painful shadowed his expression. "Seeing you out my window, standing like that, frankly, I didn't know what to think, and I could see you were crying." He sighed, dropping his chin. "I knew a little about what you'd been going through the last few months, but I also knew there was a lot I *wasn't* being told." He lifted his chin, still wearing that dark expression. "I was so worried about you, Abby. Every day. Every minute. But seeing you here . . ." He took a beat. "I was more relieved than anything."

My hands slid under his arms, around his back. Slowly, we sat up together. The end result was me on his lap.

"To be honest," he continued, his voice lighter, "I was ready to pounce on you the second I stepped outside. It was all I could do to refrain as long as I did." His strong arms tightened around me. "It looked like you had something you needed to say, so I let you talk first."

"And then you pounced."

From the street, a car honked. Todd unleashed his hold for just a moment as he tilted his head to one side, looking past me and out at the street. He raised one hand and waved.

I turned around in time to see Chandler's silver pickup pulling away from the curb.

"Small town," Todd said, and we both laughed.

I leaned in, laying my head on his shoulder. It was amazing how different I felt being with him now. I felt so good. So strong. So much more myself.

"I want you to know, I'm sorry, too," he said.

When I pulled back, his expression was oddly rueful. "For what?"

"I wanted to tell you what Nate told me that night, about Christian, but I thought the situation was bad enough already for you. I didn't want to make it worse, especially since you said you would never quit."

"It wasn't your fault."

He shook his head. "There hasn't been a day I haven't regretted leaving you like that. It killed me."

I didn't let him continue. I took his face and drew the two of us together, our foreheads touching so we could see nothing but each other.

"I'm sorry," he whispered once more.

"Shhh, it's over."

"I did try to forget you."

This startled me. I pulled my face away.

His expression was teasing. "But my house still smells like you," he added, repositioning me on his lap. "And there's that twelve-foot-tall reminder in every Gap store window."

"You saw that billboard?"

"This is America." He smiled crookedly. "There's a Gap on every corner. That first month away, I traveled a lot. Trying." His voice faded out. He rubbed my hair and then my back in slow circles. "That red bathing suit of yours is still hanging over the showerhead in my guest bathroom. Pathetic, I know, but I never had the heart to take it down. I basically just stopped going in there."

"You knew I'd be back," I explained, leaving two strategically placed kisses on his dimple.

"I hoped you would," he admitted, touching his finger to the tip of my nose and then sliding it down to my lips.

It felt like my pounding heart wanted to break through my chest and latch onto his.

"Abby." His eyes flickered away and then back to me as a streak of lightning flashed through the sky. Thunder rolled a moment later. "Abigail Kelly," he said in a rush. "I love you." His lips pressed together, but not tightly enough. I could clearly see that they were trembling. "I was afraid," he said, his voice low and hoarse, "that I would never be able to tell you that. And I wanted to. Every day." When he pulled me in, only one arm was around me; his other hand might have been wiping his eyes.

But it was no use. He'd already showed me, unmistakably, that no matter how tough we said we were, no matter how hard we could punch or how high we could climb or how well we could sing, we were breakable, and we'd both been broken, broken in two.

I hitched my chin over his shoulder and hugged him with all my might, attempting to meld his broken pieces back together while fusing my own. Perhaps blending some bits of ourselves in the process.

"I hate to ask this," he said a moment later, "but how long will you be staying here this time?"

His question caught me off guard. Didn't he understand? Could he not see into my soul? I gazed into his expectant eyes. How well he knew me. He knew it used to be hard for me to slow down and stay in one place, that I used to have moments of guilt for simply being me.

"Well, you have Internet and fax, right?" I asked. He nodded once, skeptically. "I'm sure Molly has always wanted to drive a U-Haul moving truck cross-country. I'll fly her back to L.A. first-class. Oh, if you don't mind splitting time between here and Malibu," I added. "The band is meeting again in six months. The Marine in you usually keeps enough supplies on hand to last that long, right?" I cranked my head like I was assessing his house. "We'll never have to leave home." I turned back to him. "The rest is details."

I paused here, allowing my message to sink in. If I had the guts, I might have made us both stand up, just so I could have fallen down on one knee and made it official.

My former life had been all about rushing and running, following unreasonable orders, beating deadlines. I didn't know how long we sat on that porch. Time seemed to stand still for us.

Todd whispered something in my ear that made me quiver in delight, and my mind drifted. Inside my head, I saw something distant, yet not too far away.

Chinese lanterns twinkle in the twilight, with soft candles, white lace, and me in my bare feet. I see Todd holding my hand as we stand together in the sand. Our families and friends are here, too.

There's a flash of light, and I see Todd again, bent upside down, kissing the Blarney Stone. I'm barefoot again, bright green Irish grass between my toes.

Another flash.

I'm staring into bright lights, a guitar in my hands. Instinctively I know Hal is to my right, Jordan to my left, and Yosh's steady drumbeat taps with my heart. Through the bright lights, I see all the way across the small venue. Todd is standing at the back. I automatically wave to him, but then realize he's not alone. A little girl with brown, springy curls is perched on his shoulders. Todd waves back to me as the little girl squeals, "Mommy!" through the crowd.

I can't tell if it's the future me or the present me, but one of us gasps in rapture.

"Abby? Abby!"

Todd's concerned voice yanked me back to the present. After he assessed me for a second, his expression relaxed. "What were you thinking about?"

I couldn't help laughing, wondering if I should tell him that I had just been given a precious glimpse into our future. Or maybe I should let him be surprised.

"I'll tell you later," I promised, making a mental note that we'd be going to Ireland on our honeymoon.

"Okay." Todd eyed me curiously. "I think we'd better take this inside before we both get hypothermia." He moved to stand, but then turned to me. "Would it sound too horribly crass if I suggested we get you out of these wet clothes immediately? I'm only worried about your health, of course."

"Of course." I returned his grin. "But remember what Sinatra said."

Todd snorted, and together we stood.

"Which reminds me," he said. "I finally got around to officially renaming the place." He pointed to a nameplate on his white picket fence, the one part of his front yard that wasn't completely torn apart. Charming script engraved with the new name looped in bright blue letters.

I spun around to him after reading the sign. "Really?" I exclaimed, clapping like an ecstatic four year old. "No 'Fly Me to the Moon' or 'Summer Wind?'"

"Har-har. Well, actually, both those names were in the running." His hand rested on the back of my hairless neck. "But as it happens, the Beatles did turn out a few noteworthy albums." He gestured to the sign. "Particularly that one." He lifted his chin, looking lofty. "I was finally inspired."

I twirled myself into his arms, my mouth at his ear. When I felt his breath catch, I pulled back. "I hope you kept your receipt," I whispered.

"Why?" he asked, his expression twisting.

I grinned, eager to relieve his confusion. "It was a sweet thought, but you do realize that your sign is misspelled, right?"

Todd let out a breath, his fingers combing through my hair. "I am perfectly aware of that, my love." His hand skimmed down the side of my face and stopped at my chin. "The spelling is intentional, because I didn't name my home after the Beatles." He tilted my chin up. "I named it after *you*."

As shocking as it seemed, this magnificent man loved me, even more than his precious Rat Pack. Todd's home was now called Abby Road.

> "And in the end
> The love you take
> Is equal to the love
> You make."
> —LENNON & McCARTNEY

EPILOGUE

FROM *THE WALTON BEACH SUN:*

After a month-long hiatus, our town's most prominent couple made its first appearance since disappearing from our sleepy shoreline, as well as from their other home base in Malibu. Yesterday Abigail Kelly and Todd Camford were not necessarily keeping their return to Seaside low-key. This reporter was lucky enough to be eating lunch at the outside village green when the couple strolled up and sat across from me at my table, which can happen when you live in a tiny town year-round. Abby might have been trying to be inconspicuous about it at first, but there was no hiding the dazzling new gold band nestled next to the diamond ring she began sporting six months ago. I didn't know at the time, but I was the first member of the press to offer them official congratulations as newlyweds.

Mustang Sally's new album, and the first off its independent label, was written entirely by the band. After the album exploded two months ago, its third single is still screaming up the charts and is sure to be the band's tenth consecutive number-one hit. When I asked the smiling couple how they could afford to fall off the map for a month like they had, while the album was going so strong, Todd explained that they wanted a real honeymoon before the tour began, while Abby was quick to add that this touring schedule will be smaller and much more intimate, matching the vibe of the new record.

Before the twosome left to continue their stroll, Abby made sure to point out the orange flyer taped to the window of Todd's Tackle. Of course I didn't need the reminder, but in case you do, Mustang Sally will be playing the Seaside Amphitheater on the 25th. Tickets will be available starting midnight the 20th. This is a free show.

ACKNOWLEDGMENTS

Mom and Dad, thank you for being excited about my writing and for knowing when to ask me about it. And also when not to. (Kind of like my love life.) Your support has meant the world to me. Love!

Thank you to countless friends and family members who read this manuscript in its earliest, most hideous versions. There just might be a special place in rock 'n' roll heaven for you.

Stacy, my editor/rock star. You push me to be a better, more honest writer, and help me realize the importance of staying true to my readers. Thank you for everything. All the smexy is dedicated to you. Meet ya on Canal Street. Same time, same creepy phone booth.

Heather and Debbie, my publicity team: thank you for all your cool ideas and hard work at getting my books out there.

Sue, my critique partner. Thanks for being brutally honest (puke), insightful, and pretty much the best writer I know. How did I get so freaking lucky? This book would not be what it is without your input. We'll make it to that writers' getaway up in the mountains (or was it the beach?) one of these days.

Nancy, my tireless beta, can you believe we're finally here? I remember the day I brought you the final chapter of *Abby* (it had a different title back then), and I sat across the short/ass conference table from you, watching you read. No pressure, right? You've been such a good sport, reading every word I've ever written over the years. CWC! Thank you for all the times you allowed me to drone on and on over pancakes, heartful chocolate chip cookies, eggs Benedict, and cupcakes.

Thanks to everyone at Entangled Publishing for your encouragement and support, and for making this writer chick's dreams come true!

Thanks to the sassy girls of Mustang Sally for sharing your name.

Special thanks to The Walrus, Sir Paul, Dark Horse, Mr. Starkey, and The Voice.

Sara Bareilles and Mandy Moore, thank you for keeping me company while I wrote.

Keep reading for a sneak peek at Ophelia London's short romance, *Playing at Love* . . .

Show choir teacher Tess Johansson loves three things: music, her job, and sharing that passion with her students. But when a school budget crisis forces funding to be pulled from either the sports or music programs, she finds herself going head to head with Jack, the gorgeous new football coach who broke her heart fifteen years ago.

Jack Marshall wants two things: to be closer to his young daughter and to make his mark as a football coach. Taking the new job, with the promise that he'd have time to build a solid team, gave him both. But now he must win the season with a group of boys who aren't anywhere near ready or he'll lose everything he's worked so hard for. Being pitted against Tess, the summer love he never forgot, is like being fourth and long with only seconds on the clock.

On opposing sides of a fierce battle and with everything at stake, Tess and Jack find themselves torn between doing what it takes to win and doing what it takes to be together.

Available from e-retailers everywhere!

T ess slid into the chair next to Mac at the far end of the second row and dropped her heavy bag full of the sheet music for "Breaking Up Is Hard to Do," a song she planned to teach her show choir that semester. It was a funky yet safe arrangement that was sure to sit well with the judges at the Invitationals in October and then Regionals later on in the month. And after that: Fiestaval.

Once seated, she crossed her legs, causing the front slit of her new dark gray skirt to split apart and reveal too much leg. She quickly pulled the two slits together, making a mental note that this probably wasn't the best outfit to wear to work. Lesson learned.

Tess was only half listening as Joe Walker stood at the front of the room, sifting through a stack of papers on the lectern in front of him. She toyed with the band of her watch until it suddenly came unclasped and fell to the floor, causing everyone in her row to turn and stare.

"Sorry," she mouthed. When she leaned forward to pick it up, she noticed one person was still looking at her. *He must be one of the new teachers,* she thought. And wow, he was gorgeous. Dark wavy hair, nice jaw, and built like a quarterback. At least, that's what she could detect from her distance of ten chairs away. After messing with her watch, she glanced his way again. He was still watching her, and when their eyes met, he pulled back a sexy half grin. Despite herself, when she smiled in return, her stomach made a tiny flip.

Talk about spark. If only he had backed me into that coatroom the other night.

She felt instantly attracted yet comfortable, which she found just a little odd.

Wait a minute. Did she know him? Had they met? Oh snap, he wasn't one of the guys she'd gone out with earlier in the summer, was he? Their faces were all starting to blend together. She couldn't quite place this guy's face, but she knew she'd met him. Somewhere. When she took another glance

at him, the guy lifted his hand a few inches and actually—
though very subtly—waved.

Tess knew her cheeks were about to turn an embarrassing
shade of pink as she sat back in her chair, feeling slightly
flustered now. Maybe he really was one of her dates from the
summer. Had she become that forgetful? And why hadn't she
bothered to look over the teachers' roster that was finally e-
mailed last night? She might have recognized his name. She
smiled and looked down at her lap, imagining him as the new
sex ed teacher. If a man so incredibly handsome was teaching
a bunch of hormonal girls, heaven help the poor guy.

As everyone else around her was listening to the principal,
Tess played with a strand of her hair, nonchalantly glancing
down the row. She could only see the guy's right leg now. He
was wearing khakis—pretty casual for the first day of school.
Most teachers tried to make a good impression at the beginning of the year. Just as she was about to slyly lean forward to
check out what he was wearing on top, the guy stood up. Tess
gasped, wondering what he was doing. Did he realize she was
checking him out and was giving her a better look?

It was only then that she realized Walker was talking
to him, or *about* him, introducing the new members of the
faculty.

"I'd like you all to meet," Walker said in his dry voice,
"our new head football coach."

A-ha! I was right. Tess inwardly congratulated herself. *He
probably was a quarterback once upon a time. But where?
Why does he look so familiar?*

"We're very excited to have him aboard as a last-minute
team member," Walker continued. "He was the assistant
coach at his last school, which went all the way to State."

The other teachers were murmuring in approval.

Tess vaguely remembered something about the previous football coach stepping down in the middle of July,
right before summer training camp, but she didn't follow
the sports program much. Although now—and she couldn't
help looking across the room at him—maybe she might start

attending the football games and not skipping out after half-time when her choir was finished.

"So please," Walker went on, "join me in giving a warm welcome to Jack Marshall."

While everyone was giving the new coach a round of applause, Tess felt all the blood drain from her face.

"He's gorgeous, don't you think?" Mac said, jabbing an elbow into Tess's ribs. "And look at his hands; they're huge. Tess, why are you wringing the front of your shirt?"

"I'm ..." But Tess didn't know how to finish. She was staring at Jack Marshall—the boy she'd met the summer she was fifteen. The boy who was her first *real* kiss. The boy who swore he would meet her that last night in August but never showed up. Jack Marshall: the very first boy to break her heart.